What Others Are Saying...

"There's a new name in biblical fiction! Dana McNeely peels back the mysteries of Ba'al's temples and Queen Jezebel's reign in her debut novel, Rain. Brilliantly weaving together the prophet Elijah's story with the widow of Zarephath and her son, McNeely explores a tale not widely told but brought to life with impeccable research and fascinating fiction. Biblical novice and scholar alike will be enthralled."
~**Mesu Andrews**, Christy Award winning and bestselling author

"A splendid debut from Dana McNeely. This engaging, fascinating tale takes us back to a time of idol worship and sacrifices. Rain entertains as well as challenges the reader to ponder life's deeper questions long after the last page. A must read for all seeking to understand the past as well as the present."
~**Rachel Hauck,** New York Times Bestselling Author

"Welcome to ancient Israel like you've never imagined it! McNeely has done the research, pulling aside the veil of time with astonishing insight and depth. You'll never forget the days of Elijah after reading RAIN."
~**Linore Rose Burkard**, award-winning historical fiction author

"Dana McNeely has crafted a story of faith, love, and courage so thrilling it literally kept me up late reading it! Realizing Melquart is no god, young Aban travels throughout Israel trying to find the prophet who promised a drought. Encountering danger at nearly every turn, he fights to save his mother and baby brother from the clutches of Israel's Queen Jezebel. In the end, he finds much more than he was ever searching for."
~**Carole Towriss,** Author of *Sold into Freedom*

Mantle

Mantle

Whispers on the Wind series

Rain—Book One

Whirlwind—Book Two

Mantle —Book Three

Mantle

By

Dana McNeely

Mantle
Published by Mountain Brook Ink
White Salmon, WA U.S.A.

The website addresses shown in this book are not intended in any way to be or imply an endorsement on the part of Mountain Brook Ink, nor do we vouch for their content.

This story is a work of fiction. All characters and events are the product of the author's imagination. Any resemblance to any person, living or dead, is coincidental.

Scripture taken from the Holy Bible, NEW INTERNATIONAL VERSION®, NIV® Copyright © 1973, 1978, 1984, 2011 by Biblica, Inc.® Used by permission. All rights reserved worldwide.

© 2025 Dana McNeely
ISBN 9781-953957-60-3

The Team: Miralee Ferrell, Tim Pietz, Kristen Johnson, Laurel Burgess, Cindy Jackson
Cover Design: Indie Cover Design, Lynnette Bonner Designer

Mountain Brook Ink is an inspirational publisher offering fiction you can believe in.
Printed in the United States of America

The Lord warned Israel and Judah through all
his prophets and seers: "Turn from your evil ways.
Observe my commands and decrees, in accordance with
the entire Law that I commanded your fathers to obey and
that I delivered to you through my servants the prophets."
But they would not listen and were as stiff-necked as
their fathers, who did not trust in the Lord their God.

2 Kings 17:13-14

The voice of the Lord strikes with flashes of lightning.
The voice of the Lord shakes the desert; the Lord shakes the
Desert of Kadesh. The voice of the Lord twists the oaks and
strips the forests bare. And in his temple all cry, "Glory!"

The Lord sits enthroned over the flood;
The Lord is enthroned as King forever.
The Lord gives strength to His people;
The Lord blesses His people with peace.
Psalm 29:7-11

Acknowledgements

It might have been impossible for me to write these books without my husband's avid support. Not only was he a cheerleader, he was cook, cleaner, and constant gardener. Even when he was sick, he did all he was able. Thank you, honey.

Another thank you to my pastor, Dr. T Scott Christmas, who listened with ever widening eyes when I approached him after church with a question about 2 Kings chapter three. He joked about my expecting an off-the-cuff response to a confusing Old Testament passage. He said he'd get back to me. Not only did he write several paragraphs of his own thoughts, he also provided a new resource to add to my library—Dale Ralph Davis has become a new favorite for his "Focus on the Bible" commentaries.

Betty and Laura, longtime critique partners, stuck with me during Mantle's prolonged birthing. Thank you, my friends, for sharing your book-wifery talents.

Special thanks to the busy team at Mountain Brook Ink. Miralee Ferrell is the perfect editor. She praises my writing while advising how to make it better. Lynnette Bonner has crafted another gorgeous book cover. Finally, my appreciation to Tim and Kristen for all you both do to support authors at Mountain Brook Ink.

Chapter One

Jericho
Elisha

A HAND TOUCHED HIS SHOULDER. *ELISHA, you must wake.*

At the whisper, he bolted upright, blinking in the dark.
From the far corner where they stored the pots and
provisions, he heard Elijah moving things around. Water
glugged, being poured from pot to waterskin.

Elisha stood, felt his way to the hearth, and lit their
lamp.

Elijah squinted into the light, his aged face haloed by
still-abundant white hair. "Why are you up?" His black eyes
reflected tiny images of the flaming wick.

Still groggy from sleep, Elisha nearly asked, *Why are
you?* Instead, he answered, "Yahweh told me to wake." He
paused and, when there was no response, asked, "Shall I
pack provisions for a journey?"

"Oh, perhaps." Elijah's answer sounded offhand, as if
they might walk only to the well. But as Elisha wrapped
bread and cheese, his master came to stand beside him.

"The Lord has sent me to Gilgal. He did not say you
should come. Stay if you wish."

"Did He say I should not?" Elisha slid the food into a
travel sack.

"No."

"Then I'm going with you. Is there time to make your
morning brew?" Each night, Elisha nestled a water crock into
the banked coals for the concoction of herbs Miriam
instructed the two prophets to drink each day.

"As long as we leave with the dawn."

Elisha stirred the herbs into the warm water. He had
learned to tamp down his curiosity. There were many things
Elijah could not tell him. But Yahweh had wakened him for

a reason, so he asked, "Is everything all right?"

"It is good." Elijah tipped back his head, then smacked his lips.

Elisha slowly shook his head. The drink or the day? He swallowed his own brew, noting the first glow of dawn through the lattice. A strange color, tinged with green. Was a storm coming?

He quickly cleared away the cups. "Anything else?"

No answer, and when he glanced behind the room was empty. Tossing the food parcels into a travel sack, he rushed to the window. Elijah was walking toward the road. Though the prophets were early risers, they usually broke their fasts at this time. But several clustered around Elijah, speaking to him as he continued to press his way through their midst and toward the ridge route.

Grabbing the sack, Elisha trotted after him, pausing to pick up the staff Elijah had left leaning against the doorframe. "Wait!" he called.

Outside the air felt heavy, as if rain was coming. But when he inhaled, his nostrils felt parched. Elisha adjusted his head covering against the tugs of a gusty wind.

Ahead, Elijah's hair and mantle were barely visible in the pre-dawn dimness. Elisha hurried to catch up and handed him the staff. It would not do for his mentor to stumble.

The prophet Micaiah stood at the open door to his house. "Where you headed, Elijah? Elisha, too, I see. Off to preach to the Ephraimites?"

"No, my friend," Elijah said. "Yahweh is sending me to Bethel."

Micaiah snorted, and it turned into the wheeze he'd fought since his release from Ahab's prison. "Bethel—*cough, ehz, ehz*—needs to hear the word of the Lord even more—*gasp*—than Ephraim."

More of that odd greenish color swathed the sky. Doors across the settlement swung open and prophets emerged. Elisha looked behind him at the small crowd which had fallen into step. Fragments of conversation reached his ears.

A storm is coming.

I know, and not just any storm.

What do you think it means?

Elisha trudged along, hearing the measured thuds of the staff. *Lord, what is happening? Like the others, I sense this is an unusual day. Will you reveal your plan to me?*

Thunder growled in the distance. Yahweh's whisper again filled his mind. *I am taking your master today.*

Elisha's stomach clenched, as if he'd been kicked. *Take him?*

Elijah paused, turned back to Elisha, and took hold of his arm. "Please wait here, my friend. I was to teach this afternoon, but the Lord has sent me to Bethel. There's no reason for you to walk so far."

Too far to walk? As if they hadn't crossed Israel together, many times. Why was Elijah trying to discourage him from following? It was almost like the time—

He was plowing in his father's rain-softened field, his the last oxen team of twelve. He recognized Elijah standing at the field's edge by his grizzled hair, camelhair tunic, and leather belt. All Israel had been talking about the fire and rain on Mount Carmel.

After all the teams passed Elijah, he walked up to Elisha, removed his mantle, and arranged it over his shoulders. The prophet was calling Elisha to be his successor! Elisha left his oxen and ran after him. 'Please let me kiss my father and mother good-by, and then I will come.' And Elijah had said, 'Go on back. What have I done to you?'

What had he done, indeed? Only called him into Yahweh's service. Only changed his entire life.

Elisha went back that day and kissed Abba and Imma good-by. But then he followed Elijah. Elisha killed his oxen and burned his plowing equipment to cook the meat and feed the gathered people. He destroyed his farming tools. There was no going back.

Now his mentor was testing him again.

"As surely as the Lord lives, and you live, my master, I will not leave you."

Lightning sheeted the sky. Elijah slanted a glance overhead, nodded, and after giving a double tap with his staff, walked on.

Hearing shouted greetings behind them, Elisha again

looked back. He slid his gaze over a growing crowd—not only fellow residents from Gilgal, but folks coming to join the procession from remote villages tucked away from the main thoroughfare. In the distance, he saw Dov and Miriam urging their animals to a faster pace. He didn't see Jaedon or others from his family.

When they finally reached Bethel, all the prophets came out to meet them. Several went immediately to Elijah, greeted him with kisses, and offered food and drink. Two of the younger prophets, bristling with excitement, hurried to Elisha. In their enthusiasm, they talked over each other.

"Do you know the Lord is going to take your master today?"

Feeling his face heat, Elisha did not bother to hide his irritation. "Of course I know. Be silent! How can you behave as if his departure is a festive event? It is a day of sadness for all Israel."

The two prophets stepped back, frowning.

No one had offered Elisha a drink. He didn't blame them. He felt the scowl creasing his face. He uncorked his own waterskin and took a long swallow. When he straightened again, Elijah stood before him, smiling kindly. "My friend, stay here. Teach. Micaiah is right about Bethel needing instruction, but the Lord has sent me on to Jericho."

"As the Lord lives, and you live, I will not leave you," Elisha said.

The prophet shrugged and walked off briskly, with little trace of the limp that had plagued him in recent years. He whistled, light-hearted and in a hurry to get where he was going, thumping his staff against the ground. Not as if he depended upon it for balance, but to keep time with his tune.

Elisha's own steps dragged. Briefly, he chided himself. Yahweh was taking his faithful servant to his reward. But then he thought of Moses and his assistant Joshua when Yahweh was going to take him. Did Joshua rejoice? No, he mourned.

Elisha heaved a sigh and strode after his master.

Heavy clouds had gathered by the time they reached Jericho. As at Bethel, the prophets waited at the city gates. Two of the elder prophets, charged with teaching the less experienced seers, approached Elisha.

As if revealing a secret, the first cupped his hand beside his mouth. "Do you know the Lord is going to take your master today?"

The other searched Elisha's face for his reaction.

He didn't attempt to hide his misery. "Of course I know, but I don't want to speak of it." Their question seemed a challenge, but he would not argue his case. Elijah had said he would succeed him and laid the mantle on his shoulders. No other confirmation was needed.

Elijah walked over, took his arm, and pulled him aside. "Yahweh is sending me on to the Jordan River. Stay here."

Wearily Elisha shook his head. "Let's go. As the Lord lives, and as you live, I will never leave you. No, not ever."

Elijah smiled gently, squeezed his shoulder, and they walked on.

The other prophets, along with those who followed from the settlements, hung back at a distance from the river, watching.

Elisha gazed at them and slowly shook his head. "I think they fear you will call down fire on their heads."

"Fire is always a possibility." Elijah chuckled softly. "Besides, I do not like the way some have treated you."

Elisha recognized the subtle teasing but couldn't summon a smile. "You have been my teacher and my very dear friend. I will greatly miss you."

"And I will miss you." Elijah removed his mantle, rolled it up, and then struck the surface of the flowing water. The ground trembled under their feet, and the river seemed to sigh as it heaved up, gathering into furrows, left and right.

Elisha gasped, then glanced at Elijah, whose face was as composed as if he had only unrolled the Torah. He stepped between the waters, motioned to Elisha, and they crossed together on dry ground.

Elisha heard surprised shouts from the Jordan's other side, but his attention was fixed on his master. After this great miracle, his time would be near.

"You wonder why I asked you to stay behind," Elijah said.

"Three times," Elisha replied.

"Yes, three. If you would have stayed and ministered at one of the schools for the prophets, perhaps I could have departed alone."

Elisha lifted his gaze to the crowd of followers, pressed together on the opposite bank as if an invisible wall of fear encircled them. Prophets rubbed shoulders with farmers and vintners. Yet, though dust-covered and worn, they exhibited a common air of expectation.

"I promised to follow you always."

"It has been a lonely and difficult life. Not ... not one I would choose for one I love."

Elisha gazed into his eyes. "My friend, I have seen what's ahead."

"So you have, and you have proved yourself faithful. Now tell me quickly, what can I do for you before I am taken?"

Elisha slid both hands over his face, not wanting to ask for anything but knowing what he needed. "Let me inherit a double portion of your spirit."

"The first-born's inheritance," Elijah mused, nodding slowly. "A spiritual birthright."

"If I am to accomplish what the Lord calls me to do—"

"You will need a strong spirit. Yes. What you have requested is good—but difficult." Elijah stroked his beard. "It's not in my power to give. Yet, if you see me when I am taken, you will have it. Otherwise, not."

They walked on. Elijah spoke seriously about the persecution, scorn, and hatred he had faced at the hands of rulers and from the people. "You will suffer too," he said. "But always remember, you serve the LORD God Almighty. The God who answers by fire."

Suddenly, a sheet of light cracked open the sky, twisting into a burning stream that poured into the ground between them. Elisha stumbled away, his gaze riveted on the inferno, his forearm partially shielding his face.

Thunder crashed, shaking the earth. Flames outlined a chariot pulled by fiery horses. Elisha fell to the ground, watching in awe as his master stepped into the chariot and was immediately swept by the conflagration into the highest heavens. A mighty wind fanned Elijah's grizzled hair and the flaming horses' manes and tails.

Elisha clamped his hands over his head covering, desperate to keep its wind-flailed cloth from blinding him, causing him to miss even one moment of Elijah's miraculous departure.

The wind's roar dropped to silence just before the chariot disappeared into flame and sky. Elisha stared into heat and light, his face burning, as the heavens folded around the fiery apparition. In an act of finality, Elijah's mantle slid through a crack in the heavens and, flung this way and that by a few errant gusts, finally settled at Elisha's feet. He bent to gather the garment of ancient sheepskin, smoothing its pelt with trembling fingers.

Prophets and followers from three cities watched him from the other side of the Jordan.

Why had they stayed, content to watch from a distance, as he and Elijah crossed? Yes, the river was rain swollen and tempestuous, but he would have followed the old prophet anywhere, even if the waters had not drawn back when Elijah struck their surface with his mantle.

What if he had missed that charged moment when the old prophet parted the river and they strode through churning waves that peeled back like ends of a scroll?

He knew his request was bold, some would say arrogant. A first-born son received a double portion of his father's inheritance. While Elijah had no earthly riches, he had led the schools of prophets with wisdom and strength. He had summoned fire from heaven. The others would ask, who is Elisha, to follow such a one? He was keenly aware he was not the man his mentor had been. If he were to lead in his master's place, he would need a double portion of his authority. Even then, would another challenge him for leadership of the prophets?

All along the road, at Gilgal, Bethel, and then Jericho, men from the schools of prophets had shown they doubted his calling, with jibes barely disguised as questions. "Do you know the Lord will take your master from you today?"

Do you know? Because we know.

Elisha did not blame them for doubting his call. Was he ready? He was only a tremulous breeze, to Elijah's thunder.

Elisha hesitated on the bank of the Jordan, staring

down at the spot where his master had commanded the water to clear a path. The same place the Israelites had first crossed into the Promised Land with Joshua—their priests forging ahead bearing the Ark of the Covenant.

Over six hundred years ago. But today the Lord had parted the Jordan through Elijah. Throughout the ages, Yahweh was God.

Elisha's gaze fixed on a broken twig carried by rushing waters, one bruised leaf lifted hopefully. When it sank, he sighed. The trouble was, he was not Elijah.

Are you here, Lord? I am not worthy to carry the mantle of Elijah, a man as fiery in your defense as the chariot and horses you sent to carry him away. He told me I was your choice. But am I? Will your power flow through me, as it did through him? Please show me now.

Raising his voice so that all could hear, Elisha feigned confidence he did not feel ... in himself. But he knew on whom to call. "Where are you now, God of Elijah?"

He folded the mantle and grasped one end. It had come to him twice. Once at Abel Meholah, as he plowed his father's fields. And today, sliding from the shoulders of the departing prophet, it had fallen from heaven like a second ordination.

The mantle weighed heavily as he stood on the bank. He would never see Elijah again.

I will miss you. You were the chariots and horses of Israel. Our people's only defense against corrupt rulers, idolatry, and the judgment God vowed to send. Who will protect us now?

Then, as his master had done, Elisha struck the Jordan. Once again, the water curled back. He stepped forward. Although the ground was not dry, gravel held firm beneath his feet. The current gurgled above banked waves, and a twig whirled in an eddy. Elisha lifted his gaze to the waiting prophets, as he strode between the waters.

Chapter Two

Gilgal, earlier that day
Jaedon

IT WAS A STRANGE STORM FOR the season of early rains. Just past dawn, the sky glared, with no soft edges, no clouds as of yet. Intermittent gusts of wind tossed debris into the vineyard.

Jaedon rushed among the vines, laying them flat against the ground for protection. Glancing up, he willed his fingers to move more swiftly. Imma and Dov worked the opposite side of the vineyard, his younger siblings playing at their feet. If the storm progressed, Imma would take them home. One less worker.

He glanced across the shallow ravine that separated the two hills of Gilgal. A crowd of prophets milled about the mudbrick house where he and Imma used to live with Elijah. His forehead tightened. What was going on? Something more than the storm. He continued to work against the wind's pull, quickly settling as many vines as he could along the shallow irrigation furrows. A bad storm so early in the season could wreak havoc on tender plants.

Across the way, Elijah emerged from the house, fixing his sheepskin cloak over his shoulders. Raised voices greeting the old prophet carried on the wind. Not pausing, he pressed through and headed south.

Movement pulled Jaedon's attention back to the vineyard. Imma stood up, leaving a vine unfastened at her feet. She grasped Dov's arm, and he leaned toward her. She spoke in his ear, then she reached for Gershoni's hand. Dov nodded and picked up Yuval. Settling the baby on his shoulders, he strode toward their house. Imma hurried behind, Gershoni trotting at her side.

With another glance at the sky, Jaedon turned back to the vines. There was enough time to finish the storm preparations. His little sister and brother must be gotten out of this wind. Imma, too, for she must consider her condition. After Dov got them in the house, he would be back to help.

On the opposite hill, Elisha hurried after his master, calling something indiscernible. Elijah turned and waved him back. "The Lord has sent me to"—wind stole his destination, but—"I do not know when I will return" rode the breeze. Elisha shook his head in violent refusal and strode after the old prophet.

Jaedon cocked his head, staring. Despite Elijah's advanced age, he still traveled all throughout northern Israel, Elisha at his side. But usually in fair weather. Something felt wrong.

Prophets girded their garments and trotted after the old prophet and his constant companion. Jaedon scrutinized the vineyard once more. Although the sky was cloud free, the hair on the back of his neck prickled, as if warning the time was short. He secured the few remaining vines, slung his water skin over his shoulder, and headed for home at the edge of the vineyard.

But as he approached, he saw Dov and Imma leading the warhorse and the white donkey toward the clearing. Were they planning to follow Elijah? Engrossed in conversation, neither appeared to have seen him. When he called out, Imma lifted her head, a slight frown creasing her forehead. His stepfather ducked into the nearby lean to, returning with thick blankets and saddles. Then Jaedon's gaze dropped to the supplies lying on the ground. Two waterskins, one pack.

"Jaedon, we almost forgot you," his mother said, smoothing her lips into a smile. "I know you will want to come. I will ride behind Dov. You ride Sheleg."

Dov shook his head. "No, my love, your donkey's stride is more comfortable for you. Jaedon can ride behind me."

Jaedon looked between them. Did Imma plan to travel despite her condition? He studied her determined face, then Dov's besotted one. No help there. But more significant was his always attentive mother's remark. *We almost forgot you.*

"Did you see something, Imma? What do you know?"

She waved her hand vaguely at the harried movements across the way. "Only that—the turmoil, the confusion—and the sky." She turned her face up and gestured. "The rest is only that special sense all women have. Call it … conjecture."

Jaedon repositioned the waterskin and felt for his sheathed knife, next to the slingshot nearly everyone had carried since childhood. Imma's *conjectures* were not to be ignored. If she thought he should come, it was because she worried about Elijah. They were alike in devotion to the old man who had saved them.

Still, he had to ask. "Shouldn't I stay behind with Gershoni and Yuval?"

"No. The grandparents are happy to care for them. Savta Yaffa has gone up to help Maalik and your other grandmother." Then, breathlessly, "Hurry. Elijah may need us."

Jaedon stiffened. So, she must have sensed something.

He gestured toward their packs. "No need for me to burden Uriel with a second rider. Go on ahead. I must refill my water and pack food anyway. I'll catch up with you."

Dov nodded. "You are swift enough. We will see you on the road."

Jaedon walked into the house and packed for a long journey. It was quiet without his siblings or his grandmother. The clip-clop of departing hooves sounded outside.

After grabbing his walking stick, he hurried up to the second house, where Savta Hadassah was slicing fruit, Savta Yaffa held a squirming Yuval, and Maalik chased Gershoni with a toy bear. Jaedon explained the hurried decision that he would follow his parents.

"Can I help with anything before I leave? I heard Elijah say he didn't know when he would return."

"Then you cannot know when you will," Maalik said with a shrug. "Don't concern yourself about matters at home. As you know, your grandmother is a very capable woman, and I will help her with everything."

Savta Hadassah bustled to her food shelf, wrapped something round in cloth, and dropped it into his pack.

"Bread," she said, unnecessary information now that he breathed its warm nutty aroma. "Travel with one of the prophets if you cannot catch your parents." Her black eyes peered at him sternly.

"Yes, Savta." Although she was actually his father's grandmother, her snapping eyes could still intimidate. He hugged her, not minding that he would always be her little boy.

Slipping the packs over his shoulder, he hurried outside, squinting at the bright, almost greenish, cast of the sky.

He walked through the vineyard once more, studied the neat rows, then knelt to fill his hands with rich, dark soil. He let it trickle through his fingers. The vines were snug, nestled against the earth. He'd done his best.

Yahweh, protect these vines you've given us.

A flock of sparrows careened across the sky, flying low. They headed south, toward the distant travelers on the Ridge Road.

He couldn't make out individuals among them, only a blurred mass of tunics, cloaks, and head coverings moving together, now apart. He didn't see Dov's horse nor Imma's donkey. They must be ahead, gaining ground.

He set out at an easy jog, a pace he could maintain all day. The rhythm of arms, legs, and breath blended with thought and landscape. He breathed in the storm's scent, the tremor of the Almighty's barely suppressed power. Exhaled a prayer that became a question. *What is happening?*

Elijah and Elisha often traveled together, sometimes even taking him. He'd grown familiar with the surrounding hills, and later he began delivering missives to the settlements. Like a proud father, Elijah praised Jaedon's strength, speed, and wiliness in evading enemy detection. The prophet always included a scroll which Jaedon read to the settlers.

They never traveled with more than two or three other people. Today they were followed by a crowd, and they carried with them a strange air of excitement. Something different, something of great importance was happening today.

As he left the outskirts of Gilgal, he spotted two familiar

figures. Binyamin's hulking frame was unmistakable. Also unmistakable was the tiny form of his wife. Eden appeared to be berating her husband, sometimes poking his chest with a bony finger. After a while, Binyamin, whose strength was reputed to rival the legendary Sampson, threw up his hands in surrender.

Jaedon grinned, remembering Savta Hadassah's directive to travel with one of the prophets. They'd be entertaining company. He picked up his pace. Spotting him, they waited while he caught up.

"I want Eden to go home," Binyamin muttered. "She is with child"—realizing what he'd said, he first reddened at his impropriety, then pushed on like an ox—"and will slow us down."

"Do you know where they are going?" Jaedon jutted his chin toward the walkers, careful not to smile. No point touching on the first part of his friend's remark.

Grasping his huge walking stick, Binyamin set off at a brisk, long-legged gait. "Days like this, I think I'm just a carpenter with a gift for teaching the Torah. Many claimed they received a message from Yahweh. I did not. Eden seemed troubled and insisted on coming, but she won't tell me more."

With clamped lips, Eden picked up the front of her long garment and set out at a jog. Soon she led them by several paces. Binyamin threw back his head and sighed.

Though not married, Jaedon lived with three generations of women. Well, four, if he counted Gershoni. There were times it was wise to give Imma, Yaffa, and Hadassah free rein, like a headstrong donkey. And it seemed good to let Eden take the lead for now.

He chewed on Binyamin's remark that he felt more teacher than seer. But he was one of the school of the prophets. Didn't they all hear the voice of the Lord?

What about his other statement, that Eden seemed troubled … but wouldn't speak of it? As if he thought her a prophetess, that she saw a vision. Had she? Perhaps she was only like Imma, peevish when with child.

No. Imma's *conjectures* were more than peevishness.

Jaedon had never seen a vision. But his place in the

school of prophets was different than the seers. They had come asking to be taught the Torah and were accepted as students. They had a calling.

He, along with Imma and Savta Yaffa, had been thrown into Elijah's path. At first, Jaedon felt like something muddied and beaten, washed up on the prophet's doorstep after a storm. Yet Yahweh had shown Elijah where to find the wounded family and the eaglet, Hevel, waiting near a spring. That was almost a calling, was it not?

There were times when Jaedon had hunted with the eagle, when he sensed that Yahweh also found pleasure in the beating of her wings. Had He not placed her in Jaedon's path as a gift? As He'd later provided the vineyard.

Like her name, Hevel was gone now, like a breath on the wind, after a mate caught her eye. But the vineyard was … well, Jaedon knew better than to describe it as permanent, even though he had planted it alongside Dov and Imma.

Beside him, Binyamin muttered something under his breath.

"What is it?" Jaedon asked.

Approaching a hill, Eden glanced over her shoulder as if gauging her lead. Her body was poised to again take flight. Trudging along, Binyamin sighed. "Let's hold back for now. Better let her catch her breath."

After the hill, their gradual descent turned rough where wind and rain had gouged ruts. For a while, Jaedon turned his attention to the ground under his feet. When the road leveled out, he turned his gaze across the forested landscape. In the distance, he spotted a few stragglers, and Eden was rapidly closing on them.

Binyamin said, "She's too far ahead. Come on."

They ran in silence for a while, Jaedon looking over his shoulder ever so often, but the road behind was always empty. Before long, they caught the tail-end of the stragglers. Eden was not among them. After learning that Bethel was Elijah's destination, they quickened their pace, leaving the others behind. Soon they spotted Eden resting under a scraggly acacia, taking a dainty drink from her water skin. When they uncorked their skins, she leapt up and again took the lead.

"Eden," yelled Binyamin. "Slow down! The child."

She did not turn, but shouted, "The child is not running. I don't want to keep you waiting."

A burble of laughter fought to erupt. Jaedon fought it, not wanting to undermine his friendship with Binyamin. The path continued its downward slope. A thicket of trees edging the path dappled Eden's garments as she ran beneath them.

"Let's walk a while. Until she gets a little ahead," Jaedon suggested.

Binyamin slowed. "Right. She'll slacken her pace after she proves her point." But he kept his eyes trained on her.

"Though she is small, Eden seems ... strong." Jaedon wisely avoided describing her as fearsome, the first word that had come to mind. "Imma continued to work the vineyard and hunt game each time she was with child, to no ill effect."

"Miriam has had two children and is now expecting another." Binyamin twisted his lips in a wry expression. "This is our first, after several years of marriage. None lost, thank the Lord, but we had resigned ourselves to a childless household."

Ah. So there was the source of Biny's concern. Jaedon paused, then said, "When Imma and I came to live at Gilgal, your recent marriage was a topic of every conversation."

Biny's expression grew soft, as if remembering a pleasant dream. "I met Eden while traveling with Elijah. She is the daughter of an olive farmer in a remote part of the northern hill country. A shy young girl who hid in the house when she saw us climb their hill."

Jaedon shot him a look. Eden, shy? Best not reply to that.

When Binyamin started chuckling, Jaedon joined in. "I take it you are not sorry to have found a fiery side to that demure girl."

"Not at all. I recommend it." He gave Jaedon a speculative look. "She has a little sister, if your father is ready to make arrangements on your behalf. The family lives in the hills near Lake Chinnereth."

Jaedon averted his gaze. A wife? The idea seemed distant, but right somehow. "Something to consider. What about you? Are you ready to be called 'Abba?'"

"Very much. I have already made a cradle."

"If it is as beautiful as the wedding chair you made for Imma, Eden must be pleased." Jaedon glanced ahead, noticed she'd slowed to a brisk walk, and tipped his head in her direction.

Binyamin grinned. "For such a young man, you are wise in the ways of women, my friend. Looks like we can pick up our pace again. Don't forget what I said about the little sister. Ziva was a pretty little girl playing with dolls, last I saw her." He made a show of counting on his fingers. "She will be close to marriageable age by now."

Jaedon thought on *marriageable age.* Not every man in the settlement was married, and of those who were, Eden appeared youngest. But what did he know? One night, he'd heard Imma and Dov whispering about a future wedding for him.

"Surely not yet," Imma had said.

"No, my love," Dov had murmured. "But soon perhaps. He will never be a soldier."

"I hope not," she had retorted. Then the straw mat had rustled, as he imagined her turning to sleep, and their whispers had slowed and faded to silence.

As they continued along the ridge road, Jaedon recognized an ancient olive tree. It marked a turnoff down which he'd traveled with Elijah and Elisha the previous summer. Deep into the hills three families had settled, raising sheep and farming wheat, barley, and vegetables. They welcomed the prophets, listened thoughtfully as Elijah read the Torah, and asked for news of other settlements.

They invited them to stay the night and begged Elijah to speak words of blessing over two young people who would wed.

Under a star-speckled sky the father of the bride played a willow flute. Elijah danced with the men of the settlement, his sinewy shins sometimes flashing beneath his garment while he merrily planted his staff here and there like a third leg. Later that night, he blessed the bride and groom with long life, bountiful harvests, and many children.

In the morning, Elijah gathered the elders and told them about a time he'd fled from Jezebel. But the Lord had come to him at Mount Sinai and asked why he had run.

"I told Yahweh all His prophets had been killed, and I alone still served him," Elijah said. "I was wrong. He gently explained that others faithfully obeyed. That He had reserved seven thousand in Israel who would not kiss the Ba'als. You, and more who will come to believe, are among those seven thousand, who will shine in heaven like the stars. The Lord bless and keep you."

As they passed the gnarled olive tree, Jaedon ran his hand across its bark. He smiled at the memory of Elijah trying to keep up with the flute player who kept playing faster. The couple had been married a year. *Bless and keep them, Yahweh, and bless your servant, Elijah.*

They passed two more turn offs with no sign that the crowd had left the path. Bethel was the next settlement. Jaedon was sure Elijah would speak there, and he wanted to hear what he had to say. When Elijah spoke to the farmers and shepherds in the hills, he taught from the Torah, emphasized trusting in Adonai and obeying His commands. But when he taught at a settlement of prophets, he answered questions about living as a prophet that Jaedon found even more interesting.

Such as how to humble oneself before God in preparation for the infilling. How to meditate on a portion of scripture, quiet one's mind, and listen for the voice. He had seen prophets strum an eight-stringed kinnor while gazing into a flickering fire. He had watched Elijah, sitting on a rocky outcrop that overlooked the Road from Gilgal to Samaria, staring into the distance and praying alone.

Well, not always alone. Once, when Jaedon followed at a discrete distance and hid behind a boulder, Elijah paused in his prayer. "Sit beside me, Jaedon. The Lord will listen to us both." They talked to Yahweh, short bits of conversation coming from one, then the other, as if the Lord sat there with them in the clearing. That simple method appealed to Jaedon. Since then, each day he spent time alone talking to God about everything. Though he had never heard the voice, when peace settled around him like a warm fleece, he knew the Lord heard.

As he tried to recall the substance of that first prayer

meeting with the old prophet, an eagle cry snagged his attention. A pair soared high overhead, winging their way southeast.

His footsteps faltered. No. Though he wished it, the eagles probably weren't Hevel and her mate. He took a deep breath, filling that place left empty by her departure. He was glad she'd found a partner. She'd been there when he needed her most, but she was a wild thing. Gift or not, the time had come for her to live free. Untethered.

Ahead, Eden stood waiting as Binyamin approached. Jaedon bent and, pretending to adjust his sandal, studied them obliquely. She motioned for Biny to turn, and one hand lingered on his shoulder as she rummaged through his pack.

Jaedon hid a smile as he straightened. Despite Eden's strong-minded ways, the couple shared an obvious bond.

As he approached, Eden retrieved a cloth parcel which contained several boiled eggs. She shared, and they strolled a while, munching, but then Jaedon increased the pace to a ground-covering walk.

"I'd like to catch them before Bethel," he said. His companions followed without hesitation.

They soon reached Bethel but did not find Elijah and the others there. A woman standing at the gate fixed her gaze on Jaedon, then tottered in their direction. Her lined, sun-browned face was framed by a head-covering, but its sky-blue color, a shade often woven on his family's looms, raised his interest.

"I am your Savta's friend, Naomi. You're Miriam's boy, aren't you? You just missed them. Her white donkey was easily keeping pace with your father's warhorse. I invited them to stop for refreshment, but they wanted to press on with the others."

"Did they say where they are headed?" Jaedon asked.

"Jericho. What of you three? Will you stop for honeyed wine and raisin cake?"

Jaedon shook his head. "I thank you, but we'll move on. I want to catch them before they reach the next town."

Binyamin made a strangled sound. Jaedon turned, guiltily. He shouldn't have spoken for everyone. His big friend was always ready to eat. Besides, Jaedon had eaten a good share of the boiled eggs.

Suddenly, shrill barking and yelps sounded from a nearby wadi. A dog fight, from the sounds of it. A band of young men rushed through the gate, shouting out bets and jostling one another.

A broad, red-haired man plowed into Naomi. She staggered back from the impact.

Jaedon leapt forward and steadied her. "Are you hurt?"

The brute continued running after the others, without glancing back.

"No, no. It may bruise, perhaps. Ne'er-do-wells!"

Binyamin growled under his breath. "He was twice your size. Not even an apology." He took a step as if he would go after them, but Eden grabbed his arm. "There were many, Biny, and Naomi has to live among them after we are gone."

"She is right. It will do no good." Naomi smoothed her head cloth back into place. "They are sons of wealthy businessmen and barely respect their fathers. Why would they care about an old woman?"

Jaedon took hold of her arm, feeling its frailty beneath the coarse cloth. "Where do you live? We will escort you."

"But you wanted to join the prophets—catch your parents—"

He waved his hand, making little of his intention. "We are not in such a hurry that we cannot see Savta's friend safely home."

Her mud-brick house hugged the city wall. Her arm in his, Jaedon led Naomi through a sagging gate into her narrow courtyard. The lattice fence appeared flimsy, but the fat goat that lazily munched a stack of scythed grass showed no interest in escaping.

Inside, light winked into the room through a tiny window covered by the lattice. Jaedon insisted Naomi sit to recover from the blow. Glancing around, he spotted a pitcher which, he guessed, held the recently offered honeyed wine. She protested when he handed her the first cup, attempting to rise and serve them.

"Please rest." Binyamin gently touched her shoulder, and Eden bustled about as the old woman settled back on the stool.

Jaedon pressed the drink between her wrinkled hands. "Tell us where to find the raisin cake, and we all will refresh ourselves."

She gave directions, her voice crackling like an autumn leaf.

Eden found and unwrapped the fruit-filled bread. "Strange that those young men did not follow the prophets." She broke and served pieces of the bread.

"Not so strange," Naomi replied. "They are among those who still worship at the old shrine."

"In the high places?" Jaedon frowned when she nodded. He'd heard about the golden calf idols at Bethel and Dan.

Elijah traveled throughout Israel, including Bethel, teaching the prophets and townsfolk about Yahweh. Especially His commands against worshiping idols. How could any live alongside the Lord's prophets and still practice the old ways? Yet, Jaedon couldn't discount Naomi's observation.

The food and watered wine seemed to refresh the old woman, but they tarried a while longer, watching her closely as Jaedon questioned her about the city and her neighbors. Finally satisfied she had no lasting injury, he asked if there was anything they could do for her before they resumed their journey.

Hesitating, she asked, "Can you milk the goat?"

When Jaedon grinned, Naomi limped across the room to a wooden shelf and returned with a squat, two-handled vessel.

"Where is its halter and rope?" He glanced around.

She handed him the vessel, smiling. "You will not need it."

He walked outside, Binyamin on his heels. The goat eyed the clay vessel, made a sound halfway between a bleat and a sigh, and ambled toward a low stool in a corner.

"Will we leave after this?" Binyamin rocked on his heels. "I'm afraid we'll miss the excitement—whatever it is."

"Agreed. So while I deal with the goat, will you two go next door"—Jaedon jutted his chin—"and explain what happened to Naomi? She spoke of being friendly with that family. Ask them to check on her this afternoon."

When Jaedon finished with the goat, Biny and Eden returned. "Her neighbors were very concerned," Eden said. "The woman asked me to tell Naomi they expect her for supper."

They brought Naomi the milk, conveyed her neighbor's invitation, and then left bearing gifts—a skin filled with half the milk, a lump of cloth-wrapped goat cheese, and several rounds of flatbread.

Jaedon studied the road ahead. Although the sky still bore that odd, greenish cast, the storm seemed to have paused, but long shadows crossing the path spoke of evening approaching. "Night may fall before we come upon the others. Shall we jog until we tire? Carrying messages between settlements, I've learned I cover more ground and maintain the pace longer at a slower speed."

"I can run all day," said Eden. Binyamin shrugged, clamping his lower lip between his teeth like someone who knows he's in trouble. He started out gamely, matching Jaedon's pace.

"I did not like to leave Naomi." Jaedon glanced at Biny, hoping to glean his opinion. "Still, her neighbors seemed kind."

Binyamin nodded, keeping his eye on his wife, who had pulled ahead once more.

"She did not mention a husband," Jaedon continued. Nor had she spoken of children. Had she never married? Or was she a barren woman, now widowed? He thought of his grandmothers. Though each had been widowed, a ladder of family supported them. Did Naomi have anyone?

As if responding to his unspoken question, Binyamin said between puffs, "The neighbors said they owe her a supper. It seemed as if they often share meals."

"She lives alone." Jaedon leapt over a protruding root "In Gilgal, neighbors care for one another. Even a childless widow is never destitute. With a school of prophets in Bethel, I expect the same."

The corner of Binyamin's mouth tightened, and he shrugged.

"I know." Jaedon ran a while in silence. "Surely those young men will be more heedful when the prophets return to the settlement."

Yet, if all the prophets were gone from Gilgal, would any man behave toward a woman in such a way? As if his friend read his thoughts, Binyamin huffed out. "Should not matter."

No, it should not, but was his community the exception among the hill country settlements? Elijah was a force for good in Gilgal. He and Elisha often traveled to the scattered schools of prophets in the hill country. But did their influence wane when they left?

No. The towns were not left without a leader. If Elijah and Elisha journeyed together, they assigned a trusted prophet to take charge in their absence. A similar practice must exist for the other towns. Then where was the leader of Bethel?

Jaedon scoffed under his breath. What was he thinking? Could any system of rule be depended upon to care for the vulnerable? He, who had lived in Jezreel, a great city, should know better than most. There, the king and queen, rather than protecting their citizens, had plotted and killed most of his family.

Jaedon mulled over the memory, listening to the muffled thuds of Binyamin's sandaled feet, the twitter of birds in the shrubs, and then, the shrill cry of an eagle. Again! He flicked his gaze upward, catching the distant shapes of another pair heading north. Could these be Hevel and her mate?

Jaedon's thoughts returned to those early days, when a younger Elisha had run laughing, dragging a lure made from a freshly killed pigeon, as an orphaned lad signaled his young eagle to hunt.

Now Jaedon trained his attention on the eagles flying overhead, hoping for some sign of recognition, but they only continued winging their way north. He sighed quietly, turning his eyes back to the uneven ground ahead of him.

Even if neither pair were *his* eagles, something about this day seemed important, akin to the day he met Elijah.

Binyamin tapped his shoulder. "I thought, for a moment, we might entertain feathered visitors. I am sorry."

Everyone in the settlement had watched with interest when Elisha and Jaedon worked with the eagle. He had not been the only one disappointed when Hevel left.

"It's for the best," he said.

I know that's true, Yahweh. Help me feel it.

They ran a while longer in silence. Then Eden, running ahead, began singing a Psalm of ascent. Binyamin, breathing heavily, growled under his breath.

Jaedon smiled. What would it be like to live with such a woman? Amused, he wondered about the girl, *Ziva.* How much was she like her sister?

"Look!" said Binyamin, his voice urgent. He pointed where a cloud of dust rose from a ravine intersecting the ridge road. "Riders are coming."

Chapter Three

"—and anoint Elisha son of Shaphat from
Abel Meholah to succeed you as prophet."
~ 1 Kings 19:16b

Enroute to Jericho
Jaedon

"Quick!" Jaedon hissed. "Could be raiders!"

Eden glanced over her shoulder. Biny flung his arm toward the dust plume, then gestured for her to hide. Silently she picked her way down the slope's opposite side. With surprising agility for one his size, Biny hustled off the trail and hunkered behind a clump of bracken, grasping his walking stick like a club.

Jaedon took refuge behind a fallen tree, twigs jabbing his side as he loaded stones into his slingshot. Who was coming? An Aramean cohort? Edomites? He'd stand beside Binyamin in a fight any day, but two men would be outnumbered by one of the bands of marauders that recently hit outlying Israelite villages, dragging off captives to sell. He couldn't let himself think what they would do with Eden. *Lord, make us invisible.*

A magnificent war horse, glossy with health, was first to top the ridge. A familiar animal, the color of flame, ridden by—

"Dov!" Jaedon jumped to his feet, catching his sleeve on a twig. Behind him, Binyamin crunched through the underbrush.

Imma, on her white donkey, Sheleg, followed Dov. "Were you both hiding?" She chuckled, with the low warm rumble he had loved since childhood.

Binyamin's ruddy face flamed even redder. "We saw dust from your animals and, well—"

"Ah, the ravine is steep," Dov said. "You couldn't know who approached. A sound decision."

"Eden! You can come out," Binyamin called.

Grasping handfuls of grass and the tops of half-buried boulders, Eden pulled herself up the slope. Regaining the road, she hurried toward them.

Jaedon swiped his forearm across his brow, shifting his weight awkwardly. He'd overreacted. Dov slid off his horse, handed Jaedon the reins, and lifted Imma from the donkey. "You did right, Son. Better watchful nine times than captured once."

His stepfather's reassurance lifted his spirits.

Dov seated Imma on the fallen log, then retook Uri's reins. "We watered the animals at a stream not far back. Do you need to refill your water skins?"

He led the stallion to a patch of deep grass, slid off his bridle, and hobbled his front legs. He turned the donkey loose to graze. Somewhat timid, she would stay near Uriel without tether.

Jaedon unstrapped the bag from his shoulder. "We filled them at Bethel, and your friend Naomi sent us away with milk and raisin cakes. Would you like some?"

"Oh, yes! Fresh goat milk." Imma reached for the skin of milk. After slaking her thirst, she said "I have much to tell you, Son." Finished with the animals, Dov sat on one side, Jaedon on her other. Binyamin and Eden settled where a pile of leaves had drifted to soften the ground.

Miriam took another swallow. "Ah. Naomi's goat gives such sweet milk." She took a final sip then offered it around, along with the raisin cakes. When everyone was munching contentedly, she said, "We should have waited for you. I don't know why I did not, except I felt the need for haste. But we followed the prophets to the end. To Jericho," Imma said.

Jaedon set down the raisin cake, untasted. *The end? Elijah was dead?*

"We watched it all," Dov said

"Where shall we start?" Imma asked. "They saw the beginning—the turmoil in Gilgal, Elijah telling Elisha to stay behind."

"Tell us," Jaedon said.

She summarized the start of their journey, from Gilgal. "When Elijah told Elisha not to follow, that he didn't know when he'd be back, I thought ... well, that Elijah had seen his own death."

Binyamin nodded. "Several of us heard them arguing. We thought the same. We decided to follow in case we needed to bury him."

Jaedon shot him a glance. Bury him? Why had he said nothing of that?

Binyamin stared at his feet.

Imma said, "Prophets continued to emerge from their houses. I saw Eden, shouting for you to wait."

"I thought it would be too hard on her," Binyamin said. "Not only the journey, but to see him die. But she insisted. He turned his gaze upon Eden and his whole face softened. "And I am afraid of this woman." He took her hand.

"I know what you mean." Dov bumped Miriam with his shoulder.

When Eden and Imma shared an indulgent smile, Jaedon suspected they relegated men to a rank slightly above a pet lamb.

"I told Dov something important was happening, something I didn't understand."

"I begged her to stay behind," Dov said, "but she only said, 'Hurry.'"

She took Jaedon's hand. "By the time the children were settled, the prophets were far ahead. We pushed the animals hard to catch them—you would never have done so on foot."

Imma described more of the journey. The crowd, the prophets, and the sky—like a fractured clay lamp.

"At Bethel, people streamed out of the city to greet us, as if we were long-expected guests. Dov and I puzzled over this—how could Bethel expect us? But we've all noticed—if the Lord sends a vision, many in the community experience it. Even I have sometimes caught a glimpse. I have come to believe it is not so odd. If rain falls in a city, more than one person gets wet."

Imma described a disturbing event at Bethel. "A townsman handed Elijah a waterskin. While he drank, someone asked Elisha, 'Do you know the Lord is going to take your master from you today?' As if he thought Elisha was not privy to a vision they had seen. I could see the question pained him."

Miriam paused and swallowed hard. "It was then, Jaedon, that I feared for Elisha, if his master should die on this journey. Those at Bethel seemed to consider him a poor replacement for our friend. Would other prophets challenge him for leadership?"

How could it be? Among those called *Sons of the Prophets* Elijah had openly shared what Yahweh revealed on Mount Sinai. All the prophets knew Elisha was called.

At Jericho, Imma said, more prophets confronted Elisha. This time, he snapped at them.

Jaedon frowned. A strange reaction from the peaceful prophet. Did he mourn his mentor's imminent death? Or did he mistrust the prophets' intentions?

Jaedon had little time to dwell on those questions. He was soon captive to his mother's tale as she described the day's end—her skin prickling as the storm intensified, Dov insisting they dismount and plant their feet on firm ground, Elijah smiling despite the gale, which threw his hair about like a fisherman's net.

Imma touched Jaedon's shoulder. "Despite the wind's rising volume, I heard an eagle cry."

Jaedon covered her hand with his.

"I looked up, and there it was—an eagle floating on the wind, skimming over the crowd, and dipping over my head. When it circled back toward Elijah, I knew. It was your eagle. Hevel."

"And then?" Jaedon prompted.

"A chariot of fire pulled by flaming horses landed between the prophets. Elijah stepped into the chariot, and it carried him away. I saw his cloak fall from the chariot, and it landed at Elisha's feet." She continued a story too amazing for belief.

"Then Dov reminded me ..." she nudged her husband. "Tell him."

Dov propped his elbows on his knees. "Elijah once said, 'I have always wanted to journey in a chariot.' Do you remember, Jaedon? You were there."

His voice rasped. "I remember."

How could he take this all in? Elijah, who had been like a father to him, taken to heaven in the sight of all in some sort of fiery conveyance drawn by angelic horses? And Hevel a part of the scene! Any who followed to Jericho, and all the prophets who lived there had watched it happen.

But he had missed it.

"What else?" he asked. "What happened next?"

"We were stunned. Elisha, clearly distraught, tore the neck of his tunic in mourning and shouted, 'My father! My father! You were the chariots and the horsemen of Israel.'"

Imma paused, as if unsure how to go on. Despite the day's warmth, she shivered.

Jaedon asked, "Are you all right, Imma?"

She made a gesture of dismissal. "Hear the rest." She turned toward Dov. "Tell them what you learned."

Dov nodded. "A group from Bethel argued against following Elisha. While they had seen a whirlwind, they saw no miracle. No chariot of fire, no horses. They surmised that a frail Elijah had been swept away by the storm's strength, that Elisha had brazenly taken his mantle and, possessing it, was trying to bolster his claim to leadership. Any who spoke as witnesses, they called fools or liars. When we left, they were still arguing."

Jaedon lurched to his feet. "The prophets are divided? Some favor, others oppose Elisha?"

"For now," Dov agreed. "Especially one loud-spoken group. But they must come round. Elisha was Yahweh's choice."

Jaedon considered this. Elijah had spoken of the prophecies Yahweh whispered on Mount Sinai. He had heard the story many times. But Elijah spent much of his time in Gilgal. Had he made Elisha's call as clear to all the settlements of prophets?

"What of the others from Gilgal?" he asked Dov. "Why did none return with you?"

"As I said. When we left, they were still arguing with those discontent with Elisha as leader. Likely they will stay 'til morning."

Jaedon exhaled slowly. At least Elisha had the support of friends from Gilgal.

He hated that he'd missed Elijah's departure. He could not fathom he would never see the old prophet again. He smiled. Hevel had been there, soaring in the same stretch of sky.

God had taken His prophet home—alive—carried by a conveyance of the fire that had marked his leadership. And Elisha might be facing a battle.

He turned to Binyamin. "I want to press on. Get to Jericho before sundown."

Binyamin glanced at Eden.

Jaedon extended his hand to him. "I understand if you need to see to your wife. I may stay several days."

"He does not need to see to me!" Eden declared, hands on hips.

"Correct." Binyamin hesitated, studying her a while. "However, now that we know what has happened to Elijah, I think it is best if we return together." He turned back to Jaedon. "All of us."

"You should stay together. I will go on," Jaedon said. "Elisha may need my support."

Jaedon clasped Binyamin's shoulder, hoping to reassure him, because he felt constrained to go on alone. If Elisha needed him, it might be for more than a day or two. If there was real resistance, he would stand with the man who had, with Elijah, been a wall of protection for him and his mother. He walked to her, and she stretched out her arms.

"I will not worry about you, Jaedon," she said. "You're not far from Jericho, and we met no one on the trail."

Dov added, "He can disappear into the landscape like a summer stag."

She shook her finger. "When you return home, see to it you travel in company."

Jaedon bit back a protest and bent to kiss her goodbye. "Agreed, Imma."

Dov gave him a slow wink. "You are a young man with conviction. No longer a boy."

Jaedon stood tall, shouldered his pack, and ran down the road toward Jericho.

Chapter Four

After the death of Moses the servant of the Lord,
the Lord said to Joshua son of Nun, Moses' aide:
"Moses my servant is dead. Now then, you and all
these people, get ready to cross the Jordan River
into the land I am about to give to them.
~ Joshua 1:1-2

Jericho, late in the day
Elisha

ELISHA SLOWLY CLIMBED THE JORDAN'S BANK, his gaze fixed on the prophets. Behind him, the twice-parted waters whooshed back together. As the prophets eyed the mantle, still rolled in his fist, their voices, whispers at first then growing in volume, became a chant. "The spirit of Elijah rests on Elisha. The spirit of Elijah rests on Elisha."

A cluster of prophets moved his way, tentative at first, then surging forward. They knelt in front of him, vowing allegiance, a pledge not made by those who stood apart conversing in sharp exchanges like a flock of herons tussling over a fish.

Another group approached. He recognized the spokesman being nudged forward. Gehazi, one of the married prophets who settled in Jericho, father of three sons and husband to a sharp-tongued wife.

"Master," he said, bowing his head. "The storm must have taken the body of Elijah far from here. Let us go search that we may give him the honor a great prophet deserves."

"There is no reason for searching." Elisha stared at Gehazi. What a request. Hadn't he seen Elijah ascend? Had none of these followers? The dissenters stood apart still arguing amongst themselves. They certainly had not seen.

"But master," said another. "Of course, we must bury him. It would be disrespectful not to. If you fear raiders, know that we have fifty able men here, armed and ready to go."

"You don't understand." He was careful to speak patiently. "The Spirit of the Lord has taken him."

"Yes," said another. "And who can know where the Spirit of the Lord has carried him and set him down? Perhaps he lies on a mountaintop. Or injured in some valley. We cannot leave him for lions and scavengers."

Hadn't he spoken plainly? "You will not find his body. The Lord has taken him to heaven."

Gehazi bowed again. "As you say." As if preparing to make camp, he walked a short distance into the trees and busied himself gathering sticks and kindling which he stacked in the clearing.

But a man behind him muttered, "Perhaps Elijah's assistant wearies of service and does not care if his master is found." Disgruntled murmurs followed.

Elisha turned up his hands. "Go, then. Search." Sighing, he went to sit beneath a large oak. He leaned against the wide trunk, overcome by exhaustion. It had been a long and arduous journey, but more than that, he mourned Elijah. How he'd miss their late-night walks, talking about the Lord, the king, the people. He could hardly believe his friend was gone. But he had seen him go.

The fifty, seemingly, had not. They gathered weapons, supplies, and waterskins. They consulted among themselves, then took off in different directions. Some to search mountaintops, some to search vales. It might be days before they returned.

This was a poor start to his leadership. Nearly half the prophets did not believe his wisdom came from Yahweh, or they would not have gone on their fruitless search. Rolling his shoulders, he tipped his head back, gazing at the last rays of light filtering through lobed leaves. A golden dusk, as if it reflected from the vanished chariot. He chided himself for moaning about Elijah's departure. It had been glorious, really. A beautiful close to his ministry. And yet such a day.

He expelled a breath, recalling Elijah trotting along the final approach to Jericho, his staff encouraging, emphasizing, or chastising just as often as it aided his progress. All day, he'd led younger prophets in a chase to keep up with him. He had been tireless.

Yahweh, help me. I need a double portion of Elijah's spirit.

Gehazi came and squatted beside him, laying a travel pack between them. He uncorked a water skin and offered Elisha a drink. "Are you hungry, Master? I brought bread and figs."

Elisha tipped back a draught of cool water, eying Gehazi's lined face and stooped shoulders. He'd been recruited by Elijah sometime after Arameans attacked Gehazi's village. They had captured some of its citizens and, before departing, set fire to what was left.

When Elisha handed back the remaining water, the prophet said, "Let me wash your hands so you can eat."

As the remaining water trickled, Elisha rubbed his hands underneath. A humble gesture and kind, but was Gehazi implying more than simple courtesy? To be his servant? Despite what Gehazi wanted, was he Yahweh's choice?

Elisha dried his hands on his sash. "I understand you joined the prophets here after your village was ransacked."

Gehazi pulled a cloth-wrapped parcel from the pack and laid it on Elisha's lap. Unfolding it, he revealed seven figs and three flatbread rounds. "Yes, shortly after that. Many of our friends were captured and carried off. Although our house and vineyard were burned beyond salvage, we were unharmed. We had gone to a neighboring village to help with olive harvest. The Lord protected us."

The right answer. Gehazi had lived with prophets long enough to know to attribute his family's safety to Yahweh rather than happenstance. Not sensing deep spirituality, nor a desire to learn, Elisha studied him. Why would he want to serve, this man who had lost everything?

"My family is content to live and work among the prophets. I would be blessed to serve."

Elisha nodded and felt his eyes drift down.

"You have journeyed all day," Gehazi said. "Come to my home for the night. There is room before the hearth fire."

Behind Elisha's closed eyes, a vision flashed. *The wife of Gehazi, surrounded by half-grown sons. A travel pack over her shoulder, the boys also burdened—she shook her finger at her husband. No! We will stay with my father until you give us a suitable home.*

Yes, there was plenty of room in the house assigned to Gehazi. Yet, he offered hospitality, although the empty house would expose his marital discord. So, an honest man, though not entirely forthcoming.

The sweetness of the fig still on his tongue, Elisha thought over the omission as he bit into a flatbread. He had not asked for details, but he would not stay under the prophet's roof tonight.

"I thank you, but I will stay here to watch and pray for the others' return. Perhaps another will accept your kind offer." He gestured toward clans from Gilgal and Bethel.

Gehazi nodded and left. The Jericho settlement stood aways off, but he returned surprisingly soon with a sleeping mat, a blanket, and sticks to build a small fire. Others from Gilgal or Bethel who had not returned home also made camp nearby. Many wrapped themselves in their cloaks and lay on bare ground, although Gehazi and other residents of Jericho either invited the visitors home or brought mats and blankets.

One of the Jericho prophets began to strum a lyre. Sitting near the fire, the prophet picked out a simple tune, one of King David's Psalms of praise. Other prophets pulled out reed whistles, ranging from deep croaking akin to a frog chorus to bird-like trills.

> *As a father has compassion on his children,*
> *so the Lord has compassion on those who fear him;*
> *for he knows how we are formed,*
> *he remembers that we are dust.*

> *But from everlasting to everlasting*
> *the Lord's love is with those who fear him,*
> *The Lord has established his throne in heaven,*
> *and his kingdom rules over all.*

Elisha's thoughts drifted with the music. During this day, the procession from morning to evening, Elijah leading the prophets in a parade. Most thought it a funeral procession, but it was more a celebration, like a wedding. Praise Adonai, who carried His servant Elijah past the gates of Sheol to heavenly realms. He allowed me, though unworthy, to witness such a miracle.

I thank you, Lord.

A deep-voiced prophet sang the words to the Psalm, interrupting Elisha's thoughts. He opened his eyes, seeking the source. Before he found him, however, another voice lifted higher, an alternate tune that twisted around the first like strands of wool thread. A voice he knew well.

Jaedon came walking down the ridge path, his youthful voice the melody. Elisha stood to embrace the boy who at first had come to his waist and now looked directly into his eyes.

As they clasped each other, kissing cheeks in welcome, he said, "Elijah is gone. Taken to heaven."

"I heard," Jaedon answered. "Imma said he went in a golden chariot pulled by fiery horses."

Elisha gaped. "She saw?" Warmth spread through him.

"As did Dov. She described it as glorious." Jaedon pulled back, one eyebrow raised. "Some did not?"

"I think, perhaps, no one else. Many are looking for his body tonight, sure that Yahweh has flung him on a mountaintop."

Jaedon grinned. "More likely a cloud in heaven. My Imma makes no mistakes."

Elisha heard footfalls behind him, and he sensed two conflicting desires residing in the prophet behind him and Jaedon.

Yahweh, who is your choice?

"You sing with the voice of an angel," Gehazi said. "You transformed my simple song with your melody, but we have not met. I am called Gehazi."

Chapter Five

For I know the plans I have for you," declares the Lord,
"plans to prosper you and not to harm you,
plans to give you hope and a future.
~ Jeremiah 29:11

Jericho, three days later
Jaedon

THE MASSIVE OAK BECAME THE PLACE where the prophets gathered in Jericho. It was a good meeting place for two important reasons—its wide backrest for Elisha and a dense canopy giving shade.

If only Jaedon could reach it before he collapsed. Sweat dripped from his headband, down his neck and back, and under the shoulder yoke that balanced the huge water jars.

He found it no easy task to quench the thirst of the many prophets who hadn't returned to their homes. He'd lugged water morning and evening since the searchers departed, especially after he heard women of the city mutter various versions of, "It is not our duty to draw water for able-bodied men who left their own wives at home."

Trying not to pant, but even more careful not to spill a drop, he lowered the jars to the ground. Prophets began to make their way toward the water. Jaedon felt his lips curl in displeasure but quickly smoothed his expression. It was not for him to chide older prophets for laziness. Perhaps they were more tired than he or had an unknown illness.

To the first three who lifted the ladle, Elisha said, "You, you, and you—take over this task from Jaedon for the next three days. As he has done, ensure the water does not run dry. Do not look to the women to help you. They have families of their own to look after."

Jaedon held back the sigh of relief. Better Elisha choose and instruct the prophets, not him, a younger man than most of this company. He flung himself on the ground beside the prophet and leaned against the trunk. Immediately, the stench of his own sweat assailed his senses. He planted his palms, ready to shove to his feet and step away.

"No, lad," Elisha lay a hand atop his. "Sweat from hard work in the service of others is a pleasing aroma, to the Lord and to me."

In the service of others. Would this be a good time to talk to Elisha about apprenticeship? "I have wanted to speak to you about that."

Elisha tipped his head, listening without comment.

"Elijah was like a father to me. Taught me the words of Yahweh. To be a man, pleasing in His sight. I am sorry to have missed his departure. And you … you have been my elder brother."

Elisha shifted to bump him with his shoulder.

Jaedon smiled, righting himself. No need to be nervous. He cleared his throat. "Though you came after Elijah took us in, you know how my father was taken from us."

While I hid in a tree. At first, fear had consumed him. Then, overwhelming uselessness. Like half a clay pot. Broken. Filled with vengeful thoughts, but too weak to carry them out.

"I had two men to guide me. Elijah … and you."

Elisha studied him, as if peering into his soul.

Jaedon stared back. *Does he know my dark thoughts?*

"Not to mention the other prophets." The corners of Elisha's eyes crinkled.

Jaedon slid his hands down his face. "They delighted in sending me to retrieve forgotten tools," he groaned.

He swallowed hard. *Stop babbling.* "My best memories were of you helping me train Hevel."

Elisha cleared his throat. "I wish you could've seen her. I wondered if she and her mate would follow Elijah through that crack in the heavens."

They both sat silent for a long time. Finally, Elisha spoke. "There is something you wish to ask me."

Jaedon dipped his chin. "When Dov married Imma, he treated me as a son. So, although Yahweh allowed my own father to be taken, I have been blessed with fathers. But our vineyard is small, and I have two siblings with another on the way. Perhaps it is not big enough to support all of us."

Jaedon fought a frown. Why did he say that? He loved the vineyard, and if it was small, he didn't need Elisha to point out that he and Dov could easily add terraces to expand it. His motivation wasn't *this* vineyard, and it wasn't *the other* vineyard. He was no longer a damaged child, filled with vengeful thoughts. The prophets had showered him with kindness. He owed them a great deal.

"I have always felt close to the school of the prophets. I want to study and learn. Now that Elijah is gone, and the Lord has given you his mantle, you need a servant. I want to serve you."

Elisha murmured, "I would like that if ..." He shifted his gaze to the leafy bower overhead.

"If?" Jaedon's breath stilled.

"If Yahweh wills it. I have asked Him to show me who He has planned to follow me. May I suggest that you also seek His will?"

Jaedon's self-assurance crumbled. "How shall I? I cannot play the lyre." He exhaled. Why was he making excuses?

"Gehazi said you sing like an angel, and I agree. Yet, you need not sing or play an instrument, only talk to the Lord, just as you talk to me. Go apart from the others. You and Yahweh. Walk by the Jordan. Talk aloud or speak only in your heart. When you return, read from the scrolls, listen to teachings. He will answer from the scrolls, the teachings, or His whisper."

Elisha made it sound like two friends talking. Was it really that simple?

The prophet stood and walked to an area with a fire ring, water jugs the prophets had refilled, and a pile of various-sized baskets. He sorted until he apparently found one to his liking. Sauntering back, he presented it to Jaedon as though it were a prize.

"Your lyre."

Jaedon peered into the basket. Cloth sacks lay folded inside. "I don't understand."

"Take this and walk into the forest. You and the Lord. Hunt for cumin, wild onions, anything to add to the pot for supper. You have foraged with Miriam since you were a boy. Your fingers are as skilled at finding edible plants in the hills as the musicians are plucking their instruments. Music relaxes them, but you relax when you roam the hills."

Jaedon nodded as understanding filled him. He would disappear into the hills, find herbs for supper where Yahweh had planted them, and inquire about God's plan.

Chapter Six

Then Moses cried out to the Lord, and the Lord showed
him a piece of wood. He threw it into the water,
and the water became fit to drink.
~ Exodus 15:25a

Jericho, later that evening
Gehazi

As twilight settled, Gehazi stood in the clearing stirring an enormous pot, supposed to be stew for supper. A few prophets had shared the sparse contents of their travel packs, but it was a thin gruel. Elisha had told him not to worry, that he'd sent the young man, Jaedon, to forage.

Gehazi bent over the steam and inhaled deeply. It smelled more of dirty tunics than supper. Was it burning? Quickly he swiped the paddle around. He knew little about cooking, and it seemed he would need to know such things. If Lital were here, he would quietly ask for her help. Would she give it?

Knowing her nature, yes. Despite his failings.

He willed himself to ignore the sudden clench in his chest. Having lost everything, he had few options. He would follow the only path open to him with the same dogged grit he'd used to build a home and plant a vineyard.

A few of the missing prophets trudged back into camp, one carrying a young lamb. He watched as they approached Elisha. They had been gone three days. Were these all who would gather around the new leader?

Just then, the boy, Jaedon, emerged from the forest carrying a basket. Nodding curtly, he unwrapped a lumpy cloth parcel, revealing a dozen cleaned partridges. Pulling a knife from his scabbard, he sliced between joints and dropped pieces into the bubbling water. Then he lifted a sack of root vegetables and herbs, still dripping from being washed in the river. He knelt by a stump and began chopping.

Gehazi nudged him aside. "I can do that. Thank you for the meat and vegetables." He jutted his chin at the pot, and then realized he had no knife. Jaedon had brought everything except the water. He sputtered a little. "Next time you forage, will you show me how to find"—he indicated the vegetables—"whatever these are?"

Jaedon eyed him, slowly extending his knife, hilt first. "The red bulb cooks well with meat, but do not use it alone in lentil stew. This is wild garlic, this here, onion." He held up a handful of grasses and indicated a pile of what appeared to be old wood chips. "The herbs give flavor to the broth, and the mushrooms give substance, especially when there is little meat."

Gehazi took the knife, mumbled his thanks, and resumed chopping the vegetables and dropping handfuls into the emerging stew.

Jaedon stood aside, shifting his weight from one foot to the other, then retrieved his basket. "I am going to speak with Elisha. Use the knife as long as you need."

Gehazi kept chopping. They now had more prophets to feed and more food with which to feed them, and Elisha had known the boy would find it.

Gehazi slid a pile of vegetables into the steaming pot. There should be enough, but how could he be sure? Well, he would find out when they ate tonight. If not, next time he would adjust.

Over the quiet burble of the stew, he heard one of Jericho's prophets describing the lengths they'd gone in their search. Gehazi looked toward Elisha, who appeared to be tending the lamb he'd seen earlier. Jaedon was helping, holding it about the neck while Elisha dipped his fingers in a jug of what must be olive oil. He proceeded to rub the oil into wounds. Gehazi studied the boy's demeanor, his head tilted, nearly touching Elisha's shoulder. Gehazi felt his forehead tighten. Were Elisha and the boy close?

"We looked on mountains, in valleys ... covered many miles, but we did not find him." The returning prophet sounded weary but hopeful, as if he expected to be praised for a difficult job well performed.

Elisha sighed, looking up from the lamb. "Didn't I tell you not to go?"

The prophet's shoulders sagged. "I will not doubt you

again. You are the Lord's chosen prophet."

Releasing the lamb, Elisha stood and clasped him by both shoulders. "Welcome back, my friend."

To Gehazi, it sounded as if the welcome had more than one meaning. Well, he would not make that one's mistake. When Elisha spoke, Gehazi would always pay heed.

Elisha bent over the water jar, dipped in the ladle, and extended it to the man to drink. Jaedon stood a little apart, watching and listening.

Some of the others hung back, but Elisha motioned for them to approach. Then he glanced at Gehazi, one eyebrow quirked, but Gehazi understood the silent question and answered loud enough for all to hear. "There will be enough."

The flames under the pot had burned low. He walked to where Elisha, Jaedon, and the others stood. "I think it will take a while to cook. Perhaps I should make bread." At least he'd learned that from times he'd helped Lital.

"Yes, please do." Elisha settled under a tree. One after another, the prophets came to speak with him. By their humble demeanor, it seemed they were making amends.

"I will help," Jaedon said. "Do you have grain?"

Gehazi nodded. "There is enough at my house to feed the prophets for this meal and perhaps one more." He glanced at Elisha. He would look to him for replenishment when it was needed.

It was a short walk from the clearing to the house Gehazi had been lent. They walked in silence. He darted the boy a glance. "You're a hard worker. You filled the water jars morning and evening, sometimes more than once."

Jaedon tilted his head, a slight smile curving his lips.

"And you found the game and vegetables for tonight's stew. Without them, we'd be sipping hot water tasting of dirty tunics."

Jaedon laughed. "Dirty tunics?"

"I think I burned the water." Gehazi felt his face crease into a smile. "None of the other prophets worked as hard as you."

Not even he. It occurred to him that the lad might be a better servant for Elisha.

No. That mustn't happen.

"Two of my sons are near your age." And not as hard-working. Lital used to protest when she thought he'd assigned them too many chores, saying she needed their help, since she had no daughter. A jibe at him, for not providing her with one. But was he God?

"I have seen seventeen winters. Your sons?"

"Eighteen, sixteen, and eleven. Perhaps you will meet them some day."

"Are they not in Jericho?"

"No. I ... no."

Jaedon eyed him curiously but did not press him. When he showed him inside, the boy glanced around, spotting the grinding stone and worktable. "It will be easier to prepare the dough here and carry it to the clearing."

They divided the work. Jaedon offered to grind the grain. Meanwhile, Gehazi mixed dough using grain he'd milled previously. As Jaedon neared completion, Gehazi jumped to his feet.

"The stew! I forgot to ask someone to watch it." He gathered his dough into a clean cloth Lital had left behind, along with everything else, except clothing for her and the boys.

"Go see about it." Jaedon poured the grain he'd milled into the bowl. "I expect Elisha will have assigned it to someone, but assure yourself. I'll be along as soon as I mix the next batch."

"Blessed are You, Lord our God"—Gehazi quickly bowed his head. He'd become distracted, when he needed to be focused always on Elisha.

After the blessing, Gehazi ladled out stew to the line of prophets, silently numbering them as they filed past, pulling out wooden or clay bowls from their travel packs. He noted the troublemakers were no longer in their midst. Though Lital had disapproved, he'd been right to choose Jericho. The cult of the Bulls was too near Bethel for his liking.

When the prophets finished eating, Gehazi cleaned the cookpot with leaves and sand. The boy sat by Elisha, the two talking back and forth, smiling in friendly camaraderie. It had been bandied about that the boy's father had been stoned for some sin, and the boy taken under the wings of first Elijah and then Elisha. He snorted quietly, amused at a sudden thought. There'd been an eagle, that also took the boy under its wings.

Could the boy become a problem? Hard-working, kind, intuitive … and a shared history. Gehazi looked around for some helpful task. One of the jars was nearly empty. He picked up the yoke, prepared to settle it over his shoulder, then stopped.

He walked over to Elisha and the boy. Jaedon. They looked up, the boy losing his smile. But Elisha's smile stayed warm. *Good.*

"Master," he waved his arm to indicate the clearing, the trees, and beyond, where the city rose above a staunch retaining wall. "This is a beautiful area but hard to inhabit. It is a long walk to the river, and though there is a closer spring, its water is tainted. Crops wither if its waters are used to irrigate. And there have been … miscarriages." For once, he let himself feel everything, her pain, her desolation. A child, not just a bloody mass, a baby, discernible as a girl. *Forgive me, Lital.*

Someone muttered, "The spring continues to suffer the effects of the curse."

A ripple of whispers swept through the clearing. "Ah yes, the curse lingers."

And Lital would not return to him, would not return to Jericho where she had lost the daughter she yearned for.

The curse lingers–in me.

Elisha said, "Bring me a bowl. A new bowl, which has never been used. Put salt in it."

"I have one." Gehazi ran back to the house he had, for a short time, shared with his wife and sons. Lital had made him a clay bowl, its rim engraved with grape leaves and vines. She had baked and polished it until it was very smooth and hard. Like she had become.

He had salt hidden on the top of a shelf, pressed against the wall, where the small sack could not be seen. He poured half into the bowl then, reconsidering, poured it all.

He ran back to the clearing, lungs laboring. Would someone else have hurried to fulfill Elisha's request, surpassing him? Was another, even now, basking in the prophet's favor?

Elisha stood as he approached, stretching out his arms. Gehazi settled the bowl in his hands.

"Your wife's parting gift." He nodded in approval. "And all your salt."

Then Elisha walked past Gehazi. He quickly followed behind. Jaedon and the other prophets trailed after them.

Elisha strode up the gentle slope, never outstripping his followers. They were a procession, moving together past Jericho and its walls toward the spring.

When they finally reached it, Elisha turned his face and lifted his hands up to heaven.

"Yahweh, Jericho's curse was fulfilled when you judged Hiel. Now, we ask you to remove the remaining vestiges of judgment on the land. We bring salt, in recognition of your healing power, in a never-used bowl, symbolic of a new beginning."

Then he swung the bowl, and salt arced in a fine spray across the murky surface. The water bubbled and popped like a caldron over burning coals. Then the waters cleared. The prophets moved closer, looked down, and saw their astonished reflections. Murmurs of *thank you, a miracle, God is good.*

Elisha held the bowl close to his chest. "This is what the Lord says, 'I have healed this water. Never again will it cause death or make the land barren."

Then Elisha tipped the rest of the salt into the spring, dipped the bowl, and sipped. "Delicious," he said, pouring the rest on the ground. Gehazi recognized the gesture. A thanksgiving offering.

The others hurried forward, cupped their hands, and drank the water, laughing delightedly and declaring its sweetness.

Gehazi knelt at the spring's edge, dipping his hands in the cold water, but bathing his teary eyes rather than drinking. He whispered his own thank you to Yahweh. A blessing to the city. Did using his salt, his bowl mean his guilt was removed?

Elisha turned to him. "Yahweh has said a man separated from his wife cannot serve Him. Go and see to your wife. Convince her to return to you, with her sons. Then we shall see."

Chapter Seven

*If you remain hostile toward me and refuse to listen
to me, I will multiply your afflictions seven times over,
as you sins deserve. I will send wild animals against
you, and they will rob you of your children, destroy
your cattle and make you so few in number
that your roads will be deserted.
~ Leviticus 26:21-22*

*Road to Gilgal, next morning
Jaedon*

THE NEXT DAY JAEDON ROSE BEFORE dawn. The sky was dark with rippling clouds that would burn off with the sun. But now they cloaked all but the brightest stars that hung low on the horizon.

He was not the only one awake. Though he intended to be first up, freshen the fire, and prepare Imma's herbal-infused beverage for Elisha, he spotted Gehazi already bustling around, shaking grain out of a sack, and kneeling to grind it.

Jaedon frowned and warmth rushed to his face. He was glad of the dark that hid his unworthy attitude. They both wanted to serve Elisha. That made them allies, not antagonists.

He touched his new ally's shoulder. "Need some help?"

"Ho, Jaedon!" Gehazi crooked his head around. "Yes, glad of it. Build up the fire, please, unless you would rather"—he indicated the grinding stone.

The prophet was not too proud to do women's work. Gehazi showed admirable humility. *Apprentice* prophet, Jaedon reminded himself. Older than he, but no more learned.

Again, he felt a rush of discomfort. He dipped his head. "I will gladly tend the fire."

With kindling and a few nearby logs, he stoked the fire in short order. "Are you making bread or porridge?" Jaedon asked.

"Porridge for so many. Although, this morning our numbers are fewer."

Jaedon settled the pot over the flames and added water. He would need to trek to the river soon. Glancing around the camp site, he noted more empty spots than before he turned in. Early departures.

"We've lost most of the Bethel contingent," Gehazi said. "I heard them leave during the night, squabbling as they went. I cannot fathom why they are so displeased with Elisha as leader. There is certainly no one more qualified among their number. Those remaining from Gilgal are content to stay another week and help with the building project."

"Will you stay?" Jaedon had heard several of Jericho's residents, prophets and townsfolk alike, talking of the plan to build a stone retaining wall around the spring to prevent mud seepage.

"Until the project is complete. Then I will do as Elisha said. See to my family."

Jaedon nodded. He had heard Elisha's instruction. If Gehazi offered more personal stories, Jaedon would listen, but he wouldn't question Gehazi about private matters. Jaedon didn't want to feel he must share his desire to become Elisha's follower. The prophet had told him to seek Yahweh's will, and he had heard him tell Gehazi to see to his wife. They both needed to attend to their own affairs.

"And you?" Gehazi asked. "Will you wait until the other Gilgal residents are ready to go?"

"I haven't decided." It would be safer to travel with such a number, but Jaedon wanted to keep his options open. He filled a smaller pot with water and, glancing at Gehazi, moved the large pot aside, and set the other over the flames.

"If you are not ready to begin the porridge, this will not take long. It's my Imma's special concoction she brewed for Elijah and Elisha. Gave the prophets strength and kept their lungs clear, so she said."

Gehazi motioned for Jaedon to proceed, so he sprinkled the herbs on top and stirred the brew.

Soft snoring from Elisha's mat quieted, then he stirred. As the pot began to simmer, Elisha sat up under the oak and stretched. "Do I smell Miriam's beverage?"

"Yes. I found the herbs and flowers by the river yesterday." Jaedon poured a cup for Gehazi as well as Elisha, watching anxiously for expressions of approval. Pleasure expanded his chest when Elisha sighed and asked for more. Gehazi, however, let his drink grow cold.

It couldn't be helped. Only one could be chosen to serve Elisha, as he had served Elijah. Of course, others would receive special assignments, be asked to help with a project, or prophesy to a town. But there would be one designated as Elisha's right hand, to carry messages, perform errands, see to his meals, and sit at his feet. That man would likely be Elisha's successor.

Jaedon gripped his cup tightly, realizing his also was cool—and empty. Distracted, he'd neglected to fill it. He had been close to these two prophets since he'd fled Samaria, and he wanted that to continue with Elisha. He would be a follower no matter what, but he wanted to be *the one* who followed most closely.

The problem was, Gehazi wanted that, too.

Oh, Lord, keep my heart right. Jealous thoughts come easily, please help me turn them away. I desire to follow Elisha, but most of all, to follow You.

The gruel was delicious, a combination of finely ground and coarsely cracked grain. Jaedon cleaned the pots while the prophets Elisha had designated brought water for drinking and washing. After all in the camp had finished eating, they gathered to hear Elisha read from the Torah scroll *Viyikra*.

The sun moved above the oak as Elisha read what Adonai said to Moshe from Mount Sinai. With eyes closed, Jaedon listened intently, checking his memory against the reading. The land must observe *Shabbat* rest the seventh year, after six years of sowing and gathering. The people would live on what the land produced itself without planting.

More rules—the seven *Shabbats* of years, rules for buying and selling, and land not to be sold in perpetuity, because it belongs to Adonai.

Jaedon's heart clenched at the memory of his father knocked to the ground, his head blossoming red.

Grandfather and uncle fell under a hail of stones, murdered for obedience to this holy law. Sometimes the dark shadow returned, the fear that paralyzed him as a boy in the tree where his mother had hidden him. He had remained frozen.

As Elisha continued reading rules for redeeming slaves, Jaedon felt again the rough bark skinning his thighs, remembered twisting his small fingers into claws, desperate to hold on.

A murmur from the crowd claimed his attention. Jaedon blinked, willing himself to return to the present.

"If you remain hostile toward me and refuse to listen …" Elisha continued the Torah portion that forbade worshipping idols. Then the covenant with Adonai and promises of blessings, oh, so many blessings, for obedience. Rain in season, plenteous crops, no threat from wild animals, peace and safety in the land.

But for disobedience—terror, disease, and discipline seven times over for their sins. The words drew Jaedon like a tether. Who would choose hard discipline over blessings?

When Elisha had finished reading, he gave final instructions.

"The Lord is sending me north for a time. I have given some of you specific tasks that may take you weeks to complete. But until I return, these are my final words.

"You who are prophets, teach others, with prayer and attention to the scrolls. Perhaps they will also receive the call. Visit settlements in the hills, particularly those far off and most in danger of exalting false gods.

"Prophets, never forget you are Yahweh's servants, and you speak for him. Let no one disrespect you. Remember Elijah, who dared to confront King Ahab for idolatry. He called fire from heaven several times to prove he stood before the Living God.

"Apprentices, servants, and other followers—listen to and obey your teachers. Never forget you must teach your families to follow the Lord."

Elisha walked back to the oak, greeting some who came to thank him or assure him of allegiance. Gehazi lingered until the crowd around Elisha cleared, then moved close and, though he spoke too quietly to be heard, seemed to ask some favor, hands outstretched.

Whatever the question, Elisha shook his head in refusal, tilting his head toward the west. Gehazi picked up the grinding stone and mortar and trudged up the path toward Jericho. Going toward his house?

Well, it was none of Jaedon's business. He had his own concern, and Elisha, now stowing his belongings in a travel pack, was alone. He strode over, whistling softly, more an announcement of his approach than anything else. "I would like to come with you."

"Are you sure? The Lord's prophet has enemies everywhere."

"But the Lord is with His prophet."

Elisha nodded once and secured the mantle around his shoulders.

Jaedon hurried to pack.

Imma would have been proud of him. "Be sure not to travel alone," she had said. "Travel in company." He was pleased to be traveling with the best company, Elisha, Yahweh's prophet.

Exhilarated, Jaedon had volunteered to carry both packs. Elisha had refused, but agreed to let Jaedon carry both water skins. The dripping skins cooled him, but the straps grooved his shoulder. An honor, he reminded himself, to bear some of the prophet's burden.

They walked in silence, questions filling Jaedon's mind, which he considered then discarded. He would not ask again to be Elisha's servant, at least not yet. Somehow Jaedon felt that, having given Gehazi that half-promise, that Elisha would not speak to Jaedon on the subject.

He felt certain Elisha's "we will see" did not mean "probably not" as it did with Imma.

Elisha looked at him sideways and chuckled.

Had he heard Jaedon's thoughts?

"Where are we going?" he asked, then wanted to clap his hand over his mouth.

"*You* are going home to Gilgal, and I am going beyond. But first, we need to deal with something up ahead. Stay close to me. Very close."

Elisha's tone was grave, and Jaedon cast a quick glance at his face. However, the prophet's gaze was fixed on the ground.

"Where will we stop?"

"You will know."

They continued in silence a while longer. Tangled thickets lined the banks of the ridge. They passed a patch of calanit, a fox skull half-hidden in their crimson blooms, and a narrow foot trail which departed from the ridge. Would they turn off the main route for one of the hidden settlements? It was common for the prophets to impart teaching as they came across such tucked-away places. No doubt Elisha knew of many that Jaedon had not visited on the few trips he had taken with Elijah and Elisha.

Just ahead, trees loomed tall and dense. Heavy shade fell across the road. As he often did, when in forested areas, Jaedon searched the skies. No sign of his eagle, Hevel, and her mate. But there was no birdsong, either, so he'd keep a lookout. The turnoff leading to Bethel was not far, around a curve in the ridge. He thought of Naomi, hoping her neighbors had checked on her as they promised. Perhaps he and Elisha could do so.

"When we came past Bethel on the way to Jericho ..." Jaedon hesitated, hearing a rustle in the woods. He turned but saw nothing but trees. Elisha glanced at him, one eyebrow hiked. Jaedon shrugged, and the two walked on, but he did not resume the interrupted thought.

Then came the sounds of crunching footfalls, snapping twigs, and raucous laughter. Both turned to face what was coming.

A mob of young men emerged from behind trees, fifty or sixty in number, many carrying clubs or staffs, others hoisting fist-sized rocks. Jaedon felt his mouth gape.

"Remember," Elisha said, "Stay close."

Jaedon recognized some faces—the lout who had run into Naomi, others that shouted bets as they raced toward the sound of yelping dogs.

Elisha stood quietly, facing them. They shouted insults and jeers. "Get out of here, *Baldy*. Why not rise up in the air, like your friend? You can do that surely, *Man of God.* Or if you cannot, get out of here. Go on back to Samaria, where you belong. Deal with the rich rulers and King Joram. That is your job, *Baldy.* We don't want your lying predictions."

Jaedon's whole body trembled. What was this about? Elisha was on the road, not on the turnoff to Bethel. He was, in fact, on his way to deal with the rulers of Samaria. If that was what they wanted, why come out of the city all the way to the ridge road? Their disdain bordered on hatred. They meant Elisha harm. He reached for his sling and bag of stones, tucked in his sash.

One of the Bethelites hooted with laughter. "Oooh no! The boy's got a sling. Watch out for his pebbles, lads." The others joined in.

Jaedon loaded his sling. Elisha held out his hand, splay-fingered, restraining. Jaedon waited.

The youths moved in closer. "Two of you, against all of us. Fair odds against a *Man of God*—with all those *powers.* Show us what you can do, Baldy."

They strode toward Elisha and Jaedon, jumped up the slope, and circled around, hemming them in. The miscreants stood so close he could see their patchy beards. Most were about his age, a few younger.

So many, primed to do harm, and they kept moving closer.

Elisha cleared his throat, turned his attention from the young brutes, and gazed into the sky. In a loud voice, he invoked the ancient warning. "If you are hostile and refuse to listen"—the young men bent over with laughter, slapping each other on the backs.

"Listen to the man," one said, nearly choking on his laughter. "Better be careful—it could be a *genuine* curse!"

Elisha said, "I will multiply your afflictions seven times over, as your sins deserve. I will send wild animals against you …"

A few on the circle's backside looked over their shoulders.

Jaedon smelled something rank, like rotting flesh.

Elisha continued, "they will rob you of your children… "

A whimper sounded from behind a bush, then a small, golden furry creature scampered behind the circle, quickly followed by a second animal emitting frenzied yips. Twin bear cubs tumbled over one another.

A few chuckles. But some Bethelites in the back turned away, trotting back toward the city, glancing over their shoulders.

Behind the cubs, two female bears waddled up over the ridge and into the mob, the hair on their wheat-colored backs bristling. They moved slowly at first. Silently, each bear swatted left, right, and men went flying against their companions. One bear grabbed a culprit by the arm, the other bit a screaming youth in the throat, abruptly silencing him.

Then the bears picked up speed. They galloped, lunged, grabbed, and tore at their victims. Screams and blood-curdling, savage roars surrounded them.

Elisha flung his arm around Jaedon's shoulder. His hand shaking, Jaedon reached up and clung.

Panicked, the would-be attackers tried to flee, but except for the few who had first turned away, none escaped. The bears clamped down on ankles or arms, shook, tore, ripped, and slashed.

When it was over, mangled bodies were strewn across the road and down the slopes on each side. Jaedon had never seen such carnage. Each bear grabbed a carcass and hauled it into the woods, their cubs cavorting behind.

Jaedon pressed his palms against his forehead, trying to staunch the throbbing, trying to make sense of what he had seen. "How did you…" His muddled thoughts choked all words.

"Not I." Elisha rested his hand on Jaedon's shoulder. "Yahweh did it. No one can stand against God's purpose or his prophet. Let that be a lesson."

A lesson! Jaedon would never forget this day.

"They were angry with you."

"Elijah spoke against their immorality. They were warning me not to do the same. To leave them be." Elisha shrugged. "But I do what Yahweh tells me."

He gripped Jaedon's arms, and they silently bowed their heads together until they touched, the closeness comforting.

"Come now, let us be along before the bodies are collected for burial. Their fathers will be enraged and I … I don't want to see more bloodshed today."

Chapter Eight

*Yea, though I walk through the valley of the shadow
of death, I will fear no evil: for thou art with me;
thy rod and thy staff they comfort me.*
Psalm 23:4

Road to Gilgal, towards evening
Jaedon

ALTHOUGH HE HAD MADE THE ENTIRE journey from home to Jericho in one day, the incident outside of Bethel sapped Jaedon's strength. If this was what it was like to be a prophet, he didn't want any part of it. Even Elisha walked with slumped shoulders, but Jaedon would not be the one to suggest they stop.

When the sun dipped below the treetops, Elisha finally said, "There is a cave down this path and fallen leaves to cushion our cloaks. Shall we stop for the night?"

Jaedon felt a smile loosen his lingering tension. They stepped and slid down the slope, walked through knee-high grass to a stream, and bent to dip handfuls of cool water to drink and splash over their faces.

Wading into the stream, Jaedon found patches of watercress. He pinched off leaf clusters, heaping them into a fold of his tunic. When he had enough, he climbed up the bank, wringing water from his hem, and drying his feet on the grass.

The evening was fair, so instead of taking shelter in the cave, they scooped together piles of leaves, wrapped themselves in their cloaks, and sat quietly under the streaked sky.

Twilight faded into night, and stars dotted the heavens. Elisha pulled flatbread from his travel pack. In case enraged fathers pursued, they lit no fire, eating cold, peppery watercress atop broken pieces of bread. A night thrush trilled a high-pitched vee-vee-veeer-pip-cheree, each quatrain soaring up like a question. *Where are you, my mate, my love?*

What might have been soothing, instead seemed sad.

Seeking one lost. Jaedon sat on his pallet of leaves, glad for its cushion over the cold, hard ground. Nothing could cover the day's horror. Today had changed everything.

No. That was untrue. Yesterday, he had witnessed Yahweh's power flow through Elisha. A little salt, a new bowl, and the prophet's words invoked grace and healing. Today his words brought judgment.

Jaedon knew prophets weren't always honored or believed. Well, *he* wouldn't want to chance not honoring, not believing.

The day's events replayed in his mind and bile soured his throat. But without that terrible intervention, they both could have been killed. Those brutes seemed driven by a different kind of blood lust from the men who killed his father for money and to please a queen. These could laugh while they planned mayhem.

Elisha had said the Lord's purpose could not be thwarted, but Jaedon knew Jezebel had killed many prophets. His Uncle Caleb told the story of how Obadiah, the king's steward, hid fifty in their family's cave. His friend Binyamin had been one of those, and Jaedon could not reconcile Elisha's words with his own experience.

Elisha broke the silence. "It was a hard day for you."

Jaedon bit into the watercress. "Not for you?"

"Yes, but I knew to expect it."

Of course he knew. "Why didn't you tell me?"

They chewed a while in silence. "I did say, 'The Lord's prophet has enemies everywhere.'"

So he had. "You couldn't have said, 'There will be bears'?"

Elisha chuckled. "That would not have stopped you."

"True." Jaedon smiled in the dark. "I would have imagined bears running into the forest. Adventure. Hunting, perhaps. Not ..." Tears stung his eyes, and he was grateful Elisha couldn't see. "I will never forget what I saw ... and heard."

"Nor I. Have you changed your mind, then?"

Jaedon hesitated. He had told himself not to again bring up his desire to serve. Had Elisha read his mind?

"I don't have to see everything in visions, lad. Many

secrets are written on faces, revealed in a tone of voice. Perhaps because I have watched you grow from boy to man, you are more open to me."

"I have not changed my mind. Elijah often talked about the seven thousand Yahweh 'reserved for himself.' He worked to bring Israelites into that number. It seemed an honorable calling. Now you have taken his mantle. His calling. I *do* want to follow you. Learn all I can about serving Yahweh."

"You are young," said Elisha, "Still, I would gladly make you my apprentice. But Yahweh has not yet revealed His will in this matter."

Jaedon felt his forehead crease. Living closely with the prophets had taught him the importance of obeying Yahweh without complaint or hesitation. "I understand."

"Let me ask you this. How well do you remember your uncle Kadesh?"

A strange question, but unusual questions and remarks were commonplace in a community of prophets. "He was a hero to me. An adventurer, a spy, who spoke Aramean like one born in Damascus. He taught me a little of their language. Drew maps of all the countries he visited. Taught me about weapons, but said it was important to find weapons all around you. A fist-sized stone, a fallen branch, a pot bubbling on the hearth. I was just a boy when he was murdered."

And that day, he had found no weapons to hand.

"You remember the tasks I gave the prophets in Jericho. Study the scrolls, commit all you can to memory. Teach others."

"I do."

"Now I give you one more. Stir up your memory of all your uncle taught you of Aram. The land, the language. Which may not be that difficult for you, as it has similarities to our own. Ready yourself, as best you can. The Lord says He will use that knowledge, like your uncle's everyday weapons."

Stir up childhood memories? A breeze tousled the hair that fell over his forehead. Was he to be a spy like his uncle? Something coiled inside, preparing to spring. "When will Yahweh use me?"

Elisha sighed. "*When* comes after He tells you *what*. Until then, you wait."

Soon. If that was how God worked, Jaedon needed to be always ready. To travel light. Carry only commonplace weapons—his bow, hunting knife, and sling. This was how Uncle Kadesh used to consort with Aramean traders.

Jaedon lay awake a long time, looking at the stars, trying to order his thoughts. He should find someone who spoke Aramean. But how could he? It wasn't as if he could befriend a passing raider.

He chuffed at the idea. He had to become one of them, yet his Aramean was rudimentary at best. It was hopeless.

"Elisha?"

"Yes."

"Do you know Aramean?"

"I do. As we journey tomorrow, we will speak it together. But when we reach Gilgal, I must go on alone to Mount Carmel. Yahweh has said I will spend time there, talking with Him."

"Mmm." Jaedon rolled on his side and slowed the pace of his breathing. He wanted to be rested in the morning. Make the best of the few hours he'd have with the prophet. For the first time since he realized Gehazi was his competition, he felt at peace. God had shown Elisha a glimpse of what was in store for Jaedon.

In the morning, they ate more watercress, and Elisha found a patch of berries. Then he did something strange. With his mouth stained red, he asked Jaedon a garbled question—in Aramean. Stranger still, Jaedon answered without thinking, "I am a shepherd. I live wherever I find fodder for my sheep."

"You understood me!"

"I suppose I did."

After they ate, packed, and set out toward Gilgal, their discourse consisted of naming everyday objects, questions and responses, asking and giving directions, and adjusting his pronunciation. Elisha included lists of medical terms, words for wound, blood, and bone, terms for cut, sew, and heal.

Jaedon remembered a drinking song Kadesh taught

him. Taking a deep breath, he boomed it out, fighting laughter as Elisha's eyebrows shot up.

> We are poor as shepherds
> We smell twice as bad
> Let us drink together, all we can hold
> Let us start in the morning
> Drink through the night
> Until we know we are kings.

"Your uncle taught you that?" the prophet asked.

"A terrible song, I know. But I was sick, and Imma stirred up a dreadful-tasting medicine. Could not get me to drink it, and she was worried. I remember *dod* taking the cup from her, telling her to leave it to him. He started singing and staggering comically around the room"—Jaedon demonstrated—"until I laughed uncontrollably. He pretended to take a sip, grimaced, then held my nose and poured the foul stuff through my lips."

Jaedon blinked away the memory's sting. Elisha chuckled. "You even got the accent right."

"No, really?"

As they walked, conversing in the enemy's language, long-closed doors in Jaedon's mind swung open revealing a surprising store of half-remembered knowledge. Many Aramean words were similar to Hebrew, but their clipped, harsh pronunciation made them sound foreign.

"They say everything two ways," Uncle had said, striking the air twice to demonstrate. "Once in words, again in motion."

Jaedon smiled at the memory. How much of that was Uncle and how much Aramean culture?

Elisha adjusted the mantle over his shoulder. "Kadesh could capture a crowd with his storytelling. Used his hands like a flock of birds, sometimes."

"Did you know him? I don't remember you or Elijah from that time before they died."

"We met him in the north, years before. The Lord directed us to a campfire with a mixed group of Aramean and Edomite shepherds. Kadesh happened on us. He thought we were with them!" Elisha threw back his head and laughed.

"He had your father's wine to trade and honey from an orchard hive. He learned much about troop movements that night with his finely tuned questions."

Jaedon stopped in the road, turning to look at Elisha. "He didn't know you were prophets?"

"Not until later. One of the Edomites challenged him, said he was Hebrew. That his accent gave him away. Elijah intervened."

"Intervened? Like—"

Jaedon raised both arms to heaven, then wheeled and slashed a condemning arm toward Elisha, assigning him the part of the Edomite.

"You think Elijah would wield fire upon the man?"

Jaedon walked on. The question was a test. He considered the times Elijah had used fire. Two instances that he knew of. Although he was too young to recall what happened on Mount Carmel, he knew the story. The god who sent fire would be proved as the One True God.

Elijah allowed the prophets of Ba'al to go first, to choose their sacrificial bull and call on their god to send fire. Hours later they admitted defeat.

Then he made Yahweh's job harder.

Elijah built an altar of twelve stones, laid the slain bull on top, and called for barrel after barrel to be poured over the sacrifice. Water drenched the bull and flowed into the trench he ordered dug around the altar.

Then Elijah prayed that Yahweh would hear and answer, would send fire to prove that He was God in Israel, and Elijah was His servant.

At this point Abba, Savta, even Imma, who had been a young girl at the time, would talk over one another describing how thunder rumbled like a thousand rivers at flood, lightning webbed the sky then pounded the altar with flame, and the roaring flames consumed the altar, wood, stones, and even the water in the trench.

Jaedon did not need to deliberate upon the other time Elijah brought down fire. He knew the answer to Elisha's question.

"Yahweh will not share His throne with any other so-called god. I think also, He will protect His prophet. But ... not always. Jezebel killed many of the school of prophets. Micaiah was thrown in prison, although he did not die there and was later released."

The corner of Elisha's mouth tipped infinitesimally. "You begin to understand."

Begin to understand? What had he missed? Jaedon glanced sideways at his companion's set expression and decided to take another tack.

"Before we fell asleep, you said after we reach Gilgal, you will go on alone to Mount Carmel. That Yahweh will talk to you there."

"Actually, I did not say I would go alone. I know two things—I am to spend time with Yahweh, and I am not to bring you."

Don't ask. Don't—"Will Gehazi be with you?"

Elisha cut him a sharp look. "Do not concern yourself with another man's path."

Jaedon looked at the ground. "It's only—he and I pursue the same goal."

"You are mistaken in that. There is no need for you to envy Gehazi. Listen for the Lord's voice to you."

Jaedon kicked a pebble off the ridge, hearing it bounce once against another stone. What did that even mean? He didn't hear the Lord's voice. Was that why Elisha didn't want him?

Elisha's voice gentled. "You know enough now. Obey the Lord."

Did he mean about Aram? Stirring up childhood memories of what Kadesh had taught him? What good would that do?

"Must I remind you again? The Lord will only tell you one thing. Until you obey, you will hear nothing else from Him."

"But I have never heard His voice." There. Now Elisha knew the worst. An unworthy thought clawed its way into his mind. *Had Gehazi heard the Lord speak?* Jaedon threw back his head and sighed in exasperation. "Does it make me unfit to serve?"

"Why do you want to?"

"To learn from you. The ways of Yahweh."

"But why do you want to follow in that path?"

A gust of wind skittered leaves across their path and grains of dust filled Jaedon's eyes. Squeezing them shut, he rubbed with his fists. With his eyes still closed, he saw the vineyard, the murderers, the stones, Abba shielding Saba's body with his own, filtered through the branches and leaves of his hiding place. Merciful, the way the foliage shielded him, the child, from the gory scene.

"You see?" said Elisha. "Now answer."

Jaedon pulled his hands away, drawing a deep breath.

"I want to learn to wield power—like you. To summon bears, if I need them. I want justice—" He stopped himself from finishing *for my family.*

"Did you hear me summon bears?"

"I *saw* you."

"No. The Torah warns those who are hostile to God. I reminded the mob of one such warning. They could have turned from their rebellion but continued to threaten us. The power was not from me. Yahweh sent *His* justice."

Jaedon's breath quickened, but not because their pace had increased. He fought down further argument that threatened to erupt. He was glad the mob from Bethel had been stopped—whether by bears or fire from heaven. But he wanted the mob from his father's vineyard punished—and the queen who paid them.

Elisha said, "Listen to me now. I have not changed. If the Lord allowed it, I would gladly choose you as my servant. But He has a different path for you. Do you remember everything I told you?"

"Study the scrolls, memorize all I can. Teach others. Stir up my memory of all my uncle taught me of Aram."

"One more thing. There is no coincidence."

Jaedon didn't know what to say to that, so he closed his mouth.

"I want to help you with your training. Some of the prophets have copied scrolls for their own use, but I know you have not. The scrolls belonging to Elijah and me are stored in our house. Don't remove them, but you study there whenever you like. Live in the house, if you wish. I doubt I will be there often.

"As for your continued study of Aram's land and

language, I remind you the Lord said He will use that knowledge. Since He has need for the knowledge, He will help you acquire it."

Jaedon had more questions, but he had already spoken too much without thinking things through. What had possessed him to blurt out his desire to bring long-delayed justice?

It is vengeance you want, not justice. Truth settled on his shoulder like Hevel used to, nipping at his conscience like the eagle had nipped at his clothing.

He thanked Elisha for the offer of his house. Perhaps he would stay for short periods of study, but he couldn't imagine living away from home indefinitely. If he couldn't be with Elisha, he wanted to be with his family.

They walked a while in silence as he turned his thoughts over and over, like Imma kneaded dough. Though only a few days had passed, he was returning home changed. But was he more whole? Or still struggling?

He scoffed under his breath. When it mattered, he could not save his family, nor could he serve up vengeance.

Justice, he corrected himself. No, nothing had changed there.

Finally, Elisha turned off the ridge, taking the slower way. As they meandered through the hills, they came across a slain deer. The doe had been taken down with a single arrow, her nose stretched out, legs still poised in flight. Jaedon recognized the arrow's fletching—golden-brown feathers he had harvested from his eagle, Hevel, when she molted.

Elisha held up a finger to indicate silence, and Jaedon nodded. Then the prophet walked past the carcass and led through a narrow, heavily forested path. Ahead, a rocky outcrop jutted into the path. A shaft of light penetrated a gap in the trees, and Jaedon squinted into the glare.

A big man stepped from behind the boulder, his bow raised, arrow nocked. "Stop right there," he growled.

Jaedon gasped. "Binyamin! I should have known."

Binyamin quickly lowered the bow. "Jaedon, my friend. And Elisha! Oh, I am sorry. It's only that—" he motioned behind the boulder.

Jaedon slowly walked forward. Three men, bearing the wounds of a brawl, lay unconscious on the ground.

Chapter Nine

Just outside Gilgal, same evening
Jaedon

AS THEY PRODDED BINYAMIN'S PRISONERS THROUGH the forest, Jaedon studied their foreign clothing. The padded vests probably substituted for scaled bronze, so they could move more stealthily through the forest. Cone-shaped helmets were brass smeared with clay. These were Aramean raiders. Did that mean—

"Sure glad you two came along," Binyamin said. "Didn't know how I was going to get them back to the settlement when they woke."

Jaedon slowly expelled a breath. Then Gilgal had not been attacked. That made sense, with only three prisoners. Then what were they doing here? Advance scouts? And Binyamin wanted to bring them in alive.

"How did you come across them?" Jaedon asked. "Did you see footprints? Smoke from a fire? Hear them?"

Binyamin glanced back at the prisoners with an expression of something like shame. Two of them carried the deer between them on a pole. Elisha brought up the rear.

Binyamin leaned down and whispered. "Don't want them to hear. I suspect they understand Hebrew. I saw and heard nothing, until they attacked me. They slipped through our guards as if they were invisible. If they'd reached any houses on the outskirts, they might have sneaked in and carried off hostages before the rest of us knew what was happening."

"How did you fight all three?"

His friend laughed, shrugging muscular shoulders. "You know, first threw the short one into his crony. Grabbed a large rock and threw it at that one." He indicated a fellow with a huge lump over one eye. "Picked up their dropped swords, swung with both arms at whoever moved, striking with flat edge where possible." He indicated lumps, bruises, and a soldier with a slashed vest. "Blade edge if not."

"Why are you bringing them into camp?"

"For questioning. Another village was attacked yesterday. If we can make them talk, we'll rescue our kidnapped countrymen before they are taken too far."

Jaedon said, "I speak their language. I'll help with the questioning and so will Dov." A good opportunity to test and broaden his language skills. And timely. He glanced back at Elisha. The prophet winked.

No coincidences.

Elisha had watched the whispered conversation between Binyamin and Jaedon. He drew in a deep breath, almost as strengthening as when he felt the *ruach* of the Spirit. Jaedon would do fine, back here with his family, but also with Binyamin and Eden.

He motioned for Jaedon to drop back. The lad almost bounced, ruddy-cheeked with excitement at a new challenge.

"That was Yahweh, wasn't it?" Jaedon whispered. "He put the enemy into Binyamin's hands—the one man in Gilgal who could subdue all three."

"Then He brought you here to help, again at just the right time. You see, now. The Lord has graciously shown you how He works. Trust Him."

Words he needed to remember himself. Much would happen to the boy before Elisha would see him again.

"I do trust Him. I think … I will not doubt Him again."

"Good. I want one more word with you before I go."

The boy's face fell. "You are leaving today?"

"There is daylight yet. Farewell, Jaedon. Our paths are parting now, but we will meet again. For now, we each have work to do. The Lord has shown us."

Jaedon tipped his head toward the distant north. "For you, Carmel."

"Yes, for a time. Then Samaria and ..." Elisha looked at the three Arameans. "These are troubled times. Israel needs the Lord more than ever. That is our task. To turn Israel back to the Lord. No Asherah poles in the high places, no golden calves." He looked hard at this boy he had treated as a younger brother, starting with the times he helped him train the eagle, continuing as he taught him all he could about following the Lord. Was the boy ready for what would come?

Was he leaving him defenseless?

No. *Yahweh, I leave him in your hands.*

Chapter Ten

If your enemy is hungry, give him food to eat;
if he is thirsty, give him water to drink.
Proverbs 25:21

Gilgal
Jaedon

JAEDON HAD NO TIME TO MOURN Elisha's departure. Immediately after the prophet left, Dov arrived. "I saw you approaching from the vineyard." He clapped Jaedon on the shoulder and squinted at the three Arameans. Then he turned his back to them and whispered. "Where is Elisha?"

Binyamin hailed two burly prophets to guard the prisoners, then pulled him and Dov aside. They went to stand under a grove of tamarisks apart from the village where neither spies nor prophets would hear them.

Binyamin sat beneath an ancient tree whose wide layers of feathery branches shaded them all. Speaking quietly, he told Dov how he'd come across and captured the prisoners. "Let's bring them to Elijah's—I suppose it's now Elisha's house. A perfect place to question them."

Jaedon nodded. "Elisha told me I can use the house while he is away. We should make the house secure. Remove any weapons they could get their hands on."

Both Dov and Biny glanced his way, seeming surprised. If they asked about Elisha's decision, he would try to explain, but really, even he didn't understand why the prophet offered him the house.

If Binyamin was curious, he tamped it down, instead expressing a thirst for vengeance toward the foreigners. "Let me have a turn getting information out of them. Jezebel killed many of my brother prophets, and she sent soldiers to kill me."

"Don't put Jezebel among the Arameans," Dov said. "She is from Tyre." He had agreed to help because of his experience interrogating enemy soldiers. It was hard to remember what he'd been like as a soldier. He had softened considerably as a husband and father.

"The Arameans are killing our people, too," argued Binyamin. "Kidnapping and selling peaceful Israelites from outlying settlements. Now they planned to attack one of the schools of the prophets."

A breeze gusted under the trees, flinging scouring dust. They paused their conversation to shield their faces. Jaedon breathed through the tail of his head covering, surprised to smell sweet grass. An idea formed slowly around Elisha's last instruction.

"I speak and understand some Aramean, but perhaps we should question them in Hebrew. You said one of them spoke our language, Biny. If we each speak only Hebrew, he will be forced to interpret their answers for us. He may lie, but I can tell you later what they said among themselves."

Dov chuckled. "Do you remember the Aramean Kadesh taught you as a child, my son? I also speak a fair amount of several languages, and I understand more than I speak. Between the two of us, we should learn where they have taken our countrymen."

Why had Jaedon never known this? Dov had spoken little of his life as a soldier in Ahab's army. After he wed Imma, he happily immersed himself into the staid life of a vintner, leaving battles and carnage behind. But he had also been ignorant about Jaedon's knowledge of Aramean, though it had been but a smattering. It seemed he and his stepfather had more to learn about each other.

The first round of questioning the spies returned nothing. Jaedon quickly realized none of them could stomach violence, not even Binyamin. He made a few threats, even grabbed one fellow roughly by the throat, but he seemed relieved when Dov said in Hebrew, "This is getting us nowhere, and I am hungry. Come, my friends. Let's roast that deer for the settlement. The runner from the village these evildoers attacked can guard them while we eat. They are tied securely, and we'll see to it our guard has a club."

A prophet with a club. Jaedon stifled a smile. Not much threat there. He and Dov were the only two in the settlement who were not prophets or in the family of one. If the Arameans understood the gentle souls of the men in this settlement, they would never reveal the route of the raiders.

The prisoners protested being left with a man they expected would be glad to loosen their tongues by means less polite than they had faced thus far, but Binyamin shrugged, flipped one hand palm up, pointed at his ear with the other, and shook his head.

Jaedon covered his mouth, pretended to cough, and hurried outside. The three went off talking loudly of roast venison, making sure to build their fire upwind of where the prisoners were being guarded.

Several hours later, they returned. "Succulent meat and the finest wines of Gilgal's vineyards." Jaedon patted his stomach. "Too bad there is none left, but we cannot short our hungry families to feed these who wanted to kill us."

"Of course not," Dov said. "I suppose we should give them water, though. They must be thirsty by now."

"Not watered wine?" Jaedon laughed, a sarcastic snort. At least his sarcasm came easily. There was no need to mingle wine in the drinks, because the water in Gilgal was sweet and clean. But the interrogation, trying to intimidate enemies, that was not easy. They deserved it. They'd carried off or killed peaceful Israelites. This was justice. "I don't care if our tainted water makes them sick. They haven't answered our questions."

"True." Dov stroked his chin. "Why purify the prisoners' water by adding wine. Let them suffer distress of the bowels."

The Arameans eyed him warily.

"You're right, my friend," said Biny. "Plain water will keep these enemies alive. Why should they be comfortable when our captured countrymen are suffering?"

Jaedon excused himself and went to see Imma. She looked up from showing Gershoni how to grind emmer. His little sister's cheeks were pink from the work, and she ran to hug him around the knees.

After patting her head, he explained their problem gleaning information from the prisoners.

"You want them to think our water is tainted?" Her lips quirked. "I can certainly mix a potion you can add. It won't kill them, but it might loosen their tongues ... and other things."

He returned with a large jug and set it before the three Arameans. Each sniffed its contents and refused to drink, proving they understood at least basic Hebrew. "As you wish," said Dov in Hebrew, making many hand gestures as he spoke. "If you want wine in your water, answer our questions."

Two of the Arameans clamped their lips together, but the third muttered in Aramean. "We should tell them what they want. Our lives are forfeit if we do not." A change of guards arrived, so Jaedon and his stepfather left for home.

As they walked along, Jaedon said, "I mostly understood what he said, except for"—he attempted to pronounce the unfamiliar word.

"It means forfeit, lost," Dov said. "They think we will kill them."

Jaedon nodded. So he had understood well enough. "Will we?"

"If they help us find our countrymen before they are sold into slavery, I am inclined to release them. I heard them talking amongst themselves. Their king will assume they talked, whether they do or not, so they believe a death sentence will greet them when they return. They like the land they've come through, and they spoke of finding homes in Moab or Edom."

That confused him. Moab and Edom were allies of Israel. Uneasy allies, to be sure, because their kings had been slow in honoring wartime treaties. If the Arameans thought Moab and Edom would welcome them, Israel's alliance was likely weak.

If the prisoners would not talk, could he stomach violence, even killing, however just? He knew, better than most, how it felt when powerful people used violence to take what they wanted. To save their lives, he and Imma had fled Samaria, sought refuge with the school of prophets. They were far from the rich and powerful, hidden in these remote hills. Now, violent men had invaded their sanctuary.

Lord, when the time comes, show me what I must do.

It took two days before the Arameans were ready to talk—one day before they were thirsty enough to drink the polluted water, and another half day to sicken and beg for a healing potion. Jaedon brought Imma's healing concoction and watered wine. Watered only slightly, the wine started the prisoners describing the route the rest of their band was taking toward Aram with the captives. None had been killed in the village, they swore. They stole captives by stealth, from their sleeping mats. They were to be sold as slaves.

Several prophets were brought in to listen to the testimony. When asked if the Lord spoke, their answers were the same. None could tell if the prisoners told the truth about killings, but the route described was correct.

A band of twelve agreed to go in pursuit at first light, Binyamin, Dov, and Jaedon among them.

Before they left for their homes, Binyamin prayed.

Lord God, lead us in the right paths and lead us quickly,
for the sake of our brothers. Keep them safe while we seek them,
and help us return them to their families.

Then he said, "Except for Dov and Jaedon, we are all prophets, with little experience in maneuvers such as this. I suggest they lead us in planning."

The prophets quickly agreed. Dov stood and motioned for Jaedon to stand alongside. "Though there are only twelve of us, I propose an army-style flanking maneuver. Six runners take the forefront and six bring up the rear on horseback. I will ride with the last group on Uriel. He is a seasoned warhorse and will take the lead and give your mounts confidence."

Jaedon considered the few horses owned by villagers. By no means warhorses, they were cast offs—injured, diseased, or found wandering the hill country. They'd been nursed to health and used for plowing or carrying loads.

"Two of the runners will take the lead as scouts," Dov continued.

Jaedon volunteered, quickly followed by Binyamin. They'd be a good team. He was fast and silent. Binyamin was a good man to have at his back.

And Dov was a man approved by Yahweh, else he would be like those prophets who did not see Elijah ascend.

This adventure offered another opportunity to follow the Lord's leading.

They were ready.

Chapter Eleven

When Abram heard that his relative had been taken captive,
he called out the 318 trained men born in his household
and went in pursuit as far as Dan.
Genesis 14:14

Gilgal, the next morning
Jaedon

AS THE RISING SUN FILTERED ITS soft light through an eastern window, Jaedon met with the volunteers at Elisha's house. Though they had discussed ideas until late the previous night, he went over the strategy once more. "Biny and I will scout out the general direction the Arameans disclosed. We'll watch for signs and send back reports when we have new information.

"As we decided, you four prophets, because you're skilled in archery, will follow on foot a little behind us. Should we be discovered and attacked, you are silent backup which may save our lives. Finally, you six horsemen will bring up the rear. What weapons do you bring?"

"We have bows, swords, and battle axes among us," Dov said. "Everyone remember the importance of maintaining distance from the group ahead of you. The first scouts can be most silent but also nearest the enemy and likely to be discovered."

Jaedon watched his stepfather's face as he discussed the danger of detection. Was that worry creasing his brow? If it was, Jaedon suspected the veteran of many wars was not concerned for his personal safety but for those under him. The prophets ... and him.

His attention jerked back to Dov's concluding instructions—"those following have the element of surprise on their side."

Tense with energy for the task ahead, Jaedon set out, carrying only a light pack of provisions, a waterskin, and knives strapped at waist and ankle. He could barely hear Biny behind him, moving more silently than he had when they traveled to Jericho.

The archer-runners would wait until they judged he and Biny were at least a half mile ahead. Meanwhile, the horsemen would break their fast, then follow the others at a slower pace. They would make camp at dusk, and the others would return to them with news.

Following the Arameans' directions, Jaedon shortly found large, sharply defined prints, indicating eight to ten soldiers wearing sandals similar to the prisoners held in Gilgal. In their midst, he found small prints, likely a group of children.

Thank you, Yahweh! They are alive.

Biny came to kneel beside him and Jaedon pointed. "The soldiers seem to have hemmed in the captives and are driving them," he murmured. "The children will be terrified."

"At least we're on the right path," Biny said.

Jaedon stood and proceeded carefully, watching for more prints. What if Elisha had said yes, and Jaedon had gone with him to Mount Carmel? He'd been disappointed to be left behind. Now he was keenly aware that Yahweh had a purpose and was using him in this moment.

Late that afternoon, he spotted a broken twig on a bush. Snapped to point away from the trampled path, it caught his attention. Carefully he stepped away from the trail in the indicated direction and found a small Hebrew sash, carefully folded, pressed into a depression, and weighted with a rock. A single *tzitzit* was knotted to one corner. The tassels had been chewed from the other three.

Jaedon shrilled an eagle's call to covertly draw Binyamin's attention. They had agreed to use the muted whistle Jaedon perfected when training Hevel. Quickly, he cast his gaze across the heavens, for she would be fed when she answered the summons. Though she now had a mate and likely a family, he could not resist searching the sky.

Exhaling, he returned his gaze to the sash as Biny neared. "Look," he whispered. "Three tzitzit were removed. See how it is positioned?"

Binyamin nodded. The remaining tassel pointed a little east of north.

"Go back and let the others know the path veers off here.

I'll go on. If I come to another marker, I'll wait for you."

"Not a good idea. What if you run into trouble?"

"Then I'll do my best to stall and wait for you. If I'm taken captive, I'll leave a trail, as this little one did. But you must tell the others."

With a curt nod, Binyamin hurried back the way they'd come. He'd intercept the archers soon. Jaedon took his bearings on a rocky outcrop where two trees looked like twin sentinels. Leaving the sash where he'd found it, he ran silently in the new direction it indicated, wondering about the child who had left the sign.

After reaching the sentinels, Jaedon selected a new tree in the distance and resumed running. Black, craggy, and leafless, the tree appeared diseased or burned by lightning. He scanned the ground for another tassel, also watching for a broken twig or other sign left by the captive.

He stopped a few times and listened for the sound of soldiers driving a group of young prisoners. The children would have been threatened into silence, but a sob might escape, or a soldier might bark an order. He hadn't seen hoof prints thus far, but it was possible mounted soldiers might travel south from Aram to take charge of the hostages.

The sun sank behind the trees and dusk surrounded him. He slowed but kept moving in the same direction, hoping to find another wool fringe.

There! Laid out pointing straight in the direction he'd been following, it was half covered by elm leaves, easy to miss if you weren't paying attention. He moved into a clump of trees and shrubbery and settled down to wait.

The archers arrived after dark. Binyamin stretched and repositioned his bow. "I thought you were going to wait for us at dusk."

Jaedon motioned for him to step closer. "I reasoned there would be three more markers. Hoped to find the second—which I did." The archers gathered around the tzitzit, nodding their understanding of its meaning.

"Now that we know the direction, Binyamin and I can leave before dawn heading in that direction. If we turn from the course, I'll leave markers—a broken twig angled to point the way, or three stones positioned like an arrowhead." He demonstrated.

"How do you know the child won't lay another marker

before dawn? You could miss it."

"I could. But I don't think I will. I ask you to pray for the success of our mission, now and until we find them safe."

The prophets murmured agreement and gathered in a circle. Jaedon held the tassel in his hand, lifting his face to heaven.

O Lord, we pray for the child who placed this tassel in our path. If he leaves more signs, blind the soldiers' eyes. Remind the older children to help and comfort the younger. Mute the sounds of our pursuit with Your own breath churning the wind.

A light rain began to fall, as if in answer, plinking and humming enough to mute their footsteps. With no place to shelter, they decided not to wait for dawn. They'd get just as wet walking as sleeping, so why lie in the mud?

The moon hung low, peeking through clouds and lighting their way. Still, they could not run full out. When dawn pinked the sky, they noted more broken twigs on both sides of the path. Not secretly pointing the way, but haphazardly stepped upon, as if the children had been driven blindly in the dark. Wet and exhausted, they must have been pushed hard all night, with the amount of ground they'd covered.

"Look here." Jaedon pointed out the imprint of a small body, fallen in the mud. Something internal prodded him. Anger blurred his vision, and he shook his head to clear it.

Binyamin scowled. "They must be on their last legs," he whispered.

Then they heard a sharp crack, a child cried, and a soldier bellowed.

Time to act.

He signed Binyamin to silence, then to follow. He ran toward the sounds, which had seemed to come just over a hill. Stopping, he gestured for a circular maneuver and approach from the north.

He heard more furious shouts and the child's whimpers. An idea began to form. He motioned Binyamin to hold and then follow his lead. Then Jaedon strode up and over the hill, taking on the persona of a captain.

Jaedon gauged the size of the soldier who, as they

crested the hill, struck the boy across the face. A little taller than he, but reedy looking.

He could take him.

"Fool!" Jaedon barked Aramean with the authority of an officer. Good thing he had one for a stepfather. "Do not mark the slave. He is young and beautiful. Your superior will not thank you for reducing the price he will bring at market."

Cursing, the soldier barked, "Who are you?"

A broad-shouldered man stepped beside his mate. If Jaedon distracted him, Binyamin would take over.

"Who are you, soldier? I am a trusted servant of our king, Benhadad. He will want to know who treats his merchandise so roughly. This is my Hebrew slave, Binyamin. Devoted fellow. You can speak freely in front of him. He knows very little Aramean. Except 'attack' and 'kill.' Those are usually enough."

Not impressed, the soldier strode forward, reaching for his sword. Swiftly, Binyamin slid his knife from his sheath, stepped in front of Jaedon, and with a blur of his wrist, sent it flying to lodge in the Aramean's shoulder.

"Aaagh!"

The other soldiers grabbed for their weapons.

"Hold, big fellow!" Jaedon reached out to grasp Binyamin's wrist, already grasping his hidden dagger. "We don't want to *kill* all Benhadad's soldiers."

"KILL!" Binyamin flung the dagger, picked up two rocks and set them flying.

How did this escalate so fast? Jaedon had meant to do a little more talking. He pulled both his own daggers, and with one in each hand, pivoted to face the approaching swordsman.

"Our king will have your heads if you harm me," he shouted, still in Aramean. It didn't look like they believed him. Or cared. Did he get a word wrong? Was his accent off?

Lord help us.

Suddenly, a shofar blew, and the archer-prophets topped the hill. Raining down arrows as they came, they neatly picked off soldiers while avoiding screaming children.

By the time the horsemen arrived, many Arameans lay dead or wounded. Others had fled. The horsemen advanced on the remaining soldiers, who turned and ran with the speed of distance runners.

Jaedon, Binyamin, and Dov watched them go. "Thanks for stepping in like that, Biny. You should have seen him, Abba. He played his part well—big, stupid Hebrew slave."

Jaedon gave him a playful shove.

"Stupid! Ha!" Binyamin shoved back, sending him flying into Abba's side.

Jaedon glanced at the circle of children, who gazed at them with round eyes. He arranged his face into what he hoped was a kind expression, draped an arm around each man, and nodded toward the children. He counted nine boys and two girls. He hated to think what might have happened to the young girls, if they'd been sold.

Jaedon asked the prophets to see to the children, until they'd gotten over their fear of him and Biny. After removing the children's bonds, the prophets gave them water, food, and reassurance. Their peaceful manners helped. After a while, even the smallest child stopped trembling. Then they placed the children on the horses, sometimes two children with an adult rider or three with a prophet leading the horse.

The pursuit and recovery of the captives had taken two days but delivering the children to their families would take at least three or four. It was evident they were exhausted. Jaedon hid a scowl. These little ones had been treated roughly by their captors.

The day's travel was made as easy as possible for the children. Jaedon and Binyamin walked together, each leading a horse and steadying the smallest child on his animal.

"Soon we'll be passing the settlement where Eden's family lives," Binyamin told him that afternoon. "They would celebrate with us. Perhaps we should stop for the night." He paused, waggling his eyebrows. "For the children's sake."

What was that look for? Jaedon squinted at the sun. "There are hours of daylight left."

"But the children have been through a terrible ordeal," Binyamin argued. "Eden's family are known to be welcoming when travelers come by. And what an opportunity for you to meet her sister," he continued. "Her name is Ziva."

A jolt shot through Jaedon, as if he'd been plunged into an icy stream. He remembered Biny's pointed reference to Eden's little sister on their way to Jericho. He'd been interested, even then, but his goal had been to apprentice himself to Elisha. Now that would not happen. They were passing her home, bringing home captives, and since Yahweh sent no coincidences, what was he meant to do?

Slowly, Jaedon said, "Perhaps it would be good for the children to have dry clothes, eat a warm meal, and rest tonight among our own people. I will ask Dov."

Binyamin hailed another prophet to take over leading Jaedon's horse. When he found his stepfather, he explained Binyamin's suggestion.

Then he decided to say more. "On our way to Jericho, Biny and Eden mentioned her younger sister." He felt his face grow warm. "She is not spoken for."

"I see. What is it you want, my son? Do you want me to speak to her father?"

"I … think so. If she is anything like Eden—and Biny says she is—we might suit. Is it done? Could we simply talk? I would not like her to feel forced to accept a betrothal, when she does not know me." He hesitated. "Or I, her."

Dov stroked his beard. "I will speak to her father and ask if you and his daughter might be allowed to speak—with an approved chaperone."

Jaedon allowed a discreet smile. "Her name is Ziva."

Chapter Twelve

What a person desires is unfailing love
Proverbs 19:22a

Gischala, the next day
Ziva

A SOFT BREEZE RUSTLED THE OAKS as Ziva searched the dew-dampened ground for acorns. She loved the hills surrounding Gischala, especially at daybreak. Layers of color streaked the land and sky—shades of green, gold, crimson, and blue. She filled the pouch she'd brought and tied it to her waist. Imma had promised to show her how to bake sweet bread studded with acorns upon her return.

The tasty bread was Abba's favorite. Last night, he'd brought wildflowers picked from the date orchard, nuzzling Imma for a kiss as he reminded her he'd had no sweet bread for a month.

"A month, Shimon! I made it only last week." But she patted his chest. "If Ziva finds acorns tomorrow, we will see."

When Father handed her a red *calanit* from Imma's bouquet, Ziva had determined to rise before dawn and glean fallen nuts before the other girls came to the well. There was something almost magical about date and acorn bread, at least where her father was concerned. It was worth rising early, to learn something of the practical steps needed to invoke the magic.

After ensuring the acorns were secure, she lifted the yoke to her shoulders, looped the bucket handles over dangling hooks, and hurried down the pine-studded path. When she arrived at the well, she caught her breath in the clearing, gazing at the austere pines. It was eerie, being here alone. Although she'd wanted to gather acorns early, she missed gossiping with the others. Never mind, they would retell their stories tomorrow.

She filled her buckets and climbed the path toward the village. If she hurried, her baby brother would still be sleeping, Imma would have finished grinding the day's grain, and they could make the bread without him fussing for his morning porridge.

She smiled, envisioning Aharon's round face and toothless grin. Even when fussing, he was no trouble, really. If he woke, he would be satisfied gumming broken pieces of last night's bread until the baking was finished. She liked carrying him on her hip around the settlement, laughing at his excited squeals at a locust, a singing bird, or a brightly colored leaf.

Still, she enjoyed the times she and Imma worked alone preparing meals, especially mornings when it was cooler and quieter than any other time in their busy days. Imma would describe how to prepare various meals the family enjoyed, and between grinding, soaking, and cooking, she would whisper memories.

Your father said I first caught his eye when I shoved him to the ground for teasing a friend ... Imma said to mix honey into bread, and my marriage would reflect its sweetness ... my grandmother said to pray for each person in my family while grinding grain and to ask Adonai to make my husband kind and wise.

Hearing her mother's memories was like looking through a window into another world. Ziva tried to imagine meeting her future husband as a young child, but she couldn't. None of the village boys were near her age, so perhaps she would never marry. While she would be happy to care for Abba and Imma in their old age, she couldn't imagine marrying one of her settlement's old widowers who wanted a young wife to keep their house and care for their children—some nearly as old as she!

She often imagined her mother and father in the moment they noticed each other. "What did he do then," she had asked Imma. Her mother had kneaded the dough a while, her eyelashes feathering her cheeks, then she said, "He sat on the ground, leaning back on his hands. And then he laughed."

Ziva smiled.

Adonai, if I am to marry, please make my husband kind and wise. And make him a man who laughs.

Stopping at the top of the hill, Ziva drew a few deep

breaths while casting her gaze over the village ahead and the forested hills layered into the distance. Then her eyes caught movement on the road ahead. Two runners, one quite large, headed toward the village. Their pace was rather fast if they carried only messages. Her pulse stuttered. She had heard the stories of Aramean raiders, but her village was safe. Hidden among the hills.

No, she would not fear. Only last night, Abba had read to her, from the *Ketuvim.*

He will cover you with his feathers,
and under his wings you will find refuge;
* his faithfulness will be your shield and rampart.*
You will not fear the terror of night, nor the arrow that *flies by day,*

Squinting into the distance, she looked for evidence of bows and quivers. None. Perhaps there was no reason to fear. She rested her hands on each side of the yoke and set out at a brisk pace, determined to get the water home. They would need water, no matter who these men were. Had she been foolish to go to the well alone? *Yahweh, if these men bring good news, bless them. If harm, protect us.*

Instead of continuing on the main path, Ziva decided to take precautions. She approached the village from the forested side where the thick growth concealed her from the road. Casting about for signs of the strangers, she carried the water into her house. Where had they gone?

Before she need ask, Imma greeted her, breathless and smiling, slipping the first bucket from the yoke. "We have visitors, little one." She tipped the bucket into a tall clay jug.

Comforted by her mother's tender greeting, Ziva slowly removed and emptied the remaining bucket. "I saw two runners."

"Yes. Your brother-in-law, Binyamin—"

"Biny!"

"—and his *friend.*" Imma's voice lingered on the last word as if it were important. Then she took a corner of her head covering, dipped it in water, and wiped Ziva's forehead and cheek. "He seems nice."

"A prophet?"

Her mother pondered. "I am not sure. But there is more

news! Coming behind them, others of their company bring children captured by Arameans—freed by our own Biny and his fellows."

Children captured? She'd felt safe with their village far away from the road leading to Hazor. She hadn't thought twice about walking alone to the well. With their village tucked among rolling hills, it seemed they had no reason to fear Arameans, though nearby Hazor connected two routes into Aram. Had the villagers whose children were abducted also felt safe?

"The prophets have gone to confer with the village elders," her mother continued. "I know there will be a feast. I already spoke to some of the women. Did you find acorns?"

Ziva handed her the pouch and poured grain onto the grinding stone. The rescued children would be hungry. Men were always hungry, and who knew how many came with the rest of their company? The village women would already be preparing. She and Imma would do their part.

By the time the elders and prophets had conferred, Ziva estimated she had ground enough grain for at least half the visitors, and Imma had mixed a triple portion of the date and acorn dough.

Binyamin rapped on the doorframe. Ziva looked up from her grinding stone, and her brother-in-law shot her a grin before turning to her mother.

"Imma Chedva, the elders say the children should be bathed and ... examined. They have taken the boys and prophets to the river. But the girls"—he stepped through the open door, bringing two girls with him, one taller and one younger than Ziva—"require a woman."

He bent his head toward Imma. The two conversed at length, but Ziva could not make out what was said between them. When Imma hurried toward the girls, clucking and holding out her arms, he thanked her and backed out of the house.

Ziva hurried after him. "Biny, will you carry our table to the meeting area?"

"I will," he said, but he kept going.

Shaking her head, she went back to help Imma, who had led the girls behind the screened area where she and Abba slept. She had removed their soiled tunics and was gently bathing them with a cloth and basin of water while murmuring questions. Had they been hurt? Were they hungry? Thirsty? Gently, her mother went on to ask about their families.

They were sisters and had been playing together in an orchard while their father tended the trees. He left them briefly to saw limbs from damaged trees a little apart. When he was out of sight, Arameans had snatched the girls at knifepoint, threatened them into silence, and flung them atop two camels. Then they galloped off at unfathomable speed.

"I wonder how long until Abba realized we were gone," said the older child, her eyes glistening with unshed tears. She held herself stiffly, as if she would crumble if she did not.

Ziva enfolded the girl in a quick hug. Thankfully, they had not been hurt in the way Biny had insinuated. Likely, the Arameans meant to sell them at premium prices, possibly as temple prostitutes. A hateful destiny. Because they were rescued early, other than being exhausted, dirty, and hungry the girls were physically unscathed.

But their souls had been wrung dry.

Blinking back tears of compassion, Ziva searched through a storage basket and found an outgrown tunic that fit the smaller girl. A neighbor, who had seen Binyamin bring the girls to the house, brought one belonging to her grown daughter for the taller girl.

As the neighbor left, Abba filled the doorway. He entered, followed by Biny, his young friend, and an older man Ziva had seen among the prophets.

Biny said, "Chedva, Ziva, this is my friend Jaedon and his father. Dov and Jaedon tend a vineyard on the hill opposite our settlement."

Suddenly empty of words, Ziva hung back as her brother-in-law finished the introductions.

Imma came forward, an arm around each of the girls. "Shalom and welcome to our home. We are so grateful for what you've done for these children. You were very brave."

Biny's friend glanced away, his ears turning red at Imma's praise. Jaedon. A good name. *Thankful. God will judge.* His dark hair went every which way, like a flock of birds startled by a fox. He and his father bowed slightly to her and Imma.

Abba said, "They came to help move the table and carry food for the celebration."

Ziva and Imma watched from the opposite side of the room, the girls still clinging to Imma. The men soon were lifting, grunting, and angling the table through the small door. At one point, Jaedon's father let go his side of the table. A big man, he couldn't fit through the opening with the table and the other men. But Jaedon, though not as tall or broad as his father, hefted his side of the table effortlessly, and they crossed the threshold.

Not wanting to be caught staring, Ziva bent to whisper to the younger girl. "Are any of the boys in the group your brothers?" It was a diversionary tactic, but she did hope the older boys had watched over them.

"No," said the younger, Dina. "I have no brothers. But Ethan held our hands when the path was steep or we were afraid." The older girl's mouth trembled and drooped, then she hid her face against Imma's arm.

Ziva swallowed against a wave of sympathy. A long fearful journey had beaten their bodies and hearts.

Yahweh. Please. Only You can heal them.

Chapter Thirteen

But let all who take refuge in you be glad;
let them ever sing for joy. Spread your protection over them,
that those who love your name may rejoice in you.
~Psalm 5:11

Gischala, the date orchard
Jaedon

STANDING UNDER A TAMARISK TREE, JAEDON surveyed the area where Ziva's father said the village would gather. They had placed the table on a knoll overlooking a shallow valley where a date orchard grew. A seasonal stream watered the palms, and village children led the newcomers in a game of running, hopping, and whirling upon rocks and over the trickling water. Joyous shouts at certain leaps indicated a point system, but falling in the water received no penalties, other than becoming wet.

One of the prophets sat beneath the date palms playing a flute, while another strolled about strumming his lyre. The table on the knoll quickly filled with bowls of dates, almonds, and grapes. Music and food. Lost children, found. Cause for celebration.

Much like the harvest festival Jaedon attended when he was a boy, as there had been food and music then, and *Abba* was courting Miriam, before she became *Imma*. He'd given her a bracelet strung with shells that clicked when she danced through the vineyard with the maidens of Samaria, and his father had danced with the men. Jaedon had looked down on everyone from his perch on his grandfather's shoulders.

Once again, Jaedon tried to evoke his father's face but could not coax it from the shadows. Two emotions warred within. Anger that he could not recall his dead father's face yet could not forget his stoning. Gratitude that these children lived, with no need to *remember* a father's face.

Gratitude won. He watched village women add lentils, root vegetables, and herbs to an iron pot simmering over a fire built in the center of the gathering. He breathed in the savory aroma of stewing goat meat flavored with cumin.

More villagers emerged from houses bearing planks loaded with flat bread, some spread with cheese or honey. His stomach growled. How long had it been since any of them had eaten more than a handful of grain and a swallow of water?

The Gilgal prophets walked to the table and Binyamin introduced them to his wife's parents. Jaedon wondered if he should join them. Biny had introduced him and Dov, although casually, when they carried the table outside. He glanced around, hoping to spot Ziva.

Then she emerged from her house carrying a narrow-necked jar. She was small, like Eden, and very slender, like willow shoots that grow on the banks of the Jordan. She moved like a willow gracefully bending to the coaxing of a breeze. She leaned to place her jug amid the sweet breads.

His feet felt rooted to the ground.

When Biny motioned for him to join them, her gaze flitted up to meet Jaedon's. Kind eyes, the color of chestnuts. She leaned to whisper to the rescued girls, making them both smile. He wondered what her voice sounded like.

Two of the littlest boys shrieked with excitement, jostling against him as they ran by, their trauma seemingly forgotten ... for now. Laughing, he turned to watch them head for the table, helping themselves to the treats, probably realizing this was one time when no one would reprimand them.

When he returned his gaze to the table, Ziva was walking away. Her eyes were trained on her father, whose hand was lifted in a beckoning gesture.

Dov was walking away from Ziva's father and toward him. His pulse skipped a beat, guessing why Dov approached. Jaedon glanced back at Ziva. She was now walking arm-in-arm with her father toward the door of their house.

"Come with me, my son." Dov stood before him, gesturing to a steep slope, likely leading down toward the village well. They stopped by the side of the path as soon as their heads were hidden from the gathering villagers.

"I have talked to Ziva's father, and he has agreed the two of you may speak in the date orchard."

With all the shrieking children and splashing water? Jaedon grinned. "Plenty of sentries there."

"We thought it best to avoid gossiping tongues. I know you, my son. If you were alone with the girl, it would seem of greater import. Words would fail you."

"When?"

"Soon. They will send her to the orchard with the little girls, so they might cool their feet in the stream. Then I will send you to keep order with the boys. You should have ample opportunity to speak to each other. Learn a little of each other, as friends might. But that is all. Her father insists she is too young now to consider betrothal. Perhaps in another year. As for you, I know you are a man"—he paused—"but I think your time is yet to come. Another year will not be amiss."

Ziva walked through the village, holding the hands of the two rescued girls. She stopped to include neighbor girls in their number, sometimes speaking into a doorway, other times approaching a family group and explaining it was time the girls had a turn at the trickle of a stream. Ziva was glad to have these younger girls with her, to clasp their warm hands in hers. Comforting them, as an elder sister might, like Eden had always comforted her. Suddenly, her stomach felt empty, as if she had not eaten for days. But no, this was a different kind of hunger. She longed to have her sister's counsel before she talked with the boy. Not boy—young man.

Abba had explained his discussion with Dov—Jaedon's stepfather, he told her. So that was why she hadn't seen a resemblance. She had felt her face warm and wondered if Abba and Imma could see her blush in the dim light of their mud brick house. They would just talk, surrounded by herds of children. She felt her lips curve. She had questions.

She didn't see him waiting when she looked down the knoll, but a score or more of boys dashed around the date palms, splashing each other, not caring that formerly clean tunics were now speckled with mud.

"We will wait," Imma said. She had insisted she would accompany her daughter, that she would allow no one to say Ziva was not carefully watched.

Behind her, Ziva heard footfalls on the packed earth of the knoll.

"Shalom," Jaedon said, pausing on the other side of Imma. He sent a quick glance at Ziva, then fixed his attention on her mother. "If you allow, I will go down first and establish shalom in the date orchard. Before the girls join them."

"I thank you," her mother answered. Ziva watched as he strode down the shallow grade. He put two fingers in his mouth and whistled sharply. The boys startled to attention, and no wonder. The whistle sounded like a hawk or eagle who had spotted its prey. Her lips twitched into a smile. One of her questions might touch on that whistle.

He spoke kindly as he walked among the boys, but placed a firm hand on a shoulder here, grasped an arm there, and gathered their attention. Soon all quieted and swiveled their necks to stare up at the girls.

Then Ziva followed the girls as they picked their way down, shyly blushing at the attention. They stooped carefully to remove their sandals, hooking their fingers through the leather straps. Ziva said, "Leave them here, if you like, while you play with the others."

She went to lean against one of the palms. Her mother walked a short distance away and sat on a flat-topped rock. Jaedon came to stand between them, watching the children. As if guarding them, he stood with his back to her.

"I like your sister Eden."

She felt the corners of her lips twitch. Good, he spoke first. She disliked silent men. "Biny said you are a good friend."

Jaedon turned to face her then. "He is the best kind of friend."

She looked at him from beneath her lashes, liking his frank approval. She thought the same of Eden's husband. "You tend a vineyard? Do you have brothers?"

"I have an infant brother. We will share the vineyard, I suppose. Unless I ... unless later I serve Elisha."

Serve a prophet? Her curiosity burbled up like the

stream splashing under the palms. "How did you come to live among the prophets? I saw your father on that big red horse. He seems more a soldier than a prophet." She inhaled a soft breath. "You say you want to serve Elisha?"

"We came when I was very young. A story for another time. But I grew up following Elijah and Elisha as if they were my father and elder brother."

Jaedon leaned forward, his gaze earnest. "Elisha now leads the prophets. Even though he has received Elijah's mantle, there is resistance to his authority." And then he told her a strange and frightening story about his return to Gilgal with Elisha, a mob of young men, and bears.

Before she could form a reply, Jaedon had continued, his changeable face playing every emotion across its surface as he spoke.

"You are right about Dov, he was a soldier. Now he tends vines, and I with him. As for following Elisha, it seems that may not come to pass. At least he has said, not now. Yahweh has not commanded him."

She nodded. He had not completely answered every question, and she was confused. What exactly would it mean to serve Elisha? Could a man support a family that way? Oh, what was she thinking? Why did it matter? They barely knew each other. But he had indicated he would tell her more, another time, and she wanted to know more about his family now. "Tell me about your brother."

"His name is Yuval. Imma has great hopes for him becoming a musician, but now he is a toddler who makes his way through the vineyard, clutching at rocks, fence posts, and falling in the dirt." He had parodied every movement as he spoke. Then he laughed aloud, and Ziva ducked her chin, struggling to hide her smile.

"I have a young sister, Gershoni, who tries to follow me everywhere," he continued. "And you? Do you have brothers? More sisters?"

"I have a brother, Aharon. He is yet an infant and very sweet. No more sisters, just Eden and me. We were very close before she married. It is hard for us"—she stopped.

"To be separated?" he finished.

She nodded and, feeling her eyes sting, turned away.

"Ziva," he said quietly. Slowly, as if unsure whether to continue, he said, "Your family is important to you. We are alike in that." He hesitated again. "Yet there are vast differences between us. Both my parents died when I was young. The ones I call Abba and Imma are unrelated to me, as are my siblings, save one. Yet I love my family as if there are no divisions of blood among us."

She stared at him, surprised he had told her such a story, one that weighed so heavy. How hard it must have been to tell her. Why did he? There was more, she was sure, and perhaps he felt the enormity of it tainted him, somehow.

She gazed deep into his eyes trying to communicate acceptance. More than that, the approval that warmed her more than the sun filtering through the trees. Then she gestured toward the children, and toward Imma who was grasping the hem of her long tunic and wading into the shallow water. "We are the only ones who have not cooled their feet."

"May I?" He knelt to remove her sandals, then stood, and took her hand.

They walked together to the stream.

Chapter Fourteen

*So Ahab sent word throughout all Israel and
assembled the prophets on Mount Carmel. Elijah went
before the people and said, "How long will you waver
between two opinions? If the Lord is God, follow him; but
if Baal is God, follow him." But the people said nothing.*
~ 1 Kings 18:20-21

Mount Carmel
Elisha

TWO DAYS AFTER LEAVING JAEDON, ELISHA hiked past twisted
oak and terebinth trees to stand alone on Mount Carmel.
This was what he needed. The wind swept from the sea to the
top of the mountain, cleansing his troubled soul. Crashing
waves spoke of Yahweh's power, gulls' cries of his creation.

Below, the sparkling water was dotted by red, blue, and
white bleached sails. A solitary Phoenician merchant vessel
led the smaller boats. He was glad to be so removed from
them. Glad to be alone with God.

Elijah had described a similar scene, but he had not
been alone on that day. Had he stood here, in this very spot?

Elisha turned and walked slowly to the stone altar. His
master said he had rebuilt the broken-down altar with the
original stones. Twelve stones. One for each tribe of Israel.
As he placed them, he had called out the names of twelve
tribes, representing the undivided kingdom, not only the ten
in the north. A plea for Israel to come together again, one
nation worshipping Yahweh.

How Elisha wished he had been here that day. Instead,
he must piece together stories passed by word of mouth.
Unfortunately, he had not seen it for himself.

He ran his fingers over the altar's rough surface.
Charred ash covered his hand. Other sacrifices had been
offered here, but this was not Elijah's altar. It had been
consumed by the fierce fire from heaven which consumed
everything—bull, altar, barrels of water that drenched the
offering and flowed into a surrounding trench. Even the dirt
underneath.

People from all across Israel witnessed that scene, and their hearts were changed.

Nothing and no one can withstand God's power.

Elisha tried to imagine walking beside his master on this mountaintop. But it was after Elijah fled from Jezebel that Yahweh had told him to anoint Elisha as prophet in his place.

All things happened as the Lord willed—and when.

Elisha had been right to come here. The prophets' mixed acceptance and the Bethel youths' overt hatred had saddened him. He needed spiritual strength. Yet, he'd felt Yahweh's power pour through him in the matter of the Jericho spring. So why was he again filled with trepidation? Why must he seek affirmation from this place? Why walk the mountaintop, evoke the image of Elijah walking the same ground? Why imagine the prophet standing in front of King Ahab, a crowd of priests, and onlookers from across the land, invoking the covenant 'As the Lord God Almighty lives, whom I serve ...'

Elisha turned his face up to the sun, the wind off the sea simultaneously cooling his face. He could almost hear Elijah telling stories, his voice filled with excitement, fear at times, but always with awe for the God he had revered all his life. Here, in the place where Elijah waged the ultimate battle against the Ba'als, Elisha felt he stood on holy ground.

He wrapped himself in the mantle he always kept nearby. Yahweh had given it to him. Wasn't it a sign to pick up where Elijah left off? Yet, how could he follow in the footsteps of one such as his master? His heart sank under the monumental undertaking.

Before Elijah called fire from heaven, he prayed before all who gathered to watch. He reaffirmed God's almighty power and his own lowly position. Elisha closed his eyes.

Lord God, as I serve you, let it be known that you are God in Israel, that I am your servant, and I do all things at your command. Please Lord, let me do nothing but what you command. Answer me, Lord, that your people may know that you are God, and that you are turning their hearts back again.

He retraced his steps past the spot where the Lord God Almighty had answered Elijah's prayer with fire. He walked on to the boulder near the precipice where, after the sacrifice was consumed, Elijah prayed all night for rain. Then he sent his servant, Aban, seven times to the cliff's edge to search for a cloud.

He slid to the ground, leaning against the boulder's warmth. Once more, he bowed his head. *Lord, give me your wisdom, your strength. Without you, I am not fit for this task.*

Sitting in the place where Elijah had prayed all night, a warm breeze swirled around him. Could it be *Ruach Elohim,* the Spirit of the Lord?

Elisha prayed for Jaedon, who had wanted to serve him, though the time was not right. For Gehazi, who also asked to serve, but was unprepared in a different, more troubling, way. He prayed for the hearts of each prophet who determined to follow Yahweh, but their hearts were not steadfast. How could they turn Israel's heart, if their love for God was not pure?

Lord, what about me? I am not fit to lead, but you have chosen me. I am not resolute, so you must make me strong. My love for you is tarnished, so you must purify. Make me a true man of God, such as you had in Elijah.

He was answered by the crash of waves, whisper of the breeze, and caress of the sun. His eyes drifted shut.

While the indigo sky was still dotted with stars, he awoke, more rested than he'd been since he followed Elijah on his journey to Jericho.

The Lord has heard you, Elisha. Go now to Samaria. The armies of three kings prepare to war against Moab. Follow after the armies as they travel south, but do not present yourself to the kings until they send for you.

Elisha rubbed his eyes. *Will you go with me, Lord?*

The breeze tickled his ears. *I am with you always.*

When dawn tinted the sky gold and gray, Elisha picked up his travel pack, made sure his waterskin was full, and began the winding walk down the mountain path.

He heard the long scree of an eagle's cry from the thick forest on the rolling hills, reminding him of Jaedon's Hevel. A breath, a vapor. The boy said the name fit the way the eagle floated in the air. He gazed overhead but saw nothing more than sun and sky.

Chapter Fifteen

Now Mesha king of Moab raised sheep, and he had to pay the king of Israel a tribute of a hundred thousand lambs and the wool of a hundred thousand rams. But after Ahab died, the king of Moab rebelled against the king of Israel.
So at that time King Joram set out from Samaria and mobilized all Israel. He also sent this message to Jehoshaphat king of Judah: "The king of Moab has rebelled against me. Will you go with me to fight against Moab?"
"I will go with you," [Jehoshaphat] replied. "I am as you are, my people as your people, my horses as your horses."
"By what route shall we attack?" Joram asked.
"Through the Desert of Edom," Jehoshaphat answered.
~ 2 Kings 3:4-8

From Mount Carmel to Samaria
Elisha

IT WAS A LONG DAY'S WALK from Mount Carmel to Samaria, though the Lord had told Elisha he need not hurry. Plenty of time to pray and think.

Shall I follow in disguise, Lord, as Micaiah did before Ahab?

Yahweh did not answer—but did He need to? Elisha knew the Lord did not lay out His entire roadmap, but only the next thing. In the instance of Elijah, he was first to go before Ahab and invoke the curse. He obeyed, setting aside all reason and fear. Next, he was to flee east of the Jordan, to a place the Lord would show him, the Brook Cherith. There he'd be fed by ravens. No questions about clean or unclean. His master didn't allow himself to think where the bread and meat had come from. Then, after the brook dried, he was sent to Zarephath, where the Lord had told a Canaanite widow to feed him. He was told to present himself to Ahab and to summon all Israel to Mount Carmel. In all this, he obeyed.

But Elijah's problems began when he fled from Jezebel rather than wait to hear from the Lord. He had told this story many times to the school of the prophets.

I will remember his example, Lord. Elisha had been told to go to Samaria, but not to present himself to the kings. He had not, however, been told to go in disguise. So he would not.

Finally, he stood outside Samaria, gazing openly over the multitudes of soldiers, animals, servants, and other camp followers who had gathered in the broad valley outside the city walls.

Hmm. Other than oxen, Elisha knew little of caring for cattle, horses, or donkeys, but he knew about sheep and goats. These herds and flocks followed armies as food for the soldiers. He was capable of skinning, butchering, and dressing sheep and goats and experienced at making stews. He would be most useful among the shepherds.

Without delay, he made his way toward the outskirts of the army, walking through the trampled summer grass, getting the lay of the camp. He passed well-groomed warhorses, tied between trees to picket lines and tended by self-important stableboys who understood the worth of their charges. Next, he passed cooks, secure in their value to the soldiers, mounted or on foot. Soon he came to a herd of cattle, and finally the flocks of sheep and goats, meat on the hoof. He spotted a red-haired man instructing a group of shepherds, probably the head shepherd. When a few of the others glanced his way, the red-headed leader turned. Elisha immediately recognized a shepherd who had once worked for his family.

"Tobiah! What are you doing in Samaria?"

The shepherd snapped his head around and ran to embrace him, smacking a kiss on each cheek. Stepping back, he displayed a gap-toothed grin, then stepped back to inspect Elisha from head to toe.

"I think you have put on some flesh, my friend." He patted his own middle. "I expect you live a soft life as a prophet. Or have you taken a wife?"

Elisha tilted his head, considering Tobiah's changes. Silver streaks at his temples, in his beard–and the lisp.

"No wife, but a kind neighbor who often invites me and Elijah—" He stopped, feeling the clutch in his stomach at the still-fresh realization, as if he'd been kicked. He cleared his throat. "Even now, I forget. Have you heard? Elijah was taken by the Lord."

"Taken? When? How?"

So, the news had not made its way to Samaria. Elisha was glad to shine a torch on the truth before rumors made it only a tale.

As Tobiah exclaimed in surprise and asked questions, his lisp became more pronounced. Finally Elisha, indicating the missing front teeth, asked, "What happened there?"

"Raiders hit our village."

"Not Abel Meholah!"

"Yes. Even our peaceful, remote valley was attacked by Aramean raiders. One soldier demanded I slaughter a sheep for their supper. When I moved too slowly, he struck me across the mouth with the flat of his sword."

Elisha waited. Tobiah's temper was as fiery as his hair.

"I hit back with the hammerstone I held to kill the sheep. Flung his body over the cliff, where a pair of jackals made short work of him. When his accomplices came looking, I shrugged and quickly butchered and packed up a diseased ram who died the previous day. They were none the wiser."

No, even had they known it died of disease, the Canaanites would eat the ram, having no respect for Yahweh's law. "I'm sorry they hurt you, old friend. Were others injured?"

Tobiah's expression grew more somber. "Six were killed. Families who fought when their children were being carried off. I intervened, was beaten unconscious, and left for dead. I can only pray my diseased meat carried off twice as many Arameans."

Elisha shook his head sadly. King Ahab had pardoned Benhadad in exchange for a land and trade agreement instead of executing him as Yahweh commanded. The king paid for that disobedience with his own death, but worse, his nation continued to suffer at the hands of the Arameans. How could it end, when each ruler of Israel was worse than the last?

Ahab's son, Ahaziah, reigned only two years before drunkenly falling through an upper-room lattice. He made matters worse by seeking help from Baal-zebub instead of

Yahweh. After he died, his brother Joram took the throne. While he was a stronger military leader, cut from the same cloth as Ahab, he also shared his father's faults. Would there never be a ruler who followed the Lord?

"—and so your father sent me with a flock to support our country's army."

What was that Tobiah was saying? Elisha's attention shifted away from rulers who strayed from the Lord.

"My father sent you? Tell me how my parents fare."

Tobiah launched into a description of plenteous crops, growing herds, and his younger brother's expanding family. A longing to see them again jabbed like thistle. Immediately, the mantle warmed his shoulder, and a breeze brushed his ear. *Yes, you shall.*

Thank you, Lord.

Gazing over the flock, Elisha said, "I need a job, my friend. Can I help with the sheep?"

"You!" Tobiah crossed his arms and guffawed. "A wealthy farmer's son turned prophet! I assumed you were here for more important matters. But of course. I can always use help with these unruly animals."

"I am Yahweh's servant. Right now, there is nothing more important than shepherding the sheep."

The head shepherd laughed again. "Four or two-legged?"

Elisha grinned. "The four-legged variety will provide a respite."

Tobiah punched him in the shoulder. "We will see."

After several days, many in the camp came to recognize Elisha as a prophet. He spoke of teaching, traveling, and serving with Elijah every chance he found. As he worked among the sheep, he constantly taught his companions about the Lord's commands and promises.

As word about Elisha spread through the camp, he found more interested listeners among the handlers of cattle, horses, and donkeys, especially when he recounted Elijah's miracles that ended in fire from heaven.

One day as Elisha spoke, he recognized the red and gold uniform of an officer of King Joram among their number. He also noticed the camp had nearly doubled in size. Later that night, the Lord spoke to Elisha in a dream.

"Soon, you will be summoned before King Joram of Israel and Jehoshaphat of Judah. Joram has strengthened his army and called Jehoshaphat to partner with him in war against Moab. They have planned to join with Judah's vassal state, Edom. All three kings plan to move their armies and attack Moab from the south, traveling around the south end of the Dead Sea through the wilderness of Edom.

"In all this, they have not consulted Me nor sought My will. So, I have left them to their own devices.

"When they summon you, go. Listen and answer as I tell you."

Elisha tried to speak, but his lips would not move. When he awoke, though it was still night, a warm light surrounded him, like a thumbprint in the darkness. He held a soft blue sack tied with string. When his fingers fumbled with the knots, they fell loose on their own. Inside the sack were small round wafers, soft, like bread made of finest flour and smelling of honey and coriander. *Manna?*

He ate and was strengthened.

Chapter Sixteen

*Joram son of Ahab became king of Israel in Samaria in the
eighteenth year of Jehoshaphat king of Judah, and he
reigned twelve years. He did evil in the eyes of the Lord,
but not as his father and mother had done. He got rid of
the sacred stone of Baal that his father had made.
Nevertheless he clung to the sins of Jeroboam so
of Nebat, which he had caused Israel to commit;
he did not turn away from them.*
2 Kings 3:1-3

En Route to Battle
Elisha

ELISHA BOLTED UPRIGHT. THE FIRST THING he thought upon awakening was, "I must tell Elijah!" Then, a stone pressed on his chest. They had spent hours talking each time Elijah heard from God, whether in a vision, dream, or the voice like a whisper on the wind.

Elisha had dreamed of war and eaten manna, but he had no one to tell.

As he rubbed his eyes and stretched, he contemplated discussing the dream with Tobiah. His old friend could keep a confidence. But Elisha immediately felt a need for constraint. Yahweh had not told him to discuss the dream with Tobiah, nor with anyone. No, the secrets of Yahweh were to be kept between them alone, unless the Lord instructed him differently.

Between them alone. The stone lifted off his chest. *Yahweh. I see why you have not yet given me a servant. I am your servant, you are my master. It is only us, now. Thank you for giving me direction about the kings. Without you, I am only an ignorant farmer—without a farm.*

Elisha imagined he heard a soft chuckle.

He would wait to be summoned and then listen for the Lord's next instruction. He was content, still he wondered how long the army would tarry outside Samaria.

As the sky lightened in the east, Elisha heard the

tremulous bleat of a lamb and the throaty response of its mother. An hour before the time of his watch, he rose from his sleeping mat and decided to walk the camp's perimeter to get his bearings. Heading south, he came upon herders driving cattle to drink. A shallow spot in the stream had been widened for their use. Beyond their broad, red-brown backs, the slow-moving water reflected the pale light of morning. He walked past the herd and came upon army tents, where captains were ordering soldiers to dismantle the camp and pack for moving.

As he approached a stand of pines, he smelled and heard horses. When he rounded the trees, handlers were feeding and watering the animals. Some had been hobbled to graze the thick grass. He continued south until he spotted royal tents flying flags in the reds and yellows of Israel and Judah. The flaps were rolled up and Elisha observed servants bustling around inside, while soldiers guarded the entrances. Hearing hooves approach, Elisha stepped aside. Hostlers led two royal steeds to the tent entrances. Horsemen gathered in formation.

Elisha watched as King Joram exited his tent and vaulted onto his dark bay. He still retained the vigor of youth, but King Jehoshaphat, now gray-haired and stooped, clambered onto his steed with assistance from a captain.

The mounted troops of the two armies headed south. Elisha waited until the foot soldiers mustered and followed the horsemen. Then he returned to the sheep camp to advise Tobiah to ready the herd for moving.

Elisha jumped in front of a wayward ram that had somehow broken past the sheep dogs and was heading toward pasture. They tussled until a pair of the dogs intervened, saving him from the embarrassment of losing an argument with a sheep. A big one.

"You're out of condition, my friend." Tobiah motioned for another shepherd to step into Elisha's place.

He felt his face warm. So much for avoiding embarrassment.

"Stand in the shade with me a moment," Tobiah said. "I

have questions about what you told me. I'm not surprised we're going to war. King Joram must have finally decided to teach Moab a lesson. After all, King Mesha refused to send his taxes these past two years. But to attack from the South? Now that's strange. The northern approach is more direct. Makes more sense to cross the Jordan, then travel south on the east side of the Dead Sea to the Arnon River."

"You are right. The northern approach is faster." Elisha stopped there, knowing it was not for him to reveal what the Lord had said. At least not yet.

Tobiah whistled to one of the sheepdogs, pointed at an escaping lamb, then turned his attention back to Elisha. "I'm worried. It is late in the season to mount such an offensive. Summer grass is still thick in Samaria, but what will we find on the banks of the Dead Sea?

"At least I and the other herdsmen have been told we will move soon—after the troops. The army will move faster than the flocks and herds. We've seen the route maps. The march is longer, about a hundred miles around the south end of the Dead Sea. Through the desert of Edom." He shook his head and they both stood silent, contemplating the wretchedness of bringing all these animals through the desert.

"Who came up with this idea, anyway?"

"The king of Judah." Tobiah shrugged. "I suppose I can see Jehoshaphat's reasoning. For one thing, his plan means a march through Edom, his vassal and ally. He can enlarge his army and remind Edom of Judah's strength, in case they were contemplating a rebellion of their own. Plus, there's the element of surprise. Who would expect a march through the Desert of Edom—in summer!"

Somewhat amused, Elisha listened to this reasoning without comment. It was reasonable for kings to take stock of their army and discuss various strategies before considering war, but not to consult Yahweh was foolhardy. That was the plan's major flaw. Elisha suspected the kings of North and South were next to be surprised.

Tobiah crossed his arms and squinted up at Elisha. "You are being very quiet. I am going to ask you one question, and I want you to answer me truthfully. Everyone knows you hear the voice of the Lord. Have the kings asked you what Yahweh has to say about their plans?"

Elisha hesitated, unsure if he could answer. Then he felt a breath of approval.

"No, they have not."

Each day, further information about troop movements trickled back to the herdsmen. The armies of Israel and Judah planned to quick march for seven days, with the intent to get to Edom, pick up reinforcements from Judah's ally, and pass through the desert of Edom as quickly as possible. Then attack Moab.

To reduce stress on the sheep, goats, and cattle, they followed at a slower pace behind cook wagons that surged ahead. Each night, prepared meat and grains were hauled ahead by mule teams for the next day's meals. The rest of the camp followers caught up by late afternoon, then the cycle repeated the next day.

The army generals had made provision for extra water for the longer route. On one of his rounds of the camp, Elisha came upon thousands of camels, added to carry extra water and supplies for men and beasts. Good planning, as far as human wisdom went.

Five days into the march, he walked again through the camp, no longer upon grass, trampled or otherwise, but upon sand that scuffed into his sandals at every step. He observed cattle with drooped heads and hollowed flanks. The animals lowed with thirst. When he came to the camel drivers, he heard rumblings that water supplies were low. That night the driver of the cook wagon said the wadi near their final destination, where they planned to replenish, was dry.

The next afternoon, Elisha took a break from his flock and sat in the shade of a tamarisk tree. Tobiah and a deeply tanned camel driver walked slowly through the camp, each leading a camel. One carried large water containers for animals. They sloshed as they passed, indicating they weren't full. The other camel carried waterskins for the men.

Tobiah untied one and sat beside Elisha. "Drink, my friend."

Elisha unplugged the skin, peering inside to gauge how much was left.

Sunlight struck the water surface. Elisha squinted against a bright and moving reflection as he tipped the skin this way and that. Voices floated up from the waterskin, almost as if he stood at the door of the kings' tents.

King Joram complained to the king of Judah, "Now what will we do? We have no water for men or animals. The Lord has brought our three armies to this dry desert only to let the king of Moab defeat us."

Elisha glared at the wavering vision and raked his fingers through his hair. The king was just like his father Ahab. Blaming God for events brought about by his own stupidity. Did the Lord tell Joram to take a southern route? Did Joram or Jehoshaphat ask for the Lord's advice? No, they considered their own wisdom sufficient until their plan went wrong. Then they blamed God.

Elisha peered back into the water.

"Now that's not the way a king should talk," said King Jehoshaphat. "Listen, is there a prophet of the Lord among us?"

Elisha expelled a breath. The king of Judah meant well, but he kept bad company. He should stay away from the kings of Israel.

Someone else answered. "My king, I have seen Elisha, son of Shaphat among our company. He used to be Elijah's personal servant."

King Joram swore silently. *Servant of Elijah! Cursed be that troubler of Israel.*

Elisha stiffened, hearing Joram's every thought. How dare he speak thus of the Lord's anointed prophet!

King Jehoshaphat had not heard his fellow king, and he said, "I know the Lord speaks through Elisha. Let us have your officer take us to him."

"Very well. Ocran, take us to the fellow, if you know where he is."

Ocran brought his fist to his chest in salute. "Yes, my king."

They are coming for you, Elisha. Do not trouble yourself over what to say. I will put words in your mouth.

Elisha took a sip of the water and handed it back to Tobiah. "You drink the rest." His voice rasped and he felt a hand press him down. The vision continued.

An officer was leading a company of soldiers, trying to break a path through the water-bearing camels, but sheep, horses, and cattle smelled the water. They kept surging forward, as did thirsty men.

But the officer and his soldiers persisted with shouts and the brunt of their swords. Grudgingly animals and men made way. Following behind the soldiers strode King Joram of Israel, then Jehoshaphat of Judah, and finally the king of Edom.

Elisha stood at their approach, shaking himself out of the trance. The ground under his feet wavered as vision and reality merged.

Tobiah scrambled to his feet and disappeared into the crowd.

King Joram pushed his way forward. "There you are! Are you aware that the Lord has called us together? And yet, it appears He meant only trickery, to deliver us into the hands of our enemy, Moab. We have no more water for ourselves or the animals."

This king. He dared to accuse Yahweh of unfaithful treatment. Yet, when he took the throne, he performed only a token cleansing of the temple at Samaria. Yes, he removed his father's pillar of Ba'al. But he continued to worship the golden calves at Bethel and Dan.

Elisha stood, breathing in the *ruach ha-codesh*. The infilling, as the Lord promised. "Why are you coming to me? Go to the pagan prophets of your father and mother!"

"No! We come to you, the prophet of the Lord. For it was the Lord who called us here, only to be defeated by the king of Moab. Why has Yahweh treated us thus? Isn't this pagan nation, this treaty breaker, His enemy as well as Israel's?"

Elisha scowled. "As surely as the Lord Almighty lives, whom I serve, I would not bother with you at all, except for my respect for King Jehoshaphat of Judah."

Elisha sat again and leaned back against the tree.

"Bring me a harpist," he said to King Joram.

Joram gestured to a servant who ran off presumably to find a musician.

Elisha could have played the harp himself, but Joram's arrogance needed addressing. He would benefit from being on the receiving end of a prophet's orders, and besides, it would be restful for Elisha to close his eyes and listen to another's music.

The harpist strummed and sang a *maskil* with all the emotion in his heart.

As the deer pants for streams of water,
  so my soul pants for you, my God.
My soul thirsts for God, for the living God.
  When can I go and meet with God?
My tears have been my food day and night,
while people say to me all day long,
"Where is your God?"

Elisha's eyes drifted closed with the haunting music. Why must it always be so? The psalmist thirsted for God's presence, but Israel did not. The psalmist repented for his nation's sins, but they did not. There was still hope in Yahweh, for those who would turn, trust, and praise Him for the blessings showered upon them. But Elisha feared they would not.

The power of the Lord again came upon him. He spoke loudly so all assembled could hear.

"This is what the Lord says: Make this valley full of ditches. You will see neither wind nor rain, but this valley will be filled with pools of water. You will have plenty for yourselves and your cattle and other animals. But this is only a simple thing for the Lord"—Elisha shrugged—"so He will also make you victorious over the army of Moab. You will conquer the best of their towns, even the fortified ones. You will cut down all their good trees, stop up all their springs, and ruin all their good land with stones."

The rest of that afternoon and evening, herdsmen, camel drivers, cooks, and soldiers dug ditches. Even the kings took a few turns. There weren't enough shovels for the task, so battle axes, swords, and soup ladles were also employed.

When there were sufficient ditches, Elisha told the kings and soldiers to camp near one end of the valley, but for the herdsmen to move the animals far behind the battle line where they could not be heard nor smelled. "Get what sleep you can," he advised everyone. "Tomorrow's battle will be long."

The sky was cloudless the next morning, and the sun glared hot and red. All had heard Elisha's prediction, but they watched the sky, even though Yahweh had said there would be neither wind nor rain.

Elisha urged Tobiah and the other shepherds to pack their tents and other belongings and hang them from trees to avoid being soaked by the coming flood. Some laughed, but others obeyed.

At exactly the time the morning sacrifice would be offered in Jerusalem, water began roiling toward the camp, flowing down from the direction of Edom.

At first, Tobiah and his shepherds laughed, splashing about in the spreading water. Soon there were pools of water everywhere, flattening, becoming mirror-like. The sun flashed rosy red upon their surfaces.

But not everyone in the camp had believed the word of the Lord. As a result, soldiers, cooks and others were scrambling to retrieve their sodden possessions from the flowing water.

"Tell your soldiers to prepare for battle," Elisha instructed the kings and officers. "The Moabites will arrive soon planning to collect plunder. Then you will attack."

Elisha had seen another vision, as clear as if he stood in the midst of the Moabite tents. Every man in Moab capable of strapping on a sword had been conscripted. They stood, poised to fight, along the border of their ancestral land. But at daybreak, when they saw the pools of water gleaming red, they were deceived, thinking it the blood of their enemies.

"The three armies must have attacked and killed each other," they said amongst themselves. "Let's go and collect the plunder."

So they came, laughing and shouldering huge sacks for pillage, just as Elisha's vision portrayed. When the first wave of Israelite soldiers jumped from behind trees, rocks, and sodden tents, they had the surprise advantage. More ally soldiers rushed out and attacked from the flanks, forcing the Moabites to turn and run back to their country.

Elisha climbed to a knoll above the valley and watched as the vision became reality. The Israelite coalition pursued the enemy, killing them as they fled. They did as they'd been told, destroying the towns, cutting down the trees used for building siege ramps, and stopping up springs.

Finally, only the Moabite stronghold of Kir-hareseth stood. Israelites with slings surrounded it, raining down stones. Elisha watched sadly, knowing what was coming next.

The vision swept Elisha inside Kir-hareseth. The ground under his feet shook with the rattle of falling stones where he stood next to the king of Moab.

Inside the fortress, horses squealed, bucked, and charged as stones rained over its walls. Many fell, rolled, and struggled to rise with flailing hooves, crushing riders and soldiers to death. The horsemen were devastated. When King Mesha realized his army was losing the battle, he assembled his most skilled swordsmen.

"Men, in our weakened condition, the armies of Israel and Judah are unbeatable. There is one chance for us. Of our opponents, the army of Edom is not as strong, and they fret against their bond to Judah. If we can break through the lines near their king, perhaps we can convince him to join us against our mutual adversary."

So they poured out through the gate into the waiting swords of the Edomite, but King Mesha's entreaties to the king of Edom failed. What remained of the Moabite army retreated again behind the stone walls of Kir-hareseth.

Once inside, King Mesha called his captain. "Bring my son, the crown prince."

When they brought the prince, a stripling of about twelve summers, nausea grasped Elisha. He wanted to turn away from the face of darkness, but the Lord had placed him here. He forced himself to watch, to witness the divide between dark and light.

Mesha addressed his decimated force. "Our god Chemosh demands an ultimate sacrifice. Surely if we do this, he will give us victory." Then he ordered his officers. "Build a fire atop the wall."

Outside the wall, the three allied armies watched in confusion, then horror, as the pile of kindling grew, the struggling boy was tied to the post, and a torch lit the bonfire.

Elisha put his hands over his ears.

Then, he was mercifully carried away to the herders' camp, where his ears were filled not with screams but a whisper.

Tell my people. Ask them, 'Do you see where pagans go for help? See what their god demands, he who is no god? Is this what you want, you faithless people, with your high places and idolatrous sacrifices?'

Elisha opened his eyes. He stood in the midst of the herdsmen, still trembling from what he had seen. But now he breathed in the good smell of warm animals, and he felt the refreshing breeze—the Lord's Spirit—come to fill him with peace. He fixed his gaze on Tobiah, then turned slowly to look upon shepherds, camel drivers, and cooks, their faces inscribed with confusion and fear.

Taking a deep breath, he told them everything he had seen in the vision and how the Lord's spirit had covered his eyes and carried him away before the boy's end. However, their kings and their armies had watched, horrified. Would they learn?

As much as Elisha could in that moment, he tried to explain to the people. That worshipping the Ba'als, Chemosh, and Molech led to this wretched end. Was this what they wanted to exchange for the God who brought them out of slavery in Egypt, gave them a land of their own, and who they had sworn to faithfully serve?

Then he began to pray the *Shema*, taught to his people in ancient days as a daily prayer of praise and allegiance.

Their voices joined his.

Hear, oh Israel, the Lord is our God, the Lord is one.

And as for you, you shall love the Lord your God with all your heart,

with all your soul, and with all your strength.

Chapter Seventeen

Show me the wonders of your great love,
you who save by your right hand
those who take refuge in you from their foes.
Keep me as the apple of your eye;
hide me in the shadow of your wings
Psalm 17:7-8

En Route to Samaria, after the battle
Elisha

ELISHA WALKED WITH TOBIAH AMONG A ragtag crowd of Israelites returning to Samaria and other northern towns. Before they left camp, he had watched officers of King Joram's army forced to bury their dead. They dug trenches, stripped bodies of weapons, rolled them into the graves atop one another, and quickly covered them with dirt against scavengers. The grisly task was a soldier's duty, but many Israelites who had joined for the stipend—farmers, vintners, and tradesmen—fled from the last battle when they watched the Moabite king burn his own son alive.

Would there be punishment for deserters? Perhaps. But fearing this, it was also likely that the men would leave Samaria and disappear into the hills of Ephraim.

Elisha sighed. He would never forget what he'd seen. The killing, the bodies, the waste. Worst of all, an innocent boy burned by his own father.

"Something troubling you, Master?" Tobiah slowed, and Elisha matched his pace.

The title did not rest easily on his shoulders. Tobiah and others had begun to call him Master after he had explained how the terrible sacrifice was the bitter end of following other gods—darkness rather than light. Chemosh would not answer prayers without a human sacrifice. Yahweh accepted the death of an innocent lamb to pay sin's penalty. Although the Lord blessed Israel many times despite their disobedience, He had sternly warned them against worshipping other gods.

I, the Lord your God, am a jealous God. You shall have no other gods before me.

And Elisha had led them in the *Shema*.

Last night, he had taught the troubled herdsmen in the same way Elijah taught the prophets in the settlements of the hills of Ephraim. He took them slowly through the scrolls, beginning with Adam and Eve. He spoke of blessing, rebellion, and consequences, then ended with Yahweh redeeming His own.

Perhaps, through practice, Elisha would grow comfortable with the responsibilities of the title. But for now, he was grateful for the company of an old friend.

"You know I left my father and mother to follow Elijah."

"Yes, and a prosperous farm. I never understood why. I thought it was because you wanted adventure."

Elisha shook his head and chuckled. "You know better. I was happy working my father's fields from daybreak to nightfall. No one could outwork me. A quiet life suited me. Did I ever leave the valley of Abel Meholah? No, even on market days, I asked my father to send his trusted servant."

"Me." Tobiah grinned. "I served him well, and I enjoyed the city's excitement. But your brother is poured from your mold."

Elisha felt a pull, like a peculiar sound behind bushes that prompted one to investigate.

"My brother is a good son to my parents?"

"The best—after the son who left."

Elisha was glad, especially for Imma's sake. He tugged the mantle around him, seeing again the tears on her brown cheeks when he left to follow Elijah, his father's arms holding her close.

"One thing I lacked. I loved my quiet life, but I felt more awaited. I never understood what it could be, until Elijah placed the mantle on my shoulders. Then I knew."

Tobiah nodded knowingly. "Just as I said. Adventure."

Elisha shook his head emphatically. "I never sought it. But when one hears the Call, and from one such as Elijah, the only answer is, 'Yes.'"

"You answered, 'Yes, I will come today,' as I remember. You held a feast for all in the valley but left with him that same evening."

Elisha smiled softly, remembering. It *had* been an adventure—learning from Elijah, traveling among the settlements, teaching other prophets, and Elijah's fiery flight.

Tobiah scratched his ear. "But you have not answered my question."

Elisha turned his attention back to Tobiah. "I am afraid I've forgotten."

"What is troubling you?"

Elisha felt his smile broaden. Talking to Tobiah had reminded him of his longing to do more, of his joy at receiving The Call, and yes, the adventure of following the Lord each day, never knowing what would come next. Whatever the Lord planned would always be a step designed by the true Master.

Elisha's answer would always be, 'Yes. Yes, Master. Today.'

"Nothing worth discussing, after talking with you," Elisha said. "You have lightened my spirits, my friend." He turned the conversation to Tobiah's children, grandchildren, and how he missed his wife's cooking.

Elisha could not stop his mind from returning to the war and the sacrifice of Moab's crown prince. Both were stark warnings of the direction the Israelites headed, if they did not turn.

Still, he couldn't bring himself to discuss with Tobiah how he was troubled by the visions. It would be like discussing an intimate conversation with one for whom it was not meant. If he was troubled, there were two remedies. Converse with the One who sent it. Pursue His commands with all vigor.

It took three days to reach Samaria. They arrived Friday, just before the Sabbath began, and stayed with a friend of Tobiah's on the outskirts of the city. Monday morning Elisha woke early. His mat was near a window in the main room of the house, and a ray of sunlight penetrated his dream. Although other travelers lay head to toe across the room, he forced himself to wait quietly, listening, as if he were alone.

Go down to Gilgal today. Others will join you for the journey. You are to train Gehazi to be your servant.

Yes, Master. Right now.

He laced his sandals, donned his mantle, and shouldered his waterskin. The woman of the house handed him a sack and then dropped in three wrapped parcels. "Cheese, dates, unleavened rounds," she said. "Something told me you would leave without breaking your fast. Often visitors want to leave before the heat of the day."

He glanced around, quickly searching for Tobiah. He was nowhere to be seen. Was he one of the *others* who would join him on the road to Gilgal? No, his friend longed for his family, and Abel Meholah lay in the opposite direction. Still, Elisha would have liked to say goodbye. His steps lagged as he walked through the marketplace past fruit stands and cloth vendors and headed toward the iron-reinforced city gates.

"Ho! Ox-driver!"

His lips turned up. Tobiah used to call him Ox-driver when he plowed with his father's teams. *Almost* an insult, from the ginger-haired shepherd, who loved his sheep and thought oxen stupid. Elisha wheeled to look behind. Tobiah loped toward him, his gap-toothed grin making light of any insult. "Didn't want to divulge your identity to the entire city," he murmured when he grasped Elisha's shoulders. "You will forgive me for the awful appellation?"

"I consider it a blessing." Elisha grinned and held his friend a moment longer, memorizing the face he might never see again. "The Lord is sending me back home to Gilgal."

"And me to the home of your youth. I thought we might have the morning together. I bought this"—he held out one of two large packs—"apples, very rare." He tipped his head toward a vendor's stall, where round, yellow and reddish striped fruit were carefully bolstered by cushions and guarded by a burly merchant.

"I've heard of them but never seen one." Elisha began to unwrap the parcel.

Tobiah's eyebrows shot up, and he grabbed Elisha's hands. "No, no, you've seen them right there in the booth. Leave these wrapped until you're home. Can't you tuck them there?" He indicated the sack of provisions his friend's wife had given Elisha. "They are rare, I tell you, and some might consider you easy prey. You *can* smell them right through the cloth. I've heard you can grow trees from the seeds."

Elisha brought his nose to the cloth wrapper, breathing in sweetness and tart freshness at the same time. *Yahweh, I would like to grow apple trees.* But he heard no answer.

"I am taking these to your father," Tobiah went on, indicating the second parcel. "Traded one of his sheep. He will be pleased, will he not?"

Elisha prolonged their conversation until he felt the Lord's gentle nudge. Tobiah agreed to carry greetings to Elisha's family and convey his promise to visit them in Abel Meholah when Yahweh permitted. The two said their goodbye.

Elisha headed south to Gilgal. So it would not be Jaedon but Gehazi. Ah, well. *You know best.*

Slowly he inhaled the mountain air, forcing his taut shoulders to relax. As he strolled the ridge road, his gaze swept over a seemingly endless expanse of layered hills and narrow valleys. A peaceful sight. It was only that he was weary, and no wonder. Between his travels to Jericho, back to Gilgal, Mount Carmel, Samaria, and to the battles with Moab, he had been gone from home several months.

Soon he would have a servant. A partner for the Lord's work. Perhaps he could rest a while at Gilgal before the Lord sent him off again.

A breeze lifted his hair. Overhead, a shadow crossed. He glanced up, catching sight of an eagle floating on the air. His gaze followed its flight until it ducked into a stand of cedars in a valley ahead, its weight causing the top branches to dip and sway like a boat on a choppy lake. He did not think it was Hevel. But would he recognize her?

The sighting was fleeting, as her time with them had been. He missed the hours he'd spent with young Jaedon training the eagle to hunt. Their laughter at her antics. The boy's grim expression at her inevitable departure, though he assured everyone he understood that freedom, living out her purpose in life, was best. The lad had the makings of a fine man.

There was much to appreciate about Gehazi, as well. He was hardworking, willing, and had obeyed without argument when Elisha sent him to fetch his wife and sons.

But there it was. *Why* had he separated from his family? Elisha would wish his servant to be ... settled. Well. He would ask him about that.

One thing reassured him. If God meant for Gehazi to serve him, all was well.

The sun had passed overhead before he finally decided to break his fast. Ahead, an acacia tree offered dappled shade. He sat and leaned against its broad trunk, then he reached into his sack. Spreading cheese on a bread round, he took a huge bite. The bread was dense, filling, and flavored with salt, as he liked it. The creamy cheese caused him to close his eyes in pleasure. He heard chittering in the branches above and squinted against filtered sunlight. A nest with a small round head peering over its edge. Imma finch and, if he were not mistaken, two or three chicks inside.

He took another bite, let his eyes drift closed again, and listened to the bird song. Was she praying? *Thank you Lord for that delicious worm.* Or was it a message to her mate, carried on the wind? *Where are you, Amos? The children are hungry.* Or, was she talking to him? *Ho, fat stranger. Can you not spare a bit of that bread for me and my children?*

He took one more bite, then curled his hand around the remaining morsel and tossed it a few paces away. Shortly, the little brown bird darted down, grabbed it in her beak, and swooped back to the nest.

He must have dozed off, for when he opened his eyes, the chittering had doubled with the arrival of a colorful male with a reddish belly and a gray cap. The sun slanted lower in the sky. Elisha twisted the stopper from the waterskin and poured a long, cool drink down his throat. Before taking another, he stood to peruse the landscape for a tell-tale band of deeper green. It would be good to find a spring or stream and replenish his supply. He saw none, but his search revealed a small party of travelers approaching him from behind. Two donkeys. A tall man led one laden with bundles, and a woman rode the other.

He often preferred walking alone. Gave him time to think. To pray. He had much to think and pray over. But Yahweh had said he would be joined by others.

The man studied him as they passed. No use pretending Elisha hadn't seen them, so he raised a hand in casual greeting. The man lifted his, fingers splayed. Shaking her head, the woman leaned over to speak to him. The man shrugged and kept walking, but they had slowed their steps.

A single man on the road might mean a band of fellow ruffians hid down the slope, waiting to attack. Likewise, two travelers might not be man and wife, but two men, one disguised as a woman to appear innocent and conceal weapons under flowing garments.

Elisha listened for a word from the Lord.

Gather your belongings. Walk on.

He bent to grasp the mantle, which had slipped to the ground while he dozed. After fastening it around his neck, he pulled his head covering forward to shield him from the sun. Then he shouldered the half-empty waterskin and sack of provisions.

Lengthening his stride, he settled into a pace that would get him to Gilgal before nightfall. It appeared he had no reason to fear the travelers, but he understood their concern. And he welcomed time alone to contemplate—

Clip clop, clip clopity.

The man cast a backward glance and stopped. One of the donkeys lowered its head, the other cocked a hind leg.

"Ho! Elijah! Is that you?"

Elisha also stopped, maintaining distance. Had anyone in Israel not heard?

The man tipped his head, as if uncertain and said, "Not Elijah. Is it ... you Elisha?"

Who was this?

"I am sorry. I recognize you now. Do you remember me? Ocran. I heard Elijah had gone. But when I recognized his mantle, I thought for one moment he had returned."

Elisha walked toward the pair and, reliving Ocran's stealthy entry in the dead of night, tried not to scowl. "Yes, I remember Dov's friend from the army."

And that Elijah stopped you in your plot to kill Miriam and Jaedon. He felt a twinge between his shoulder blades, like a tap from a strong finger. *Yes, Lord. I remember. You have forgiven him, and Jezebel had imprisoned his family, so I will do the same.*

"You have Elijah's mantle," Ocran said.

Ocran's garments were also confusing. A poor man's tunic, and no visible sword on a soldier?

"The prophet threw it over my shoulders when we met. The Lord gave it again when he left."

"I would like to hear about his leave-taking. I have heard stories but not from an eyewitness, especially one who wears his mantle."

"We can talk on the road. I am headed for Gilgal. Where are you going?"

The woman smiled for the first time, her face transforming from concerned to lovely, although she was not a young woman. Something moved under her cloak. He had begun to wonder if its fullness concealed a pregnancy, but that was too much movement. A child.

"We should arrive around sunset," Elisha said. "If you are going farther perhaps you would like to spend the night in the settlement. There are many who could house you. Even I, unless Jaedon has already invited others to stay."

"A coincidence," said Ocran. "We are going to Gilgal. I hailed you at first because I needed directions—forgot where to turn off. My wife warned me you could be a bandit."

Elisha smiled, wanting to erase the blush of embarrassment that spread across the woman's cheeks. "You needed directions. I have them. And a place to stay, if you have none."

"I thank you. Dov urged me to settle here after"—he glanced at his wife. A child peered from behind her cloak— "well, you know why I came before. Before I returned, he and I talked about my life in the army, about the danger in Samaria. I went home ready to move to Gilgal right then. But then things changed." Ocran glanced meaningfully at the child, who now was nearly uncovered. A pretty little girl of about three or four summers, curls falling across her forehead and down her shoulders.

"We can speak more of it later," Elisha said. "I am sure Dov will welcome you and help you settle in, but if his home is too full, we have room for you elsewhere."

Interesting. Another soldier to settle with the school of the prophets. *What use do you have for them, Lord?*

What is that to you? Tend to the work I have given you.

Elisha hid a grin. He had plenty to tend to. He was to train the prophets to preach. Teach Gehazi to serve with him. Build up the seven thousand who had not worshipped the Ba'als. Yahweh had given him enough work to occupy himself. He had no doubt there would be more to come.

He smelled Miriam's lentil stew before he saw the settlement. She had finally told him her secret—wild cumin—but even so, the taste of his stew never matched hers. She had probably held back another secret.

Was it coincidence she was cooking his favorite dish the day he returned from Samaria? He chuckled. *Prophet, remember your own teachings. There are no coincidences.*

When the road curved, he saw the two halves of the settlement, like twin nests laying against each side of the ridge road. But smoke curled, not from Miriam's mud brick house on the west side, but from a smaller, new residence up the eastern slope, behind Elijah's ... behind *his* house.

Ocran said goodbye and led his family toward Dov and Miriam's home. "Don't hesitate to come to me if they are crowded," Elisha said. He exhaled and turned for his own house. It would be good to take off his sandals and be alone.

But a prophet came hurrying out the door of the new house, waving. No, not a prophet. Gehazi. His apprentice.

Elisha ran his hand over the folds of Elijah's mantle, the cloth warming his hand. *Forgive my human impatience, Lord. He is not yet a prophet, perhaps. Thank you for trusting me with his training.*

He paused, dwelling on his thoughts and feeling out of step. Out of sorts. He was tired. Surely, he did not doubt the Lord? *Help me see him as You see him.*

Forcing the corners of his mouth up, he lifted his hand. "Shalom."

Gehazi hurried down through the hillside settlement then up the few steps of the slope to meet him on the road. "Welcome home, Master. My wife has prepared your favorite dish. We hope you will honor our home."

"Gladly." Elisha breathed in the aroma wafting from the little house. Perhaps Miriam had shared the secret of cumin with Gehazi's wife.

The mud bricks were dark, with squared-off corners, obviously new. Built quickly, for Elisha had only been gone a few months. The prophets would have teamed up to help build it. But it was very small. Did he not have three sons? Well, they could add a room, if needed.

A goat poked its spotted head out from a lean-to at the left, a rope tethering it to a post. A young one sidled alongside, then darted behind the doe. Good, they would have milk for drinking or cheese. The settlement had embraced the newcomer.

As they neared the house, a woman came to stand in the doorway drying her hands on a cloth. Gehazi introduced his wife, Lital. Her head cloth was slightly off-center, as was her smile. "Welcome, Elisha. Come sit. Have a cool drink while Gehazi calls the boys."

Elisha hesitated, watching Gehazi walk behind the house. Two young men dug in a garden running aslant up the slope. A boy of about ten or eleven summers watered a row of seedlings at one end. An older boy was spreading manure over bare earth at the other end. The eldest, a young man sprouting a beard, came behind and spaded the dirt, mixing in the fertilizer.

Then, smiling at Lital, Elisha ducked to enter the new dwelling. A narrow window at right gave light as did a small opening above the hearth.

"Your sons are certainly industrious."

"They are happy to have a garden again. And the goat and kid were a gift from Eden. Such kind neighbors."

Elisha studied Gehazi's wife while sipping the sweetened beverage she handed him. It tasted of mint and lemongrass. Lital's face was round and pleasant, not at all fitting the description he had heard of a sharp-tongued woman. She chattered, fluttering plump hands, asking if the sea was visible from Mount Carmel, what was the news of Samaria, and did he have stories of his travels?

Hmm. He doubted she would enjoy battle tales, so he mentioned his times with the herdsmen and sighting the eagle. "I wondered if it was the one belonging to Jaedon," he said.

"Is it true that you and the boy trained the eagle to hunt? Not only for its own food, but for you?"

"All true."

She laughed, a merry sound like a cluster of brass bells the prophets sometimes used to accompany the lyre. "How useful."

Just then, Gehazi entered with his three sons. The eldest washed Elisha's feet and hands, and Gehazi asked Elisha to bless the food. Lital distributed bowls of stew, while the young men and the boy exclaimed at the idea of a trained eagle and asked questions. Elisha sat back, enjoying the conversation. The one he would shortly have with Gehazi might not be as pleasant.

"Will we see it?" The youngest boy leaned forward, enthusiastic and very like Jaedon at that age.

"I do not know if we will see Jaedon's eagle again. But perhaps you will see another flying overhead, as I did today."

"It is a wild thing, son." Gehazi set down his bowl. The sons applied themselves to eating, discretely eyed the stew pot, but did not ask for more. Shortly, the three excused themselves, wanting to finish their planting before sunset.

The adults talked a while longer, but weariness clouded Elisha's thoughts, and he found it difficult to listen.

Gehazi shot him a glance, then stood, moved to the hearth, and raked a few coals into an iron pot.

Elisha eyed the pot, grateful he would not have to start tonight's hearth fire.

Gehazi turned to his wife. "Elisha and I have a few things to discuss. And then, I am sure he longs to rest in his own home."

Elisha shoved to his feet, suddenly weary beyond reason. "Yes, the journey was tiring. I am glad to have finally met your family. Thank you for the meal, Lital. Most delicious."

The moment Elisha emerged through Gehazi's door, he was hailed by several prophets. He greeted each warmly, promising to meet with them on the morrow.

The house was as he and Elijah had left it. Though he had offered it to Jaedon for his own use, it seemed untouched. There was Elijah's seat by the hearth, a three-legged stool with a curved back. Elisha had carved it himself for the old prophet's comfort. He went to sit in it now, leaving his own stool for Gehazi.

Gehazi looked around, set the iron pot near the hearth, then asked, "Would you like water, Master? I drew some for you this morning."

Elisha glanced toward the rimmed jar where he and Elijah had kept drinking water. "This morning?"

"Yes." Gehazi walked to the jar, one eyebrow raised as he gripped the handle.

"Please." Elisha waited.

Gehazi filled a cup, handed it to Elisha, then sat facing him, hands on his knees. "I knew you were coming. I saw you." His voice sounded like his young son's, excited about the eagle.

"From one of the taller hills?"

"No. Last night. *I saw you.*"

Elisha tipped his head. "A dream?"

"Yes." Gehazi shifted his weight from foot to foot.

"What did you see?"

"I saw you standing in the marketplace, talking to a red-haired stranger. A smallish man, in a faded, brown tunic past his knees. He wore no cloak. He handed you a cloth-wrapped parcel."

Tobiah. The apples. "Anything else?"

Gehazi looked taken aback at the question. He cleared his throat. "What do you mean?"

So he had not heard the Voice, or he would have told. Few had, other than Elijah. And him.

"Anything else at all?"

"I woke up. I wondered what it meant. You had your waterskin and mantle—was that what you meant? So I saw those and thought it meant you would travel. I watched for you all day, and I asked Lital to cook your favorite dish."

"How did you know that was Miriam's stew? Or is it a dish Lital often cooks?" Was it a part of Gehazi's dream?

"*I* know nothing about cooking. But, no, she has never made it that way. Several women have befriended her, Miriam among them. Lital asked her what you would enjoy."

Feeling a smile crease his face, Elisha leaned back in his chair, encouraged. Not so much at Gehazi's dream but by his reaction. Eager. Trying to understand. Not making more of it than what he saw.

"I am glad your wife has already found her place in the community."

"As am I," Gehazi said. "She did not want to live at Jericho, even though I told her you cleansed the spring. Our child, our only girl, was born dead there."

"Because of the spring. Yes, I know. I am sorry."

Gehazi looked at him steadily. "I did not tell you about the child before."

"No." Elisha stood, selected some kindling from a basket, and began layering it into the hearth.

Gehazi moved beside him. "Master, will you allow me?" Carefully he removed the pot's iron lid, placed the hot coals he'd brought from his hearth, and finished building a fire.

Elisha nodded and returned to his stool. Gehazi's willingness to serve others came easily. Feeling lighter than he had, he said, "The Lord has told me to train you as my servant. That is why I sent word for you to settle in Gilgal."

Gehazi turned to gaze steadily at Elisha. "I did not know. But I hoped—and prayed."

A good answer. An honest answer.

"So you will teach me to serve you?"

"Yes, but more important, I will teach you to serve the Lord. Can you read? Do you have a copy of the scrolls?"

"I can read, but my father did not have a copy of the scrolls, nor was there one in the settlement where we lived before the Arameans burned it. When we came to Jericho, the prophets who had scrolls read to the others."

Elisha nodded. "That was kind. But now, you can make your own copy from my scroll. One who follows Yahweh must study His teachings and spend time in prayer."

"Will we remain here? Or will we travel?"

"Yahweh does not reveal His plans far ahead of time. We serve the Lord at His pleasure and must be ready to go where and when He commands."

"Yes. I understand." Gehazi's expression appeared open and willing.

"Your wife must have been glad she need not settle in Jericho. Sad memories for her."

"Yes, we are all happy to have come here." He positioned a few small logs over the flickering flames.

"Yet, your house is small for five people."

The corner of Gehazi's mouth twitched. "Yes, but it is enough. We are grateful."

Elisha nodded. If the quarters became cramped, Gehazi would find many willing hands among the settlers to enlarge it. His expression of contentment spoke well for him.

But ... he had answered too glibly when asked about Lital's sad memories. And just now, he was guarding a secret.

The fire flickered, and Gehazi sat back on his heels. "Do you have more for me tonight? Or would you like to rest?"

"No, that is sufficient. Thank you for the fire."

"Would you like to break your fast with us in the morning?"

"I have other plans, but I will find you later. Until then, tend to your family's needs."

Elisha smiled as Gehazi bowed and departed, glancing back once more.

Tend to your wife.

Elisha sat and stared a long time into the crackling, orange flames, praying for the one Yahweh had given him to tend.

Chapter Eighteen

*Like apples of gold in settings of silver is a word aptly
spoken. Like a gold earring or a gold ornament
is a wise reproof to a receptive ear.*
Proverbs 25:10-12

Gilgal
Elisha

THE NEXT MORNING, WITH APPLES NESTLED in a bit of cloth, Elisha hurried across the road dividing the settlement. Sunlight warmed ripening grapes in the small vineyard tended by Dov and Miriam's growing family. He inhaled the sweet aroma mingled with—yes—Miriam's leavened bread. His favorite way to break his fast. As he approached the door, he heard Miriam speaking. Did she sound irritated? He hesitated. Was it eavesdropping when the couple spoke loudly and the door stood open?

"What I want to know is, was there an understanding with the girl's father or not?"

"Not exactly," Dov said.

"What then?"

"More of an understanding ... to have an understanding."

"And you came to this after you trailed kidnappers through the northern hills and rescued captives? After you, oh let me see, stopped off to discuss this 'understanding to have an understanding' with her father on the way to return the poor captive children to their homes? Why did you not explain all this to me at first?"

Elisha cringed at the irritation in her voice. He should come back later, but his feet were rooted where he stood.

"It is not so strange as it sounds. The girl is Eden's sister. Remember she told us about her as we returned from Jericho?"

"Yes, and that is why I thought—"

"It is only that the situation changed. The captured children were weary and hungry. On our way back, we approached the settlement where Eden's family lives, and Biny mentioned to Jaedon that the girl's family lived there. Our first concern was the children—here was a known settlement where they could be fed and rest safely. It also seemed right to check on Eden's family—give them news of her. Of course, it would not be the proper time to arrange a betrothal. In truth, the girl's father considers her too young. As do I. Even Jaedon said he would like only to speak with her. To see if they could converse as … new friends. It seems they did so. That is why I—"

Elisha cleared his throat and stepped into the open doorway just as Miriam huffed and propped her hands on her hips, the action tightening her tunic across her belly. Miriam was a tall woman and the child she carried did not make her appear—swollen—as did some. Still, her time was very close. Perhaps even before the day's end. He felt his ears warm and quickly moved his gaze to her face.

"Hello," he said quietly, rapping twice on the wooden frame. "Is this a bad time? I can return later."

"Of course not," Miriam snapped, and then her hand flew to her mouth. "Come in," she added, in a milder tone.

Hesitantly, Elisha took a step inside and looked around the room. "Where are the children? It is too quiet in here."

The corners of her mouth trembled with what seemed a stifled grin. She rolled her eyes at the ceiling.

"You must have heard plenty of noise coming from this room a moment ago. However, Gershoni and Yuval are visiting their grandparents. Well, except for Savta Yaffa—she is across the way visiting a friend. And Jaedon is building a house for a young woman to whom he is apparently not actually betrothed. As he has been doing every morning since he and Dov returned."

Unshed tears gleamed in her eyes. He could not ignore her obvious emotion, she was like family. Neither did he want to step between husband and wife. But perhaps a question.

"Do you object to the girl?"

"No. Of course not! What I object to is Jaedon pouring his heart into building a home when he has no assurance that a wedding will take place. All he needs is another agonizing loss. Mostly I object to being misled."

Elisha swallowed. Was he meant to answer that? Then Dov turned a hand upward, as if in supplication.

"My love, forgive me. I did not realize I led you to believe a *ketubah* had been signed. However, the girl's father assured us Ziva is not spoken for. He was pleased when I asked if the two could speak, properly supervised by her mother and in sight of others. He is a man who loves his daughter and truly wants her to be happy. As we want for our boy. I think we both understood, though nothing was written, that we would be welcomed if we bring a *ketubah* in a year. He liked Jaedon. Who would not? You have raised such a fine son."

She blinked and wiped her eyes. "You have been like a father to him since we wed."

"Yes. But all his good qualities come from you."

She chuffed and turned her back to them. "Go see about him and the others. The food is almost ready. I have only to peel the figs."

With a final touch to her shoulder, Dov headed for the door.

Elisha glanced around and took a furtive sniff. He could clearly see rolls cooling on the hearth, but he didn't see or smell figs.

"Wait, I'll come with you, Dov. I'd like to—say hello to Maalik and Hadassah." Elisha almost said *see the house.* He didn't want to bring up any part of that discussion again. At least not within Miriam's hearing. He disliked disagreements between husband and wife. He'd never heard them between his own parents. But they had been childless many years before he and his brother were born, and they were raised by grateful, settled parents. Some disagreements were probably inevitable, especially when people were very different from each other.

Perhaps this was why many of the prophets did not take a wife. Elijah had never married. Elisha supposed he would not either. He grinned at a sudden thought. *Who would have had either of us? Who could have understood our ways?*

Dov shrugged and gave him an uncertain smile as they began to climb the hill. Was he embarrassed his marital discord had been overheard?

Elisha felt the package still tucked under his arm.

Perhaps a gift of the apples would smooth any remaining ruffled feathers.

"Look here, Dov." He folded back the cloth. "Apples from the market in Samaria. A gift from a friend."

Dov peered down and smiled. "Once, as a young soldier on a campaign with King Ahab, we came across a vendor with a cartload of apples. The king bought them all, but only officers got a taste."

"I want your family to have these," Elisha said, extending them. "Will you try to sprout the seeds? I would love to see apples growing on a tree."

"It was your gift." Dov held up his hands in refusal. "I won't take the fruit. But save the seeds, I will enjoy planting them for you."

"I have more. We will all have a taste!"

As they climbed the hill, they passed the home of Maalik and Hadassah. Muffled giggles and bumps sounded from inside. The children at some game. He also heard intermittent strikes of a hammerstone.

Behind Maalik's house, a deep swath of land had been freshly terraced. Jaedon was on the slope above the cleared area, searching through a rocky outcrop and rolling melon-sized rocks downhill. In the cleared area, Maalik carefully fit one atop another in a growing rectangular structure, now about five stones high.

"Ho, Elisha!" Jaedon bounded toward them, looking taller somehow since his God-sent assignment to reclaim the children.

"How do you like my house?"

Taller ... and embracing a new focus. Elisha had seen the change when God put Binyamin and the three captured spies in their path. He was at once proud of the lad and regretful. Had he completely lost his desire to serve the Lord? But wasn't he right to accept Yahweh's choice?

Thoughtfully stroking his chin, Elisha walked the home's perimeter. "Stone. It should last for generations." He ran his hand down hewn logs that defined the sides of the doorpost, feeling a niggle of concern. Miriam was right. Jaedon would be hurt if the girl's father turned him down. But Dov had spoken to the man, and he was also right. Why would anyone refuse Jaedon?

Elisha nodded his approval. "Fine sanding job."

"There will be two windows," Jaedon said. "One facing south for light. One here, overlooking the vineyard."

"And a play area for the children," Maalik said. "Here between our two houses, where they will be closely watched."

Color spread up Jaedon's neck and face, but he grinned and nodded.

Elisha surveyed the area. A wide, level expanse that would be bordered on one side at least by the vineyard wall. "Well planned. One must always keep the children in sight."

Dov cleared his throat. "Jaedon, if you can take a break now, Imma has food ready. Maalik, Miriam asked that you and Hadassah join us."

"No, my wife is expecting me for the midday meal," Maalik said. "But may we keep the children with us a while longer? Hadassah wants to help Gershoni make a tunic for her doll, and I promised to occupy Yuval with a willow flute. Jaedon, I know you are anxious to catch up with Elisha. I can use a brief rest from placing stones." He reached for his back with an expression of mock pain. "Old bones, you know. Stop by the house when you are ready for our next stint."

As they walked to the house, Elisha answered their questions about the war with Moab. When he described the three kings running out of water upon reaching the desert of Edom, Dov spread his hands wide. "So, they only thought to consult with the Lord's prophet *after* they ran out of water? Then what? Because here you are."

Elisha shook his head. "Many times, the Lord sends miracles to those who do not deserve them. Yahweh told me to command the three armies to dig ditches, then He sent flows of water to fill them by daybreak."

"Water without rain? And the battle was won?" Dov was not truly surprised, because the Lord had given him a similar victory years before. "I suppose the king gave you a huge reward for your part."

Elisha laughed. "Yes, something like that. We can talk more later." He gestured toward the house, then tapped his ear. He didn't want Miriam to overhear him speak of the battle's end at Kir-hareseth, nor how King Joram did not so much as speak to him after he had delivered the word of the Lord. He glanced at Jaedon, who had remained silent. The boy had his own experience with a godless king.

Kings did not often reward prophets. After Elijah's prayer on Mount Carmel brought rain, Jezebel swore to kill him with Ahab's tacit support. Still, Elisha would rather be on the Lord's side, regardless of the outcome.

He redirected the conversation. "Ocran and his family joined me on the road as I approached Gilgal. He said he planned to stay with you."

"That is right," Dov said. "He stopped by last night. I was surprised to see him. So much time has passed since we spoke of him moving here, I thought he had changed his mind. I welcomed them to stay with us. But as we were eating supper together, Micaiah stopped on his way to the ridge. He will be teaching for several months from Jericho, making the rounds of settlements in the south."

"Oh yes, I had nearly forgotten. He would want Ocran to watch over his empty house while he is away. A good solution for both."

"They will have more privacy. But our daughters are of similar age, and Micaiah's house is not far. Our families will see each other often."

When they approached the house, Dov stood aside for Elisha to enter. He ducked beneath the doorframe. Miriam turned to face him, a cushion in each hand. "Sit here, Elisha. It is the best place."

As always, she was thinking of his comfort. She plumped the cushion and placed it between the hearth and the window.

"I am sorry you had to hear me earlier," she murmured. She sucked her lower lip between her teeth.

"On the contrary, I am always pleased to see"—he fought a grin—"and hear from you, Miriam. Here. Please take these apples." He handed her the parcel and settled on the cushion. "I brought them for you, but Dov insisted we all share them."

She took the parcel, smiling. "Thank you. I thought I had set aside figs for this morning, but I forgot that we ate them yesterday. Right now, I am forgetting a lot." She peered down at the swell of her belly. "Four children. How ever shall I manage?"

Jaedon, who was over at the hearth ladling something savory into wooden bowls, whipped his head around. "You count me among the children, Imma?"

She pursed her lips. "There are times."

Elisha raised one eyebrow. "Hmm. So you have Dov, Jaedon, and three grandparents to help."

She nodded. "The Lord is good. But I do hope for another girl."

Should he tell her? No.

Miriam unwrapped the cloth, revealing six red and gold orbs. "Oh, how pretty they are."

Dov hunkered down beside Elisha. "He wants you to save the seeds for planting."

"Of course we must. If only they will grow." Miriam carried the apples to her table, sliced them into crescents, and layered them on a round wooden tray.

Jaedon quickly handed them bowls of what smelled like lentils seasoned with foraged greens and spices. Then he sat on Elisha's other side, angling toward the apples.

"Will you bless the food, Elisha?" Dov asked.

He spread his hands and turned his face up, replacing the smoke-darkened ceiling with his memory of blinding light that had filled the heaven as Elijah departed. "Blessed are you, Lord our God, King of the universe, who creates the fruit of the tree, and who has brought forth bread from the earth. Lord, I thank you for this family and their friendship. Please bless them with health and safety."

It had been a long time since Elisha had taken a meal with this family. He broke a chunk of bread from the loaf and dipped it into the stew.

"Mmm," he hummed. "Never better. What is your secret?" He hid a smile, waiting for the tart answer that would come.

"You know there is no longer a secret. I add wild cumin to the garlic, onions, and whatever other roots and greens Jaedon or I forage. I have told everyone they must look for it. Is it my fault that Yahweh's birds always plant it in hidden spots?"

Elisha grinned. "Well, it has been said that you do talk to the birds."

She rolled her eyes.

"It also has been said that both you and Jaedon generously share the cumin you find. You are great favorites in Gilgal."

Elisha's first taste of apple was a surprising burst of sweetness on his tongue. And the bread! Would it be greedy to ask to take a loaf home?

He enjoyed the banter and hearing all the settlement's gossip. He was most interested in Dov and Jaedon's story of retaking the hostages from the Aramean spies.

"Their strategy was similar to wolves who snatch outlying animals in a herd and run," Dov explained. "In this way they captured twelve children from various settlements without any confrontation, until Binyamin happened upon them and took the three spies prisoner. I am sure the parents chastised themselves for not being more vigilant, but thankfully, the result was no villagers were killed, and we were able to recover the little ones."

"This is not the first I have heard of raiders, but I don't understand," Miriam said. "We are not at war with Aram."

"Not a declared war," Dov said, biting into a roll. "In this way they keep us unsettled without much risk to themselves. Aram has often been an adversary and our lush farmland in the north a temptation. When Ahab was king, his military prowess kept Aram in check. But his son, King Joram, does not command the same respect."

"True," Elisha said. "Yahweh allows a pagan nation to harass Israel, because they still worship golden calves at the high places."

As they munched apple slices, the conversation turned to safety within city walls as opposed to remote settlements tucked away in the hills of Ephraim and Naphtali.

"It depends on whether the enemy comes with chariots or on foot," Dov said.

Jaedon stared out the house's window, his expression revealing troubled thoughts. Was he thinking of the young girl in her tucked-away village?

"May I remind you all," Elisha said, his voice gentle. "Whether we reside in a walled city or humble village, the eternal God is our refuge, and underneath are the everlasting arms."

"Right," Dov said. "When the battle plans of Kings Joram and Jehoshaphat failed, the Lord gave them an undeserved victory." He bowed his head. "Lord, we look to you for our safety—and that of our friends and family. Please keep our country safe, even though we do not deserve it."

When they opened their eyes, Elisha chuckled. "My work here is done."

"Yes," said Dov. "Today's lesson delivered and received."

"Now I must get back to my servant. I promised him we would begin his training today."

As he strolled to his house, his mind lingered on the end of their discussion. Jaedon and Miriam had been most unsafe within the walled city of Samaria and were forced to flee. They found their safety here in Gilgal with the prophets.

Was it any wonder if Jaedon thought safety lay in these hills? That they had left all danger behind in a wicked city?

Well, no. He had been there for the confrontation with the Bethel youths … and the bears. He went on a quest to retake the stolen children. Did those events only teach him that Yahweh always steps in to save his children?

No again. His father and grandfather were murdered, and Yahweh did not spare them from *physical* death. But did Jaedon understand Yahweh had stayed with them until the end?

Yahweh, some things only You can teach. Is this one of them? If you command, I will try. Please give me the words.

Elisha rubbed his forehead, which had begun to throb. Death would come for all men. The Lord expected His people to be watchful, but He did not want them to worry needlessly. Come a time the Lord did not step in to save those He loved, that was the time to seek understanding, and if it did not come, to remind oneself. Whatever happened, despite all.

Underneath are the everlasting arms.

Chapter Nineteen

*"Cursed is anyone who withholds justice
from the foreigner, the fatherless or the widow."
Then all the people shall say, "Amen!"
Deuteronomy 27:19*

Gilgal
Elisha

ELISHA STEPPED INTO HIS HOUSE REVELING in the quiet. Too big a house for one alone. He was willing to share, should the Lord ask, but for now, he sank onto Elijah's three-legged stool and leaned on the backrest with a grateful sigh.

The wood was smooth, but Miriam's stuffed cushion had felt good under his knobby bones. He glanced around the room. No cushions anywhere. Probably, he had only to ask, and one of the prophet's wives would show up with a freshly sewn cushion stuffed with feathers or dried grass.

Or even one of the unmarried prophets. They had learned many talents fending for themselves, but their sewing skills mostly tended toward awkwardly mended clothing.

Besides, he didn't like to ask.

A knock sounded on the door frame.

He stood and ambled toward the door. Probably Gehazi, although Elisha had said he'd find him. Wasn't that what he'd said?

Another knock. "Master Elisha. Are you home?"

A feminine voice. One he didn't recognize.

He swung the door open to reveal a woman of middle years. Her gray-streaked hair peeked from beneath a moss-colored head covering. Oh, yes. Obadiah's wife. Widow, he reminded himself.

"Come in," he said, motioning for her to take his more comfortable stool. But as if sensing it belonged to him, she lowered herself onto the other. Her face was drawn in worried lines, and her eyes glistened with pent-up emotion.

"What is wrong, dear woman? Is there something I can

do for you?" Obadiah had been dead for about a year, and she had two young sons. Did she need food? Were not the residents of Gilgal helping her?"

She twisted the fabric draped over her knees. "You know my husband, your servant, is dead, and you know he revered the Lord."

He knew. Obadiah had been King Ahab's steward. When Jezebel was killing prophets in Samaria, he secretly hid one hundred in caves. Further, he saw to it the prophets had bread and water each day, discretely buying their provisions with his own funds. When his actions were revealed to the queen, he had to go into hiding himself. The school of the prophets had welcomed him.

"My husband borrowed money and was unable to repay it before he died. His creditor showed me a signed agreement. I must pay him, or he is coming to take my two boys as his slaves."

This was wrong. Obadiah would have borrowed from a fellow Israelite, and the law prohibited the lender from taking advantage of a helpless widow. "How much is the debt?" he asked.

"Sixty shekels of silver."

He felt his jaw gape. Why had no one in Gilgal helped her? She was well liked. Perhaps she had told no one, ashamed to admit she was so deeply in debt. To be fair, even if all Gilgal took up a collection, it would not be enough. But how could Obadiah have incurred so much?

By feeding one hundred prophets in hiding. You seek how to help her. I am with you.

"Tell me," Elisha said. "What do you have in your house."

She blinked. "Why, nothing of value. No silver, nor even bronze. Even my food stuffs are gone. There is nothing left except a small jar of olive oil."

He inhaled, clasping her hands. The answer was there. He saw flashes of many empty jars, the excitement of knowing.

"That's it! Listen to me. Go around and ask all of your neighbors for empty jars. Don't ask for just a few, go to everyone in Gilgal. Then, just as you approached me in private, take your sons into your house and close the door behind you. Pour oil into each jar, and as it is filled, set it aside. Secretly, you understand?"

Staring at him in confusion, she nodded her head. "Yes," she whispered, still nodding. Then in a stronger voice, "Yes, I will."

She stood and they walked together to the door. His hand was on the latch, but he hesitated, then said, "Wait here a moment."

He went to the table where their water jugs sat. He only needed one, now that Elijah was gone. He came back with the large jar and two smaller ones he found stacked inside. "You can start with these."

Smiling, she nestled the vessels against her hip and hurried away.

He shut the door behind her, leaning against it a moment.

You are going to send another miracle, aren't you? You can work with anything. Even a small jar of oil. Or nothing … like me.

Then he opened the door and walked outside. It was time to find Gehazi.

Elisha found him in the first place he looked. The garden plot behind his house. All three of his sons were working with him, and his wife was carefully ladling used wash water over seedlings.

When he saw Elisha, Gehazi touched his wife on the shoulder and whispered to each of his sons. Instructions to help their mother, no doubt. Then he followed Elisha to his house.

Elisha moved the water jug from the worktable and spread out the first scroll. "Since this is our first lesson, I ask that you read from the beginning, and we will discuss." They stood shoulder to shoulder, bent over the scroll as Gehazi read aloud.

"In the beginning God created the heavens and the earth. Now the earth was formless and empty, darkness was over the surface of the deep, and the Spirit of God was hovering over the waters."

His reading voice was pleasant, but Elisha listened to the currents running beneath. *Resistance.*

Gehazi went on reading until he got to the scene with the woman and the serpent, where he slowed.

"The woman said to the serpent, 'We may eat fruit from the trees in the garden,' but God did say, "You must not eat fruit from the tree that is in the middle of the garden, and you must not touch it, or you will die."'" He stopped reading, pressing his thumb against the place.

"Why did you stop?" Elisha asked.

Gehazi looked disturbed, perhaps even angry. "All the trouble she started," he said. "She had everything. A beautiful garden, where she could eat without planting or harvesting. All she had to do was stay away from the one tree."

"Well, the Lord did not say not to touch it, just not eat it."

Gehazi raised an eyebrow. "Then where did she get that idea?"

"We are not told. From Adam, perhaps. Or her own reasoning. She clearly knew she should not eat the fruit. So why do you think she did?"

"Because she was greedy. Or … because her husband told her not to. You may not know this, not having married, but sometimes a woman is driven to go against her husband's wishes."

"That may be, but I find your other idea more interesting. Greed is the cause of many sins. Perhaps you are right about that." Elisha pondered a while. "Still, I wonder. Not having married, I am sure I lack understanding, but could it instead have been weakness?"

"No, you are right," Gehazi said. "Women are weak."

"I meant Adam's weakness. Not wanting to lose her."

"Lose her?"

"Because he thought she would die after her disobedience, he ate of the tree. Neither of them understood death, never having seen anything die. But on some level, Adam realized death would separate them."

"Still, it was her fault. The fall. The death."

Elisha sighed. "They both blamed each other, and both were at fault. Now read here." Elisha moved Gehazi's thumb back several columns of characters.

Gehazi read, "The Lord God took the man and put him in the Garden of Eden to work it and take care of it. And the Lord God commanded the man, 'You are free to eat from any tree in the garden; but you must not eat from the tree of the knowledge of good and evil, for when you eat of it you will surely die.' The Lord God said, 'It is not good for the man to be alone. I will make a helper suitable for him.'"

Elisha watched Gehazi's expression, saw understanding dawn. "Oh. God commanded Adam, not Eve. He had not yet made Eve."

"Well, perhaps He commanded her also, later. If not, Adam told her, because she told the serpent she was not to eat. Who added the bit about not touching, Adam or Eve? It is not written about in the scrolls, wherein we find lessons of life and light. So the Lord did not think that point was urgent. The lessons He has given us in this reading are, to beware of our weakness, watch out for greed, but most of all obey the Lord our God."

"I am sorry. What point was not urgent?"

"Placing the blame."

Gehazi frowned thoughtfully, nodding. "But how can we beware of our weakness? Might we be unaware of our areas of weakness?"

"Perhaps. Do you think you are?"

He shrugged. "I am not sure. I can see others who are unaware of their weaknesses."

Elisha chuckled. "That is easy. Do you know what Yahweh tells me when I dwell on the shortcomings of others? He says, 'What is that to you? Do as I have told you.'"

Gehazi looked at the floor between his feet.

Elisha patted him on the shoulder. "This is enough for today. Write a copy of what you have read so far, then take it home with you. Tonight, and every night, read your copy to your sons and Lital."

"But I do not have enough knowledge—"

"Just read and tell them what you learned. You can ask the Lord for more knowledge, and we will have more lessons.

If you pay attention throughout the scrolls, you will find examples to follow and mistakes to avoid. Remember how I told you the Lord does not always reveal his plans to me before I need to know?"

"Yes, Master."

"We understand the scrolls and learn of Him in a similar way. At the right time."

Late the next morning, the widow returned, knocking and calling his name as before. When Elisha opened the door, she entered, smiling as if she would break into laughter, her gray-streaked hair braided and falling over one shoulder. Both hands were tucked behind her back.

"Tell me," Elisha said.

"I did just as you instructed. After leaving your jars in my house, I went to all my neighbors, even those in the hills across the ridge road. I visited every house in Gilgal and did not stop as long as there was another neighbor. The sun was setting, and my house has only a small, high window for light, but I shut the door anyway. Just as you said."

She took a deep shuddering breath. "My sons brought me the jars one by one, and I filled them. I filled each to the brim, even your large water jug, all from my small jar of oil." She paused, and her work-worn hands cupped empty air, as though she held a small jar between them.

"The oil smelled sweet and clean, like the first press of the season. As my arms grew tired, I feared I would have to ask one of my boys to take over. But I told myself. 'I must do exactly as the prophet said.' I felt I must make no changes at all. Instead, I prayed, 'Lord, give me strength. Thank you for your great kindness to me, a poor widow.' I continued to pour into one vessel after another. Finally, I said, 'Bring me the next.' The boys laughed and said, 'There are no more, Imma.' I remembered my empty oil lamp, which I had stopped using for the sake of economy. 'Then bring me our lamp,' I said, even though I had no fire or stick to light it with. As soon as I filled the lamp, which was the last empty vessel in our house, the oil stopped flowing. And"—her eyes glistened and she tucked her chin—"God lit the lamp."

Elisha felt his chest expand with joy. "Now you must go, sell the oil and pay your debt. You and your sons will be able to live on what is left."

She laughed. "We will indeed! The house is filled with the odor of sweet oil. The Lord did this. I do not know what to say, except the Lord is good. So good."

Then, tilting her head shyly, she removed a long cushion from behind her back. It was the color of moss, the same color as her missing head covering.

"This is for your chair," she said. She positioned the rectangular cushion across the seat and back of the three-legged stool, smoothing it into place.

He settled into it, stretching out his legs with a sigh. "It smells of fresh grass."

"Yes, I stuffed it with grass, but I had dried it first. I suppose I knew I would be making a cushion." When she smiled, her brown cheeks creased into familiar lines. A good way for a face to map itself.

"Well, I thank you. I will enjoy sitting here in the evenings, reading my scrolls by lamplight. Perhaps I need to buy a little of your oil for my lamp."

"Oh no," she said. "It will be my gift to you."

"Are you forgetting what I told you? Sell the oil, pay your debt, and live off the rest. But perhaps I have something of value to trade."

He walked back to the worktable and picked up the three remaining apples.

"Take these," he said. "And be sure to plant the seeds."

Chapter Twenty

Many are the plans in a person's heart,
but it is the Lord's purpose that prevails.
Proverbs 19:21

Gilgal
Jaedon

JAEDON HAD EXPECTED DOV'S HELP ON the house today. He'd planned to finish the walls, frame the windows, and maybe start the roof. But nothing was going as foreseen. Fine prophet he would have made.

Instead of starting after breaking their fasts, they began building before sunrise, after Hadassah, Yaffa and Eden put them out of the house.

Imma's baby was coming!

One would think the extra time would hurry the project along. But Dov kept heaving sighs and dropping tools, boards, and stones. When he nearly dropped a rock on his foot, Jaedon suggested, "Let's go to Elisha's house before you lame one of us. The prophets' wives are always bringing him food. He will have something to eat and a calming drink for you. Perhaps we both need one."

Jaedon gathered the tools. Dov was fit only for staring in the direction of the house. Jaedon also worried about his mother, though she was as strong as her long-legged white donkey. He and Dov had prayed for her, along with the grandmothers, before they left them to their ministrations.

However, things sometimes went wrong during childbirth. One of the prophet's wives had died last winter, and the women of the settlement still took turns nursing the boy.

He glanced at Dov, who had picked up and dropped the same mallet twice. Was Dov thinking about the motherless boy? He hoped not.

Jaedon reached for the mallet. "Give me that and wait here. I will put the tools in the shed and tell the women where we are going."

Hopefully, time with Elisha would ease Dov's mind.

When Jaedon rapped on Elisha's doorpost, the prophet called "Enter" from inside. He sat on his stool, a large cushion draped over seat and back. No wonder he didn't want to answer the door—he looked very comfortable.

Except for one thing. He clutched the rolled ends of a scroll and was reading a little awkwardly from the center. Jaedon glanced toward the empty table where he and Elisha had read and discussed a lesson last week. He glanced back at the prophet and visually measured where he held the scroll. A shorter table was in order.

"Imma is having the baby."

"Yes," Elisha said. "I am looking for names." Then he colored and rolled the scroll shut. "Sorry, Dov. That is for you to do. I was just passing time until you arrived."

Growing up among prophets, Jaedon had almost grown used to remarks like this being tossed off, especially from Elijah and Elisha.

Almost.

If Elisha knew what he was thinking—

Elisha chuckled. "I don't always know what's going on."

Jaedon carefully schooled his expression, saying nothing.

Dov squinted, glanced between the two of them, and started pacing in front of the window.

Elisha stood, plumped the cushion, and walked to the hearth. "Will you help me, Jaedon? I've brewed a relaxing drink that Elijah used to enjoy." He ladled the concoction into two cups, handed them to Jaedon, and poured himself another.

Jaedon handed Dov the warm drink. If only Elisha would stay away from the topics of death, babies, or midwives. If only he could talk about something that would engage Dov's mind. War maneuvers, maybe.

Elisha quirked a smile at him. "Jaedon, have you shared your Torah lesson with your household?"

Well, that hadn't worked. Taking a deep swallow of the herbal brew, Jaedon tried again, thinking hard. *Not Torah.*

Battle plans interest Dov.

"Your thoughts on creation and the fall were very interesting, Elisha," Dov said, pausing from his pacing. "I would like to hear more."

Elisha jumped to his feet. "You would? Finish your drink and come over here." He gulped his cup's contents, then spread the scroll on the same table from which Jaedon had read. "You, too, Jaedon. I want you to read again."

Jaedon felt two things, and he tried to push the second out of his mind. He wanted to read the passage. He did. He liked reading the words of Moses written long ago. Words the Lord had meant for His people to live by.

But ... no, do not think that. Do not worry about another. Yet the question forced its way out of the dark corner where he had banished it. Had Gehazi been taught this lesson first?

Elisha held his gaze a long time, his thumb pressed to the parchment. Slowly, he shook his head. Not much, but enough.

Knowing he was first should have made Jaedon feel better, but instead he felt shamed. Jealous over being second to receive the Torah lesson. Forcing his chin up, he stepped forward and began reading.

"Then the man and his wife heard the sound of the Lord God as He was walking in the garden in the cool of the day, and they hid from the Lord God among the trees in the garden. But the Lord God called to the man, 'Where are you?'"

Jaedon paused, feeling he knew what Elisha would say. *Why bother to hide from God?* He looked up, waiting.

Elisha smiled. "Read on."

"Adam answered, 'I heard you in the garden, and I was afraid because I was naked; so I hid.'

"And God said, 'Who told you that you were naked? Have you eaten from the tree that I commanded you not to eat from?'"

This much had been in his lesson from last time. He put his head down and doggedly read about the blaming again. He understood, better than last time, that when Adam blamed the woman that God had given him, he was actually blaming God. *What kind of gift is this you have given me, God?*

Jaedon paused before reading on. Elisha had once told him that every day, every moment was a gift from God. So, one should think before complaining ... about anything?

He could not wrap his thoughts around that, so he began reading again.

"So the Lord God said to the serpent, 'Because you have done this, cursed are you above all the livestock and all the wild animals!'"

Jaedon stepped back. "I am glad the serpent was cursed." Then, remembering, he clamped his lips shut, realizing too late it probably made no difference, that a man such as Elisha could hear his very thoughts. *Queen Jezebel should have been cursed, as well as King Ahab, her evil husband.*

"And, of course, they were," Elisha answered.

"They?" Dov questioned.

"There is more," Elisha said. "Read on."

"'You will crawl on your belly and you will eat dust all the days of your life. And I will put enmity between you and the woman and between your offspring and hers; he will crush your head, and you will strike his heel.'"

This was new. He did not understand it, but it sounded like a future fight the serpent would lose.

"What does that mean?" Dov asked.

His stepfather, though born to an Israelite, was orphaned before his father could teach him the Torah. Maalik had done the best he could to train Dov in the practices of his people, but Maalik was a Canaanite.

"It is a prophecy of One who will reverse the curse of death," Elisha said, "the Messiah."

As they walked up the hill, they heard women's exclamations, an infant's cry, and then "You have a son!" Dov rushed toward the doorway, but Savta Yaffa must have heard him coming because she appeared to block his way. "Give her a moment," she said, laying a hand against Dov's chest. "The babe has only just arrived."

"Do you think I care that the child is unwashed?" he

argued. "I want to see my wife."

Yaffa put a hand on his chest. "She is fine. We will not be long." Still holding her hand up, she pulled the door closed.

Dov paced back and forth until she opened it again and motioned him inside.

Jaedon hung back, concerned for Imma's modesty, until he heard Dov shout, "Come in here and meet your new brother!"

He rushed to the other side of the pallet from where Dov stood. Imma, looking pale and exhausted, held the newborn in the crook of her arm as she stroked and inspected him.

"What do you think, my son?"

Jaedon laughed "I think the vineyard will prosper with three sons. Especially one so handsome and strong."

She raised one eyebrow and gave him a look. "The wrinkles and redness will go away. He will love and look up to you, as Gershoni and Yuval do their elder brother."

Eden, who had been neatening the room, came over to say goodbye. "You did well, Miriam. He is a beautiful boy. Is there anything else you need?" Though she held Miriam's hand, she looked at Yaffa.

"Go home now and rest," Yaffa said. "You are close to your own time and have done enough. Hadassah and I will wash the little one."

Eden smiled, kissed the baby's head, and patted Miriam's hand once more. After she left, the two grandmothers quickly cleaned the little one with damp cloths, rubbed him with salt, and alternately laughed and cooed at his angry squalls. Then they swaddled him tightly and tucked him back against Miriam's side.

Jaedon watched the baby a while longer, smiling at the ever-changing expressions on his face, and listening to Dov and Imma discuss names, none of which suited the little fellow.

"I hope you will not name him for another musician," he blurted. "We need workers to help with the vineyard, not two brothers thinking it is their duty to lay about strumming lyres and reciting poetry." Immediately he clamped his jaw. Where had that come from? He loved Yuval.

Dov's face seemed to express the same surprise, but Imma burst out laughing. "How about Reuben or Noach?" she asked. "Those are robust-sounding names."

Jaedon shook his head. "I am sorry. It is not my place to comment. I love Yuval."

"Despite his name?" Imma laughed again, and Dov gave him a shove. But now he was smiling.

Imma looked thoughtful. "Do you remember Nathaniel, your great-grandfather? You were so young. I'm not sure you had seen two winters when he died."

Savta Hadassah pressed her hands over her heart, the lines on her face creasing into a smile. "My Nathaniel."

"I think I do," Jaedon said. "He was very tall and had a big laugh."

"He was tall enough," said Savta Yaffa. "But I think it was more that you were ... very short."

Imma cast her gaze around the room. "Is that yes, Hadassah?"

"Oh, but surely, Dov would want ...."

"Don't fuss, Hadassah. It is settled. His name is Nathaniel," Dov said. "But if he starts singing in the vineyard, I want no complaints from you, lad." He gave Jaedon another shove.

Seemingly bored by the conversation, the little fellow stretched both arms and yawned. Spiky eyelashes fluttered and drooped. When Jaedon touched his open palm, the baby grasped his finger, and a lump formed in his throat. *Yahweh, thank you for this child. Please protect him always.*

After a while, Jaedon pried loose his finger. "I could spend the afternoon watching him, but I want to get another layer of stones on the house."

"Ask Maalik to help you, son," Dov said. "I will stay." He pulled a stool beside the bed, where he could watch mother and son.

"We will walk with you," Savta Hadassah said. "Yaffa and I will make supper at our house so Miriam can get some rest. When you are hungry, come up, Dov. We'll give you food to bring back for Miriam. One of us will spend the night, to help with the ... with Nathaniel."

Jaedon took each grandmother by an arm and started up the slope, keeping in step with those he loved.

Chapter Twenty-One

*By wisdom a house is built, and through
understanding it is established; through knowledge
its rooms are filled with rare and beautiful treasures.*
~ Proverbs 24:3-4

Gilgal
Jaedon

Jaedon woke before daybreak, quietly donned working clothes, and slipped out the door. He stood a moment orienting himself by the moon, stars, and the rooftop of Maalik's house, touched by indistinct light.

It was enough. He headed toward the patch of land that was his. Theirs. His and Ziva's.

As the light spread, he made short work of the pile of stones he'd tossed down the hill yesterday. Two more rows placed and mortared. He'd gathered rocks of similar size, and some were of unusual coloration. He ran his hands over the top row. Could he lay another? No, Biny had told him to wait between every couple of rows, let the mortar harden. Though he was anxious to finish the house, he also wanted it to stand for generations, as Elisha had said.

He stood, stretched his back, then carried two stones to the door frame. He'd left a spot for them on either side. He placed one imprinted with long-decayed leaves to the left of the door. Had it seen the time of Father Abraham? Another imprisoning an ancient sea creature went to the right. Had the creature been carried to this hill by Noah's flood?

The rocks spoke of permanence, a symbol of his devotion, which grew stronger by the day. Gauging their height from the ground, he pictured their children tracing tiny fingers over the rock-encased remains.

His hands kept moving, smoothing the mortar around the last two stones, not unlike his thoughts which had begun to churn upon one word. *Time.* It moved so slowly as he waited for her. Did she feel the same? He called forth the picture of her face. Kind, honest, yet also secretive, as if a veil shrouded her innermost thoughts. What if she did not think of the time between now and then? What if she thought of it with trepidation? Worried it was not long enough?

Oh Yahweh, for whom a thousand years are as a single day. Let this year pass in such a way for me.

He breathed her name. *Ziva.* Like the whisper of a night breeze. He wanted to talk with her again, but he couldn't visit her until he brought the ketubah, and he had nothing to offer until he finished the house. He thought of all the messages his Uncle Caleb had carried between Samaria and Jezreel. Jaedon had carried some among the settlements, but even so, he doubted he'd be allowed to carry one to her. But when Elisha sent messengers to the outlying settlements, one of them could carry his message.

He would write a letter. Tell her all his thoughts. Then he remembered the secrets in her eyes. Well, perhaps not all, but he would tell her all about the house. Ask about the plaster and what tree she would like to shade the entry.

He had thought to face those rocks into the house, but not if she wanted the interior plastered. Perhaps he should write her and ask. When would the next runner go to the settlement? Why couldn't he carry his own letter? He imagined seeing her again and grinned. Why not?

He shook his head, doubting such an action was appropriate. He did not want to dishonor Ziva's parents or sully her reputation. He would ask Imma what was right. Dov was raised by Maalik, and they both confessed to gaps in their Hebrew learning. But somehow, they were well-liked and respected among the school of the prophets. If none of his family had advice to give, he could ask Elisha.

A wooden door flew open. Dov walked out of his house, shut the door behind him, and started toward Jaedon. The sun had climbed past the mountain tops, lighting a cloth-wrapped bundle in his arms.

As if he'd been watching from his window, Maalik came out and waved.

"Bring a jar of water," Dov called.

Briefly, Maalik ducked back inside, emerging again with

the large jar.

Jaedon paced the length of the plot, excited to show off his progress and hear their suggestions. Usually, they'd spend a few hours helping with the work.

"What is that?" he asked, when Dov reached him.

Dov folded back the cloth, grinning. "Your first row of vines."

Immediately, Jaedon grabbed the long stick they used for planting and gouged a long trench. Dov laid the parcel near one end, and the three of them planted the cuttings. Jaedon counted a dozen, taking note of roots already growing on a few, several that had nodes, and a few that appeared thin and weak. They doused the plants three times before reciting the blessing of fruit Elisha had taught them.

Baruch atah A-donay, Elo-heinu Melech Ha'Olam borei pri ha-aitz.

Blessed are you, Lord our God, who creates the fruit of the tree.

Then Jaedon brought them over to his newly laid stones. After nodding at their compliments, he said, "What do you think of these?" He pointed out his prized stones. Grunting, Maalik bent over to inspect them and nodded his approval.

"Why not put them at eye-level?" Dov asked. "Not many will notice them here." He touched a finger to the mortar. "But it is not set. You can still move them."

Before he had a chance to respond, Maalik answered. "He put them where he wants them, my boy. You should know why."

A slow smile crossed Dov's face. He glanced at his house down the hill. "I suppose I do."

Maalik stepped through the doorframe. "You will want to put the hearth here, Jaedon. You'll have a large room in front for keeping warm in winter or enjoying a breeze through the window in summer, and a bedroom or two off to the side."

"That reminds me about furniture," said Jaedon.

Dov looked surprised. "There is plenty of time for that after your roof is on."

"Oh. No, you misunderstand. Remember when Elisha taught us from the scroll?"

Dov looked at him, puzzled.

"He has a worktable upon which he can unroll the Torah when he stands to read it. But he likes Elijah's chair, especially since the widow gave him that grass-stuffed cushion."

Chuckling, Dov described for Maalik how awkwardly the prophet had held the scroll, nearly dropping it at times, just to keep from leaving his comfortable seat.

"Although I have to wonder, how comfortable could it be, stretching out his arms and craning his neck like that?"

They all laughed.

"Yes, we will ask Biny to help us build it," said Dov.

"Build what?" Maalik asked.

"A low table," said Jaedon. "So Elisha can read sitting in his chair."

Maalik shook his head, as if uncertain. "Are you sure he wants such a thing? Maybe you should ask."

"I would like to surprise him," Jaedon said.

Dov grinned. "Surprise a prophet?"

When they all finished laughing, Dov reached into his sash and pulled out a small, folded cloth. "Now where shall we plant these? To shade your door?"

They all looked at what he'd wrapped.

"No, not by the door," said Maalik. "Every woman wants a fig tree to shade her courtyard."

"Is that so? Why have I never heard this before?"

"I expect because you don't have Hadassah to tell you how things should be."

"Hmm. What does she say about apples?" Dov asked.

"None of us can know about apples," said Jaedon. "But Saba Naboth said no tree should shade the vines. So if the fig shades the courtyard, we must plant the apple seeds where the children will play." Children with Ziva. He pictured a tiny version of her crawling under trees.

Dov raised his eyebrows and Maalik chuckled. Then warmth bloomed red in Jaedon's face.

Chapter Twenty-Two

The name of the Lord is a fortified tower;
the righteous run to it and are safe.
Proverbs 18:10

Gischala, early autumn, a few months after the captives' return
Ziva

HEADED TOWARD THE WELL, ZIVA SHIFTED her shoulder yoke as she and the others trudged behind Mara's father. She slowed her pace even more, wishing the elders had chosen someone else to accompany the women on their short walk to the well. His skill with the bow and sling earned him the role of protector, but his limp made him slow.

She looked behind, noticing how they bunched together in places. She'd taken the position behind Mara to be near the head of the line with the swift walkers. Not this time. She heaved a sigh.

Abba said Lotan had been a soldier, wounded in the battle that killed King Ahab. Ziva was too young to remember that history, but she knew one thing—it would take twice as long to fetch water with this old soldier in the lead.

She sighed again, her impatience at the slow pace growing. Did they really need a guard? Then she lifted her gaze and saw Mara glare back at her.

Ziva sent her friend an apologetic smile and mouthed, "Sorry."

It did not help to tread on the man's heels or insult her friend. Slowing, she turned around to gaze at Mount Merom in the distance. Snow had fallen during the night and dusted its peak. The air held a chill, pleasant while walking. Workers picked the last grapes from terraced vineyards. Harvest was nearly finished. Winter would come soon.

Last year she'd been allowed to travel to the mountain with her father and the village hunting party. She'd enjoyed the half-day walk, camping overnight, and sampling the venison they'd shared with everyone in Gischala upon their return. When they arrived in the settlement, she and Abba were surprised to meet her baby brother, Aharon, who had arrived early. Now he was fat, healthy, and loved to walk, as long as she held both his little hands.

When she turned back, Mara's father was eyeing the tangle of scrub juniper, gorse, and dill as he plodded down the winding path, sometimes poking into the thatch with his walking stick. A stand of old trees loomed over the undergrowth. Ziva supposed their depths might provide cover for Arameans. She peered through the crowded trunks and shivered.

Brushing aside a trailing branch, she started down the hill. Perhaps the elders were right to put precautions in place. The captive children had been snatched on the outskirts of their settlement. But Gischala was deep into tree-covered hills. Hadn't Abba said that was why his grandfather had put down roots here? Plenty of water, timber, and rich land safely hidden in the forest.

At the well, Mara helped Ziva hook her filled buckets on the yoke's dangling hooks. "You are too impatient, my friend." She balanced her full jug atop her head. "My father is slow of step, but his arrows fly straight, and one after another. We will be glad of him, should the enemy strike."

Ziva clenched her fingers over the yoke's wooden curve. Sometimes Mara seemed older, although her friend had seen only thirteen summers, two years less than Ziva. She looked away, shame stinging her eyes.

"I am sorry, Mara. I was wrong to be impatient. The brambles and woods could easily hide an enemy. Even one on horseback might ride close before we realized. Abba told me your father was a distinguished soldier. That we are safe with him." She paused. "I suppose I dislike admitting that our hills are not safe."

Mara started to nod, then clutched at her wobbling water jug. "I understand. An armed guard reminds us of danger we would like to forget. But two of those girls were close to our own age. It could happen to us."

Others moved to take their turns filling jugs and buckets, while Mara's father stood guard. When all were ready again, the two friends took the lead, walking a while in companionable silence. Then Mara asked, "You never told me who the man was you talked to at the celebration."

Ziva scoffed to gain time. "Back then?"

"Not that long. Only a few months."

She hesitated, not sure she wanted to talk about Jaedon, but if she refused to answer a simple question, Mara would think it more important than it was. "His name is Jaedon. He and his father are friends of Binyamin."

"Your sister's husband? Isn't he one of the school of prophets?"

Feeling a tightness in her throat, Ziva gazed ahead, measuring the distance to her house. She wanted to excuse herself, claim that Imma needed her ... for something. "Yes," she said slowly.

"Jaedon—is he a prophet?"

"No. He and his father tend a vineyard."

Mara slanted a gaze at her, seeming to approve. "Then your young man will be able to support a family. A prophet has to depend on Yahweh."

Ziva blinked several times. What did that mean? Was her friend saying the Lord could not provide as well as a farmer? Why did she think it should matter to Ziva? What did she mean by ... *your young man?* She felt her face flush. "We are not betrothed."

"Did they not make an offer?"

Now her cheeks burned. She had thought on this often, but she did not wish to speak of it. Not even with Mara. "Not exactly. They stopped here for the children to eat and rest, and so Biny could relay greetings from Eden."

"I understand, but my mother watched you in the orchard. She said he had the look of a young man who brings a *Ketubah.*"

"I assure you—"

"Or who might soon bring one."

Ziva clamped her jaw. Was the whole settlement whispering and supposing? At first, Abba had told Jaedon's father she was too young, that he could not consider a betrothal contract at present. Yet after she and Jaedon had spoken in the orchard, her father had told Dov to return with his son the next year, in mid-summer, when she would have seen sixteen summers. If she were honest with herself, Mara was right. Jaedon *might* soon return with a *ketubah.*

Did she hope he would?

Ziva knew why Abba said she was too young to marry, although girls in their settlement had married even younger. Late one night, she had heard him whisper to Imma. "I can't bear to see our girl married to Laban. Though he is a good man and kind, he is twice her age."

Her mother had responded breathlessly. "And with four children. Absolutely not! Tell him I still need her help with Aharon. If you turn him down, I have it on good authority he will ask Hezi's widow. A far better match for both."

Silence stretched until Ziva thought they had fallen asleep. Then she heard her mother whisper, "But it is not only Laban you object to. You can't bear to let your little girl leave."

Ziva heard a soft chuckle. "Nor you."

"Nor I." Then a drawn-out breath, the rustle of one rolling over, and silence.

It was clear, Ziva's prospects in their settlement were either younger boys or older widowers with children. Jaedon was not too much older than she and spoke lovingly of his family. She liked him. She thought of the way his left eye squinted when he grinned, as if the sun shone in his eyes. Yes. She wanted to wait for this good-looking, kind, young man, who was a friend to her sister's husband. She hoped he would return.

Still, many things could happen in a year. There was no *ketubah* and might never be.

Friend or no friend, Ziva would say no more of the matter. If the betrothal did not occur, she did not want to be an object of discussion or pity to her neighbors.

Until they reached Gischala, Mara continued to ask questions and Ziva to dodge them. She was relieved when her friend's attention was captured by a runner coming from the north. She remembered Jaedon sometimes acted as runner between the cities and settlements. As she eyed the messenger, she noted his speed, his clenched fists. What was this about? Dripping sweat, he ran down the main path through the village to the home of the chief elder.

A chill ran through her. Not news of another attack on a village.

She stared after him. Mara laid a hand on her wrist,

clearly meaning to question her further.

"Imma is expecting me with the water," Ziva said, pulling away. "And I ... I am to mind Aharon while she ... tends to other tasks."

She hurried off, slowing as she passed the elder's house in the hope she might hear something of the message. Though she heard the deep voice of the elder and breathless responses from the runner, she could make out nothing. She picked up her pace. She would tell her parents that a messenger had arrived. The news would spread soon enough.

Much later that night, Ziva lay on her mat, curled on her side and breathing in slow, even breaths. Imma had just checked to be sure she was asleep. That meant she and Abba wanted to talk without her overhearing, but Ziva wanted to know what the messenger said that had caused the adults in the settlement to whisper together all day.

Abba began to murmur, so softly that, at first, she could not make out what he said. Soundlessly, she rolled to her back so she could tune both ears.

"—not more than a half-day's journey from us. This time horsemen ransacked the village, set fire to roofs, and herded the villagers together. They chose young, unmarried captives. Tied them to be taken away on horseback. When parents interfered, they herded families together and killed them, children first, then the parents."

Ziva shoved her fist against her mouth, swallowing convulsively.

Her mother choked on a sob. "What can be done?"

"Pairs of armed sentries will patrol the village. If they spot intruders, they will raise an alarm and attack."

"At night?"

"Day and night. No one is to leave the village alone as long as the threat remains. At least two armed men will accompany women to the well. The herds will be brought in close, and all remaining crops will be harvested and distributed among our households."

Her father paused. "In the stricken village, the attackers set fire to the crops as they fled with captives."

Nausea welled in Ziva's throat. Abba was worried, though he tried to reassure Imma. Their village wasn't hidden, not safe. Not if terrible men had torched their neighbors.

What could the pillagers want from her village? There was no gold or silver here. Not like the rich, walled cities of Samaria or Jezreel.

That was just it. Like the destroyed town, Gischala had no walls to besiege. An easy victory, with little risk to the bandits. Captives would bring silver in the slave market.

What if her baby brother was taken? Her mother and father would try to save Aharon, and the attackers would kill her parents. Tears began to run down her cheeks and drip onto her sleeping mat.

Would they take a baby on a long and strenuous horseback ride? No, no, no—they would kill him! They would take only young men for slaves and maidens for brothels. They would take her, and she would be forced to—

She heard a rustle of cloth and her mother's hand on her cheek. "Are you awake, daughter? What! Are these tears?"

She grasped her mother's hand, struggling to choke back another sob.

Imma lay down beside her, snuggling close on the mat. "Yahweh will watch over us. The men have a good plan."

"But others were killed."

"Yahweh will see that our enemy receives justice."

Ziva tucked her chin close to her chest. Justice or not, whole families were dead. She imagined little Aharon, bloody and unmoving on the ground.

"I am sorry I complained about caring for my brother. I will watch him whenever you say."

"Thank you, my sweet. We will all be watchful. But our men will care for us. Do not worry."

"I heard what Abba said about sentries. I want a weapon of my own, and I want Abba to teach me to use it."

Her mother was silent a few heartbeats then drew a deep breath. "Your father will protect—"

"She is right, Chedva."

Abba was standing over them.

"I will make daggers for each of you, and I will show you how to use them," he said. "We will teach all the women to use weapons and other ways to fight with what is at hand. A hot cook pot. A handful of dust. Where to hurt a man with an unexpected blow."

"Are you angry with me, Abba? I am sorry I pretended to sleep and listened to your conversation."

He lit a straw from coals in the banked hearth and held it to the lamp wick. After tossing the straw back into the hearth, he shoved his hand through his hair, making it stand on end. "I am not angry, little one, but I am sorry you heard me and were frightened."

Abba finished their knives three days later. Mara had volunteered to watch Aharon in exchange for a dagger of her own, so Ziva hefted her brother on her hip and set out. He struggled to get down, but she jigged and sang along the path to Mara's house.

Aharon was giggling and grabbing for her hair when they arrived. He scowled when he realized he was going to be handed off, but Mara scooped him from Ziva's arms and closed his fingers around a date.

"He will be fine," she said. "But you'd better learn all you can today, for I will show you no mercy when we spar!"

Ziva laughed and waved good-bye. Mara spoke lightheartedly, but she meant what she said. With her father's fighting experience, he would make of her a fearsome opponent.

When Ziva returned, Abba was already showing Imma how to hold the knife for three different thrusts. Then he demonstrated for Ziva. Their handles were smaller than his, to fit their hands, but the blades were as long and sturdy. "Not too long to hide," he assured them, and he slid the knife into the leather sheath fastened to Imma's thigh.

He explained how to quickly pull the weapon despite their tunics. "There will be no time for modesty," he said. "Get the weapon into your hand and then into your enemy."

He affixed ripened gourds for targets all over a rotted tree.

"Where should I aim?" Ziva asked.

"Anywhere you can reach. Stab him again and again, kick him here and here if he falls, stomp on his head, his hands—make sure he cannot come at you again."

Ziva felt the blood drain from her face. Her father took her hand and pulled her to him. "Do not give a care for the enemy, my daughter. He is not a man, he is a demon who wants only to destroy. If you are threatened, fight without compunction. You, your mother, and your baby brother are all that matters."

"Father," she began, her face against his tunic. "We are so close to the enemy. Their cities are less than a day's ride on horseback. I can't bear the thought of our little town being overrun, of losing you."

"Yahweh will protect us. He has given us warning, and we are making preparations. No more talk. Let us try again."

The three practiced for hours, until the sun dipped below the treetops and Ziva quivered with—truth be told, with fear. The longer they trained, the greater her anxiety grew. She would never be skilled enough to fight off a real attack.

Although an hour remained before dusk, Abba wiped his brow and said, "Enough." Then sliding an arm around each of their shoulders, he walked them to Mara's house. He presented her with her dagger and sheath, thanked her for caring for Aharon, and set him on his shoulders.

It was time for supper, but nothing was prepared. Her mind filled with the afternoon's activity, Ziva couldn't bear the thought of food.

"I am not hungry," Abba said. "But I think we could use music and"—he feigned a lunge at her mother—"dancing!"

Imma squealed and kicked him, a perfectly executed strike to his thigh—although Abba had said to aim for the kneecap. Ziva put her hand over her mouth, glad her mother had not actually maimed him.

"Whether or not you are hungry, Aharon surely is, and we all need to eat. I have leftover bread from this morning, cheese, and watered wine."

"A feast!" Abba made a pretense of limping to the shelf where he kept his flute. He began to play a cheerful tune, and he shuffled his feet to the music. He paused when Imma popped a morsel of cheese in his mouth and handed him a bread round and cup of watered wine.

Ziva ate slowly at first, but Imma had been right. The food and drink strengthened her and lifted her mood. When they finished, Abba swung Aharon back to his shoulders and picked up his flute, she grasped Imma's hands, and they danced in the tiny area near the hearth. Finally gasping for breath, they all sank onto the floor.

Abba handed the flute to Ziva. As dusk turned to night, he built a fire while she played tunes he had taught her since childhood. Her fingers were at home on the willow her father had carved into a flute. Aharon crawled beside her, lay his head on her lap, and fell asleep.

Ziva finished by trying to copy the song her father had played for dancing. When she missed a phrase, he lifted a hand to stop her, then sang to her, his voice deep, rumbling, and surrounding the room with peace.

The Lord is my strength and my shield ...

She lifted the flute, repeated the melody while he sang with her, then lifted her lips from the smooth cylinder.

"Abba, I know we should look to the Lord. But perhaps instead of training to fight, He meant for us to flee before the enemy comes." She rushed to complete her thought, before her father would shush her. "Perhaps the Lord meant us to take refuge with Binyamin and Eden, with the school of the prophets."

There, she'd said it. She didn't want to be disrespectful, but she did want her father to consider a different idea. What seemed to her a safer plan.

His hand slid to stroke her hair. Then he kissed her forehead and tipped her face so she would look at him. "It is a good idea. We would be safe. But we would leave our home and our land unprotected, our neighbors without our support." He slowly shook his head and tears stung her eyes.

"Yet, our neighbors do not need the support of women and children. I will speak to the town elders. They may agree that the most vulnerable should be sent to the prophets. They will be safe with the Lord's servants. Yes, I will speak to them tonight."

Ziva clutched the front of his tunic. "No, Abba! That is not what I meant. Imma and I will never leave you."

"Hush, now. Nothing is decided. But daughter, remember King David, when he was pursued by his enemy, wrote, 'The Lord is my light and my salvation—whom shall I fear? The Lord is the stronghold of my life—of whom shall I be afraid?'"

How could he think of sending them away and staying to fight? Instead, she curled her fingers into the coarse cloth of his tunic and answered hoarsely, "Yes, Abba. I will remember."

Chapter Twenty-Three

Hear, O Israel: The Lord our God, the Lord is one.
Love the Lord your God with all your heart
and with all your soul and with all your strength.
~ Deuteronomy 6:6

Weeks later, autumn, enroute to Mount Carmel
Gehazi

RAIN HAD FALLEN RECENTLY OVER THE fertile plain of Esdraelon. Gehazi lifted one foot, then the other, shaking water from wet sandals. He didn't mind, for the sun was shining. His sandals and the grass would soon dry. And every step took them closer to a town where Elisha would teach on their way to Mount Carmel.

The view across the plain was always admirable, but rain had washed it clean and it sparkled in the sunlight. Ripening crops blanketed the valley with gold and bronze, a shepherd and his dog guarded a flock of grazing sheep, and date palms lined a path to the town of Shunem.

Built on the gentle slope of Mount Moreh, it snuggled close to its sister-city, Nain, on an adjacent slope. Two communities would allow for many listeners for Elisha's Torah lessons.

Gehazi had looked on this day with anticipation. He would be publicly seen as Elisha's chosen servant. His assistant, really, standing by to step in as teacher and prophet. When the time was right, of course.

"Have you decided on your topic, Master?" On the way, they had discussed whether Elisha would teach one of the lessons he had taught Gehazi—creation, the fall of man, or God's promise of a future deliverer.

"Elijah placed great importance in teaching the Shema, so I shall follow his example."

Gehazi nodded, glad he'd learn something new. "I regret never having sat under Elijah's teaching. I would have liked to observe you with him." He gazed ahead at a few houses on the top of the hill and more clinging to its slope. "I have never thought to ask how I can help when you teach. Would you like me to run ahead and announce your coming? Ask the townsfolk to assemble?"

Elisha chuckled. "Good questions. We may need you to speak to the elders, since I am not well-known. It seemed everywhere we went, people were already waiting for Elijah." Elisha continued talking about his time with Elijah.

Gehazi stepped around a puddle and smiled, heartened by Elisha's approval and liking hearing his reminiscences. There was much he didn't know. Of course, everyone had heard about Jezebel's fury and attempt to find Elijah. But none had dared touch him, gold or not. No surprise there. Fire appeared at Elijah's command. Even after the fire on Mount Carmel, hadn't his fire slain one hundred soldiers? Or was it one hundred fifty?

Elisha's miracles, however, seemed more … kindly. He parted the Jordan, cleansed a spring, and helped a widow. He made things better wherever he went. Except one mustn't forget the bears. A wise man should not touch the Lord's prophet.

Another good reason to become a prophet.

A bothersome thought shoved its way forward. While Jaedon had walked beside Elisha during the confrontation with thugs from Bethel, Gehazi had been sent to reclaim Lital and his sons. Was he jealous of the boy? Concerned the experience had strengthened the bond between boy and prophet? But Elisha had chosen him. He was here.

"How is your family? Is the house satisfactory?" Elisha looked at him steadily, like a farmer waiting to hear a report of the day's work in the field.

Gehazi held his gaze.

"Our boys work hard in the garden and manage it well, even when I travel with you. They have told me they would like to enlarge the tilled space next spring. Lital has used many of the vegetables in her stews and was pleased to find neighbors who wanted to trade their figs or olives for our cucumbers."

He walked silently a while, deciding what he'd say next.

"The house is snug and warms easily. Though it is small, Lital is content. If we should be blessed with another child, then might be the time to consider enlarging the space. We are grateful."

Even as he spoke, he felt the warmth of well-being spread through him. Sometimes all it took was firmly marshaling his thoughts. The community of prophets had embraced his family. He was not afraid to leave them alone. Lital and the boys had friends who helped them when he was gone.

He swallowed a sigh. Still, the house and property did not belong to them. No one owned property in Gilgal. They had been lent the house to use when another prophet left for a time. What happened when he returned? Would his boys' hard work benefit another?

He would never be able to replace his destroyed vineyard.

Elisha eyed him intently.

They neared the town on the hill. The surrounding plain boasted fields of grain nearly ready for harvest. A few people strolled down the slope, and more were scattered among the fields.

"That is Shunem ahead," Elisha said. "Let us introduce ourselves without fanfare. See the farmers? Let's start with them."

Gehazi studied two men watering an ox hitched to a wagon. Had Elisha received some special knowledge from the Lord? The taller man's rolled turban shaded his head but revealed long gray hair tied neatly back, while the shorter man's unruly black hair poked from wherever it could escape. Nothing special that he could see.

A woman approached carrying a basket, probably their midday meal. She shaded her eyes and studied Elisha and him carefully, almost as if searching for weapons. Then she smiled. "Ho, travelers, can you stop with us? I brought plenty of food."

Perhaps ... the food?

The gray-haired man stepped away from the ox and grinned at the woman, apparently used to her outgoing ways. "By all means, join us. I am Samuel, my wife, Malka. This is my steward, Tal."

Smiling at the couple, Elisha moved close to the ox and

stroked its shoulder. "Shalom. What a fine fellow." He introduced himself and Gehazi, meanwhile turning the animal's head to examine its eyes.

"Elisha!" said the woman. "The Man of God?"

Gehazi stood a little straighter.

Elisha released the animal and bowed his head. "We are on our way to Mount Carmel. We will teach the words of the Lord to any who would like to listen."

"Wonderful," Malka said. "I am sure others will want to hear you." She turned her gaze on her husband and widened her eyes. Gehazi, having seen such a look from Lital in the past, wondered how her husband might respond.

Samuel cleared his throat. "Tal, go now to alert Shunem that the man of God is here. Likewise, send one of our servants to Nain."

He turned to Elisha. "Are you content for the people to assemble on the slope below the village gate? If you speak from the lowest part, they will be able to see and hear you very well. There is a tree to shade you, just as if the Lord arranged it."

As the steward left, they ate from the woman's capacious basket—bread, cheese, vinegar-soaked olives, cucumbers, and cooled goat's milk. By the time the steward returned, followed by a long stream of villagers, Gehazi felt his eyes drooping. Elisha, who had been talking with Samuel about the fine points of the ox, appeared revived and ready to teach.

Tal had brought the requested stool, which he set up under the tree where Malka directed. Men, women, and children sat on the slope in rows, nearly covering the hillside. Elisha settled comfortably on the stool, then started speaking, first introducing himself and narrating the incident when Elijah called him from his father's field, where he had been plowing with oxen. He spoke loud enough to be heard, but in his typical gentle manner. He told how he had served Elijah until the Lord had taken him to heaven.

"But not in the ordinary way," he said. "Nothing about Elijah was ordinary."

Elisha described the fiery chariot and horses in such detail that the townsfolk were captivated. Listening, Gehazi could almost imagine *he* had seen it. It troubled him that he had not. He glanced sideways at Elisha, remembering how he'd volunteered to go search for Elijah's body on that day. He wondered if Elisha was remembering, too.

Then Elisha introduced Gehazi as his servant-apprentice. Many faces turned their way, and Gehazi felt warmth spread throughout his chest. Elisha remembered, but he extended kindness. Acceptance for Gehazi's failings and a chance to learn. To be better. He applied himself to listen.

"It is important that each of you hear and learn the Lord's words," Elisha said. "What I will teach today was given to Moses by Yahweh Himself.

"These are the words of the Lord God,

"'Hear, O Israel: The Lord our God, the Lord is one. Love the Lord your God with all your heart, and with all your soul, and with all your strength. These commandments that I give you today are to be on your hearts. Impress them on your children. Talk about them when you sit at home and when you walk along the road, when you lie down and when you get up.'"

He paused and swept his gaze up the hillside. "Repetition in the oral account tells us these words are vitally important. We must do more than listen, as a parent listens with one ear to a child's prattle. We must pay close attention—hear with our heart. These are the very words of God. He tells us about Himself, and how we must interact with Him. You must be deeply engaged in your love for God and teach your children, so that God Himself will live among you, as is His desire."

Elisha repeated the Shema, asking the men to stand and repeat after him. He did so until they had faultlessly memorized the passage.

"Will you teach your children?" Elisha asked.

"We will!" Responses came from all over the hill. One man shouted, "My son has already memorized the Shema. He will teach me."

Elisha chuckled. "Come see me in eight or ten years, lad. I may have a job for you."

When the laughter died down, Elisha continued in a serious tone.

"One who loves the Lord will not worship other gods.

Made of wood, stone, and metal, they cannot hear nor answer prayers. Some worship idols because of superstition, to socialize with Canaanite neighbors, or for the lascivious rituals. But the end of worshipping the Ba'als, Chemosh, and Molech is death."

Elisha had told Gehazi the story of the Moabite king sacrificing his son on the city wall. Gehazi thought of his own sons, of whom he was so proud. How could any father do such a thing?

He wondered how many from Shunem or Nain, only a day's journey from King Joram's palace, had been conscripted in the war with Moab. If they returned here to tell the tale, would it have affected their hearers as deeply as those who witnessed the boy's senseless death?

Probably not. Just as those who had not lost everything to Arameans were not as affected as he and his family. Yes, thanks to Elisha's help, they were starting over, but that was not the same as never having lost.

Gehazi clenched his fists at his side, struggling to control the surge of anger at the memory of his family staring at smoke and rubble, all that was left of home and vineyard. Reason whispered, *'But were you loving the Lord your God with all your heart, all your soul, and all your strength? Were you grateful for what He had given you?'*

He clamped his lips, but it didn't stop the response that filled his mind. *I built that house and vineyard with years of hard work. Yahweh let it burn.*

Gehazi forced his attention back to Elisha, trying to fill his mind with the Torah. How was he to mature as a prophet if he could not control his thoughts? If his mind warred with what he was taught?

Elisha had finished talking about thankfulness for God's gifts and was explaining that sex and promiscuity involved in idol worship not only angered God, but dishonored people and destroyed relationships.

Gehazi drew a breath. Well, that sin, at least, had never been his problem. He loved Lital, and he knew she would not stand for such treatment. Nor would her father. But ... how long would either of them stand for living off the kindness of others? Owning nothing?

As Elisha finished talking, several in the crowd surrounded him. Gehazi picked up the travel bags, intending to fill the waterskins and see about purchasing food in the marketplace. Before he left, he noticed Malka and her husband standing apart, obviously waiting their turn to speak to Elisha. She motioned to Gehazi.

"It is too late for the prophet to travel to Mount Carmel today. We would be honored if you both would take supper with us and stay the night. We have plenty of room."

"You are kind, and it is a long walk. I will ask him." He thought Elisha looked tired, but that didn't mean he would consent to stay. It all depended on what the Lord told him.

As it should.

Chapter Twenty-Four

Seek the Lord and His strength;
Seek His face evermore.
Psalm 105:4

Gischala in Autumn, the Date Orchard
Ziva

RECENT RAINS HAD SWELLED THE STREAM that threaded through the date orchard, but the sun shone as hot as a summer day. Or at least as hot as it ever got in their northern hills. In celebration of the unseasonably warm weather, Ziva had donned her summer tunic but, in the event the weather turned cool, she brought her cloak. The morning sun coaxed her to twist it around her head in a style imitating her father's head covering, rolling a cloth brim that shaded her face.

They were preparing to harvest the season's last dates and knew they would sample some when finished. Several village men had been assigned to act as guards, keeping watch from each corner of the orchard plot, but Ziva and the other villagers did not let the reminder of danger dim their celebratory mood. A shared meal at midday, with the best cooks of the village bringing their most-loved dishes, eclipsed their fears, at least for today.

Ziva's family worked next to Mara's and the girls chatted back and forth about chores, pesky brothers, and what they would do with the family's date allotment. The day's work began by gathering ground fall so the dates would not be stepped on when they cut new clusters.

After dropping her gleanings into Imma's basket, Ziva discreetly slipped her fingers under her make-shift turban, feeling the smooth fold of Jaedon's letter, which had come with the messenger.

No one she knew had ever received a letter. Reading the unexpected missive brought a smile. He admired her. Was building a house. Hoped she would be agreeable to a betrothal. Each phrase was like a drop of sweet honey.

A house near her sister. A life with this young man, so

handsome and kind. When she had shown the letter to Imma, her mother had sighed while her gaze flitted over the neatly inked characters. Then she said, "Neither your father nor I wish you to settle so far from us. Yet"—she had sighed again—"it is no more than two or three days travel. I suppose that is not so bad. And Eden will be close. Binyamin spoke well of Jaedon and his family. They have a vineyard and the wherewithal to build you a separate house, rather than a room off his family's." She had paused then as if she had poured out all her thoughts on the matter. "Your prospects in Gischala are less attractive, I fear. What do you think, Daughter? Are you willing to pledge yourself to the young man?"

Her father had asked her a similar question on the day she spoke with Jaedon in the orchard. Although Eden had likewise been questioned about Binyamin, Ziva knew to be thus consulted was unusual. Other young women in her village had no say in their marriage arrangements.

There had been time, these months, to think on her parents' questions. She had liked Jaedon. He seemed polite, affable, and brave—hadn't he participated in the rescue of the captives? Binyamin's opinion weighed in his favor. After all, Jaedon was a friend and neighbor.

But Biny had known Jaedon as a friend. That was no guarantee he would be a good husband.

Yet, even as uncertainty nipped at her thoughts, she remembered him speaking indulgently of his younger siblings. Of the expression on his open face as he spoke with fondness and respect about his imma and stepfather. Of his relationship with Elijah and his successor, Elisha.

Then, there was his letter. 'Behind the vineyard, I am building a house of stone. It will withstand the years. The kitchen hearth is of matching stone, and if you wish, I will plaster the inside walls.'

"I do like him, Imma," she had answered. "His letter seems thoughtful. I think he is trustworthy, but I trust you and Abba more."

She had left the final decision in her father's hands. When she showed her father Jaedon's letter, she thought his expression revealed approval.

Mara sidled up with a stack of cloth strips. "What are you smiling about, Ziva?"

"Just"—she waved her hand at the scene—"just everything."

"Umm hmm." Mara grinned and lay several strips across her open palm. "Well, wrap your arms and let's get busy." Her friend strolled ahead, distributed the supplies, and tossed a wink over her shoulder.

Perhaps it had been a mistake to tell Mara about the letter.

With cloth wrapped around her left hand to protect her from date thorns, Ziva worked alongside her father, as she had since childhood. She quickly established a rhythm—pulled down a palm bract, sliced date clusters free, and dropped them into the basket her mother carried. With most villagers participating in the harvest, they should finish well before sundown.

After a while, she straightened and rubbed a tight spot in her shoulder. Then she glanced toward the tamarisk tree where they'd left Aharon gumming a date. She didn't see her brother, but she did see stems of yellow broom bounce back into place.

"Aharon?" She huffed, flung off the wraps, and tramped toward the clearing's edge. She'd find him crawling into the forest, as fast as his fat knees could take him, with a handful of mud smeared around his mouth. Such a troublesome little boy!

She looked over her shoulder to tell her mother where she was going. She saw her mother's mouth stretched into a wide circle but never heard the scream. A blow to the side of her head exploded in pain and hurled her into darkness.

When Ziva woke, she was lying on her belly across the back of a moving horse. Her forehead was wet with sweat and every inch of her ached. She tried to lift her head but couldn't. The ground whirled beneath her. She could barely twist to see the horse's gray shoulder, whiskered chin, and the tree trunks ahead.

"Imma," she rasped.

A leather-gloved hand grasped the back of her neck and shook her like a rat. Her teeth rattled and all went black again.

When she forced her eyes open, she was lying face-down on splintery wood. A raised platform of planks, for she could see through narrow gaps down to a dirt road. Around her, she saw sandaled feet and the hems of long tunics, unlike any woven in Gischala. Too colorful, garish even, with borders of a strange shiny fabric.

Someone rapped the bottom of her foot, and she groaned, not because the stick hurt her heel, but because the slightest jiggle sent shards of pain through her head. She thought to reach, to feel the wound for blood, but her hands were tied behind her back.

Imma. Abba. She wouldn't speak aloud this time, didn't want to be shaken back into darkness. *Aharon.* She rolled her face to look again through the crack. Those strange tunics. Raiders must have taken her. Was she no longer in Israel?

Aharon … where was he? Reliving her worst fears, she clamped her lips together, squeezed her eyes shut, to no avail. A tear squeezed through.

Again the sharp taps on her feet. A voice in accented Hebrew. "You awake, girl?" Tap, tap. "I'm going to help you up."

A hand grasped the rope around her wrists and yanked her up, as easily as if she were a small dog on a rope. The man was short, stocky, and bald and had no eyebrows. Her legs wobbled beneath her, but she raised her chin. "Where are my mother, father, and brother?"

He laughed, revealing yellowed teeth. "Look around you, girl. Do you think this is a family gathering?"

Slowly she turned her head, resolutely planting her feet against the dizziness that swayed her. She stood, as she had surmised, on a raised, wooden platform. Other captives in Hebrew clothing stood with her. A mixed group of men and women she guessed were meant to be slaves. She appeared to be the youngest. No children or older adults. No one she knew. No one from her settlement.

Yahweh, my family. Wherever they are. Protect them.

Mara. Young and beautiful, but she was not here to be sold. Had one of the attackers taken her as a prize? Ziva knew such things were done, though spoken of only in whispers. Or had she been killed? *My friend, my dearest friend.*

Below, she saw the people whose feet and hems she had glimpsed previously. They were staring at her curiously, even as she stared back. Houses stood behind them, many-colored, clustered close, and backed up to a wall. She was in a strange city. Was she even in Israel?

A helmeted soldier rode close to the platform on a black horse. Her father had described conical-shaped helmets when he recounted his stint in a battle under King Ahab. The feather at its crest identified an Aramean officer.

Her legs began to tremble, and she clenched her fists behind her, willed herself not to faint, though fear engulfed her. She had heard of slave markets in Aram. She must stand in one now. Where would she be taken next? Brothel or temple?

Yahweh, help me. Help me.

Abba's knife! Did she still have it? Not having the use of her hands, she shifted her weight, surreptitiously pressing one thigh against the other. Her heart sank. The leather sheath was no longer strapped to her leg. She squeezed her eyes shut against the image of Old Yellow Teeth feeling around beneath her tunic, finding and removing the knife, and doing who knew what else while she drowned in blackness!

Here he came again, bringing a bucket and ladle. Dipping it, he offered her a drink. She drank deeply, careful not to spill a drop, for which she was glad when he walked away without offering her a second ladle.

She gazed longingly after the retreating bucket.

A taller man came carrying a stylus and wax tablet. "What skills do you have?" he barked.

Even though this man did not speak Hebrew, she understood enough of what he said. But what skills might give an advantage? When she hesitated, he said, "Do not bother. I can see you are a maiden. You will go to the temple or—"

Ziva sucked her lip between her teeth. "I can cook, clean, farm, and know many healing potions. My father had no sons old enough, so he taught me to hunt and dress game."

The scribe tipped his head and snorted. "No one will let you hunt here, little Israelite. Brothel," he said distinctly as he wrote.

"No." The soldier on the black rode up to the platform. "Put her on my horse, Scribe. I will take her."

The scribe looked at Ziva, then at the soldier. "The captives will be auctioned. This maid will bring a higher price. You may bid along with the others."

The soldier took off his feather-topped helmet, revealing dark hair, graying at the sides. His hair and beard were neatly clipped. To Ziva, he was unremarkable in appearance, though his helmet revealed him a soldier. But she heard a sharp intake of breath from the man beside her.

She switched her attention back to the rider. He was, she supposed, larger than most, and the horse was impressive. Perhaps the scribe felt threatened.

A shudder ran through her.

"I am Naaman," the soldier said quietly. "Shall I tell the king you denied my request?"

"No, sir. My apologies, Captain, I did not recognize you. Ride closer and I'll hand her down."

He motioned to a massive guard wearing fish-scaled armor and leather gauntlets. The platform shook with his strides, but he was gentle when he turned Ziva around, sliced through her bonds, and lowered her from the platform to sit crossways in front of the soldier. Captain Naaman.

When she was settled on the horse, she tentatively felt the side of her head. It was sore and felt crusted over. She examined her fingers. No blood. Suddenly both hands flew back to her head. Her turban—her father's cloak—gone. With it, Jaedon's letter.

Naaman studied her. "Bring a cloak or a head covering," he instructed the soldier who had lowered her. "Can you also find riding trousers that will fit this little one?"

Ziva cringed at hearing her father's pet name for her from this soldier's guttural, foreign voice. Seated sideways in front of his saddle, she had the opportunity to inspect his appearance. She didn't wonder that the scribe thought him only a soldier. He wore no armor, save a padded vest that might save him from a direct blow. But what did she know of soldiers?

Only Mara's lame father, wounded in battle. *Mara.* What had happened to her?

"Yes, sir." The soldier hurried away and returned in short order with a cloak and a strange half-garment, similar in appearance to a man's tucked-up tunic meant to gird his loins. She glanced down at the captain's cloth-covered limbs, extending beneath a soldier's kilt. When she folded the garment across her lap, she felt padding in its legs.

Naaman draped the cloak over her head and around her shoulders. Then he extracted a small pouch from the folds of his clothing, checked its contents, and handed it over to the soldier. He passed it on to the scribe, who looked inside and nodded his satisfaction at the payment.

Naaman turned the horse, and they rode away from the platform toward a market backed by a residential sector. When six more military riders took stations around them, Ziva realized she would not travel alone with the captain.

None of his men wore armor, but one led a jangling pack animal. The stoutly muscled horse was loaded with bulging objects that rattled under worn and patched hides. The curved edges of bronze shields peeked from beneath the tarp.

Five of these riders wore surprisingly clean tunics, padded trousers, and leather helmets. Bows were slung over their shoulders, quivers looped over within reach. She counted four swords among them, but perhaps the fifth was left-handed or preferred a dagger.

The sixth had no blood on his plain but well-made garments, but they were dusty and wrinkled. He wore a heavy sword at his side, as did the captain.

She shivered. Where were they going? What would happen to her? Though she tried to blink them back, stray tears soon streaked her cheeks.

Keeping his horse to a walk, Naaman began to talk to

her in broken Hebrew. "Do not be afraid, little one. Yes, I am a soldier, a captain in my king's army, but I purchased you as a handmaid for my wife. She is a kind woman, and you will be treated well. It is a long ride to our home, and you cannot sit sideways for the distance. We will stop at an inn here in Hazor, and you can put those trousers on beneath your tunic. Then you can ride astride with the modesty I am sure you have been raised with."

She had never been to an inn. Her heart stuttered. Would he do to her the things men sometimes did in secret? Six men in his company! She bowed her head, thinking. If they left her unguarded at any time, perhaps she could escape through a window. Hide. Could she somehow find her way home?

She studied the other soldiers under her lashes. They appeared travel worn, but none were wounded or bloody, so they had not been the slaughterers of her village. Even so, seven men held her captive. She had no chance of escape.

Her stomach growled. She had not eaten a crust of bread, not even a date as they worked in the orchard. How long ago had that been? A sob escaped. What did food matter? What had happened to her family?

"When did you last eat?" asked the captain. "Are you hungry? Thirsty? We will eat at the inn."

"Water, please," she croaked." That was answer enough to both questions.

He uncorked a water skin and helped as she drank greedily. When she finished, she summoned courage to ask, "Sir, can you tell me ... what of my family? My neighbors?"

"The others on the auction stage?"

It had a name? Was it regularly used to sell Israelite slaves?

"No, none of those were from my village."

"What is the name of your village?"

"Gischala."

He flinched at the name, as if he'd received a blow. She glanced up, hoping to read his expression, but he had averted his gaze.

Finally, he returned his attention to the narrow pathway through the city. "I am sorry," he said, then fell silent. She watched him through half-lowered lashes. The lines in his face drew down. Suddenly, she did not want him to continue.

"All were killed." His voice was almost too low to hear.

No. No. That could not be. It was impossible that she would never see them again. Dead? Her entire town? Imma, Abba? Even little Aharon?

She sucked in a gasp of air. She had seen signs of her brother crawling into the brush. Perhaps he had escaped. But ... if all were killed, as Naaman had told her, the marauders would certainly find Aharon. He would hear the frightening sounds and cry. They would find and kill him.

Or if not ... a helpless babe alone. All in the village were dead. Except her, and she was captured. Who would feed him? Keep him warm at night?

She cupped her hand over her mouth, thinking of the cold nights, of wild beasts that stalked the hills.

If he was not already dead—no, no she would not think of it.

Then she did not attempt to stay the tears, but she held herself very erect, careful not to allow herself to sway against her new master. For though he spoke kindly, he was a soldier of Aram. He was her enemy.

Chapter Twenty-Five

Now bands of raiders from Aram had gone
Out and had taken captive a young girl from
Israel, and she served Naaman's wife.
2 Kings 5:2

Trade Route, City of Hazor
Ziva

AS THEY RODE THROUGH THE MARKETPLACE of Hazor, Ziva felt numb to the exotic goods displayed. Vendors hawked pottery painted in brilliant colors, stacks of shiny cloth, and round orange, yellow, and red fruits like nothing grown in Gischala.

She closed her eyes. These sprawling goods were luxuries for the rich, nothing she or her family had ever wanted or needed. All she could think of were her brother's dimpled hands. Her father calling her his little one. And her mother gently teaching her how to care for the husband, house, and children she would have one day.

But no longer. All she had loved, all she had dreamed of were gone.

She felt the swaying walk of the black horse. Its gait was longer, rougher than the small working donkeys a neighboring farmer sometimes let her ride. The last time she had ridden, Aharon had stretched out his hands, demanding to be put astride. Deeming him too young, her father had grabbed up her brother, settled him on his shoulders, and bounced about, promising, "Another time, another time," in comic guttural imitation of a donkey's bray.

Ziva clasped her arm across her middle. The memory ached like a physical blow. *Yahweh, please take this pain from me. It is too much to bear.*

When she forced her eyes open, the soldiers had drawn closer around the captain's horse. Their group approached a row of plastered houses. Realization seized her. She must keep her eyes open. Pay attention. Orient herself firmly to her surroundings, should the opportunity arise for her to flee.

Ahead were a gate out of the city and a path leading

northwest. Jagged mountains loomed in the far distance. Pretending the need to stretch her back, she turned and looked behind, trying to appear only weary. Another gate they must have ridden through when she had closed her eyes in pain. Beyond the path winding down a slope, she recognized the hills of Naphtali. She was certain she gazed upon the way back to Gischala. For the first time since she awoke on the auction platform, she felt a flicker of something other than fear. Resolve. It wavered, but she promised herself it would grow.

The house on the corner appeared twice as large as the rest of the row. A horse was tied to a post out front, head down, eyes half-lidded, a hind hoof cocked. Was this the inn?

A sturdy young woman stood in the doorway. Ziva thought her striking, not only because she looked so assured, but also because of the large yellow dog that stood by her side.

"Welcome. There is a stable for your horses around back, sirs." She gestured to a gate that must lead to the shelter.

Naaman did not move. "We will not stay overnight, but we will take the midday meal, if you have sufficient for me, the girl, and six hungry men."

"We have a hearty stew of fish and root vegetables simmering over the hearth. Can you smell it?" She raised her eyebrows.

He breathed in deeply. "I can. It will do nicely. With bread. Much bread."

She smiled, made a deep bow, and disappeared inside, presumably to see to food for the travelers.

Naaman slid off his horse and held out his hands to Ziva. She leaned over, and he lifted her down. The horsemen headed together for the stable.

All except one. Ziva studied him as he turned back to speak to Naaman. For the first time she noticed his clothing was different than the others. Less protective, less military.

"If we are to ride on, should I buy food for the road ahead?"

"Yes, Rafiq. Enough for three days. Include meat, if you can find it, and fresh fruit. And a clean tunic for the girl." He indicated her bloodstained garment.

"It should be larger than the one she is wearing, so it will hang loose over her trousers when she rides." He took a measuring look at Ziva. "Of course, it won't have to be very big to be big enough."

Rafiq studied her without smiling. "Anything else? A cloak?"

"No. The cloak from the slave market is a man's, but it will keep her warm. My wife will provide something more appropriate when we arrive."

As he rode off, Naaman took firm hold of Ziva's hand and addressed the innkeeper's assistant who had greeted them. "Prepare a bath for this one." He indicated her head. "Clean and apply salve to her wound."

The young woman nodded. "Come with me, girl. Emet, go to your place." She pointed to a scooped-out depression under a window. The dog seemed to grin wolfishly, dashed to the spot, and curled up, keeping his attention fixed on her.

"A moment." The captain glanced back and forth between the dog and its mistress, then bent until his face was level with Ziva's. "There is nothing for you to return to. Beasts and highwaymen patrol the way. You will be recaptured and punished if you try." He held her gaze.

She nodded, unable to speak.

"Do I have your word you will not try to escape?"

She hesitated, thinking about what he had said. Though everything in her tensed with the desire to fight her way home, she recognized the truth in his words. *Nothing to return to.* Again, she nodded.

"You must swear it."

Ziva found her voice. "I will not run, but neither will I swear. Our God has said we must not. We are to let our yea be yea, and our nay be nay."

He frowned at her. "What is your name, girl?"

"I am Ziva." She raised her chin.

He narrowed his eyes, but then the corner of his mouth twitched. "You have said you will not run, Ziva. That will suffice."

He gave her a little shove toward the inn's door.

She had never even seen an inn. Many voices rumbled

inside. Men's voices. She glanced back once. She was afraid of the captain—but at least he was known, and who knew what lay beyond this room. As she followed the young woman, he watched, his horse's reins looped in his hand.

Then they were inside, weaving their way across a public room furnished with low wooden tables, colorful plump cushions, and patterned carpets. The tables were not all filled, but men of all ages sat around them. Many men.

Passing a window, they walked toward a stout wooden door shut tight. As they passed the window, Ziva heard the captain speaking to someone. But the courtyard had emptied—one man gone to the marketplace, the others around back to the stables, settling their mounts.

She listened. He could only be speaking to the horse.

"Let your nay be nay?" he said, and then he chuckled.

The closed door hid a private room, with two sleeping mats, a stool, and a wooden box. The young woman gently cleaned Ziva's head wound with a cloth dipped in cool water. "My name is Neri."

Ziva blinked. Neri's voice sounded almost like Mara's. There was something about the confident way she spoke and held herself that reminded Ziva of her friend. On closer scrutiny, she appeared younger than Ziva had first thought. A girl. Only a little older than herself.

Neri dipped the cloth again, catching Ziva's gaze. "You are Hebrew, yet you are with Aramean soldiers. Did Captain Naaman hit you? Did he do this?" Her fingers were light on Ziva's scalp.

Seeming to pick up on Neri's emotion, the dog made a low rumble in its throat.

"No," said Ziva. "At least I don't think so. I did not see who attacked me."

"You are his captive?"

"He bought me at the slave market."

Neri scoffed under her breath. "Hazor's disgrace is in straddling the line between Israel and Aram. Many in this city seek to amass wealth more than do what is right." She wrung out the cloth until it dripped no more, then seeming to catch herself, dipped it again and resumed her gentle ministrations.

Ziva felt her eyes sting. Why was this stranger's kindness harder to bear than the matter-of-fact cruelty of the slave traders?

Neri heaved a great sigh. "I suppose I am no better. I want to help you, but I am afraid. The innkeeper runs a prosperous trade with many Arameans among his customers. If he thought me a troublemaker, he would send me packing. Or, more likely, sell me to the highest bidder."

"Sell you? Are you not also a Hebrew?"

"Yes, and so is he, but my mother and I owe him a great debt. My father required the services of a physician in the months prior to his death. The innkeeper kindly paid the fees. Or so we thought at the time. But now I am working off the debt, and he let me know, that while he would see my honor protected, in all else I must please his clientele. If I did not, I was of no use to him, and he would sell me to settle our debt." She shrugged apologetically. "So you see, I am also a slave. My mother is aged and infirm. She needs me to work so we can eat and have this roof over our heads. I must not anger him."

Ziva nodded dully. Despair had shadowed her thoughts since she awoke to the knowledge of her capture, prospective sale, and her family's deaths. It seemed God had removed His hand of protection from her. Now she waited to see where she would be flung.

Neri looked at her thoughtfully. "Are you ... are you to be your captain's concubine?"

Ziva's eyes widened. "I ... I do not think so. He told me I am to serve his wife."

Neri's shoulders relaxed. "If he tells the truth, then all may go well for you. Perhaps he loves his wife. Or perhaps, like my master's wife, their wealth is from her family, and he fears to anger her."

"I doubt Captain Naaman fears anything," Ziva said. "He is a man of war."

In the short time she'd known him, she had formed a broad opinion of the man. He also seemed proud. Not the sort to be told by anyone what to do. His men respected him.

Seemed to almost like him, although there was no familiarity in the way they addressed him.

Neri gently turned Ziva's face, then dipped her fingers in a crock of olive oil. "Hold your head just so." Leaning forward, she stroked oil over the wound. "You said you did not see who attacked you."

Ziva closed her eyes. "I was picking dates with others from our village. I saw my baby brother crawling toward the forest from the cloak on which we'd placed him. He is"—her voice broke—"was, an adventurous little boy. A babe, really, not yet walking. That is when someone struck me." She lightly touched the bump on the side of her head. Neri's oiled fingers found hers and stayed.

"When I awoke, I was among others being sold as slaves, but they were all strangers. The captain told me our entire village—my family, my friends"—her voice squeezed to a whisper—"all killed. My former life is gone. I was a cherished daughter. A doting sister. Now I am an orphan and ... a slave." Her voice caught. "I must ... faithfully serve my master and mistress." She swallowed hard. Her words were practical and true, but everything in her warred against them.

"How terrible," said Neri. "I am so sorry."

Ziva lay her hand atop Neri's. "I thank you for caring. My head feels much better, but I thank you even more for your kind words."

"Well," Neri said briskly, turning away. "Let us finish cleaning you up, as the captain ordered."

They washed away blood and dirt. Then they marveled over the strange half-garment as Ziva stepped into first one leg opening and then the other. As the padded legs slid over the chaffed skin of her thighs, the garment made more sense.

"That is a startling piece of clothing," Neri commented. "What are you to wear on the top?"

"Captain Naaman said my tunic will hang over it. It is meant to simplify riding astride."

With a scrunched-up face, Neri picked up Ziva's soiled tunic and shook out the wrinkles. No amount of shaking nor brushing could remove the ground-in dirt, let alone the blood stains. "I could wash it," Neri volunteered. "But it would not dry in time for your departure this afternoon."

Ziva's mother had woven the tunic with her own hands. The last gift she would have from Imma. "I will wash it and bring it wet. May I wait in this room, perhaps be given some food while it dries? Or I could cover myself with the cloak if I must come into the public room."

Just then there was a knock at the door. Ziva quickly wrapped the cloak around her while Neri went to answer. The man who had gone to the marketplace stood in the adjacent room, folded cloth of a soft rosy color clutched in his fist. *Rafiq.*

He looked past Neri to Ziva, holding forth the tunic. "From the captain, to replace your bloodied tunic. He specified it should be larger than you need so it will fall over the riding garment once you are on the horse."

Ziva clutched the neck of the cloak she'd been wearing, nodded, but did not approach. "I thank you."

Neri took hold of the pink garment. "She will be out shortly." The soldier stepped back, and she shut the door.

The tunic was indeed loose and nearly swept the floor. Ziva took care not to step on it. Slits on each side revealed the legs of the padded trousers, but they simply appeared to be an underskirt.

Neri stood back, a finger under her chin, and studied her. "A sash will shorten it," she pronounced, then hurried to a wooden trunk standing in the corner. She pulled out a wide girdle, embroidered in pinks, reds, and blues.

Ziva held up both hands. "Oh, no! Something simpler. Do you have a length of rope?"

"But this is so pretty, and it matches the tunic perfectly."

"Exactly."

"The new garment is huge. You need something to hold it in place, or you will stumble about. Come now, I want you to have it."

Ziva sighed. "You are kind, but don't you see? I am traveling alone with a company of soldiers. I don't want to be pretty."

Neri sighed and reluctantly returned the sash to the wooden box. Ziva was also disappointed. Her fingers had itched to stroke the finely decorated belt.

Yet as she had told Neri, she was no longer a cherished daughter, watched over by her abba. Yes, the captain meant her as a gift for his wife, and such a gift should not be sullied. Still, Ziva did not trust these men of Aram, not one. Oh, how she missed her father's dagger.

She sucked in her breath with a gasp. "I had a dagger strapped to my thigh, but it was taken from me while I was unconscious. Do you—"

"Oh no, I could not give you a knife," Neri blurted. "Why, if they found one in your possession, they would beat you, perhaps even kill you."

Ziva stared at the floor. Neri was right. Then Neri would also be punished.

"I have an idea." Neri rummaged through the trunk again and handed Ziva a plain, woven sash. Then she ran into the public room, returning shortly with a clay jar topped with a tightly fitted lid. When she opened it, the stench of fish filled the room, and she handed Ziva a handful of dried, salted fish. "Tie the sash around you. Tuck the fish inside. Keep one in your hand."

Ziva obeyed. What was this about? It was certainly an offensive smell. Was it meant to keep the soldiers at a distance?

Perhaps more concerning, what would Captain Naaman think about this smell permeating the new tunic he had bought her?

Neri deftly removed the window lattice and whistled softly through the opening. The dog poked its head through, salivating and baring its teeth. He looked at Ziva and made a deep grumbling sound.

"This is Emet, my faithful friend. Come and feed him." Neri held out another dried fish. "Don't mind his teeth. He smiles like that when I whistle. Frightening, eh? Can you whistle?"

Jaedon had taught her, that day in the vineyard. But remembering, Ziva could only stare.

Neri waited, but when Ziva did not move, she came to stand beside her and whistled again. "Come, Emet. Get ready, Ziva. I want him to attach to you."

The dog leapt through the window, rushed toward Ziva,

and tried to take the food from her fingers. She froze, trying not to jump away. His tongue felt strange on her flattened palm, like wet, slippery leather, and a strangled yelp squeaked from her lips. He made the grumbling sound again, but he waved his tail like a flag.

"He likes you," Neri said. "After you feed him another fish or two, he will follow you anywhere. He'll sleep beside you if you sneak him a fish head before you retire. And he will defend you to the death."

"He is like a wolf! They will not let him follow us."

"They will. He knows how to behave. People like him. But if you scream … well, he also knows how to misbehave."

Neri spoke to the dog. "Emet! This is Ziva. I want you to watch her." She emphasized the last two words. The dog set his hindquarters on the floor and, ears alert, stared intently into her eyes.

"Good boy!" Neri said.

Then he leaped forward and licked her face. Laughing, she pushed him away, then she turned back to Ziva. "Now he knows you are his responsibility. I will keep him tied up until you have traveled a distance from the inn, and then I will send him to you. Of course he will track the fish. He loves fish, don't you Emet boy?" Neri grabbed the loose skin on either side of the dog's jaw and shook his big head back and forth.

The dog thumped his tail on the floor, grinning stupidly. "He will catch up with you by dark, when he grows hungry. If you need him before, just call. He will come."

"Won't the innkeeper miss him?" Ziva asked.

"He belongs to me. Who do you think keeps me safe in this place? Not the innkeeper, despite his promise and that he relies heavily on me. Don't worry for me. Emet disappears for long periods of time, but our customers know he always returns when I need him. It keeps them respectful, never knowing when he will turn up. When you have reached your new mistress, you can send him back if you no longer need him. Just say, 'Go find Neri.'

"This I can do for you. He will bond to you and stay, unless you send him away. So if you come to love him, keep him with you."

"Oh, no—you need him."

"Emet is special, but I can easily find another starving dog. I seem to be good at training. I will miss my friend, but I am glad to help you in this way."

Tentatively, Ziva stroked the dog's big head. His tongue lolled and his eyes drifted half-closed. "What if the captain smells this fish on me before we even leave? Or discovers the supply and takes it from me?"

"Remember the stew simmering on the hearth, made of fish and root vegetables? No one will think the smell comes from you."

Neri raised her finger to her chin and frowned thoughtfully. "Besides," she said slowly, "Come with me and help serve the stew to your soldiers and our other customers. That way, they will link the smell to their meal. They will expect the two of us to eat together, apart from the men. Believe me, by the time you rejoin them, they all will smell like fish. But I have told Emet to watch *you*."

Neri told the dog to wait, pointing to a mat. He ran over, grabbing up what looked like an old sandal. Ziva giggled, transfixed at his speed and seeming cheerful obedience.

Neri grinned. "Smart, isn't he? He'll wait there until I call him. Or scream." She winked.

Ziva trailed in Neri's wake through the common room, now filled to capacity. She spotted the captain and his soldiers in a corner close to the door, where they all sat with their backs to the wall. They kept their eyes trained on the door as if they expected Hebrew rescuers to plunge through at any moment.

And well they should! After all, Biny, Jaedon, and their friends had retrieved the children stolen from the first village. A tremor of hope rippled up her spine. Was it possible? Might they come for her?

No. The messenger had only just come to Gischala, bringing Jaedon's letter. There was no reason for another to come for months. Unless Jaedon sent another letter. But why should he? She'd had it only days, no time to write an answer. At least she'd had time to read it over several times. Time to imagine tenderness in his description of planting apples, regard, if not love, in his offer to plaster walls. But there was no reason to expect him to come bearing a *ketubah* before early summer.

As she passed the captain's party, a soldier nudged Naaman, jutting his chin toward her. She kept her face bowed. She was a servant, after all. They must realize it was fitting that she help Neri serve dinners to thank her for treating her wound.

The smell of fish and murmurs of hungry men drifted over the room. Behind a low half wall, a sweating man stood over a steaming pot. He turned, his black beard bristling. The innkeeper.

He glared at Neri. "There you are, girl. Get your tray over here fast." Then, apparently noticing Ziva for the first time, he swung his head in her direction. "Well. You've brought help at least." He raised his voice. "Move your feet. Hungry customers out there."

Neri handed her a tray, silently mouthing, *'Watch me.'* Then moving ahead, she grabbed a stack of empty bowls, clattered them across her tray, and bustled over to the innkeeper. He filled each bowl to within a finger's width of its top, then brusquely jerked his head toward the crowd.

Ziva quickly repeated Neri's actions. Her tray was quaking only a little as she approached the innkeeper. Neri took a step ahead but seemed to be counting her bowls while she waited for the innkeeper to fill Ziva's. When he finished, she turned and followed Neri around the half wall, back toward the customers.

Ziva slid her gaze across the room. Strange, so large a crowd of men and boys. Thirty? No, nearing forty. Had they no wives nor mothers to feed them at home? Who were all these?

She began distributing bowls around low tables, playing a guessing game. Sifted wheat chaff on shoulder. *Farmer.* Smell of camel. Easy. *Camel driver.* Wide grin, silver hoops in his ears. *Glib merchant.* So many travelers. Each with his own hidden history.

This world was so different from her quiet life cradled in the hills, where a man strayed no farther from home than a hunt would take him. She picked up the last bowl in her tray, set it in front of her customer, and—

A tray's edge jammed into her shoulder—"Oof, my apologies!" Hot, slimy liquid gushed down the front of her tunic. Neri appeared, grabbed a cloth, and began dabbing it over blobs of fish stew. The rag felt wetter than Ziva's tunic, if that were possible.

With a final dab to Ziva's forehead—*had any of the stew even splattered there?*—Neri said, "I am very sorry. I will finish serving. Get a bowl for yourself. Eat by the hearth, if you wish, or in my room if you prefer. Again, my apologies." Then she winked, turned, and shoulders shaking, carried her empty tray back to the innkeeper and stewpot.

Ziva followed. As she rounded the half-wall, Neri handed her a filled bowl and a damp cloth. Well, at least she could clean the worst of the fish from her tunic before they left, but not enough for the dog to lose the scent.

As she walked back toward Neri's room, she glanced around at the patrons. Most ate stolidly, heads down, enjoying their stew. A few looked past her to Neri, who was already bringing refills. None seemed concerned with the soup-covered maid servant who trudged toward a closed door.

None but the captain, who eyed her carefully. And Rafiq, who stood and walked out to the courtyard where they'd arrived. Where he'd have a clear view of the window in Neri's room.

Chapter Twenty-Six

*I love the Lord, for he heard my voice; he heard my
cry for mercy. Because he turned his ear to me,
I will call on him as long as I live.
Psalm 116:1-2*

Trade Route, Hazor to Damascus, later that day
Ziva

THOUGH ZIVA SPOTTED EMET SKULKING THROUGH the
underbrush as the sun sank, none of the soldiers seemed to
notice. At first, she wondered how the dog knew to go to
ground, until she remembered he had growled at her at first.
She ducked her chin to hide a smile. Inherently suspicious,
that one. She respected the dog more and more.

Even keeping his distance, he should have no trouble
tracking her. The smell of fish was terrible, and though
Captain Naaman commented once that she should wash her
tunic when they stopped at a stream, he said no more on the
subject.

They soon left the well-traveled route that the soldiers
had taken to Hazor, heading across a plain with a barely
perceptible slope. Though she had promised she would not
escape, Ziva took note of the narrow road they followed, its
curious black color, and deep wagon ruts.

Next, they rode through lush fields. Barley hung over
both sides of the narrow dirt road, and the soldiers helped
themselves to the raw grain as they rode. The captain
plucked several heads, handing a couple back to her. Still
green, the sun-warmed kernels were soft, plump, and tasted
sweet on her tongue.

Wearing the Aramean trousers, Ziva now rode astride
behind Captain Naaman. Though the foreign garment
seemed strange, she felt more confident with both legs
gripping the horse's sides instead of precariously seated
sideways. Since they'd left the inn, she had grown used to
the horse's swaying walk, even the jounce of the trot to which
the captain had several times nudged it. Still, her muscles

ached, especially her back and thighs.

Thank you, Yahweh, for telling the captain I should have this riding garment.

Despite her soreness, she gripped the saddle and dared to lean over the horse's side. What strange black dirt it walked upon!

Naaman sat back in the saddle, slowing the horse still more. "Do you need to stop?"

"No, sir. I … I am only curious about the dirt. I have never seen this color."

"No?" He pointed to a cone-shaped mountain peak aways off in the distance. "That is an old volcano. There are several more throughout the land, and though my grandfather learned from his grandfather that they once spat out a fiery flow, neither of them were alive to witness the spectacle. This black dirt is the reminder of that long-ago time." He waved his hand to indicate the field. "Crops flourish in the soil."

Would the grapes of Gilgal or date palms of Gischala grow sweeter in this soil? The thought squeezed her throat like a fist, as other thoughts had done since she woke to a world without family, home, or country.

She did not forget them, not for a moment, but there were those times when the arrows struck especially deep, and Ziva ached with pain she could not banish. Oh, how she'd like to spew pain on her captors like that ancient fiery molten flow from these mountains!

Yet … Captain Naaman had treated her kindly. *Thus far.*

He had told her the truth. *But had he?* What if all back home were searching for her? She had not seen them dead.

Neither had she seen anyone from her settlement at the slave auction. Not even her friend Mara, who was so near Ziva's age. She should have been of equal value to the raiders. As she mused over the time before the attack, she remembered her brother crawling into the underbrush. Wait. Had she actually seen him? No. Only the movement of yellow broom branches falling back into place. It must have been him.

Had he escaped? No. If she had seen movement, the man who had attacked her was right there. He would have seen what she did. He would—she tried to close her mind to the image of the club that had felled her, swinging again. Failing, she choked, and then she was sobbing against the back of Naaman's tunic.

He stopped the horse, leapt off, and swung her to the ground.

"I want my brother. My imma," she cried. "What did you do to them?"

He pressed his hands to both sides of her head, trying to lock gazes with her. "No. I swear to you. No, I *do not* swear. But I tell you, I was not at Gischala."

She sneered, curling her lip. Let him kill her, too. "You are the captain of your king's armies. You are responsible for the raids." She grabbed his hands, trying to pull loose, then she roared like a beast and began kicking, trying to do as her father had taught her, but she only stumbled and fell. He grabbed her by the waist, turning her around, so her kicks flailed into air.

She heard laughter from the soldiers, but Naaman barked something in Aramean that silenced them. He set her down, murmuring words she could not understand, then she heard, "I am sorry about your imma, your brother. I was not there. It is right for you to be sad, but I promise—"

Then she heard the growling, saw a yellow flash of fur and teeth. *Emet.* The dog grabbed the captain's arm. One of the soldiers galloped toward them, his spear poised to throw.

"No, Captain! The dog knows me—thinks you were hurting me. Emet, no!"

The dog sat, held on a moment longer, then let go. Naaman shoved his flat palm into the air and shouted at the soldier. "Hold."

The soldier stopped a few lengths away but circled them.

Emet narrowed his eyes and crouched. Ziva grasped him by the ruff and felt a piece of twine. Neri must have tied it around his neck. Perhaps it would help Ziva to manage the big animal. She didn't want him to leap for the soldier and get himself killed.

"This is your dog?" the captain asked. "From Gischala?"

She paused. She wanted to lie, tell him yes. He seemed regretful. She should take advantage of that. She should—

Yahweh, forgive my errant thoughts. Help me keep to your ways.

"He is not my dog. He belongs to Neri, but she showed him to me at the inn. I fed him."

Emet shoved her with his nose, leaving another smudge on her tunic. "He must smell fish on me."

"I imagine he does." Naaman reached slowly for the twine around Emet's neck, pulling it to reveal a long trailing end. "It appears he was tied and escaped to follow you."

The broken twine seemed to tell that story, but she knew Neri had sent him. If he asked …

Emet nudged her once more, and when she stepped back, he followed and lipped the folded edge of her sash. Finally, she pulled out pieces of broken fish and offered them. The dog's tongue felt rough and warm on her flattened palm.

Ziva hadn't meant to reveal the hidden fish, but Emet's appearance had left her few options. She glanced at the captain, who watched their interaction. Had the captain worked out that the fish were intended to attract the dog? Or did he think she hid them for herself, fearful she wouldn't be fed?

"The dog wants to protect you. Good. We will keep it with us." He looked up as Rafiq rode close.

"Captain, there is a stream in the valley. Shall I ride ahead and begin making camp?"

The captain shook his head. "It is one thing to shop alone in Hazor, but in this remote location we stay together."

Naaman remounted, then leaned over to help Ziva. The dog dashed back and forth, whining. He'd been ordered to watch her, and now she was out of reach. He made a lunge for the horse's heels, nipping air.

Watching him narrowly, the captain muttered. "Can you calm the dog, Ziva? If he acts aggressive with my warhorse, he'll be kicked."

"Come, Emet." Remembering that Neri had whistled, Ziva pursed her lips and managed a whispery sort of trill. Emet cocked his ears, and when the horse moved out, he followed, bushy tail curled over his back.

"Hold tight," the captain said. He nudged the horse into a rocking gait which swept them over the ground at amazing speed. The hood of Ziva's cloak blew to her shoulders, and rows of barley blurred as the horse's hooves pounded past. She turned to look at the others, who galloped close.

Her hair whipped over her face, and she shook it behind her shoulders, where it lifted and fell with every stride.

The captain called out. "Are you all right?"

"Yes," she said tightly. She couldn't bring herself to admit she loved the wind on her face. Tangling her hair. How could her thoughts summon the feel of Imma's gentle fingers combing the strands?

The memory warred with pain. How could she enjoy a breeze on her face? Her imma was gone.

They continued loping until they reached the end of the grain field. Then they slowed for the horses to pick their way down the slope to the valley with more care.

As they descended, Ziva braced her palms against the saddle to hold herself from sliding forward. The dog trotted alongside, keeping even with the black horse who trained a dark eye on the dog, as if gauging its intent.

Horse and dog must have reached an understanding, for they walked together companionably as they reached the valley. It was carpeted with rolling layers of grass, some green and lush, others still tinged with the gold and rust from cooler nights.

A little farther, Ziva glimpsed a ribbon of blue winding across their way. The stream Rafiq had mentioned, where they'd camp. They were now deep into enemy territory. Her chances of being rescued, or escaping, grew dim. Her muscles tightened with the reflex to flee despite all the jolting they'd received. Why had she promised not to try to escape? She would not be able to sleep, even with Emet beside her.

Then she remembered what the captain had done after Emet had bit him. He stopped his soldier from killing the dog. He'd said Emet only wanted to protect her—and they should keep him.

The Lord was using this man, this godless man, to keep her safe. *Thank you, Lord. I see what you are doing.*

They neared the stream, having passed several level places she would have thought ideal for making camp. One in particular was protected on three sides by oak trees, and a ring of stones testified that previous travelers had warmed themselves in that spot, but the captain led them ahead to the stream.

Whooping, the soldiers leapt off their horses and led them to water. The animals followed willingly, splashing into the stream and slurping loudly.

The captain rode his horse toward the water, but did not dismount nor help Ziva down. Rafiq waited beside them.

Ziva shifted her weight behind the saddle. Rafiq seemed to hold himself aloof from the soldiers. He did not ride with them, nor laugh at their boasts. Instead, he constantly looked around—kept an eye on her.

Was he a second-in-command to Naaman? Or a personal servant? She knew very little of military ranks—or of servants, for that matter. The only servant she had any knowledge of was Elisha, who had served Elijah and succeeded him as leader of the prophets. Was Rafiq in a similar position?

"I am going to ride ahead with Ziva," Naaman said, speaking directly to Rafiq. "There is a quiet pool surrounded by reeds, if it is as I remember. After the horses drink their fill and the men fill their waterskins, take them to set up camp where we have stayed before."

Rafiq nodded, turned, and rode off to join the soldiers.

Slowing the horse to walk along the stream's bank, Naaman spoke over his shoulder. "There is privacy in this place I am taking you."

Ziva felt a pulse beat in her throat. She swallowed. *Yahweh, I thought you were using him to keep me safe. Please do not let me be mistaken.*

She heard a little whine from the ground and glanced down to see Emet trotting alongside, grinning up at her.

His mood was infectious. She smiled back but stayed alert.

Ahead she saw a rocky outcropping and a thicket of tall reeds. The captain stopped before the reeds, helped her down, and untied a small bag from the front of the saddle. He dropped the horse's reins to brush the ground and, as if tied, the animal cropped eagerly at the grass.

"Follow me," the captain ordered, following the stream

bank then veering behind the reeds. Heart thudding, she froze, reaching for Emet. He pushed his head beneath her hand, and she tucked her fingers under the twine. She wasn't following the captain back there. She would be completely out of sight of the others, what if he—

He strode back around the reeds and toward her. "Why are you still"—he stopped speaking. Then he spoke very quietly. "Of course. You are yet afraid of me. I meant only to show you the way."

He stepped away from the reeds, gesturing toward where he had been. "The pool is just here. You can kneel on a grassy bank and wash your tunic. Or you can get in the pool yourself. It is no deeper than your chest."

When she hesitated, he said, "I have said you will be well treated. I only want you to care for my wife, Amirah. She is … I would not … You have nothing to fear from me. But take the dog with you. I will wait by the rocks, within earshot, should you need anything." Then he extended the bag he'd retrieved from the saddle. "This is for you. Your other tunic is inside."

She took the bag, soft leather with a flap and tie closure. She felt something heavy shift when she tucked it under her arm. "I thank you."

Turning, she patted Emet, then tried Neri's command. "Emet, come." He snapped to her side and followed as she walked behind the reeds.

The pool was shallow and inviting. Grass led to its edge, with rocks on the bank and then leading into the water, where she could scrub the tunic and spread it to dry.

She untied the bag, finding her old tunic inside, but also a pomegranate, and a clay jar. The jar's lid was secured with a square of leather, around which a narrow twine was wrapped and knotted. Curious, she unknotted and removed the lid. She had inhaled this aromatic fragrance once before.

Her father had traveled near Jezreel to deliver a promised ram. When he returned, he presented her mother with a clay jar, looking much like this. When Imma lifted the lid, she had thrown her arms around his neck and kissed him on the lips, right in front of Ziva.

"Is it all right?" The captain's voice came from the

direction of the rock cropping.

"The pool? Yes... thank you for the borinth."

"Rafiq thought you would find it useful," he called. Then he said in a more hushed tone that she nevertheless heard quite clearly. "Although I did not think you would have need of it quite so soon."

"I fear it will take me a while to get the smell out," she called back. "But I will hurry."

"No need. My horse is eating, and I will rest while I wait. Rafiq and the others will see to the camp and to supper."

Ziva placed the bag near the pool's edge. She stepped out of the riding garment and decided not to wash it. After all, it had not been doused by the soup, and its thick padding might not dry overnight.

Carrying the pomegranate in one hand and the jar in the other, she waded in up to her neck, careful not to step on the long tunic. She set the jar and fruit on a boulder that protruded above the surface, then pulled the over-sized and dripping garment over her head.

Laying it against the boulder, she spread the sweet-smelling gel over the worst spots and scrubbed it. She let it soak while she took her pomegranate toward the mouth of the pool, cracked it into chunks, and bit into the sweet, juicy kernels. She admired their glistening red beauty. She continued to eat, and the red juice trickled over her hands. A gentle current led back to the stream, carrying the sticky juices away.

Emet paced the bank where she'd waded in, seemingly troubled by her distance from him. She patted the water's surface. "Come, Emet. Come." But he grew even more agitated at her invitation.

"No matter," she said. "Wait there."

Then she fully immersed herself and used the borinth in her hair. When she finished, she squeezed water through the tunic once more, wrung it out, and tossed it onto the grass. She picked up the borinth jar and stepped out of the water.

The dog ran up to her wriggling all over. "Good boy.

Good watching." He definitely did not like water. Somehow, that endeared him to her. Not afraid to tackle soldiers or horses but afraid to get his feet wet.

Well, she would just take care not to drown.

From the bag on the bank, she retrieved her old tunic, dried herself with it, and slid it on. She walked around the thicket, back toward the place she'd last heard the captain's voice.

She flinched at the sight of him splayed on the ground, unmoving, his mouth agape.

He was dead! Her hand flew to her throat. Her gaze shot around wildly for signs of a struggle. Had he been struck from behind as she had?

Where were his soldiers? Rafiq? Had they—

A loud snore interrupted her panic.

The captain yawned loudly, ran his hand over his face, and sat up. "Oh. You've finished?" Then his eyebrows creased. "What is it?"

"I … I thought you were dead."

One side of his mouth turned up. "You are disappointed, I suppose."

"No, I …" She was surprised to realize she was not. Instead, she was relieved he was not dead, even though he might have been responsible for the deaths of her family and friends.

Might be responsible? Did she believe that?

No. Somehow, she believed his assertion that he had not been there. Why? Because of a little thing.

He had started to swear, stopped himself, and then stated without oath that he did not attack her village.

There was something … honorable about the captain. Even though he was Aramean.

Rafiq and the soldiers had set up an orderly camp. At its center, a pot of what smelled like lentil stew simmered over a fire. Even Arameans ate lentils. A wiry soldier stirred and tossed in handfuls of bitter greens. A stack of cloaks and seven sleeping mats were arranged around the fire like petals on a sunflower.

The captain seated her on one of several logs placed between the mats. The warmth of the fire felt soothing and worked to dry her still-damp hair. Emet stretched out by her feet, ears cocked forward, as he watched the men line up by the kettle.

She stroked his head, gratitude filling her. Neri had taught him well.

It seemed obvious the cloaks were for her. Each man had his mat, and for her, they had contrived a bed with several of their cloaks. Not all, certainly. The nights were cool.

Rafiq walked toward her carrying two bowls. Emet stood and growled. Rafiq paused, looking to her for direction.

"Down, Emet." She put her hand on his neck, feeling for the twine. He squatted on his haunches, poised to leap up again if necessary.

Rafiq slowly closed the distance between them, handing her one bowl but holding onto the other.

"This is for the dog." He raised it to his lips and sipped some broth. "You can see that it is not poisoned." Slowly, he placed it beside her. "Perhaps you will want to observe me awhile."

Ziva's bowl was topped with a large round of flat bread. Mulling over Rafiq's comment, she tore off half and gave the piece to Emet. He swallowed it cheerfully in three gulping bites. She didn't believe any of the soldiers would poison Emet, not when the captain had spoken for him. Yet she depended on the dog to keep her safe, so she waited to give him the stew until Rafiq and the captain came to sit near her, one on each side.

She tried drinking from her bowl but found the stew to be too thick to swallow without chewing. So she tore off pieces from her remaining loaf and scooped up mouthfuls of lentils and wilted greens. The savory mixture warmed her insides. Eating slowly, she thought of home. How many times had she helped Imma make a similar stew?

She watched as the other men filled their bowls and found places around the fire. Emet swiveled his head back and forth, his dark eyes suspicious of their nearness. He stood again and leaned heavily against her side.

Signaling with a lifted shoulder and a tipped head, the captain stood and casually moved his log and mat several steps farther from hers. Nodding, Rafiq did the same, and the dog slowly lowered himself back to the ground.

The soldiers talked amongst themselves, giving playful shoves, and starting to pass wineskins. The captain pointed at one of the skins, spoke sharply, and shook his head.

Why?

Six pairs of eyes turned on her, disgruntled over the denial of wine.

When they realized she watched, the soldiers flicked their gazes away, corking the wineskins, and instead drank from their waterskins.

Thoughtfully, she studied them. She knew none of their names and couldn't understand much of their language. How would she deal with these men in the future? Were they only returning to their homes after military duty? The captain had said he was not at Gischala, but had these soldiers attacked her village?

She realized she did not want to know.

When the stew bowls were emptied, two men gathered them for cleaning. When one came to collect hers, Ziva quickly took Emet's bowl and stacked it into hers. The soldier gave her a small smile, but kept his distance from the dog, who gave him a steady stare.

The captain noisily cleared his throat, catching her attention. "Soon all will retire, and tomorrow we will leave before dawn." He shifted his gaze. "The thicket by the pool provides privacy. I will walk you there."

He lit a torch from the fire and led her to the thicket, waiting again by the rocks where he had slept. Now, he turned his back but held the torch aloft so she and Emet could see to make their way behind the reeds and return without stumbling.

She didn't suppose Emet would stumble, torch or no. It was strange to have this animal at her side wherever she went. Heaviness clouded her heart, remembering how Aharon had also followed her everywhere. He had been helpless and clingy. Now she was the helpless one.

She splashed water on her face and smoothed her hair.

How she wished she could smooth away her yawning despair so easily. She crossed her arms across her chest, embracing the roughly woven cloth. She would sleep better in the tunic her mother had woven.

Imma. Abba. Aharon. How I long to be with you.

When she finished, she walked toward the light. The captain was still standing with his back to her, his torch a beacon.

"I am ready," she said.

He nodded silently and led the way back.

They passed the dark forms of soldiers kneeling at a narrow section of the stream, washing the bowls and cooking pot.

As they walked back into the camp, Ziva observed preparations for parching grain. The fire, which had burned low after supper, had been built up with more branches. The cook-soldier spread fallen leaves over top, and the fire hissed and steamed. When tendrils of flame began to lick their way through the leaves, he grabbed a satchel and shook out heads of grain, still in their outer hulls, over its surface.

After a while, the first men returned with the pot and bowls. They helped the cook repeat the process and turn the wheat ears.

She sat on the log to watch. How familiar, this fire-lit scene. The times she had foraged with Abba and others from her village, when green emmer wheat was plump and sweet. The smell of charr from the bristle and outer hulls as they burned. Blackened hands when they threshed away the chaff.

The cook raked the roasted wheat from the fire and spread them to cool on a tarp.

Ziva's mouth watered as she anticipated parched grain. Perhaps she would be given a taste tonight, but more likely, since they were to leave before dawn, it would be kept to break their fast later.

Briefly, she wondered if she should tell the captain she could help with this task. But her throat tightened at the thought. She did not know how to speak to this man about such things, about servant-to-master things.

What would she say? 'Master, I am well versed in

parching grain?' Would she call him Master? Or Captain, as the soldiers did? He had spoken to her about her duties, that she would serve his wife. It would probably be best if she watched more, talked less. Unless the captain asked her a question.

"Ziva, try to sleep now. Keep the dog close."

"Yes … Master," she said, trying the word. She felt herself frown.

He paused and then said, "I prefer 'Captain.'"

"Yes, Captain." Allowing her to address him thus put her level with his soldiers. At the thought, a nervous giggle threatened to overtake her. What? The reaction made no sense. Somehow she restrained it.

She burrowed into the pile of cloaks, feeling immediate warmth as she wrapped herself in the thick top garment. She counted two underneath. Which soldiers had gone without to keep her warm? Emet whined, circled, then tucked himself against her.

The captain walked away, speaking first to Rafiq, then the others, one by one. Some of them looked over at her and nodded as they spoke. They were all respectful of the captain, even when he turned his back and moved on to speak with another.

Ziva closed her eyes, comforted by the warm, furry body beside her. Even his smell of dusty pelt felt reassuring. She heard diminishing sounds in the camp. Soldiers tending to horses, filling waterskins, packing items that would not be needed in the morning, all the while speaking to each other in hushed voices, words she could not understand, but that did not sound threatening.

One by one, she heard the heavy sound of bodies dropping onto mats, of turning, grumbling, and sighing. Emet nuzzled her, then lifted his head to watch. Stillness fell over the camp and her breathing slowed.

Chapter Twenty-Seven

*A wife of noble character who can find? She is
worth far more than rubies. Her husband has full
confidence in her and lacks nothing of value. She
brings him good, not harm, all the days of her life.*
Proverbs 31:10-12

Shunem
Gehazi

A FEW WHITE FLAKES FLUTTERED DOWN and soon the dry grass
was dusted with snow. Gehazi shouldered both travel packs
and slowed to match Elisha's pace. The prophet had been
favoring his right leg for the last few days. Should he offer his
arm?

They'd been on the road for nearly two months, trekking
a circular route teaching the Torah and making followers.
Then Elisha insisted they climb Mount Carmel before leaving
the area. There, he seemed to find spiritual strength, walking
where his predecessor had communed with the Lord. Much
of their journey seemed a success, but the distance and steep
trek up Carmel had taken a toll on the prophet.

Gehazi anticipated that evening's fine dinner and restful
sleep, courtesy of the kind woman who, after Elisha's first
visit, petitioned her husband to build a private room on their
roof, set apart for Elisha's use whenever he passed this way.

There it was. The nearest of the clustered houses,
highest on the hill. The snug room, with its view of Mount
Carmel's crags, perched above the other rooflines. Gehazi
noticed someone coming down the hill. Two people with a
donkey, one riding, one leading.

It appeared they were on the same path. Why would
these two leave the city so late in the afternoon, especially
since the falling snow had increased?

Perhaps the pair felt the same hesitation, for one
dismounted at the foot of Shunem's hill, and the other
jumped on the donkey's back and thumped his heels until
the animal swiftly trotted in their direction.

Before long, Gehazi recognized Tal, Samuel's servant. Was it Malka who watched, adjusting her head covering to block the falling snow?

When Tal reached them, he jumped off the donkey. "Please, Master Elisha, let the donkey carry you to the city. The mistress sent me ahead for such a purpose."

Elisha nodded, grimacing a little as he swung his leg over the sturdy little creature.

Tal handed the prophet a sack. "She also sent food. Said you would not have eaten."

Elisha reached into the sack, pulled out a folded flatbread, and handed it to Gehazi.

Gehazi's stomach rumbled. There was no reason to deny his hunger, so he thanked his master and took a bite. Fresh bread spread with warm cheese. The best thing he'd eaten since the last time they were here.

Tal led the donkey at a faster pace than Elisha had been able to walk. His hands free, the prophet now held a folded round in his hand, a bite missing from its edge. "Samuel has certainly found a wife of noble character," he said between bites.

"Yes," said Tal. "I would do anything for the mistress. She took me in as a child when my parents died of a wasting disease. I have lived with them many years. She is the best of women."

When they reached Malka, she clucked over the two of them and accompanied them back to her house. Elisha had tried to climb down from the donkey, but she said, "Do not let him, Tal. I saw him limping. Make sure he does not climb down until we reach the house."

Then she hurried on ahead, muttering that she must oversee supper preparations, and something about Samuel being worthless in the kitchen.

The three men grinned at each other and followed at the donkey's pace.

It was a noteworthy supper and Malka received appropriate praise. Afterwards, as Elisha tried to respond to Samuel and Malka's interest in their travels and teaching, he failed to stifle a yawn. "I am sorry for my rudeness. Perhaps I should go upstairs and rest."

"Of course," said Samuel. "We can hear more in the morning."

Gehazi followed Elisha up the stairs, noting he led with his good leg and steadied himself with the rail. Once in the room, he sat heavily on his bed, a folded wool blanket at its end. He did not light the lamp, though he had often sat on the chair and studied by its light before sleep.

Instead, Elisha recited the *Shema* in the dark, then prayed, *Master of the Universe, help me to forgive anyone who has harmed me, as you have forgiven me. Thank you for safe travel today. As my weariness reminds me, I need sleep, I thank you for this family and their kindness to us. Give us the rest we need, and please bring us safely to our destination.*

After he chanted a Psalm of praise, the prophet removed one sandal then paused, holding it in his hand. "I wish to do something for Malka, Gehazi. Say to her, 'You have gone to all this trouble for us. Now what can be done for you? Can we speak on your behalf to the king or the commander of the army?'"

Elisha dropped the sandal, slid out of the other, and paused. "Sometimes it is helpful to have the ear of the king. Perhaps Malka and Samuel need help with a civil grievance or Shunem needs soldiers stationed nearby."

With a quiet groan, the prophet lay back on his bed. He was already snoring as Gehazi padded down the stairs. Below, Malka bent over her worktable cleaning the dishes from supper. She glanced at him in surprise. "Samuel and Tal are seeing to the animals, if you wish to see one of them."

"My master asked me to speak with you."

Gehazi repeated Elisha's question. Although King Joram had not rewarded Elisha with riches when God helped Israel during the Moabite rebellion, Gehazi knew the king and his generals held a genial attitude toward the prophet. He could ask a favor for Malka, and it would be granted.

"No, I have need of nothing," she said. "I live among my own people, and I am content."

She was content? Gehazi felt surprise crease his brow. What kind of reply was that? The woman had gone far beyond feeding him and the prophet as they passed through her region. When offered royal favor, shouldn't she accept it?

Well, of course she was content. She and Samuel owned their house, a donkey, an ox, and a large field in Esdraelon's fertile soil. Though their house was large, they lived plainly, and the couple had only Tal to care for.

Only Tal.

Gehazi thought a moment, wished her *lilah tov*, and wearily climbed the stairs for the second time. Elisha's snores had subsided to whispers of breath.

Gehazi unrolled his mat, lay down, and covered himself with his cloak. Immediately he was chilled. The cloak was damp from the snow. He flung it over the chair to dry, then he heard footsteps on the stairs.

"Gehazi."

He walked to the door and looked down.

"I forgot to give you this." Malka handed him a folded wool blanket.

In the morning, Gehazi repeated his conversation with Malka.

Elisha threw up his hands in obvious frustration. "What can be done for her?"

How good it felt to have the solution. "Well," Gehazi said, "she has no child and her husband is old."

Elisha brightened at once. "Call her."

When Malka stood before them, Elisha said, "About this time next year, you shall embrace a son."

The woman flinched and nested her palms over her heart. "No! Do not lie to me, man of God."

Gehazi saw hope in her eyes, and he could not help smiling. He remembered Lital, when she told him she was expecting their fourth and her hope that it would be a girl.

Hope. When it seems too good to be true, but ...

Would it be true for Malka? Yes. Elisha had said.

No, *God* had said this blessing would come.

But ... why not for Lital? She was a good woman. The best. She had cared for their sons and for him, despite all. Why not Lital?

Why must his wife live in a borrowed home, not her own, not among her own people? Why must he be destitute, dependent on Elisha for their sustenance? If only he had some silver put aside, Lital would feel secure. She would look up to him again. Forget his failures. Then, perhaps, a girl child would come.

Chapter Twenty-Eight

Arise, Lord! Lift up your hand, O God.
Do not forget the helpless.
Psalm 10:12

Day 2, the road to Damascus
Ziva

EMET SNARLED AND LEAPT UP BESIDE Ziva, startling her awake. Trembling, she peered into the darkness, making out the dark form of a man standing a few steps away.

"Ziva, wake now and quiet the dog. We leave soon." It was the captain.

Her heartbeat calmed, and she stroked Emet, which soothed her as well as him. Then she rolled the cloaks, stood, and rubbed sleep from her eyes. Once again, the dog stuck to her side. The captain lit a torch and led her away from camp, turning his back as she took care of her needs in the privacy of darkness.

"It will be a long ride today," he said in the dark. "I feel the need to get home as soon as I can."

He had said the journey would take three days. Why was he changing his plan? He sounded worried ... or sad. Maybe it was only the misty dawn, which made everything seem mournful.

"I am ready, Captain. Can I do anything for you?"

He took a deep breath, as if he were seeking a response. Was he surprised by her question? Shouldn't he assign her tasks? She was, after all, his slave.

As he lifted his torch, she squinted at the light.

"Rafiq will have everything in hand. See to it your things are in the satchel."

"I will. If we leave soon, what of the cloaks? Your men were kind to lend them last night."

"Leave them where they are. The owners will reclaim them, except for the large cloak you were given at the"—he hesitated—"where I found you."

Where I found you? As if he had been looking for

someone lost. Not for the first time, he sounded awkward speaking to her. He spoke forthrightly to his men, yet he avoided mentioning the slave market as if averse to bringing her misery to mind. Why did he seem almost ... deferential?

"Yes, sir." She patted Emet's head.

The captain swung the torch away and headed for camp. A dark shape advanced through the darkness, shortly revealed as Rafiq and the black horse, saddled and ready to go.

After the captain mounted and pulled Ziva up behind him, Rafiq handed each of them a small cloth-wrapped packet. "Parched grain to break your fasts."

While daybreak slowly suffused the sky, one soldier scraped dirt over the remains of last night's fire. The others milled around at the edge of camp, where they had tied the horses. One whinnied, another answered, hooves stamped, saddles were adjusted, and the soldiers conversed amongst themselves and to their animals. Before long, the commotion coalesced, and they were on the road.

The horses seemed to enjoy the ground-covering gait that began their journey. Ziva tired long before the captain's sturdy black horse or the dog, who loped easily beside them, but she gritted her teeth and remained silent. When the soldiers finally reined in the horses, it was to a bone-jarring trot that also continued far too long. Finally, they slowed to a walk, and she breathed a prayer. *Thank you, Lord, that the horses finally tired. We might never have stopped.*

"You did well," the captain said. "Do you still have your parched grain?"

"I tucked it in my satchel."

"Good. Eat now, while you have the opportunity."

Ziva bit into smoky grain that crunched lightly as she chewed. She swigged from the waterskin as well, guessing they would pick up the pace again. Soon she learned that she had guessed correctly.

After the sun had passed its zenith, they finally stopped for the midday meal. The captain pointed Ziva and Emet toward a thatch of shrubbery and sent the soldiers and horses in the opposite direction.

Before Ziva reached her destination, she glanced back. Smelling water, the lead horse lifted its nose and began trotting, pulling his soldier down a slope. The others laughed and hurried after them.

Later Ziva walked stiffly toward their voices, her hand pressed against the small of her back. Emet trotted in circles around her, tongue lolling, as if mocking her slow pace.

"It's all very well for you, Emet. You are used to traveling long distances in search of your food." But was he really? Neri had said he ensured her safety at the inn. Had she fed him his meals and kept him close?

She came upon the captain first, walking along an animal trail. He nodded a greeting, then motioned for her to follow him.

Another stream, smaller than yesterday's, bubbled ahead. It was so narrow and shallow she could have lain in its waters, her head on one bank, her feet resting on the other. The trees bordering the stream were old and spaced apart, providing striped shade that lent a greenish cast to the water. Weathered stumps stood among them, revealing their number had been thinned in past years.

Rafiq stood in the stream's center, only his ankles beneath its surface. His horse stood on the bank, its front legs splayed so it could lower its head to drink. Behind Rafiq, she saw a bay tossing its head and snorting in an affronted manner. A gray replied with a squeal, a grunt, and a flash of hooves. Their handlers shouted unintelligible orders, to which neither horse attended.

Emet tensed beside her, but before he could move, Ziva slipped her hand under the twine. He glanced up with an impatient look as if to say, *Let me go, and I'll settle their dispute.*

The soldiers moved the horses farther apart. When all had drunk, the men hobbled their front legs and turned them loose to graze.

Ziva clucked for Emet to sit with her under a tree with roots sinking deep into the water. Leaning back, she picked tares and foxtail from his cream-colored pelt.

Rafiq and one of the soldiers apportioned food—

flatbread, figs, and more parched grain. When he came to her, he cut the ends from several figs before handing them over. After she stashed the bread and grain in her satchel to eat later, she peeled and ate the fruit. Milky sap oozed from the skins onto her hands. She didn't want to get sap on Emet's fur, so she removed her sandals, waded into the cool water, and swished her hands. Though the dog walked with her to the bank, again he refused to step in the water.

If she were home in Gischala, she would lie down and soak in the orchard's seasonal stream to ease her sore muscles, and if she had gone with the women of the settlement, no one would chide her for immodesty. In Gischala, she would not be sore from a ride, and here, on the road to Damascus, she was among enemies.

Enemies?

Yes! Arameans, who had made of her an orphan and a slave.

But none of these had treated her unkindly.

She looked uncertainly at the captain and Rafiq, talking quietly. She turned to watch the others loosen saddles to give the tired horses respite before the next leg of the journey.

Oh! She argued with herself.

Lord, here I am. Lost and confused. Bereft. Where are you? She stared up through the tree branches to the silent blue sky. No answer. Not even a whisper of breeze.

Her troubled mind framed another question. What if the captain had not bought her? On the auction platform, she had been destined for brothels or pagan temples. Had Yahweh sent the captain to save her from such shame?

What happened to Mara in Gischala? Did Yahweh forget her? She had not been sent to Hazor with Ziva. When she was knocked unconscious, had Mara been slain? Or had one of the soldiers taken her for a prize?

Forcing all thought from her mind, she trudged up the bank and returned to her tree. Gathering the cloak and the food she'd stashed, she leaned back and pillowed her head on the cloak. Emet eyed the flatbread. She shared it with him, even gave him a few kernels of the parched grain. He had trouble keeping them inside his narrow jaw, dropping them repeatedly and lapping them up again. Would such fare be enough for him?

Well, if it was not, she supposed he would hunt, but he did seem loath to leave her.

Seeing that the captain and Rafiq were still talking and none of the horses saddled, Ziva decided to rest. She wrapped herself in the cloak and stretched out on the grass. The dog crawled under her arm. His smell was not unpleasant, rather earthy and comforting. He laid his head on a paw, his breath warming her side. He thumped his tail against the ground. Thump, thump, thump. Then he was still. His breathing had slowed. So did hers.

"Ziva."

Her eyes flew open. Again, she woke disoriented, frightened at the strange voice. In moments, however, she recognized the captain, remembered all, and despaired.

Ziva shoved herself up, blinking. The captain had been reaching into her travel pack. Why?

She glanced at Emet, sitting calmly beside her. Why had he not growled?

"I am sorry for falling asleep. What can I do for you, Captain?" She glanced at the horses, quickly noticing their saddles were fastened tight.

"We are leaving. I need nothing. I am glad you slept. We have another long stretch before us. I saw you feed the dog some of your bread. Assuming you are out of yours, I fed him some dried fish."

Ziva nodded, feeling her face grow warm. How little it took to win Emet's friendship. She didn't know whether to feel betrayed by Emet or pleased at the captain's kindness to the dog ... and to her.

Oh, what did it really matter? She had little control over either, so she decided on 'pleased.' She turned her attention toward the journey ahead. Her waterskin was full and the satchel packed, except for the cloak. With another long stretch before them, they would likely travel into the night, so she tied it around her shoulders.

The captain left her and returned riding his horse. "Ready?"

She nodded.

He pulled his boot out of the stirrup and reached down. "Put your foot there as I pull you up."

She did, and he helped her until she'd swung her leg over the horse.

"Can your other foot reach? I shortened the straps."

She felt around with her right foot, sliding on leather and horsehide before she found the leather-wrapped oval. She put her weight on them, lifting herself slightly from the horse's rump. She slid backward. She tried again holding to the back of the saddle. Better.

"Yes. Thank you." She felt more secure, but then she glanced down at the captain's unsecured boots. "What of you? Your feet have no resting place."

"It is nothing. I've ridden without saddle or bridle since boyhood." The captain turned his head and barked out commands to his men, as if he no longer wished to speak of the topic. Why? Did he regret speaking of his childhood? Or consider it weakness to show her kindness?

He lifted the reins. "We'll be moving fast. You can hold on to me."

Ziva tightened her grip on the saddle. It was bad enough to sit so close behind him. "The saddle is easier."

He shrugged. The group headed out at a brisk pace. From her perch behind the saddle, she studied the back of his head, heavily threaded with gray. As her father's had been. She frowned and sucked in air.

She tried to imagine the captain as a boy, but it was impossible to imagine a boy who had a horse to ride so frequently that he became proficient without saddle or bridle. Of course, he was not a village urchin, he came from a wealthy family. They probably owned the horse, a costly animal, not a neighbor's donkey only available for rides on the rare days it wasn't needed to labor in the fields or carry goods to market. Maybe his family had owned a stable full.

What kind of household was she bound for?

It was not long before the group pushed their mounts even faster. Ziva was glad of the stirrups, but even so, as they went on, she tired with the effort of clinging to the saddle. The sun crossed the sky, and the monotony of road passing beneath them caused her eyes to droop. She forced them open—it would not do to fall asleep with the horse galloping at such a pace.

"Ziva, are you doing well?"

The voice jarred her out of her lethargy and she nodded vigorously. As the captain turned to look at her, she widened her eyes. "Yes," she said. "All is well."

He turned back to face the road. It stretched through a wide valley and continued toward a lone structure she could barely make out in the distance. So far. Yet, she dare not tell him she grew tired. She was a slave, and he had told her they must ride past nightfall in order to reach his home today. She must not be the reason for a delay.

She set her jaw and grimly held on. Her body was racked by the pounding of hooves. Her head whipped to and fro by the power of the horse's muscles bunching and extending.

Just when she thought she could go no further, the captain yelled "Hold on!"

With a mighty leap, the horse sailed skyward, and Ziva's body flew backward. Her feet slipped from the stirrups as if they'd been greased. As she fell, she saw the mud puddle. The horse cleared the water, and Ziva slammed onto rock-hard dirt.

When she woke, Emet was licking her face and the captain kneeling beside her. "She's coming round," he tossed over his shoulder to the others, still on their horses. Rafiq jumped down, handing his reins to another soldier.

Ziva tried to sit, but the captain held her shoulders. "Rest. Get your bearings."

She ached all over. Two blows to her head in less than a week left her feeling befuddled, but she must not show weakness. She remembered the auctioneer at the slave market. *Look around you girl. Think this is a family picnic?* A slave did not slow her master's progress.

"I am sorry," she said in as firm a voice as she could manage. "I lost my grip. I will hold on tighter."

"Here, drink." Rafiq held a waterskin to her lips while the captain lifted her up.

She swallowed several gulps then pushed it away, struggling to her feet. "I am ready to go on."

The captain stared at her and then nodded. "Very well, but you will ride in front this time." Then he muttered under his breath, "Foolish horse. I reined him around the puddle."

The captain lifted her onto his saddle, then he leapt behind her onto his horse's rump. Fitting his arms around her he took the reins from Rafiq. "Find the stirrups," he told her. She tried, but only gained one. Rafiq hurried close, shortened both stirrups, and guided her feet inside.

Immediately she felt more secure. "Good," she said.

They started off at a walk, Emet trotting alongside. "Do you not want to gallop?" she asked. "I am ready." She gritted her teeth.

"The horses need a breather. We will walk a while."

While Ziva felt more secure with the captain's arms around her as he held the reins, the black's long strides kept throwing her against his chest. She couldn't hold herself apart. She was simply too exhausted. How long, how long? *Lord, I am helpless. Please help me.*

As they rode, the captain began to speak haltingly, quietly, sometimes obscured by the soldiers' voices. "I have said you will be serving my wife. She has become ill. Although the physician has seen her, he has been unable to help. In fact, she grew worse under his care, and my steward sent him away."

Ziva stared at the captain's hands, clenching and unclenching on the reins. Her pain from the fall, her anxiety over the future, briefly took second place to curiosity about the woman she would serve. And compassion. The woman was ill, and a healer could not help her.

Ziva listened carefully, sensing a reason the captain spoke of his wife. A deeper intention than merely instructing a servant in her duties.

"In service for my king, I have not seen my wife in nearly a year. In my absence, I received reports through my steward and the soldiers guarding my family."

While he was off to war. With Israel? Or other nations? Ziva shifted her weight. "I am sorry your wife is not well. You know nothing of her illness?"

The horse took several steps before the captain answered. "It is an illness of the mind. Our young daughter Kala was killed, and I was not there to comfort Amirah. My dispatches tell me that she will not leave her room. Will not eat."

The horse's ears flipped back briefly, as if listening to the captain's sad tale, then flicked forward again, intent on the trail.

"I am sorry, Captain. Of course your wife is grieving her loss. How old was your daughter?"

"She had not seen twelve years. She was only a little thing"—he sighed—"about your age, I think."

Ziva's first thought was to correct him, tell him she was nearly three years older, but something stopped her. He had not asked, only guessed she was of a similar age to his daughter. Was it a lie to conceal the truth? The command was to not bear false witness against a neighbor. She intended no harm to the captain, and he certainly was not her neighbor. It seemed good that he might associate her, if only in this small way, with his beloved daughter. She would not tell. At least not now.

"When I saw you on the platform—realized you were no older than Kala—I thought your company might ease Amirah's grief."

Ziva felt her forehead crease. She felt compassion for the woman, certainly. She would do all she could to serve her. Would the captain expect more?

What madness. The woman was not her mother. Her mother was dead, her entire family murdered, and Ziva wanted to join them. She could not forget.

Yet, of all her village, she had survived. Yahweh had sent the captain to bring her to his wife, rather than a pagan temple. Was the Lord revealing His purpose?

"I ... I will do all I can to comfort her, Captain."

Yahweh, please make it enough

Chapter Twenty-Nine

*All these blessings will come on you and accompany
you if you obey the Lord your God: You will be
blessed in the city and blessed in the country.*
Deuteronomy 28:2-3

Damascus, later that night
Ziva

NIGHT HAD FALLEN BY THE TIME they approached the city, but Ziva was startled awake by loud voices, flashing torches, and clanging. Blinking away sleep, she straightened in the saddle, looking about for Emet. There. The dog trotted near the horse's right flank.

The captain tightened his arms around her. "Slaves are working night and day to repair damage to the gate and rebuild the wall. Don't be afraid, we are now at peace."

The voice of Rafiq emerged from the darkness. "That is your doing, Captain."

Ziva smiled at his tone which melded respect and warmth. Most times, he seemed as close as a brother, but he always deferred to the captain.

Torch light revealed the naked torsos of slaves who heaved beams, pounded spikes, and stacked stone blocks along a damaged portion of wall. A wheeled battering ram stood nearby, half burned and abandoned. By whom had the Arameans been attacked? Surely not Israel. This was recent damage, and when it happened, according to the stories spread by Biny and Jaedon during their brief visit, Israel would have been fighting Moab.

She had no wish to discuss matters of war with the captain. "Are we near your home?" she asked instead.

"Farther ahead." He pointed into the distance.

They rode down a long straight street. On each side buildings crowded so close they seemed attached. As they approached a decorative gate, she peered into a wide enclosure. Did each home have such a courtyard behind this length of wall? Curious to see farther into the interior, Ziva leaned over and spotted a round structure, touched by light from a lamp in a window. Her mother used to place an oil lamp in their window when Abba worked past sundown. Her throat tightened, and as they passed, she heard the splash of water. A fountain?

As they reached a section of wall that jutted forward, a wooden door swung open. A man she took for a soldier strode out, two more men behind him. "Who goes—Oh, Captain Naaman, welcome! I was just checking who was out so late at night."

The soldier saluted and the captain returned his greeting. Open to her gaze, the courtyard yawned wide, an expanse that could have swallowed Ziva's home and two others. She caught a glimpse of paved ground and plants growing from huge pottery jars before they passed.

Soon they left the circle of torchlight spilling from the gate workers. Buildings merged into shadow except a few lit by torches. As they continued, they passed a crossroad that connected rows of houses in both directions. They passed another cross street with even more buildings. Could so many people live within these walls? An urge to crawl into a hiding place seized her, as she imagined all these people swarming the city.

Almost at the street's end, they turned down a path marked by a row of palm trees, reminding her of the little palm orchard of Gischala.

They continued to the end of the path. Rafiq leapt from his horse and pounded the wooden gate with his fist. Beyond its wooden arch loomed the tallest structure she had ever seen. As if three mudbrick houses had been stacked one upon the other.

"We are home, Habib. Unbar the gates!"

Ziva heard excited voices directing one another, "Lift—shove!" In short order the gate swung open, and a stocky man flung down an iron bar which reverberated against the stone floor of a huge courtyard. One even larger than the previous house.

Rafiq jumped from his horse and threw his arms around Habib. Several other men swarmed around the captain and his remaining soldiers, welcoming them home. Ziva noticed the men in the courtyard were all older, each greeting one of the younger soldiers, almost like ... fathers and sons? It seemed so. They spoke excitedly, with no attempt to quiet their voices, so if she could speak their language, she would know all. As she listened, she realized she understood several words. Perhaps it would not be too difficult to learn.

When they quieted, Habib seemed to notice Emet for the first time. "What is this?" he asked, in an amused tone. "You are now keeping company with dogs, my son?"

So she was right, at least about Habib and Rafiq being father and son.

Not realizing she had understood, Rafiq repeated his father's question in Hebrew, explaining it was meant as a joke. Then he answered his father, translating once again. "The dog is with the girl, my father."

Habib eyed her thoughtfully but asked no questions.

Others came from the house, women as well as men. They appeared rumpled as if roused from their sleeping mats. The captain slid off his horse and reached for her. She sighed wearily when her sandaled feet touched the ground. The captain motioned to a plump woman, holding an oil lamp, who stopped beside Habib. "Gihan, does my wife sleep?"

Ziva blinked when he spoke Hebrew. He must want her to follow the conversation. Even more surprising, the woman answered in heavily accented, but recognizable, Hebrew.

"She is, Captain. I do not like to wake her. She sometimes does not sleep for days."

The captain made a deep sound of disgust. "Days? Did the physician not give her—never mind."

Ziva heard the frown in his voice, although the flickering lamp shadowed more than it revealed.

"This little one is recently orphaned. Her name is Ziva." He paused and spoke several sentences in Aramean. Curious as to why he did *not* want her to understand, Ziva watched several expressions cross the woman's face, which she attempted to interpret. Disgusted. Horrified. Sympathetic. Finally, disapproving.

The captain switched again to Hebrew. "Give her something light to eat and put her to bed. She is to help you serve Amirah. Beginning tomorrow, see to it you teach her everything. You are growing old and should not work so hard."

Gihan's anger was easy to interpret. She opened her mouth to speak, but with a noticeable tap on her arm, Habib advised silence. Again, the captain spoke a stream of Aramean. Twice he invoked the name of Kala, his deceased daughter. He gestured at the dog, who sat beside Ziva.

Then, both Habib and Gihan appraised her. The steward nodded. The woman wiped all expression from her face.

The captain put his hand on the small of Ziva's back and gave her a gentle shove. "Gihan was nursemaid to Amirah when she was a child." He lowered his voice. "And to our daughter. She is glad for your help, but she does not speak Hebrew well, my wife, not at all. Only Rafiq and myself have learned." He studied her a moment. "Will you try to learn Aramean?"

She nodded. Of course she must, although she disagreed with his appraisal of Gihan's Hebrew. Like Gihan, Ziva must be agreeable. Unlike the resentful nursemaid, Ziva was a slave, not a longtime member of the household. If she displeased the captain or his wife, she faced more than dismissal. Another sale and life as a zonah might be her punishment.

Ziva took another step toward the plump woman, trying to imagine her as one of the kind elderly women in Gischala. Like ... Mara's grandmother.

Mara.

Feeling tears pool in her eyes, Ziva attempted a smile, hoping to soften the stern visage facing her. Gihan, she feared, would be her destiny or her doom.

The nursemaid nodded briefly, motioned for her to follow, and said something in Aramean. Some of the words were similar to Hebrew, but not the accent.

Ziva repeated the not-so-unfamiliar sounds.

Gihan whirled and stared at her for a moment. Then, begrudging, she said, "Your accent is not bad." She pointed to her chest. "I said, 'Follow me.'" She pointed to Ziva. "You say"—and she rattled off a string of sounds. "That will answer as affirmation to any order you are given, whether from me, your mistress, or even the captain."

Ziva repeated the phrase, then added, "Thank you, Gihan."

Gihan tipped her head and provided another phrase. Yes … there it was … she heard it again. Ziva repeated several words in her own language, many only different by Gihan's accent. Ziva silently recited the three phrases as she followed the woman's lamp across the dark courtyard. The door opened to a huge square room lavished with red, gold, and green cushions, some fringed, others beaded. The lamp revealed they were all made of the unusual gleaming fabric Ziva had noticed worn by the auction customers.

Emet padded silently beside her. Ziva followed Gihan across a red and blue patterned carpet, spotting the gleam of polished stone where the carpet did not reach. She marveled at the wealth that replaced a dirt floor with expensive stone, only to hide it with plush carpet.

At the room's end, they walked through an arched opening. This time, there was no door, but mosaic tiles drew her eyes upward, blue and twinkling gold squares arranged like an eyebrow above the arch.

The next room was similar to the first, in size as well as furnishings, as if affording extra room for an overspill of guests. It was uninhabited though, like the first. Of course it was night. What might it be like for celebrations of harvest or weddings or births in these rooms? Such festivities were held under the sky back in Gischala, for want of a covered space large enough to contain the whole settlement. She smiled at the memory of a wedding where the bride and groom were soaked in a summer downpour, and the entire village danced in the rain.

Her heart's momentary lightness faded as she slowly crossed the opulent room. Her village was no more. There would be no more celebrations, unless … the enemy settled there–made the orchard their own. Hunted the hills. Tilled the fields. Her insides twisted, wringing her thoughts into bitterness.

She kept her gaze on Gihan as they walked through more rooms. She did not want to think any more about the splendor of what she had glimpsed tonight. She was exhausted.

Even now her thoughts ravaged her with accusations. *All this beauty is bought by blood. How will you live here? It will be like sleeping in a tomb.*

Gihan must have turned, but Ziva had not noticed. She stood in another large room, this one uncarpeted, revealing an expanse of the gleaming white floor Ziva had glimpsed before.

Gihan lifted her lamp and paused, as if to give Ziva a good view of the room. Perhaps she would be working here. By the lamplight she made out black and gray veins branching across its polished surface, like bare trees in a winter forest.

An arched window was fitted with wooden shutters, which must fold open to the courtyard. A long waist-high table stood under the window. Stacked with bowls, platters, and utensils, its purpose was clear. How pleasant it must be to prepare food by an open window. There was a hearth in the corner, but it did not appear large enough to prepare meals for the household.

Noting her gaze upon the hearth, Gihan said, "The courtyard holds an oven. This is meant only to heat water for herbal drinks." She chaffed her arms. "Or to"—she touched her hand to her mouth, looking exasperated. Perhaps the captain had been right about her rudimentary Hebrew. Would she understand a response in Hebrew if Ziva mimicked Gihan's inflections?

"To warm the room?" Ziva suggested.

"Yes, to warm the room." Gihan walked over to the hearth. "And this? Not oven, but"—she looked expectantly at Ziva.

"Hearth." Again, the Aramean inflection was slight, but it did change the sound. "An oven is"—she drew a beehive shape with her hands—"for bread."

"Yes." Gihan nodded with satisfaction. She repeated the phrase with extra words in Aramean and turned toward a door a couple steps from the hearth. "Let us go."

The door led to a windowless room, smaller than any they had passed through. Still, it was a larger chamber than where her parents slept. *Had slept.* A sleeping mat lay open, a thick covering rumpled on top.

"This is my room. You will sleep here, also."

Ziva could not conceal her exhausted yawn. Gihan must have risen hastily when wakened by the sound of Naaman's arrival. The floor looked comfortable enough, for the stone in this room was covered with several small carpets, one overlapping another.

But the woman lifted the lamp and pointed to a high shelf. The shapes looked like a mat and blanket. Gihan handed Ziva the lamp, motioned again toward the shelf, and left the room. Swaying with weariness, Ziva stared into the finger of flame.

She turned slowly, surveying the room again. A table sat to one side of the shelf, holding a basin and pitcher. A bronze mirror on the wall reflected the lamp and her shadow. As she continued to turn, she found cushions piled in a corner. A cloak and tunic hung on wall hooks. There was a second door, on the wall adjacent to the door through which they'd entered. Was that where the captain's wife slept?

Completing her circuit, she headed toward the shelf. She took care when setting the lamp on the table, not wanting a spark nor drop of oil to mar the expensive carpets. Then she reached for the bedding, arranged her pallet a few steps from Gihan's, and sank gratefully into the soft blankets. As during their journey, Emet settled beside her.

Gihan came back through the door, carrying two cups. Had her way been lit by wall torches? Perhaps, or her feet knew every step of this home, though it was so large.

"Drink." Gihan thrust one of the fragrant cups into her hands. "Warm goat's milk with"— she stretched out one hand as if grasping for a word, then she spoke Aramean, a word Ziva did not recognize.

She inhaled a nutty aroma like nothing she had experienced. Taking a cautious sip, she closed her eyes and hummed in pleasure, comforted by the creamy warmth.

Emet lifted his nose and sniffed the air. Gihan stared at him while sipping her own milk.

When she finished, Gihan took Ziva's cup and poured the dregs into her own. She extended the cup toward Emet, who politely lapped it up. With a small quirk resting on her lips, Gihan said, "I once had a dog. We cared for my father's sheep." Then as if she regretted speaking of her past, she snatched the cups and carried them to the shelf.

"Sleep now," she said brusquely. "You will meet the mistress tomorrow. And you must do everything exactly as I say."

Ziva answered using the words Gihan had taught, earning a grunt of what she hoped was approval. Then the woman tossed Ziva one of her own cushions and blew out the lamp.

"Wake now, Ziva. There is much to be done."

Gihan walked to the door from which they had entered the previous night. The small window in that room allowed light into theirs. Motioning to the washbasin, Gihan donned a robe over the tunic she had slept in, then taking stock of the tunic Ziva wore, shook her head.

"What else have you, save that stained garment?"

Ziva showed her the long tunic and padded pants that comprised her riding clothes.

Gihan frowned, looking back and forth between the two garments. "Wear this." She wrinkled her nose at the long tunic, which looked cleaner than Ziva's tunic, but smelled of sweaty horse. "We have nothing better. You are so much smaller than I or other women in the household." She shrugged. "The mistress will decide what is to be done."

Ziva nodded and quickly changed tunics. Gihan left the room and returned with a brown sash. She wrapped it twice around Ziva's waist, and pulled the fabric up so she wouldn't step on it. Eyeing the garment, Gihan tapped her chin. "Still too long. How can you work without tripping?" She tied knots at both sides of the skirt, stepped back, and nodded.

Heading for the door, she beckoned for Ziva to follow but stopped when she noticed Emet at her heels. She explained they would help draw water for the household. "Will he stay here?"

Ziva chewed her lower lip. "He has not been with me long, but he listens and does what I tell him. The captain allowed him to stay close to me on the journey. He does not run off."

"We will see. He can go with us today."

Smiling, Ziva grasped Emet by the ruff of his neck, giving him a little shake. He responded with an intense gaze that seemed to say, 'Ask me for anything. I am yours.'

"Stay close, Emet." She tapped her side and he sidled close. As soon as she moved out, he followed in lockstep. Testing him, she stopped, as did he.

Gihan, made an approving sound in her throat. "Come."

On their way out, Ziva saw servants carrying wash pots. She did not see the captain or his soldiers.

Noticing her gaze, Gihan said, "The soldiers sleep in a building adjacent to the house so as not to disturb the family. They stand watch over the household."

The captain had spoken only of his wife and the daughter who had died. If there were more children, wouldn't he have mentioned them? Did elderly parents still live? It was such a large house.

A tall woman was adjusting a yoke over her shoulders as they came outside. She flinched when she saw Emet, and her pots swayed precariously. Gihan reassured her in Aramean, patting the dog to demonstrate his tractability.

"Rima, this is Ziva. The captain bought her for the mistress. I will train her. For now, he allows the dog."

Rima. The woman looked much younger than Gihan, perhaps near her own mother's age. She seemed surprised. Was it because Emet had startled her or something else?

Ziva's head ached with trying to comprehend the workings of so many strangers in her life, so many people in this household. She knew how to be a daughter and an older sister—but a servant? She knew nothing. She must learn quickly.

Gihan showed her another yoke and made hand motions—did Ziva understand how to use it? Grateful that she knew this, at least, she hooked the buckets and fitted the yoke over her shoulders. The three of them set out for the well. Rima and Gihan chattered in Aramean. Ziva kept an eye on Emet while taking note of her surroundings.

The sun had burst over the walls of the city. Outside of their courtyard, the streets flowed with people—more than she'd seen in her life. Men in colorful long-sleeved robes and turbans, walked briskly toward unknown destinations, stood about arguing on corners, or trotted in or out of the city gate on horses. So many horses! Was everyone in Damascus wealthy? No, here were beggars, a blind man and two women—were they *zonahs*? Numerous dirty, ragged children darted about to avoid being trodden upon by the horses, cuffed by suspicious merchants, or chided by impatient shoppers. They must be orphans, such as she. Oh, the hollows in their cheeks, their bony arms and legs. Her heart lurched with longing to help them, but she had nothing to share. Not a morsel of bread, not even a cup of water.

Tomorrow morning she must come prepared. But how? Gihan decided her actions. Yet she could not see the children suffer and do nothing. Surely she would be given a portion of bread at supper. Was she willing to risk punishment? *Yahweh, please help me. Whatever I receive I will share half.*

There were many women at the well ahead of them, but they stood back when they spotted Gihan and Rima. As Ziva eyed the group, she realized they deferred to Gihan. The older woman nodded politely, then motioned to Rima to go first. Rima dropped her yoke, spoke quietly to Ziva as she drew water, then repeated slowly as she pointed toward one of Ziva's buckets. Understanding, she held it forth. After all the buckets were filled, Rima helped Gihan with her yoke, then Rima and Ziva shouldered theirs.

As they returned to the compound, Gihan explained by word and gestures that the captain, and by extension, his household, were respected in the city. Not only was the captain a man of honorable character, he was also a powerful warrior who had given Aram victory over its enemies. Even more, he had the regard of the king of Aram.

So that was why the other women had given them preference. Gihan spoke further of neighboring enemies on either side of Damascus, how they were now at peace because of the captain.

Peace. For Damascus.

Ziva looked down at cobblestones passing beneath her feet, as the yoke dug into her shoulders. They were far from Israel, and she knew nothing of the city's 'neighboring enemies.' Yet she thought it likely that at least some of the captain's conquests were Israelite villages. She believed him when he said he was not at Gischala. But he must have led raids on other settlements. Or planned and ordered them. How were Israel's little villages a threat to mighty Aram?

Yet, victory *or* loss came through the hand of Yahweh, did they not?

Pain seized her as if a knife plunged into her chest, and she stumbled beneath the yoke.

Quickly, a hand on either side reached out and grasped her arms, bearing her up. "Watch your step, little one," said Rima.

Ziva sucked in a deep breath. "I thank you."

Each woman gave her arm a final squeeze and let go. Gihan frowned. "Watch your step. Your clumsiness could have forced us to return to the well."

Ziva looked down, as an icy cold spread through her core.

Trust me. I am with you.

When they reached the household, the aroma of spices and bread baking in the outdoor ovens floated over the courtyard. Three cooks formed rounds of dough, slapping them inside the ovens and snatching them out just before they fell into the coals. Ziva wondered if, like her father, there were some who preferred the crusts charred.

Gihan handed her a tray and motioned her to follow. Emet, lifting his nose to test the air, stuck by her side, but he trembled at all the smells he must ignore.

"Food for the entire household is prepared either here or at the indoor hearth," Gihan said. "We take the first portions to our master and mistress. After we serve them, we eat."

So she would finally meet the mistress. She wanted to ask Gihan questions but something in her recoiled at the thought of discussing the unknown woman with another servant. The captain had assured her she would be treated kindly, and that was enough. Everything else she would learn directly from—she searched her memory for the woman's name—Amirah.

After Ziva filled her tray with golden crusted bread, Gihan added a pitcher filled with what appeared to be watered wine. Then she stacked cups, a pitcher of water, and folded cloths on her own tray.

Gihan explained the family quarters were next to the room they had slept in and could also be accessed through the courtyard. They walked through an open gate of ornamental iron into a smaller courtyard with a mosaic floor. Ziva could not make out the purpose of two low chairs. What a strange shape. Were they intended for sleeping? They were fitted with cushions. But they also had a back support, though it was greatly slanted. Before she could come to a conclusion, Gihan stopped. They stood only a few steps from the closed chamber door.

"The captain said he purchased you for her," Gihan said. "Likely, he will introduce you. If not, I will do so because Amirah has been my charge since her father put her in my arms."

The woman's face softened, became almost motherly as she spoke. "Losing her daughter dealt her a blow she struggles to recover from. We must try to lift her spirits. Can you sing or play an instrument?"

"I ... my father made a willow flute I played. But ... it is lost." That was enough. Telling the story of how she lost the flute would mean relating the murder of her entire settlement. No one need tell her Gihan did not want to hear sad stories.

Gihan looked toward the larger courtyard, seemed to catch sight of who she searched for, and gestured their approach. "I am sure we can find one."

Rafiq's father loped across the courtyard. Emet watched him closely, but seeing that Ziva was not distressed, he did not growl as he approached.

"Habib, we need a flute."

His gaze traveled from Gihan to Ziva and down to Emet. "Hmm. For the girl?"

Gihan nodded. "If you find one, bring it through our room. The dog will stay here."

Ziva bit her lip. What if she couldn't play Habib's flute? Her father had carved hers of willow shoots. It was a rustic instrument, one that sounded different in damp weather than days the sun shone. Likely any flute in this household would be finely crafted.

She trembled at the thought of meeting the mistress on the other side of this door. She also wondered at Gihan's confidence that Emet would remain in this small courtyard when she walked inside. Even as Habib shut the iron gate behind him, Ziva measured the low wall with her eyes. The dog could easily leap the private courtyard's enclosure and trouble the members of the household.

She reminded herself that Gihan was familiar with dogs. Despite her lack of experience, Ziva was starting to know Emet's ways. She felt her lips twitch. He was mostly obedient, but she sensed he could be willful.

Gihan tapped on the door, then reached for the latch. "Do not be afraid," she said. "Watch, listen, and be ready to act on my instructions."

Ziva's hands began to tremble. To hide her apprehension, she tightened her grip on the tray and nodded. Then, she said, "Stay here, Emet. Wait until I return."

He whined, but lay down.

She drew in a breath. This room was even more opulent than the others. The walls were stained the blue-green color of a forest pool, and arched recesses were defined with cream-painted moldings. Ziva couldn't fathom the time spent to create such beauty.

Her eyes were quickly drawn to the cushioned bed where a frail but beautiful woman lay, her wavy black hair dull and tangled on the silk pillow. Her mistress, Amirah. Though the morning was mild, her slender form was draped with wool coverings dyed shades of deep blue. A small table beside the bed held only an unlit oil lamp. A striped pelt warmed her legs and a hearth in the corner sent waves of heat.

Although the woman's eyes were closed, Gihan motioned for Ziva to place her tray on a large table in the center of the room, intricately painted with colorful birds and lush plants. Gihan set the watered wine and cups beside the tray. As she lifted the pitcher, the door to the house interior opened and the captain strode through.

Quickly he crossed to his wife's side. Though he did not wear the sword that usually swung at his side, his heavy steps woke her.

"Naaman! Oh, my love." She struggled to sit and a servant, who Ziva had not noticed standing against the wall, hurried forward to help her.

"I am sorry to have wakened you," he said.

Ziva took in his troubled expression as he reached to stroke his wife's hair. Remembering that he had not seen her since their daughter's death, Ziva suspected her mistress was much changed.

The servant tried to help her sit but was motioned aside by the captain who tenderly took her into his arms. Amirah's face, as she turned it up to receive his kiss, displayed jutting angles and deep hollows. She raised a thin arm to rake her fingers through her hair. "I am not fit to receive you. Did you just arrive?"

Even if Ziva had not travelled with him, his damp combed hair and spotless tunic answered, but the mistress did not seem to notice.

"Late last night. I did not want to disturb you." He glanced around the room, his attention fixing on the food tray. "You have not yet eaten. Good, I am ravenous."

He walked to the table and received two filled cups from Gihan. Turning to the other servant he whispered, "Bring milk for your mistress."

As the woman retreated, he turned back to his wife. "Amirah, I brought this young girl to serve you. Her name is Ziva. She came from an Israelite village and speaks only a little Aramean."

Amirah fixed her gaze on Ziva, smiling kindly, but then her eyes widened.

Ziva bowed respectfully but kept silent. She knew nothing about being a slave, but even as a child, she had been taught to remain silent around her elders if a question was not directed to her.

Though the interior door stood open, Habib knocked on the door frame before entering. He greeted the captain and the mistress and then revealed a silver flute. He held it out to Ziva.

"What is this?" the captain asked.

"Gihan asked for a flute. Said the girl can play."

Ziva took it and ran her fingers nervously over the polished surface. She fought the urge to explain she had never touched such a flute—that hers had been little more than a whistle. Even the round holes felt smooth to her fingertips. She ducked her head in awe of its beauty, then glanced first at Gihan then the captain. Was she meant to play today, without first trying in private?

"We will eat first," said the captain, returning to his wife's side. He lifted a cup to his wife's lips. "Drink, my dear."

Obediently she took a sip, then gripped his hand. "Enough for now," she whispered. "Bring the girl close."

"She is meant to serve you, wife. If you do not at least take bread and milk from her hand, I will send her to scrub pots for the cook."

Ziva selected the softest loaf and moved to the woman's side. The captain was concerned for his wife, not stern. Last winter Ziva's lingering cough had frightened her mother, and she spent wakeful nights by her bed. Impulsively, Ziva placed her palm across Amirah's forehead. "You have no fever."

The captain quickly repeated her words in Aramean. Ziva listened closely. Again, not so different.

Amirah started to reach for Ziva's arm, then let her hand fall on the cushion. "I am not sick, only tired. So weary."

Ziva broke off a piece of bread and held it over her lips. "Rest then, Mistress. But first, eat."

Again the captain interpreted.

Glancing at her husband, who loomed over her like an oak, Amirah accepted and chewed the bread. She took a few more bites and then held up her hand to stop.

Was it only sadness that made the mistress ill? A woman of Israel would not lie down and waste away. Yet Ziva had felt such despair, and if she had more strength of spirit, Abba had taught such strength came from the Lord. She hummed a little without realizing. When the captain gave her a strange look, she felt her face grow warm.

"I am sorry. It is a little tune my father taught me."

Amirah smiled. "Very pretty. Finish."

The other servant returned with a bowl of milk and set

it on the table beside them.

"She will play the flute, Amirah, and then you will take more bread dipped in milk."

Ziva's stomach turned with distress as she examined the flute. She thought again about explaining. No. *Yahweh, I don't know why you have placed me here. Is it to help my enemy? No matter. Please teach me what I must do.*

She counted eight holes in the silver barrel. She interlaced her fingers, placing one on each hole. Lifted one finger and blew gently through the mouthpiece. Lifted the others in sequence, hearing the tones ascend. If she wanted, she could limit herself to only the first four notes, but twice as many notes gave her more freedom to soar with the melody.

She closed her eyes and played the song her father had taught. She imagined his lips on his willow flute, his merry eyes creased with pleasure as she and Imma sang.

The Lord is my strength and my shield;

my heart trusts in him, and He helps me.

My heart leaps for joy, and with my song I praise him.

As she finished the stanza, she ran up the string of notes and repeated the final line.

She opened her eyes. The mistress was staring at her with lips slightly parted. "A lovely tune," she said. "Are there words?"

"Yes, Mistress, and—"

"And she will sing them to you after you have taken more of the bread and milk."

Amirah laughed, a sound like tinkling chimes. "Very well, Husband. Help me sit." He propped her with cushions then fed her all she would take before insisting that Ziva sing.

Ziva sang the Psalm twice with the captain murmuring in his wife's ear. Amirah slowly continued to eat. "Will you play the flute one more time?"

"Of course, Mistress." Drawing a deep breath, Ziva repeated the opening stanza, filling her spirit with strength and joy as she played. Then a piercing howl joined her tune, accompanied by a string of plaintive barks. The captain strode to the courtyard door and yanked it open.

Emet bounded into the room, ran to Ziva, and sniffed

her all around. Then, satisfied she was safe, he stretched out beside her, his nose on his paws.

Ziva knelt and grabbed him by his ruff. "I am sorry, Mistress. He has not heard me play a flute. It seems he thought me in danger."

The mistress held her hand over her mouth. Her eyes had widened even more.

The captain pressed his lips together. "I forgot to mention, Amirah, that the girl comes with a dog." Then he chuckled. Habib and a few others joined in.

Lowering her hand, the mistress smiled. "Very good. I think we shall all get along. I enjoyed your music, Ziva. Perhaps the dog ... does he have a name?"

It seemed they both began to understand the other, at least a little.

"His name is Emet."

"Ah, of course. A faithful friend. Perhaps Emet will come to love your music as well."

Chapter Thirty

*"There are three things that are too amazing for me,
four that I do not understand: the way of an eagle in the sky,
the way of a snake on a rock, the way of a ship on the high
seas, and the way of a man with a young woman."*
Proverbs 30:18-20

Gilgal, after Elisha's return from Shunem
Jaedon

JAEDON GRUNTED AS HE KNELT TO fit his end of the doorpost
into the socket stone, while Biny hoisted the top of the post
into the socket mortared to the lintel. It slid into the circular
stone depression with an audible click.

"Whew, heavy," said Biny. "Got it?"

"Not quite." Jaedon grasped his hammer and rapped the
lower socket, not yet affixed to the threshold, until it stood
directly under the one fixed to the lintel. "A moment." He
shoved up and checked the alignment with his plumb line.
"Done. How's your end?"

Biny slowly rotated the carved door he'd built as a
wedding present. "As a door turns on its hinges, so a
sluggard turns on his bed."

Jaedon laughed and shook his head. "You aren't
satisfied to be a master woodworker, but you must also best
me at the Torah?"

"That is from the Proverbs of King Solomon, not Torah."

"Ah, the Book of Wisdom."

Biny tapped the side of his head. "Appropriate, eh? Do
you think your bride will like it?"

"It is the best door in Gilgal, Biny. Eden will insist you
build her one."

"Already has."

"And then there is Elisha."

"Hmm," said Biny. "I'm not saying I know the prophet
better than you, but he seems a man content with what he
has."

Across the vineyard, Imma swung open her door and

swept dust outside. She paused and eyed the two of them. "You fitted the door already?"

"Come look!" Jaedon dropped to his knees and quickly troweled mortar between the socket and the threshold.

Imma clasped her hands together. "Ooh, so beautiful. The stones, the shutters, the door—Ziva will love the whole house."

"Is there anything else to be done?" Biny swung the door again and glanced inside. "Plastered walls, shelves ..." He directed a meaningful stare at Jaedon.

"Shelves for which I am greatly ... umm ... grateful."

"You know what that means."

Perhaps gratitude should include more than words. "You want me to plaster your walls?"

"Hmm. Perhaps, but that is not what I intended. Your house is finished. It is time for you and your father to take a *ketubah* to Ziva's father. And then, bring your bride home."

Biny took his tools and headed home. Then Jaedon and Dov crossed the road to meet with Elisha. The sun had not yet reached its zenith, but the village was quiet. Because the recent harvest had suffered from drought, many of the prophets had gone to set snares or forage in the hills. If they did not find sufficient food for supper, Jaedon would help after meeting with Elisha. Some worried about the continued lack of rainfall, but Yahweh would meet their needs. He threw back his shoulders and lengthened his stride, trying to tamp down his excitement before they reached the prophet's house.

Dov glanced sideways at him. "Why the hurry? You've waited nearly a year already."

"I thought it would never end," Jaedon confided, his feet light on the path.

"You have done well, building a house and planting a vineyard, my son. Since all is prepared, maybe we can bring her home instead of waiting another year. We will ask Elisha if that is proper."

Could it be so easy? Jaedon had longed for their life to begin, and now it seemed it might.

Elisha met them at his door. "Have you come for a Torah lesson?"

When Jaedon's step faltered, a smile curved the prophet's lips. "Sorry. A small joke. Did you bring papyrus?"

Jaedon had learned to expect Elisha's sometimes baffling responses. This time, he was ready. "No, a thin slab of oak." He grinned at Elisha's raised eyebrows and presented the smooth piece of wood that would hold the words of the *ketubah.* Biny had inscribed a narrow border of flowers and leaves on its edges. Both savtas had prepared colorful dyes to enhance the design. "Can you write directly on the wood? If not, I can whitewash it first."

Elisha ran his fingers over the smooth wood. "Let me try without. If the ink bleeds, we will adapt." He tilted the slab, eying it from every direction, then nodded his approval. "Fine workmanship."

He beckoned them to the worktable, removing his quill and ink from the practical *qeset* Biny had made to store his writing instruments. After mixing water into powdered ink, he wrote, mumbling to himself. "… Jaedon bar Gershon, the bridegroom, said to this woman Ziva, daughter of Shimon, be my wife according to the law of Moses. I will work, honor, feed and support you in the custom of Hebrew men …" he went on speaking, writing, and dipping the quill in the black ink, until he asked Dov, "What *mohar* do you offer?

"A talent of silver. Is that right?"

"In these times, more than fair. Most have no silver and promise their labor or animals from their flock. And the house! Rare is the young couple who does not move in with the groom's parents."

Jaedon fidgeted. When Dov had offered the silver, saved from his time in Ahab's army, Jaedon tried to refuse, reminding him, "You have sons of your own. You have already done so much for me."

Dov's expression drooped into discouraged lines. "Jaedon, are you not the son of my heart? And is not Gershoni my daughter, as much as Yuval and Nathaniel my sons? You are a man grown. I have no doubt you will help your mother and siblings, comes a time I am unable. Let me take part in your happiness. It is a father's joy."

Jaedon felt his heart swell with gratitude. He turned to Elisha, smiling. "I do not deserve such a father."

Elisha did not answer, his eyes seemingly fixed on something outside the window. He dropped the quill onto the table and swayed. Dov and Jaedon both leapt forward, grasped his elbows, and lowered him to the floor. The prophet folded his arms atop his knees and rocked back and forth, moaning.

Jaedon sloshed wine into a cup, knelt beside him, and pressed it into his hands. "What is it, Master?"

Elisha took the cup, staring into its quivering surface. "Soldiers attack the settlement."

Dov rushed to the window and looked out. After a moment, he turned and leaned against the wall. "Nothing. All is peaceful."

Jaedon asked, "Is it coming? Did you see a vision?"

Elisha nodded. "Not here. Gischala."

Jaedon felt the blood rush from his head. "Gischala? Is Ziva safe? What of her family?"

Elisha pressed the cup back into Jaedon's hands. "I do not know more. Yahweh has hidden it from me."

Jaedon's jaw fell slack. Yahweh hid part of a vision? He slammed the cup on the table. "Ask Him again. I must know what to do." One thought drove out every other—he must get to her.

"Go quickly to Gischala, my boy, that is all I know. I pray you will be in time."

Dov gripped his arm, motioned for the door, and they ran.

Dov explained to the women and Maalik, while Jaedon saddled the horse and donkey. As he led the animals to the house, Dov emerged carrying waterskins and weapons, Imma a food pack. The savtas clutched the three children.

Binyamin came running across the way, wearing his travel cloak and carrying a pack and waterskin. "I am coming."

Jaedon climbed on the long-legged donkey. "No, my friend. If we had another riding animal, there is no one I'd rather have come. But we must hurry. I fear there will be times, we must move with stealth."

"He's right," Dov said. "Three men would draw more attention, especially one of your size."

Biny sputtered and argued, but in the end he accepted the truth—to accompany them on foot would slow them.

They pushed themselves and the animals long past nightfall. Dov's warhorse, battle hardened and heavily muscled, charged up hills and along the route to Gischala with speed and strength. The donkey followed, sometimes falling behind despite her long legs, but continued her rocking gait gamely until she caught up with her companion.

When they came upon a forest-edged meadow, Dov signaled a halt. The white donkey stretched her neck down and shook all over, nearly tossing Jaedon from the saddle before he could slide off.

Dov said, "Let us water the animals. We'll leave them and approach the settlement on foot. It may be occupied by the enemy."

As Jaedon led the donkey to the stream, fear roiled through him like the water coursing over rocks. If the village had been overrun, what would have happened to Ziva? He tried to hold back pictures of her fallen, bloodied, even dead. His beautiful girl. The one on whom he had set his heart.

Jaedon hobbled the animals to graze in the valley. He checked his weapons, then they continued their quest. As they walked, Jaedon prayed. *Yahweh, I thought you meant her for me. If she lives, please protect her. Stay with her. Keep her safe.*

Dov raised his fisted hand. "We are close," he whispered.

They soon realized there was no need for stealth. Blackened rubble and scorched earth reproached them. Bodies sprawled across dirt footpaths and in houses. Jaedon ignored the stench, as he perused each face.

His hopes were raised when they did not find Ziva or her family in their home or on the city streets with the fallen. But when they searched the date orchard, Jaedon found a man's body face down over a woman's, as if he had tried to shield her. Despite the blood-crusted gash on his head, he recognized Ziva's father. Jaedon rolled him off, not caring that touching a dead body made him unclean. Shimon had been unsuccessful in his attempt to save his wife. Jaedon staggered back, leaned against a trunk, and covered his eyes.

Dov came to stand beside him. "I have searched the others. Ziva is not here, nor her little brother. It is possible they escaped."

Jaedon tried to believe that, but as he viewed the carnage, it appeared the enemy had slain everyone in the settlement. Or at least everyone who resisted.

"We must bury the bodies," Dov said.

"But you said they could have escaped. We cannot delay for the dead."

Dov nodded slowly. "You're right, although it pains me to leave them. We'll be back. For now, let's search for tracks."

As they studied hoof prints, signs of scuffle, and drag marks, it became apparent that the onslaught had begun in the orchard and ended at the village. Perhaps the initial attack had been silent. Then, having overcome the able-bodied harvesters, the invaders found the aged and young to be easy prey.

They circled the area looking for tracks, but they did not find a single set of footprints departing either the orchard or the village. Hoofprints, however, crossed each other and milled in circles.

"I am sorry, my son. If she left, it was on horseback."

Jaedon studied Dov's face. No one in Gischala owned a horse. An image of Ziva, struggling to escape her attacker's clutches, seared like a lightning strike.

His heart seized in helpless pain. He'd been powerless to save his father, grandfather, and uncle. Now he'd come to collect his betrothed, too late. *Why are those I love overcome by evildoers? What would you have me do? Open my eyes, Yahweh.*

That prayer was answered when Jaedon spotted a corner of papyrus poking out of an area of trampled mud. Falling to his knees, he clawed to unearth his letter.

"What is that?" Dov hurried toward him.

Jaedon smoothed the mud-caked papyrus against his chest, then held it out to study the fragmented lines.

... plaster the walls ... plant a tree ...

"The letter I wrote last month. About the house ... and other things."

"No message from her?"

Silently, Jaedon shook his head, studying the erratic paths of the hoof prints. It had happened fast. There'd been no time to position the fragment to point a direction. She must have tucked his letter in her sash and it had fallen, unmissed, during the attack. "We should circle the village—perhaps we'll find clear prints showing the way they took her and other hostages."

Dov pursed his lips. "Yes, we'll do so. But the nearest slave market is on the way to Damascus, in Hazor. We can reach it before nightfall and inquire."

Though having direction had raised Jaedon's hopes, at day's end Hazor revealed no real answers. A disinterested auctioneer informed them a large shipment of women, victims of famine, had recently offered themselves for sale as prostitutes and been transported to temples across Aram.

"Where?" Jaedon demanded.

The auctioneer snorted. "Scattered. No buyer would feed more than one or two of the scrawny hags. Now leave me be. It's time for my supper."

But when Dov offered some of Imma's flatbread, the man sniffed, named the most likely temples, and provided directions.

Dov looked grim as they climbed on their animals. "I brought the silver meant for your *mohar*. I pray we have the opportunity to use it."

Jaedon followed him at a brisk trot. He'd never carried messages as far as Aram, but Dov had related tales of soldiering forays into the territory. He named five likely cities. A long search. Jaedon's belly felt as cold and heavy as the silver Dov brought. To buy Ziva back, after ... whatever had happened to her. It would not change how he felt about her. But he had heard stories of taken women. How they were broken. Inconsolable.

He set his shoulders. No, they would be in time. Yahweh would care for Ziva. An eerie voice sneered from the darkness. *Care for her like He did the others?*

He thought of the dead in Gischala—her townsfolk, her family. Did their souls hover round their fallen bodies, bemoaning their untimely deaths and her abduction? Did they, as he did, petition Yahweh to bring her back?

No, Elisha had taught him the dead did not linger. King David, when his baby son lay sick, had fasted and prayed. When the child died, the king rallied himself. He answered his wondering servants, 'While the child lived, I fasted and wept, for who can tell whether God will be gracious to me? But now the child is dead, so why should I fast? Can I bring him back again? I shall go to him, but he shall not return to me.'

Yahweh, is her spirit with you, even now?

A breeze cooled his face, drying hot tears.

Again, a dark thought tried to push its way past that breath of comfort and remind him of his slain family, rotting in their graves.

No. His father, grandfather, and uncle had left their bodies. They were in the presence of Yahweh, with King David's son and a multitude of others.

Jaedon picked up the reins and *tsked*. The donkey quickened her pace. Ziva was not among the spirits. Not yet.

He would know.

On the third day, they probed their fifth temple. When Dov mentioned silver, the high priest brought forth a listless group purchased within the past year, none of them Hebrew. The women eyed Jaedon and Dov wearily, struggling to summon a smile or lift a chin. If the silver would have stretched, Jaedon would have bought each one and returned her to her family. As they made camp that night, he shared the thought with Dov.

Firelight cast shadows on his stepfather's grim expression. "It would do no good, my boy. They were Canaanites. Most likely their own fathers sold them. Would do so again if they returned."

This had been the last of the temples within reasonable distance to the slave market. Each priest had told them they would have bought Ziva, given the chance. "Young and beautiful—of course we would take her. Even if her face were scarred—" Jaedon had turned away in disgust before the priest could finish his vile remark.

But Dov had stayed behind, speaking softly in Aramean and telling the priest not to mind the young hot blood. "He is mourning his betrothed. If you hear of the girl, send word to me through the king of Samaria."

Later, as they rode in the direction from which they had come, Jaedon asked, "Why Samaria? You have not been there since you married Imma."

"Did you see the priest's eyes when I mentioned the king? Greed increases our chances of hearing news. Since Elisha often stays in Samaria, the king will consult him if a message comes for me, and Elisha will ensure we are told. I don't want to direct Arameans to little Gilgal. Have them do to us as they did to Gischala."

Gischala. Clenching the reins, Jaedon nudged the donkey's sides. His spirit drooped along with his shoulders. They had agreed this was the last temple within a reasonable distance to the slave market. "Let us return and bury the bodies."

Dov spoke quietly to his horse. They loped along the trade route, squinting into the setting sun.

They did not make camp that night, instead traveled on by moonlight. As they approached the destroyed settlement, the stench caused them to rethink entering in the dark. So they withdrew upwind, hobbled their mounts, and slept a few hours wrapped in their cloaks.

At first light they remounted and rode grimly toward Gischala. The donkey preferred to follow rather than lead, so it was Dov who first noticed the mounds. "What?" He reined in his warhorse.

Then Jaedon saw the graves. While bodies were still strewn across the clearing, several mounds lay among them with rocks piled atop.

Ziva! Could the Lord have hidden her hereabouts? Had his love been safe the whole time they sought her? But though they both shouted until they were hoarse, striding in and among the bodies and graves, there came no answering cry.

Finally, Dov said, "A traveler may have come through and buried these." He looked around. "Perhaps he was alone and unable to attend to so many. May have gone for help.”

Jaedon winced as he searched decomposing faces where they had left Ziva’s parents, not finding them now. Had the traveler chosen to bury them first? Why? Had he known them?

Remembering where there had been tool sheds, Jaedon searched through rubble until he found a shovel with its handle only partially burnt. He dug the first grave, then helped Dov move a body. A slow process and there were so many.

After several graves, Dov straightened and swiped his forearm across his brow. “We need water if we’re to continue.”

Jaedon nodded, looking around once more. “Why have we seen no old graves?”

Dov leaned the shovel against a boulder. “You’re right. In a settlement as old as Gischala, we should have spotted a graveyard. And the ground is rock, beneath this shallow layer of soil. There must be caves.”

After slaking their thirst, they decided to explore on horseback, deeming it unwise to leave the animals unattended. Once more they circled the settlement, then headed toward a cliff. A spring trickled across its base and down into the date orchard, the source of the rivulet that fed the trees and had entertained the village children. How long ago that seemed! A tangle of shrubs and vines crowded the rock, so Jaedon dismounted, handed Dov the donkey’s reins, and forced his way through the growth to investigate.

Jaedon spotted a vertical shadow ahead. “A fissure!” He turned, pointing behind him. “You were right.”

“Look out!” Dov shouted.

Jaedon spun, then dove under the shovel that slashed toward his head. Shards of pain and light exploded.

“Oh!” his assailant cried.

Jaedon shoved him to the ground, tore the shovel from his grasp, and grasped him by the front of his tunic.

Then his attacker’s turban slid sideways and long hair fell out. A girl! Ziva’s friend. “Mara?”

“Forgive me,” she said. She picked up the turban and extended it to him. “You’re bleeding.”

He did not take the head covering, instead swiping the

back of his hand against his forehead. Yes, he felt blood trickling from his eyebrow. He let his breath out in a slow whistle. She could have blinded him.

"Forgive me," she repeated. "I thought you were Arameans."

"Have they been back?" Dov climbed down from his horse, dousing water on a corner of his cloak as he came.

"Is Ziva with you?" Jaedon heard the desperation in his voice.

She shook her head, her eyes glistening. "I am sorry. I never found her. They must have carried her off. And no, they have not returned. Though I've feared every day that they would."

Jaedon swallowed, loosened his grip on her tunic, and backed away. "How did you survive?"

"I had help," she said. She stuck two fingers into her mouth and whistled, an eagle's call. Like he had taught Ziva.

An old woman emerged from the shadowy fissure. Short of stature with twig-like bones, she seemed too small to carry the burden strapped to her chest. He recognized one of Gischala's aging widows. She bent to kiss the top of the bundle, and the shape moved and cried.

A child.

As Dov shared their provisions with the survivors, Mara explained how she had seen Ziva's baby brother crawling into the bushes. "That was just before the raiders struck," she said. "I followed, and when I heard the attack in the orchard, I covered his mouth and held him close. I was so afraid he would cry, that they would be upon us. "Then Puah"—she nodded toward the old woman—"crept from a cave and pulled us inside."

"The cave is deep," said the old woman. When Dov asked if the settlement had used it for burials, she nodded. "My mother's bones rest in the deep recesses of the cave. But it has not been used for many years," she said. "There is another. Closer, and with a wider opening."

Mara looked surprised. "Why did you not tell me? I could have dragged bodies easier than piling rocks over them."

The woman pursed her lips. "There, you could be seen from the road leading to Hazor. I was afraid we would be discovered. Alone, how could I keep the child alive? But with these men—"

After Puah gave them directions, Jaedon and Dov strapped saplings together and used the donkey to carry the unburied to the cave. Stars dotted the sky before they finished the solemn duty. Finally, they moved the last body, and Dov spoke a prayer of blessing over all the fallen.

Jaedon turned his face toward heaven, listening. Attending. But he had his own prayer, one he had come across while perusing Elisha's scrolls. His gaze had stopped on the passage when visions of Saba Naboth's vineyard invaded his mind. Furious shouts. Flying rocks. His family destroyed.

Arise, Lord, in your anger; rise up against the rage of my enemies.

Awake, my God; decree justice.

Justice. He stared a moment at the burial cave, then shoved his shoulder, with Dov's, against the boulder that would seal its entrance. *Yes, Lord, once more justice is required. Will you intervene?*

"Come, let us wash," said Dov.

Jaedon followed him to the rivulet of water, far downstream from the cave where Mara, Puah, and Aharon waited. He splashed water over his head and face, inhaling its mossy coolness. Would the stench of death ever leave him?

Jaedon dunked his head once more, shaking the water from his ears when he came up. "The survivors must be taken to Gilgal."

Dov nodded. "The settlement will welcome them."

Though drought and famine had troubled the area, all of Gilgal would rally. Neighbors would vie for the privilege of caring for the refugees. Whoever housed them would find a bunch of turnips, a brace of quail, or bundle of clothing on their threshold to help meet their needs. They talked about this as they wrung out their clothes, dried as best they could, and headed back to the others.

"You must take them," Jaedon muttered as they walked. "I will keep searching for Ziva."

Dov eyed him. "But we questioned all the nearby temples."

"I will go farther. Will you give me the silver?"

Even as Dov reached for the pouch, he frowned in disapproval. "You should come back with me. Elisha may have had another vision about Ziva."

Jaedon thought on this, then firmly shook his head. He couldn't explain why, but he knew there'd been no further revelation. Wouldn't Yahweh speak to his heart? "I will not let time erase all chance of tracking her."

Before they parted the next morning, they prayed together for Jaedon's success. He felt hopeful as he tracked hoofprints east to another auction. Then another. He talked to several auctioneers, and he learned that most had sprung up temporarily when the raids were frequent. Lately, several had closed for lack of business.

No one remembered a girl of Ziva's description until Jaedon offered payment for information. Then an auctioneer said he'd sold her to a farmer looking for an attractive bride. After Jaedon found the man who was supposed to have bought her, the farmer laughed in derision. "The wife of my youth has already given me three sons, and when my brother died, I married his widow. Why would I buy a wife?" He looked Jaedon over. "If you need a wife, I will sell you this one." He pushed his brother's widow toward Jaedon. "She is comely, has all her teeth, and is as good a cook as that one." He jutted his chin toward his other wife.

The young woman looked at him hopefully. He felt sorry for her. Her new husband and brother-in-law had no compunction about trying to rid himself of her, even in her presence.

Jaedon turned aside the suggestion and went on his way. He continued his search for six months, then he returned, defeated, to Gilgal.

Elisha greeted him sadly. He had heard no more from the Lord.

After another year passed, one of the prophets approached Dov, suggesting a match between his daughter and Jaedon.

He refused. Wouldn't Yahweh have told him if Ziva no longer lived? Their hearts had warmed to each other. Yes, he would know.

He would remain faithful to the promise his heart had given.

Chapter Thirty-One

*Now Naaman was commander of the army of the king of
Aram. He was a great man in the sight of his master and
highly regarded, because through him the Lord had given
victory to Aram. He was a valiant soldier, but he had leprosy.*
2 Kings 5:1

Damascus
Ziva, about three years after her capture

ZIVA WOKE WITH A START. SHE blinked in the dark, casting her
gaze toward the hall. No light under the wooden door
separating her mistress's room from hers, no sound of
footfalls. Then, through the opposite wall, she heard a faint
sob. Emet growled deep in his throat.

Now she heard footsteps, and then the captain
speaking. "I must see the healer."

Her mistress responded in shattered fragments. "He will
say … you must … leave me."

"If he does, then I must. There is no alternative. You
know I love you."

When the captain was with Amirah, Ziva would not
enter their room unless summoned. But shortly she heard
heavy footsteps, and the outer door opened and closed.

She stood and waited, her feet itching to run to her
mistress. Emet pressed his cold nose against her wrist.

"Ziva!"

She shoved through the door and ran to kneel beside
Amirah. An oil lamp lit the plains of her mistress's face,
revealing red-rimmed eyes and tear-streaked cheeks.

"What is it?" Ziva asked. "How can I help?"

"I am afraid. I cannot lose him, too."

She heard but hoped she misunderstood. "The captain
loves you. You cannot lose him."

"He has the white spots—has gone to a healer."

Ziva's breath splintered. *Tzara'at.* The dread disease.
Isolation. Suffering. Death. Naaman could die.

She pressed her lips together. Should she ask if there

were only a few spots? It might not be *tzara'at*. He might not ... die. But what if there were many?

Would her mistress understand what it meant? Did he? Their wealth shielded them from the suffering of poverty as a boat carries its passengers above floodwaters.

Amirah had been crying. She understood enough.

What was to be done? In Israel, a priest would examine the spots and determine if it was a simple skin ailment or ... not. Did healers perform a similar function in Aram?

"I will pray it is nothing, Mistress. That the captain returns with a healing salve."

"Oh, yes. Please ask your God to help us. And I will ..." Amirah did not finish. Had she begun to say she would also pay for a sacrifice to Rimmon? A pulse beat in Ziva's temple.

Already on her knees, Ziva laid her hand on Amirah's and closed her eyes. "Lord God, Creator of the Universe, may you look with compassion upon my master Naaman, a man who has treated me, and all in this house, with kindness. Please strengthen him, restore him, heal him. May you give the healer wisdom and your servants peace. The name of the One God be praised."

Her mistress lifted Ziva's hand to her lips and kissed her fingers. Ziva stood, walked to the window, and folded back the shutters. Rosy fingers of dawn lit the room, softening the words they had spoken and those left unsaid.

"Shall I tend to your hair, my lady? Perhaps it will relax you."

Amirah nodded. As if he knew she needed comfort, Emet had stationed himself beside her, his muzzle on her knee. Absently, she stroked his head.

Ziva selected a wide-toothed comb the captain had given Amirah. As she gently worked the expensive trinket through her mistress's black hair, she admired the prowling lion carved into its handle. The captain was like a lion, fierce when at war, caring at home.

All his gifts were nothing compared to this house—the servants—the horses. All trappings of his high standing with the king. But their wealth could not shield them from this trouble.

"Thank you, child." Then her voice broke. "I am so worried."

Frowning, Ziva lay the comb on the tray and began to

massage Amirah's temples. The couple had been kind to her during the years they'd owned her. Treated her almost as family. Her mistress had even dressed Ziva in their daughter's clothes. What if the captain were compelled to leave their home? Leave the king's service? He no longer led men to war, but he was still an advisor to his king. But if *tzara'at* had claimed him—if he died—would the king's gold and silver still flow?

If it did not, how could this large household be maintained? Worse, would others fall prey to the disease?

Would she be sold? Once again face the prospect of prostitution—a brothel or pagan temple.

Her fingers trembled. Oh, she did not want him to die. He was not her father, not family, but he had become ... she cared for him. For them both. And not only for her own selfish reasons, but for her beloved mistress, who had suffered so much after the death of her only child. She had just begun to recover from that deep sorrow. If she lost her husband now, would she lose all hope?

Ziva chuffed under her breath. How strange, that she had once dreamed of escaping this household. Now she feared losing a home. A family.

Because yes. She had lost her family—Abba, Imma, and Aharon killed by raiders. Yet Eden still lived, unless raiders had struck Gilgal. But her sister was married to a poor prophet and was with child when Ziva was taken. She could not expect they could take her in.

And Jaedon. Might he have looked for her? Gone to her village? Scrutinized the site of the attack? Had he waited?

No. He would have thought her dead. Surely, he had taken another by now. It would be hard to live in the same village where the man she had planned to marry, lived with another.

Yahweh had not given her what she expected. He had taken her from her people and settled her among her enemies—like a fledgling among serpents.

She had accepted what happened to her. Believed if Yahweh had settled her in this place, she should embrace His plan. If He willed it, what was His purpose? Did he give her love for her mistress and the captain for a reason?

Perhaps it was so she could offer comfort in this season of sadness.

As the morning stretched on and her mistress paced the room, Ziva suggested they break their fast and then visit the marketplace. Anything to take Amirah's mind off the master's delayed return.

Emet trotting by her side, Ziva swung back the oak door, crossed the courtyard, and stopped by the cooking area. After learning of their destination, the cook returned with a covered dish and a heavy sack. When the cook whistled to Emet, he sat and watched expectantly. She scratched his ears, filled his bowl with scraps, and whistled again. The dog leapt up and gulped his meal.

Ziva felt her breath coming easy for the first time that day. Emet's perfect manners had gained him status with the cook and made him a favorite of the household. His presence had eased her way into the home as well. She patted his head and they returned to her mistress bearing the cook's parcels.

She set the plate on the small table and lifted the cloth. Quail eggs boiled in their shells, purple grapes, slices of golden melon, and breads glistening with honey should tempt her mistress.

Gihan had instructed her to serve the mistress and eat later, but Amirah would not allow that. Instead, as she often did when Naaman was not present, she asked Ziva to sit and talk with her while they ate together.

As they finished the grapes, Ziva said, "The captain will not want us to visit the marketplace without an armed escort. Shall I ask Rafiq to accompany us?"

Amirah nodded. "Yes. I invited Gihan also. She may enjoy an outing."

Ziva searched through the compound. She did not find Rafiq but came across his father smoothing a wood plank.

"He and the master went on an errand together, but I am happy to accompany you," Habib said. "Is Gihan coming?"

Ziva carefully schooled her expression. It seemed the two had grown affectionate of late. Might they have an understanding? But Gihan had confided nothing.

"I will ask," she said. "Will you wait for us by the gate?"

He nodded, picked up pieces of his project, and sauntered away whistling.

The sun's light had turned yellow, making it easy for Ziva to spot Gihan as she emptied a pot of wash water into the kitchen garden.

"Gihan, let's go to the marketplace. The mistress needs a diversion."

The older woman rolled her eyes as if she were impatient with the whims of the wealthy, though Amirah was not spoiled, nor capricious. For a while after Ziva had arrived, Gihan seemed jealous when she waited on the mistress. But that had changed one day when, as if concerned for her former nurse's pride, Amirah had explained she only wanted to ease the older woman's workload. Gihan had glared at Ziva for weeks until the mistress expressed a desire for a hard-to-find vegetable, and the older woman found good use for her extra time.

Ziva cleared her throat. "I know you love her as I do, so I will tell you in confidence. The master is visiting a healer. Our mistress fears for his health."

Gihan's demeanor quickly changed. "Oh! My poor dear. What is wrong? Has he a fever?"

"She mentioned spots."

Gihan's eyes widened. "A rash? Could it be—" Gihan looked around them as if afraid to be overheard.

"That is all I know, except that Rafiq accompanied the captain on his errand, so Habib will escort us to the marketplace."

Gihan glanced down and smoothed the front of her tunic. "Habib? Oh. Yes, you may need help to carry her purchases. I will go with you."

Ziva allowed herself a small smile. "Your help is very welcome. We will meet at the courtyard gate when you are ready."

They left the compound and headed for the market. Soon, they came upon a group of boys kneeling in a circle, playing a game with stones. When they caught sight of Ziva, they stood respectfully and waited to be acknowledged. Gihan, resplendent in her best tunic, stayed with the mistress, while Ziva distributed food from the cook's sack. Emet watched closely for a dropped crumb.

Over time, she had come to admire these boys. They shared food with smaller street children who were unable to scrabble for it themselves.

"You and you"—Habib pointed at two of the biggest boys—"look for me at the captain's gate before sundown. If you are willing to work, I have tasks for you. There will be more food."

One of the boys peered from under a thatch of hair the color of sunset. "And blankets?"

Habib frowned. "We will judge your work."

Ziva detected sympathy rather than ire. There would be food and blankets.

When they reached the market, Amirah stopped at a booth where she sometimes purchased fragrance. She chose a ceramic vessel shaped for pouring oil and pointed it out to the vendor. "Please remove the stopper so I can smell the fragrance."

He complied with a flourish and extended the little pitcher. The mistress sniffed and averted her face. "Too intense."

Emet sneezed. Ziva caught a whiff of a woodsy aroma that drew her thoughts to the captain. Seeing Amirah's haunted expression, she quickly suggested, "Something lighter, perhaps?" She fanned the air to dispel the familiar scent that might trouble her mistress.

The vendor nodded and quickly selected a rimmed vessel decorated with tiny squares of abalone shell. Amirah inhaled deeply and smiled. "Please wrap two for me."

After arranging to pick up her purchase on their way home, they moved on.

Ziva pointed out a hammered cook pot, delicately embroidered head coverings, and a wizened snake charmer. Amirah smiled indulgently at her enthusiasm. Ziva had intended to distract and entertain her mistress, but she continued to be amazed by the variety of goods and strange things encountered in the city.

Gihan and Habib had lagged behind and were inspecting wool at another vendor. But when they noticed Amirah walk on, they hurried to catch up. Habib took his responsibilities seriously, although it seemed doubtful anyone would dare to accost a member of Naaman's household. When Amirah realized she had drawn Habib away from a potential purchase, she insisted she also wanted to inspect the merchant's goods, and they returned.

The mistress owned many woolen shawls and soft blankets in every conceivable color. Still, she politely felt the softness and admired the dyes of the vendor's various offerings. Gihan had been examining yarn of a pale color that many spurned as being a poor imitation of purple. Ziva thought it lovely, and so, apparently, did Gihan. But when she learned its price, she refused it, and when Amirah offered to buy it as a gift, Gihan shook her head. "It is too dear. In any event, I don't see well enough to weave."

Amirah eyed her long-time servant, then shrugged.

A movement at the corner of her vision caught Ziva's attention. Something had passed between Habib and the merchant, who was tucking the pale purple yarn under a basket.

"Shall we visit the fruit vendors?" Habib asked, casually turning Gihan aside. "A caravan from the East has brought rare offerings."

Although Amirah declared the eastern fruit too bruised, they bought melons, leeks, and cucumbers from a local farmer. When Habib insisted on carrying the purchases, he brushed Gihan's hand during the transfer and she blushed. Fixing his gaze on her, he spoke quietly, seeming to pose a question. She laughed and responded just as softly, her hands flying about like birds. Years seemed to fall away from her.

Ziva looked away, pretending to be caught up in the antics of a street cat pouncing after a locust. They were even older than her parents. Neither had a living father to arrange or approve a marriage, and yet love grew between them.

Something fluttered within her. Happiness for Gihan, yes. Also, a long-suppressed memory, a girl and boy in the palm grove, and the question unfurled, impossible to ignore.

Would she ever know love? Jaedon must think her dead.? Did he even ... have a child or two?

Ziva smiled wistfully, mildly surprised that the memory of her parents and of Jaedon no longer sent her mood spiraling into darkness.

Not so when she thought of little Aharon. An innocent child. His young life, scarcely begun, ended in violence. She pressed her palm against her heart. Would it ever heal?

"Take us to the soap vendor," Amirah was saying. "When the boys have performed their tasks, Habib, I want you to give them borinth and teach them how to use it."

He nodded respectfully, but later Ziva heard him whisper to Gihan.

"Am I becoming a nursemaid to street boys?" Habib waggled his head like the snake charmer, and Gihan giggled like a girl.

Chapter Thirty-Two

*Now Naaman was commander of the army of the king of
Aram. He was a great man in the sight of his master and
highly regarded, because through him the Lord had given
victory to Aram. He was a valiant soldier, but he had leprosy.*
2 Kings 5:1

Damascus, later that day
Ziva

AS THEY NEARED HOME, ZIVA SPOTTED the captain,
accompanied by Rafiq, riding through the Damascus gates.
Though he smiled when his gaze lit on Amirah and her
entourage, there was a set to his jaw that said all was not
well.

The two groups entered the household's courtyard
together. Rafiq held the captain's horse while he dismounted
then led both animals to the stables. Amirah ran to greet her
husband, but he stepped back and raised his hand to stop
her. She halted two or three paces away and listened as he
spoke so quietly that his words were unintelligible to Ziva.

She shuffled uneasily, studying her mistress. Should
she go to her now, or would she be considered an unwanted
interruption? Then the captain glanced at Habib and
gestured, holding out a small leather bag.

Habib stepped forward, but the master again motioned
for him to stay back. He spoke to Habib for several minutes,
gesturing to the house and then to the stables. Amirah
covered her mouth with her hand.

Habib slowly set the market parcels on the stone floor.
Naaman turned and headed for the stable. Habib walked
toward the central portion of the house, carrying only the
pouch.

Ziva glanced at Gihan. "We should go to her."

Gihan nodded. The mistress stared at the stacked
parcels, then swung her gaze first to Gihan, then Ziva.

"The healer said … in order to be safe … Naaman must
remove himself from all company for a fortnight. He will stay

in the rooms above the stable. Only Rafiq, who has already been with him for several days, will see to his needs. No one else may come near." She blinked several times, then bent to pick up a package.

"Mistress, allow us." Gihan reached for the wrapped jars of scent. "We will carry your purchases."

Ziva gathered up the remaining packages, opened the gate of the inner courtyard, and the three of them walked into Amirah's bedchamber.

Ziva's mind clouded with questions. If the captain was not sick, the healer would have known. A fortnight. How would the mistress bear it?

"Shall I unwrap these?" Ziva asked Amirah as she placed the day's purchases on an ornate shelf.

"Later perhaps." The mistress sat on the edge of her bed. After Gihan wedged cushions behind her, the mistress leaned back. "I want to talk. There is a disease, more common in your country, Ziva, than in Aram. Tzara'at. Or you, Gihan. You came from eastern Aram. Have either of you heard of it?"

Shaking her head, Gihan poured a cup of watered wine and handed it to Amirah. "No. Not I."

Ziva nodded slowly. "Yes, Mistress."

Amirah sipped the wine. "The healer did not believe my husband had the disease but ... could not be sure he did not. That is why we must keep a distance from him. In two weeks the healer will come here and examine him again. He hopes the salve may heal the rash." She turned her head away and her shoulders shook silently.

Gihan stared at Ziva, her eyes as wide as Ziva suspected were her own. Emet settled next to the bed, his head on his paws, and he let loose a loud, rumbling sigh.

Ziva moved beside the bed. "It seems a good report, Mistress. Two weeks is not such a long time. And he is here, in his own home. We will see that he has all the comforts of his own bedchamber, will we not, Gihan?"

"No one is to approach him except Rafiq," Amirah said.

"He allowed Habib to take the medicine pouch," Gihan said. "He headed for the kitchen, so it must need preparation.

If the master wishes to be isolated from the rest of the household, I suspect Habib will carry what they need—medicine, food, bedding—and Rafiq will minister to him."

"You see," said Ziva. "All will be well."

"I do not believe that," said the mistress. "I think the healer was afraid to give my husband bad news. He is a much-feared warrior, after all." She paused, then choked out a small laugh. "Except in his own home."

Ziva could not even force a smile, but her mistress was right. The captain was well-liked by all who served him.

"I do not want pretty stories. What I want is the truth. Tell me what you know about *tzara'at*." She looked directly at Ziva.

Nausea roiled and her hand flew to her throat. How could she speak of the terrible things she had heard? She tried to calm herself. She must do as she was asked, but must she cause her mistress pain? "I have never seen someone afflicted with the disease," she said slowly.

"But you have heard of it. What have you heard? Everything, Ziva."

She looked down at her folded hands, one finger tapping another. "It may begin as a skin affliction. A rash or white spots. In Israel, one afflicted must be seen by a priest. The priest may prescribe treatment as the healer did. If it worsens, the sick person will be … forced to move outside the city. To live in a colony with others with the disease."

"So it is contagious?"

Tap, tap. "Yes."

"Is that all?"

Tap, tap, tap. She did not want to tell her mistress it was considered a judgment from Yahweh.

Suddenly she remembered something Jaedon had told her about Yahweh's prophet. The one he once wanted to serve. A great man, Elisha, who performed miracles. Jaedon had told her about two he had witnessed. Could the prophet heal her master? Would he? Was this Yahweh's purpose in settling her in this house? *Tap, tap.*

"Ziva, answer."

She shook her head. "I am sorry. I was thinking about—"

"You said it is contagious. Does it lead to death?"

Terribly contagious. Ziva served both the master and mistress daily. She might already be carrying the disease.

But she was young, strong, and Yahweh was her protector. Perhaps He had sent her to them for this purpose. To care for them.

"In severe cases, it has." She hoped she did not have to describe the horrors of disfigurement, of rotting noses, fingers, and limbs, of which she had heard. "I will pray for the master. That the healer's medicine will work. Reveal that all he has is a skin disease that will leave of its own volition."

Amirah's eyes drooped, then she opened them again and asked, "Is that what you were thinking about? Death?

Should she tell her? Raise her hopes? Would a prophet of Israel even see the captain of Aram's army, let alone heal him to fight future battles?

If he was not healed, would she be punished? Put to death? She took a deep breath.

"What is it? I charge you to tell me the truth. Hold nothing back." Her mistress held Ziva's gaze. Her eyes communicated anger, but Ziva did not think it was directed at her. Rather at the disease or at her own helplessness.

Ziva clasped her hands together. Her breath rushed forth, propelling her words like flotsam. "It is only that there is a prophet of God in Israel. I wish my master would go to him, that he may be healed."

Chapter Thirty-Three

*"About this time next year," Elisha said, "you will hold a son
in your arms." "No, my lord!" she objected. "Please, man
of God, don't mislead your servant!" But the woman
became pregnant, and the next year about that same
time she gave birth to a son, just as Elisha had told her.*
2 Kings 4:16-17

Shunem, Sivan, month of wheat harvest
Malka

MALKA WALKED DOWN THE HILL OF Shunem, holding her young
son by the hand, though it made him frown. She whistled a
birdsong, and he pursed his lips in imitation. His upturned
face reached her waist. "Imma." Joel tugged on her hand. His
hair curled sweetly below the rolled head covering that
shaded his earnest little face.

"Yes, son?"

"Do you think Abba will let me ride the ox today?"

Smiling, she nodded. Samuel would let the boy do
anything he asked, as long as it was not dangerous or sinful.
They both spoiled him, though he had not grown demanding
or proud. Indeed, he was a kind and generous child.

"Will he let my friend David ride in front of me?"

There. As if the Lord looked down and confirmed her
assessment of his character. Joel shared his possessions
without holding them close. She was proud of their son, yes,
but justifiably so.

"Ask him, my son. But you shall ride in the field, not on
the threshing floor. If you fall, I do not want you landing on
the flints that separate wheat from chaff."

Joel nodded seriously and Malka stifled a grin. He was
such a little sage!

Her mind on plans for a celebration, she turned her gaze
to Mount Carmel. Elisha was near enough to attend. The
Man of God prayed and meditated on Mount Carmel about
this time each year. And he *should* be here. Yes! He would be
an honored guest. She would send word. She hummed under

her breath, anticipating his appreciation of the special dishes she would prepare.

Samuel would care for the boy while he and Tal cut wheat and transported wagon loads to the threshing floor, and she would begin preparations. All too soon, they'd be home for the midday meal. She quickened her step.

Hours later, her hands were deep in the dough she'd been kneading, when someone kicked the door. Malka jerked her head up. A shout followed. "Mistress! The boy!"

Wiping her hands, she rushed to the door and yanked it open.

Tal cradled Joel in his arms. "His father says he complained of his head."

Her son blinked at her through teary eyes and moaned. "It hurts."

She reached for him, settled him on her hip, and rested his head on her shoulder. His hair smelled of sweat, wheat, and dust. His sandals brushed her thighs as she hurried to her chair.

"Where is his head covering?" she asked.

Tal squinted. "I … I don't know. Perhaps he lost it earlier, when he and his friend rode the ox."

"Never mind. Bring me some water and a cloth, and then go back to help Samuel. Make sure he is wearing his head covering." She glared up at him. "And you as well."

She dribbled water into Joel's mouth, but she thought it only wet his tunic. She wet the cloth and stroked it over his face and hair. She tried again to give him water, but he coughed it up and cried weakly. She rocked and crooned, sang and prayed.

For you will deliver the needy who cry out, the afflicted who have no one to help.

You will take pity on the weak and save the needy from death.

The words taunted her. *You will deliver the needy.* Oh, yes, she admitted her need today. Nearly six years ago, however, she had told Elisha she needed nothing. *I am content. I live among my own people. There is nothing I need.*

She stroked Joel's face. It burned.

She touched her cheek to his. "Try to drink," she whispered, then again tipped drops of water into his slack mouth. Did they trickle down his throat? Did his breaths, at first labored, grow calm? Yes, in, out, in, out, slow and gentle like the waves of Chinnereth at dawn.

She continued to sing, in her frightened, reedy voice, songs of brooks and birds, grass and sky. His fist curled around her forefinger, as he had done when a baby. A faint dimple still marked the plump back of his hand.

"*Imma*," he whispered, and his mouth fell open.

"Yes," she crooned, "yes, love, I am here. I am here." She stroked his face again, cooling now. Felt under his chin, where the baby fat had disappeared. His flat little chest. She stroked it again, then held her hand steady. She stopped breathing and listened. Put her ear to his chest, listened for his heart.

Silence.

She tipped back her head and wailed. "What have you done, God of Elisha? Did you make me glad only to increase my pain? Why have you crushed me?"

She jumped to her feet, clutching his body against her, as if she could keep his soul from departing. She looked around wildly. Where was help? Where was Elisha?

She staggered up the stairs, intent on laying her boy on the prophet's bed. *Don't mislead me, man of God*, she had told him, but he gave her a son—only to take him away? He was responsible. He must put this right.

Joel's body, white and still, sank into the cushion she had made for Elisha's comfort. Her fist pressed against her mouth, she stared at her son's face, willing him to move.

Open your eyes. Breathe.

But he did not.

Malka flattened her lips. She was not finished. She would bring the prophet here. Let him see what he had done.

But Samuel! *Oh, Samuel.* This would kill her old husband. Should she lose both she loved in one day? No, she must hide this horror from Samuel. What if he tried to stop her? She could not allow it! No, she must lay her boy at the feet of Elisha. He was the man of God. She would not let him rest until he made this right. He would. Samuel had no need to know the boy was up here. Dead.

Unless ... until ... he needed to know.

She crossed her arms and huffed. She needed Tal.

She tried to control her trembling as she ran down the stairs, out the city gate, down the hill from Shunem to the plain where Samuel and Tal were tossing the last sheaves of grain into the wagon. The ox turned its head in the traces, and the donkey, grazing at the edge of the field, flopped an ear her way. She slowed to a brisk walk. If she ran all the way, they would know.

"How is the boy?" Samuel asked.

"Nothing to concern yourself about, husband. But I ... I wish to go see the prophet up on the mountain. Give me Tal and the donkey so I can go and return quickly."

"Why go to him today?" asked Samuel. "That is no short journey, even on the donkey. It is neither a new moon festival nor the Sabbath."

"Oh, I know" she said, then forced a lighthearted chuckle and a shrug, pretending it was nothing but a foolish whim. Samuel could deny her nothing. "Never mind. It will be all right."

She pressed her lips together. She sounded foolish, even to herself. But she climbed on the donkey, leaning to whisper to Tal "Lead on as quickly as you can, and do not slow down for me—or anything—unless I tell you to."

Hours later, she hung on grimly, each of her bones feeling pulled apart from each other. The pain gave her grim satisfaction. She should ache! Why did she live when her life's light lay still? Mount Carmel loomed over them. Another hour and they'd arrive. Poor donkey, wretched Tal, running ahead. Yet he did not complain, nor did he question her. Did he know?

Ahead, she spotted someone running toward them, coming down the path that wound around the mountain. Her heart stuttered. Elisha! But soon she recognized the servant, Gehazi. Her spirit, hopeful a moment before, now bowed in despair. No! She would not give up.

"Are you all right?" Gehazi shouted as he ran. "Is your husband all right? Is the child all right?"

"Do not stop for him," she said to Tal. "Press on." She had not come for Gehazi. He could do nothing. Her son needed Elisha. "It is all right." She wheezed as she passed him.

They climbed the mountain, Malka and the donkey in front, Tal doing his best to keep up, and Gehazi coming last, talking, pricking her ire. "Mistress, Elisha sent me ahead to find out why you have come. Yahweh has not revealed it to him. If you tell me your problem, I will run ahead and lay it out before the prophet."

Each time, she nodded and brushed him off. She wished him quiet. "Everything is all right," she murmured, her anger building. She had begged God. Next she would talk to the man of God. No one else could help. She would not waste her breath.

When she reached Elisha, she leapt down, took hold of his sandaled feet, and touched her forehead against them.

Gehazi came from behind and tried to push her away, but she clung with all her might.

"Leave her alone!" Elisha rumbled. "She is in bitter distress, but the Lord has not told me why."

She glared up at him, all her misery pouring out in tears that dripped on his feet. "Did I ask you for a son, my lord? Didn't I tell you, 'Don't raise my hopes?'" Elisha shoved his staff into Gehazi's hands. "Tuck your cloak into your belt and run. Don't speak to anyone you meet, and if anyone greets you, do not answer. Lay my staff on the boy's face."

Gehazi left at once, but Malka glanced after him, shaking her head. He could not help.

Only Yahweh, through his prophet Elisha. She did not understand why the Lord, who had given her son, had now taken him away. But with stubborn faith, she understood that Yahweh was the only one with the power to help. She had asked Him for her boy's life, but He had been silent. Somehow, she knew He would be silent to Gehazi.

Her throat constricted. Would Yahweh even listen to Elisha? Would the Lord restore her boy's life, as He had done for the widow of Zarephath? Surely... surely ... *oh, please!*

Still kneeling and clinging to his feet, she looked into Elisha's face. "As surely as the Lord lives and as you live, I will not leave you."

He nodded and got to his feet. "Let us go," he said. He followed her down the mountain, moving stiffly, but refusing the offer of her donkey.

When they finally neared Shunem, Gehazi came running to meet them. His face was sweat-streaked and dusty, and he no longer held the staff. "I laid it across the boy's face as you said, but he has not awakened." His shoulders slumped.

Samuel was nowhere to be seen. Malka moaned, longing for her old husband's arms around her but relieved he was spared this sorrow, at least for a while.

The three of them climbed the stairs to the prophet's room. When they reached the top, Malka saw her boy still lying where she had placed him, like a child carved of marble. A sob welled up, but she suppressed it somehow. It would be wrong to cry here, while Elisha stood at the room's threshold. It might be taken as unbelief.

I believe, Lord, I believe. And in those little places where I do not wholly trust, help me. Help me believe.

Elisha pushed the door wide, walked in, and shut it behind him, leaving them outside on the rooftop. Gehazi turned and went to sit on the top step.

Malka tiptoed close and pressed her ear tight against the door.

She heard Elisha pray, "Yahweh, restore this boy's life. Only you have the power. Please, if his death is not needed in Your eternal plans, do not take him from his mother just now."

Malka whispered, her cheek against the door. *Yes, Lord, I beg you. Let me keep my son a little longer.*

Then Elisha stopped praying. In a moment she heard the bed frame creak. What was he doing? Then she remembered more of the story of Elijah and the widow's son. The boy from Zarephath had lain on Elijah's bed, and Elisha's master stretched himself over the body. Mouth to mouth, eyes to eyes, hands to hands, it was said. Was that what Elisha did now?

Malka trembled, fear and excitement coursing through her veins. What was happening? The room grew quiet again.

She stretched her hand toward the latch, then yanked it away, and shoved both hands behind her back.

Wait. Wait on the Lord.

The bed creaked again. Had Elisha stood? Yes, and she heard his footsteps approach the door. Quickly, she stepped back. The footsteps paused, then it seemed the prophet turned and walked the other way. Now floorboards groaned as Elisha trod back and forth, back and forth. On this side of the door, Malka restrained herself from pacing with him. The bed creaked again. Silence.

Then she heard a quiet prayer.

Yahweh, give him your breath. A long exhale.

Give him sight. She raised her fingers to her own eyes and imagined Elijah, long gone from this earth, and imagined his servant Elisha on the other side of this door. Two prophets, two boys, one God.

Restore strength to his hands. She made fists of her own, then bit down on a knuckle to stifle her sob.

And then … Aatcho. Atchoo, chooey. Not a man's sneezes. A child's surprised squeaks. Seven times in all.

Tears blinded her and she stumbled back. Gehazi leapt to his feet and hurried to grasp her arms and steady her.

"I think … I think," she said, then covered her mouth, unable to say more.

The door swung open. Apparently not seeing her, Elisha said, "Gehazi, call the Shunammite."

Gehazi gently pushed her forward.

"Take your son," the prophet said.

She stumbled into the room, her eyes devouring her son's face as he rubbed his eyes.

"Imma." He held out his arms.

She bowed first at Elisha's feet, tears wetting her cheeks. "Truly you are a man of God," she choked. "Praise Yahweh for His kindness to me, a poor woman. I will thank Him every day of my life."

Then she gathered her son in her arms and hurried off to find Samuel.

Chapter Thirty-Four

Elisha returned to Gilgal and there was a famine in
hat region. While the company of the prophets was meeting
with him, he said to his servant, "Put on the large
pot and cook some stew for these prophets."
2 Kings 4:38

Gilgal
Elisha

AFTER MALKA'S SON REGAINED HIS STRENGTH, Elisha felt the
Lord nudging him to return to Gilgal. "I want to spend time
in the company of the prophets," he told Gehazi. "They need
encouragement, and you need to see your wife."

When Malka learned of their plan, she tried to convince
Elisha to stay longer. "You hurried so from Mount Carmel.
You gave me back my son, but I fear it drained you of
strength. Can you not rest here a little longer? My sister is
coming for a visit, and she has longed to meet you."

He suppressed a smile. Malka was younger than he, yet
she mothered him. He did feel depleted, but Yahweh had
said, "Go." The Lord would strengthen him along the way.

When Elisha began to shake his head, Samuel said, "At
least take the donkey."

Elisha considered the suggestion. It would make his
journey easier, but then he'd need to return the animal. "No,
I am not sure where the Lord will send me next."

The Lord hadn't said where they'd go after Gilgal, but
Elisha thought it might be Samaria. Aramean attacks on
outlying villages grew more frequent and violent, and war
seemed imminent. If it did break out, a prophet's job was to
provide godly counsel to Israel's king.

Samuel persisted. "Then keep the donkey for your
travels until you return to Shunem. After what you've done
for our son, I don't care when. If I need a work animal before
then, I have the ox."

So it was decided. Malka packed bread and cheese, and
Samuel added a small sack with the season's first threshing

of barley. "Keep it for yourselves," he said. "I am sorry there is not more to share among the prophets."

Gehazi glanced at the sack as they made their way toward Gilgal. "If the harvest is so sparse on the plain, what will it be like in the hills?"

"It is only the first threshing." Though Elisha knew what was coming, he purposefully put a lilt to his voice, wanting to encourage his servant. "Remember, my son, the Lord will provide."

Gehazi's mouth compressed and they continued in silence. Elisha sighed. After everything his servant had seen, why was it so hard for him to completely trust God?

The donkey's pace was smooth, barely rocking him to and fro. He hooked his hand under the saddle leather and relaxed to the gentle motion. A long-ago memory emerged, faded by time and distance. *Imma*, seated in front of a crackling hearth, arms around him, hummed sweetly and rocked him. He'd really been too big to sit on her lap anymore, but that night a dream had awakened him, and the childish ritual, long outgrown, comforted them both.

The dream expanded, opened like a door, and he walked in. He trod across furrowed rows of dirt behind his father's oxen and passed his mother's kitchen where she and her servant girl sang while baking bread. *Bless the Lord, oh my soul, and forget not all his benefits …* They sounded like a pair of garden warblers. How strange to move so quickly from field to house. He strained to bend, check for mud on his sandals. *Imma* would—

"Elisha."

He snorted, opened his eyes, and saw prophets, some with their families, streaming across the road from the hills around Gilgal. Had he slept so long? They headed for the house where he had lived with Elijah.

A breeze cooled his face, carrying the familiar whisper. *I told them you would return this evening.*

Those who already crowded around the house backed away, opening a path for Gehazi to lead the donkey through. How many? Elisha turned in the saddle, counting. A hundred, at least. *What shall I do, Lord?*

Feed them.

Gehazi's stomach rumbled loudly. He smiled apologetically at Elisha. "I'm hungry. They must be, too." He glanced at the pack Malka had sent. "Bread and cheese for two will not go far. For the children?"

"Perhaps some brought food to share." He slid off the donkey and began greeting the prophets by name. Gehazi appeared to be questioning some who carried travel packs, but their gestures told Elisha they had not brought food.

He caught sight of Dov across the way and briefly wondered if Jaedon, the great hunter-gatherer, had returned.

Not yet.

Gehazi returned and whispered what Elisha had already surmised. The extent of their food supply was enough grain to thicken a stew, six unleavened loaves, and a fist-sized round of cheese. Enough for each child to have a bite.

Elisha drew a deep breath. Well. The Lord had refreshed him with sleep and a dream of his mother's kitchen. A vision from the Lord? The smell of bread still lingered. Yahweh had spoken, with that whisper that rode the winds like eiderdown.

Feed them.

"Put the largest pot on the hearth. Then ask Dov or Miriam if they have anything to add to the grain Samuel gave us."

"I will," Gehazi said. "I know where to forage for roots and greens. While the grain is simmering, I'll gather what I can."

As Gehazi hurried toward the stream, he searched for the tangled vines he'd seen blooming before their last journey. Perhaps he'd find mature squash. Tubers and wild carrots grew nearby.

Dov had offered to accompany him, but Gehazi wanted to go alone. He remembered most of what Jaedon had showed him in the early days when they both sought to serve the prophet. The competition between them lessened when Elisha made his choice. Or had Jaedon withdrawn, more interested in the girl he met in Gischala?

Gehazi frowned and purposefully closed the door on

that thought. Any remnant of jealousy was unbefitting the servant of the man of God. Elisha had chosen Gehazi, and all he had to do was continue to please him. Yet here he was, taking on tasks such as this, that a few years ago he had been ill-prepared for.

Then he spotted the squash. Ripe, round, and yellow against glossy dark leaves. Enough to feed the crowd, even without digging for tubers. Gehazi pulled his knife from his sash, chopped through coarse stems, and piled the squash atop his cloak. When he had all he could carry, he tied the corners, shouldered his find, and headed back with his contribution to supper.

When he arrived at the house, Elisha was speaking to the crowd gathered outside. Gehazi caught enough of his instruction to recognize a topic he had favored among the remote villages—the seven thousand Israelites Yahweh said would stay true to Him and not follow the Ba'als. A paltry number, when compared to the population of the northern kingdom, which was somewhere near seventy times seven thousand.

One of the older boys was stirring the pot. Good. It would be a shame if Samuel's measure of grain burned. Carrots and greens were simmering already, so his decision to forgo the tuber patch was correct. Perhaps some of the women had gleaned in the hills. Quickly, Gehazi sliced the wild gourds into the stew. He offered to take over stirring, but the boy refused with a wide grin, seeming proud to perform a task for the man of God.

Gehazi cast his gaze over the men seated around Elisha. Should he borrow bowls from neighbors? Most had travel packs beside them. They probably carried bowls or pots inside. He wouldn't ask unless he saw more were needed. All was well for now, so he leaned against the wall and listened to Elisha teach.

"Shortly after Elijah called me to follow him, he reminisced about the time he fled from Jezebel, discouraged that he had failed in his mission to turn Israel from idol worship. Having failed the Lord, or so he thought, he ran from the powerful woman who threatened to kill him. In fact, he wanted to die, but not at the queen's hand. He did not want to allow her to boast of any victory over the Lord or his servant. So he fled Israel far south into the Judean wilderness, and there he begged God to take his life. To die at the hand of the Lord was an honor, he told me. Instead of death, the angel of Yahweh fed him heavenly food and led him on to Mount Horeb."

Gehazi frowned, concentrating. Elijah wanted to die, but he wanted God to be the one to kill him? He couldn't remember hearing that. He listened close.

Now Elisha related what followed for his master on Mount Horeb, where Moses received the commandments. A rock-shattering wind. An earthquake. Fire. But the Lord was not in any of these.

Then came the Lord's gentle whisper. *What are you doing here, Elijah?*

"At first the question broke his heart. Then he realized that, rather than criticizing, the Lord had invited Elijah to be honest, to pour out his heart. So he replied, 'The Israelites have rejected your covenant, torn down your altars, and killed your prophets. I am the only one left, and now they are trying to kill me.'"

The crowd waited in silence.

"Before he was taken from us, Elijah traveled the hills, often with me. Some of you have heard what the Lord told Elijah next, a prophecy, meant to encourage my master who thought he was the only follower left. 'You are not alone. I have reserved seven thousand in Israel—all whose knees have not bowed to Ba'al and whose mouths have not kissed him.'"

Elisha paused, sweeping his gaze across the room. "Are you one of God's seven thousand?"

Gehazi watched them murmur among themselves. Some nodded and spoke excitedly to their neighbor. Yet others were silent, glancing at the pot as if the day's most important event was the promised supper. Gehazi's stomach rumbled. He was hungry, too.

Elisha stood, smiling at the prophets and their families. "Enough stories for now. God is still working among us. After your bellies are filled, I will tell you of the miracle God worked in Shunem." Then he turned his hands up toward heaven.

"Thank you, our Lord and God of the Universe, for this food during a season of famine."

Gehazi took the ladle from the boy and scooped hot stew into bowls. It was thick with squash, field greens, and tubers. Too hungry to wait for the others, a few prophets began eating chunks of gourd with their fingers.

"Stop eating!" One of them shouted. "Poison!"

From the opposite side of the room, another shouted over him, "Man of God, there is death in the pot."

Elisha said, "Bring me some flour."

Miriam ran to her house and returned with only a few handfuls. Elisha stirred it into the stew, praying.

"All is well now," Elisha said. He handed the ladle to Gehazi. "Don't be afraid. Serve it to them."

Gehazi slowly stirred the pot. His stomach felt like he'd swallowed the entire iron kettle and its noxious contents. How proud he'd been to gather the vegetables. Yet he couldn't spot poisonous gourds. Flour? Flour could not take away poison! Yet … his mentor said it was safe.

After all he'd seen and heard, couldn't he take Elisha at his word? The God of Elijah sent fire when the Ba'als could not. The God of Elisha raised Malka's son from the dead. Gehazi had been there.

As the prophets lined up once more, Gehazi ladled the stew into their bowls, but he watched the first ones eat. At first, they were slow, as he would be, lifting the chunks of gourd to their mouths with wooden spoons or speared on knife point.

Then there were grins, and soon they were teasing him as they ate, tossing out tips for identifying poisonous plants.

Gehazi shook his head. The story would travel the hills of Ephraim, always accompanied by laughter. He fixed a smile on his face as he continued to serve the prophets. When all had been fed, he spooned a little into his own bowl. Hesitantly, he tipped the contents into his mouth. How could it be? He had never tasted such delicious stew.

Chapter Thirty-Five

Naaman went to his master and told him what the girl from Israel had said. "By all means, go," the king of Aram replied. "I will send a letter to the king of Israel." So Naaman left, taking with him ten talents of silver, six thousand shekels of gold and ten sets of clothing. The letter that he took to the king of Israel read: "With this letter I am sending my servant Naaman to you so that you may cure him of his leprosy."
2 Kings 5:4-6

Samaria, three months later
Elisha

ELISHA STIRRED THE LENTILS, GLANCING OUT the window for Gehazi. He should turn the corner soon, bringing the onions, greens, and bits of meat the king's cook sent to augment the students' meals.

The hearth fire sparked and popped as a stick burned through. Elisha knelt to shove more wood under the iron pot, humming. He held an almost house-wifely pride in the comfortable home which King Joram had provided for his visits to Samaria.

Yet the king had revealed his superstitious hope that, because of this gift, he would not suffer consequences for his father's sin, Ahab's murder of Naboth.

Elisha sighed. What made Joram think he could bribe the Lord with a house? After all Elisha's instruction, did he still not understand? *God is best pleased with a broken spirit and a contrite heart.*

Well, the king would have more opportunities to repent and believe. Yahweh was merciful that way.

And—Elisha leaned to check the window again—the Torah students would be here soon. Where was Gehazi? He was never late.

I delayed him. He is bringing a message.

Elisha smiled, looking up. "You are using him, Lord?" Perhaps his mentoring approach had been right—putting Gehazi in various situations to test him. Like sending him to the palace today—Elisha hadn't sent him merely to pick up the cook's offerings.

He went back to stirring. *Lord, what was the message?*

Silence.

He should have known. The Lord told him what he needed to know. And that meant—

A hand yanked back the cloth door flap, and Gehazi ducked inside. "There was a disturbance at the palace," he said breathlessly. "I was in the hall when King Joram met with a foreign dignitary bearing a letter from the king of Aram. Joram did not read aloud, but when he finished he tore his robes, called his advisors, and said, 'Am I God? Can I kill and bring back to life? Why does this fellow send someone to me to be healed of *tzara'at*? See how he is trying to pick a quarrel with me?'"

A breeze curled through the window, and the Lord whispered the letter's contents into Elisha's ear.

He wanted to laugh.

The king of Aram sent the commander of his armies to be healed by the king of Israel. Of *tzara'at*, no less!

What do you want from me, Lord? Do you intend to heal Israel's enemy?

Elisha listened and nodded.

Gehazi stretched out trembling arms. "This means outright war with Aram. The man is a favorite—the captain of Benhadad's armies. Called on King Joram bearing silver and gold. War, I tell you. No more raids on outlying settlements. They will swarm the land—"

Elisha turned his hands palm up. "Hush, Gehazi. Do you forget whom we serve? All is well. Go back to the palace. Say to King Joram, 'Why have you torn your robes? Send the man to me and he will know that there is a prophet of God in Israel.'"

The air shimmered around Elisha, opening the roof to earth, sky, and water. He staggered as the vision unfurled. He saw an eagle—Jaedon's *Hevel*—swoop over three men— King Joram, Naaman, Gehazi. And ... there was someone else in the shadows. A young woman, too far off and hazy to recognize.

Do you bring mercy or judgment, Lord?

To each, according to their heart.

The students arrived, and Elisha began teaching from the scrolls. Each read a section, and he questioned them. Vigorous discussion ensued. He had not finished the Torah lesson when horses and chariots rolled up outside. The wooden door stood open on warm days such as this, but its hanging cloth liner afforded a little privacy and slowed flying insects. A breeze lifted the hem enough for ten heads to swivel and gasp at hooves, chariots, and armor.

"Gehazi," he said. "I have more to teach today. Tell the man, 'Go wash yourself seven times in the Jordan. Your flesh will be restored, and you will be cleansed.'"

Gehazi opened his mouth, shut it, and stood.

The students looked at each other and some shifted, preparing to follow.

Elisha motioned for them to stay where they were. "Only Gehazi. We will continue."

With a final glance at Elisha, Gehazi slipped past the wind-tossed cloth.

When Gehazi saw the number of the Aramean's attendants, his legs suddenly grew weak. Here were three chariots with spear-carrying drivers, mounted soldiers with bows, and foot soldiers or bearers. Some wore uniforms similar to the soldiers who had burned his village. In addition to the horses, several heavily laden donkeys crowded outside his master's house. Did they carry at least some of the wealth he had seen displayed in Joram's court?

The man himself sat atop a huge black horse. Naaman, the captain of Aram's armies, was resplendent in a long-sleeved tunic, scaled armor, and brass helmet.

Gehazi eyed his face and hands. Yes, although long sleeves hid much, red and purple lesions crept down his wrists, up his neck, and over his jaw.

Why had he not already been sent to a *tzara'at* camp outside his city? This man's standing must be higher than Gehazi supposed, to gain audience with the king of Aram and a letter of introduction to the king of Israel.

Or didn't the unwashed Arameans understand that

tzara'at at this stage hurtled a man toward certain death? It was extremely contagious. Gehazi retreated another step before repeating, word-for-word, what Elisha had told him.

The man's face suffused with blood and his eyes became slits. Gehazi was glad he'd moved back. When Naaman finally spoke, his voice was harsh. "I thought the prophet would surely come to me—call on the name of his God, wave his hand over the spots, and cure me."

So the pagan thought Elisha some sort of magician or sorcerer. That the prophet was inferior to himself. Surely, Yahweh would not favor a man such as this with healing.

Gehazi hid a sneer as Naaman paced about, shooting angry glares at the now immovable hanging door cloth. All could hear the words of the Shema being repeated inside. Elisha continued his lesson, apparently unimpressed with the captain's raised voice. The captain's men, however, watched their leader warily.

He stopped pacing and spoke louder. "Yet *the prophet* does not even pay me the courtesy of emerging from his hovel to greet me."

Hovel? The house King Joram gave Elisha was one of the finest in Samaria. Of course, this was a man whose coffers must be glutted by the blood of war.

The captain continued to rave. "He tells me to wash in that muddy river. Are not Abana and Pharpar, the rivers of Damascus, better than all the waters of Israel? Could not I wash in them and be cleansed? Get back in your chariots, men."

One of his soldiers, who had watched from horseback, dismounted, dropped his reins to the ground, and hurried to his master. "My father," he began, causing Gehazi's eyebrows to raise.

He squinted, taking a closer look. They could not be father and son, they were too close in age. Did Naaman's followers look upon him as a mentor, a father figure? As did many of Elisha's followers.

The captain's voice quieted. "Yes, Rafiq?"

"If the prophet had told you to do some difficult thing, would you not have done it?" he coaxed. "How much more when he tells you, 'Wash and be cleansed!'"

After a pause, Naaman nodded. His men climbed back on their horses or chariots and headed for the river. When the last charioteer waited and invited Gehazi to ride with him, he accepted gratefully. He wanted to witness whatever happened at the river, and on foot he'd arrive after dark. He'd seen many strange things while serving the prophet. There might be a healing. Yet, there was something peculiar about Elisha staying in the house, finishing the Torah lesson, while the captain railed against him outside. Unless …

Unless the Lord told him the Aramean deserved the disease. Deserved death, which he did, they all did, after their raids on Israel. Perhaps the Lord had decided to make an example of him.

One way or the other, Gehazi wanted to be there.

The horses and chariots covered the distance in less than half the time it would have taken him on foot. He would mention to Elisha how convenient and comfortable it was to travel by chariot. Yet, he supposed, even if King Joram gave Elisha a chariot, the vehicle could scarcely navigate the hills of Ephraim. Perhaps Gehazi could convince his master to ask for a horse or two. Then he wouldn't have to borrow a donkey.

"Captain Naaman!" The man called Rafiq pointed to a clearing in the brush along the river. "There's a path over here."

Naaman rode his horse to the bank, then dismounted and gazed over the surface. Rain a few days earlier had muddied its center, but the shallows shone with ever-shifting greens. On the opposite bank, two eagles ripped strips of flesh from a rabbit carcass. Palms, oaks, and acacia cast their reflections as the captain slowly stripped off armor and clothing down to his loincloth. Rafiq took the discarded items and stacked them in the chariot.

The captain's muscled torso and legs were disfigured by inflamed lesions. Gehazi had never seen worse, though he had brought food to the *tzara'at* colony outside Samaria several times. But the camp dwellers wrapped their heads and limbs with rags, like swaddling or grave clothes. It was terrible to look upon this strong man in such a condition. Even an enemy. Gehazi shook his head. There could be no healing. Naaman was all but dead.

The captain walked down the bank until he stood chest deep in the deepest part of the river. The eagles lifted their heads from the carcass, eying him with interest. When he dipped below the surface, they went back to eating.

When he rose above the water, sputtering and swiping his hands down his face, the female eagle eyed him sideways through one yellow eye, but continued to rip and gulp strips of bloody flesh as the captain dipped himself a second time.

Gehazi counted three, four, five. No change to the ugly sores, except that the river water caused them to glisten like the bloody mass upon which the eagles feasted. If Yahweh were going to heal this pagan, wouldn't the sores be fading by now?

He remembered all the diseased within the camp outside Samaria. There might have been idol worshippers within their number, but surely at least one was a believing Hebrew. Even so, no one in all of Israel had ever been healed of the disease.

Naaman paused before the seventh dip. Sudden fear gripped Gehazi. He stumbled away, poised to run. When their captain was not healed as they hoped, would the entire Aramean band seek vengeance on the nearest Israelite? Him!

Naaman went under the water. Gehazi held his breath. The eagles angled their heads and watched as the ripples expanded.

Then the captain burst from the surface, his long hair flinging droplets of water in an arc. Unblemished arms stretched above his head! With a shout, he spun in the water and faced the crowd watching from the bank. His skin was as clear and clean as a young lad.

On the way back to the house, Naaman invited Gehazi to ride with him. He kept slapping Gehazi on the back and thanking him, laughing all the while, but he insisted upon returning to thank Elisha also.

"He did it," he proclaimed, grinning. "Your God healed me. Every time I went under, I heard Elisha in my mind. 'Dip yourself in the Jordan seven times.' I knew it had to be the full seven, knew that from the start, but still I cursed the prophet each time. Well, maybe I stopped cursing after six. May God forgive me. By then I ... was afraid. That time I prayed, I think. At least I thought ... please. Just please. And I said His name, Yahweh, though I felt unworthy, but I did not want Him to mistake that I prayed to any other god. I myself am a captain, and I demand loyalty from those who serve me. Somehow, I knew this God of gods would demand such loyalty from me. Then I went under for the last time.

"I knew before I broke the surface. The river roared in my head. I was so cold it was as if ice burned my body. Even my head felt charged, as if I'd plunged face-first into a snowbank. That is the only way I can explain it." He stared at his outstretched arm, spread his fingers, and shook his head in disbelief. Then he glanced sideways at Gehazi, punched his shoulder, and shouted "Ha!" like one who has lost his mind. "Ha!"

Gehazi's thoughts were also muddled in ways he couldn't understand. Why did he hope Elisha would again refuse to see the captain when they arrived?

As their chariot rolled through Samaria's gate, Elisha stood on the stoop as if he were waiting. Naaman jumped out first, then walked hesitantly to stand in front of him. Humbly, he bowed to the ground. His voice was muffled as he said, "Now I know that there is no God in all the world except in Israel. Please accept a gift from your servant." Without lifting his head, he motioned back to the chariots and laden pack animals.

Still in the chariot, Gehazi clenched his fingers around its iron frame. Yes. This Aramean had received a miracle, and he'd brought silver and gold to pay. After what Elisha had done for him, the school of the prophets should receive some benefit. Might there even be enough to replace Gehazi's vineyard?

Elisha's gaze fixed on Naaman. "As surely as the Lord lives, whom I serve, I will not accept anything."

Gehazi fought a scowl as he stepped down from the chariot. Nothing? Why did Elisha refuse what the Aramean wanted to give? His pack animals were weighed down with riches, and who had more need of it than the schools of prophets? Naaman should pay a fair price for what he'd received. He'd been delivered from death.

And Elisha had done it. Well, Yahweh had done it. But the prophet had delivered a gift from God, and without him, none of this would have happened. He should be paid.

Gehazi stood quietly, feigning meek submission as Elisha and Naaman talked, but he fumed inside. He'd had a hand in this matter. In fact, if he hadn't told Elisha about the king tearing his clothes, his master wouldn't have known that Naaman needed healing. He wouldn't have sent the message to King Joram. When Joram sent Naaman to Elisha, he refused to even meet him. Sent Gehazi in his stead.

Without him, Naaman would have gone home unhealed.

Despite all Gehazi had done, Elisha was refusing Naaman's persistent offers. Not even asking Gehazi's opinion. He pressed his lips together and expelled a long breath.

"If you will not accept any payment," Naaman said, "Please let me, your servant, be given as much earth of this place as a pair of mules can carry. For I will never again make burnt offerings and sacrifices to any other god but the Lord."

Dirt? The Aramean wanted dirt?

Elisha smiled and nodded at this while Gehazi twisted a fold of his tunic. How pleased the prophet seemed that one gentile believed.

Naaman was still speaking.

"But may the Lord forgive me this one thing," he began, "when my master, Benhadad, enters the temple of Rimmon to bow down, and he is leaning on my arm and I have to bow there also—may the Lord forgive me this."

Elisha studied him a moment, that almost-smile still on his face. "Go in peace."

Go in peace? Healed of an incurable disease, just swore he would worship only Yahweh from this day—*except* for those times when he walks his king into the temple of the storm god of Aram.

Apostasy!

What did Elisha mean, 'Go in peace.' Was it the same as 'Don't concern yourself. It is of no great import.'

If so, why did he and the prophet tread the heights and depths of the hills of Ephram, teaching the inhabitants to worship only the Lord?

Gehazi struggled to slow his breath. His nostrils

annoyingly expanded with the effort, so he turned his back to Elisha. He was in no mood for a scolding. He watched the Arameans leave for Damascus, taking their gold with them.

"It is a long ride to the river," Elisha said. "Are you hungry? I saved stew."

He shook his head, his eyes still on the departing chariots.

"Tell me what you saw at the river."

Struggling to conceal his distaste, Gehazi described everything, adding what Naaman had related about the final moments before his healing.

"Hmm." Elisha scratched his chin. "Were you impressed by his prayer? Asking Yahweh to save him?"

"Save him?"

"The prayer he mentioned."

One word? Elisha was too easy on this fellow. Please? Please heal me from this disease. Sure, one word could be a prayer. And then he receives healing, a mercy he did not deserve, *and* goes home with his gold.

Frowning, Gehazi watched the last chariot disappear over a hill. Elisha cleared his throat. "He also said, 'there is no god in all the world except the God of Israel.' Quite a change from the man who arrived on our doorstep."

"What does he think about the rivers of Damascus now, do you suppose? Ha!" Elisha slapped him on the shoulder, right where he was still sore from all of Naaman's slaps.

Gehazi clamped his lips. No point reminding Elisha how Naaman, in his next breath, talked about kneeling in the temple of Rimmon. But he did have a question. "What did you mean by 'Go in peace?'"

Elisha was silent for a moment. Then he said, "Was he to learn all the Torah in an afternoon? The Lord will teach him what he must know. That is why I sent him on his way in peace ... as the Lord told me to do."

Gehazi looked down. His sandaled feet stood amid hoof prints and chariot ruts. "I am tired," he said.

"You should rest," Elisha said. "Remember Elijah's example. There are times one needs to eat and then nap." He lifted his hand in farewell and retreated into his house, obviously expecting Gehazi to take his advice.

Instead, he walked into the little house next to Elisha's, retrieved his waterskin and, after ensuring that Elisha was still inside his own house, he ran after the chariots.

His master had been wrong not to accept a gift from Benhadad's captain. But as surely as the Lord lived, Gehazi would not make the same mistake.

The Arameans had moved out smartly, but Gehazi ran hard. When Naaman looked back and saw Gehazi following, he stopped and rode back to meet him. "Is everything all right?"

Gehazi bent over and sucked in deep breaths. "Everything is all right. My master sent me because two young prophets have just arrived from the hill country of Ephraim. He said, 'Please give them a talent of silver and two sets of clothing.'"

"Of course, but take two talents." said Naaman, urging him as he'd done with Elisha. Gehazi protested mildly about the increased offer but allowed Naaman to prevail. The captain divided the silver between two leather bags and added a set of clothing to each.

As two of Naaman's servants carried the sacks toward him, Gehazi felt a flicker of apprehension. With that much silver, the two sacks would weigh almost as much as he. How could he carry so much back to his house?

Naaman laughed when Gehazi explained. "No, my friend, you are not meant to carry anything. My two servants will carry it for you."

His plan had worked better than he hoped. All this silver! He could buy a vineyard—replace what Aramean raiders had taken from him. He could share some of the silver with his sons, and if any were left, with some of the prophets. He also now owned two sets of finer clothing than he had ever worn.

Naaman's two servants ran ahead of him toward the hill of Samaria. Gehazi smiled, imagining they were his own servants, running ahead to announce his approach to the city, as if he were some great man. What would it be like to be wealthy like Naaman? He'd had dreams when he married Lital. To prosper, be secure. But he had struggled, all their lives. Just wait until he poured silver into her lap! Finally, she would have reason to be proud of him.

He stopped Naaman's servants before they ran through the city gates. It would not do for them to be observed running ahead of him with large, obviously heavy bundles.

He took the sacks, thanked them, and sent them on their way.

He grunted as he slung one over each shoulder. The silver pressed through the thick fabric into his back as he trudged through the back streets. When he reached his house, he lowered his burdens through the rear window, left open for the evening breeze. He climbed in after, then hid everything in a wooden chest. He had to remove his cook pots, but the chest was a good place to store the silver and clothing. After he arranged the items, he pressed a couple of pots back on top. Everything concealed, he stood back and sighed.

Fine clothes he could not wear. A fortune in silver he could not spend. He tried replaying the vision of pouring silver into Lital's lap, but now he imagined suspicion instead of pride in her gaze. For the first time since he'd joined the school of the prophets, he dreaded the morning.

The next day, Gehazi walked the few steps to Elisha's house, his tread heavy. To compensate, he tried to make his voice cheery. "What can I do for you this morning, master?"

"Where have you been, Gehazi?"

He looked around, pretending confusion. "Sleeping, of course. I did not go anywhere," he lied. What else could he do?

Elisha's shoulders sagged. "Did not my heart go with you when the man turned from his chariot to meet you? Should you have accepted from him silver, or clothing, or servants for what God meant as a free gift? You rebelled against the will of the Lord. Such hopes I had for you ... that you might take up my mantle one day. But now Naaman's leprosy will cling to you and to your descendants."

Gehazi looked down at his hands, his arms, stretched out a leg, where lesions already mottled his skin.

He tried to protest, to shout, 'Unfair!' But his throat, tight and sore, only croaked.

Chapter Thirty-Six

No one who hopes in you will ever be put to shame,
but shame will come on those who are
treacherous without cause.
Psalm 25:3

Gilgal to Samaria, a few weeks later
Jaedon

JAEDON WORKED CAREFULLY, LIFTING ERRANT STRANDS of vine and shortening or removing them as the grandmothers had instructed. Warm sun on his shoulders and soft earth under his feet filled him with contentment. His healing had begun here, in the vineyard.

Dov's house had grown crowded with three growing children as well as Jaedon under one roof, yet he and Imma hadn't pushed him to leave. But during one particularly loud squabble among the children, he decided to go hunting. As he strode past the vineyard he had planted, he saw it needed water.

Maalik and Dov had taken turns watering for him. With the dearth of rain, they had enough to do carrying water to their own plots. Painful thoughts or not, it was time he stepped up to his own responsibility.

He found the vineyard did not evoke the sad memories he expected, on the contrary his spirits lifted each hour he spent toiling. One hot afternoon, he'd stepped into the house's cool interior, walking slowly through each quiet room, a goodbye of sorts to thoughts of any future search. He'd visited every temple, each slave auction, exhausted all leads. To no avail. His heart heavy, he finally conceded. He would never find her.

It had been eerie at first, to walk alone in the pretty dwelling he'd imagined bringing her to. But Ziva was not here. Had never been.

You gave me a home and a vineyard, Lord. I thought a wife would be part of the blessing.

He listened a while after the prayer, as Elisha had

taught him.

He didn't hear the voice, but a question arose in his mind. *Because I did not receive the blessing of a wife, should I treat the first two blessings with contempt?*

Perhaps that was his own reasoning, not *the Voice*, but Jaedon asked forgiveness for his ingratitude and thanked the Lord. He glanced upward once more. *And ... a little rain would be nice.*

"Ho, Jaedon! A runner has arrived!" He set down his pruning hook as Binyamin rushed into the vineyard. His friend's eyes sparked with energy.

"A runner arrived."

"So you said." Jaedon got to his feet. Across the roadway the runner was sharing his message among a crowd of villagers, Dov and Imma among them. Jaedon glanced uphill to the grandparents' home. The three would want to hear, so he stuck his fingers in his mouth and whistled.

"You won't believe what he said." Biny said.

"Wait, unless you want to repeat it twice." Jaedon gestured toward Maalik and the savtas— Hadassah and Yaffa. They emerged from the house faster than their ages should allow.

"Something wrong?" Maalik shouted.

Biny cupped his hands around his mouth. "News from Samaria."

Good news or bad? Jaedon worried about Elisha when he stayed in the capital, though King Joram was not as evil as his father had been. How could a prophet of the Lord be safe when Jezebel lived?

Savta Hadassah was first to arrive, her strong will always driving her body to keep up. "Speak, Biny! Is Elisha all right?"

"He is well." Binyamin pursed his lips. "But he mourns the loss of his servant."

Jaedon shaded his eyes. "What? Has Gehazi died?"

"No. Though he probably wishes he had."

Then Binyamin told of the powerful Aramean soldier afflicted by *tzara'at*. His servant had told the diseased captain that Israel's prophet could heal him. "He must have been desperate to listen to a servant's advice. And he must have been a very great man in his country, for the king of Aram to allow him into his court."

"Into the king's presence? Don't Arameans isolate those with the disfiguring disease?"

Biny raised both hands. "Who can say? In fact, King Benhadad received him and then wrote King Joram and instructed him to heal this man. Naaman."

"Heal him!"

Biny nodded. "He sent rich gifts to secure the healing. Enough silver and gold to pay a year's wages for over five hundred men. Maybe because of the disease risk. Complete sets of clothing. King Joram was alarmed. 'Am I God?' he said and rent his clothes."

Jaedon shook his head. Strange foreign ways. No wonder Joram was confused. "Was the man healed?"

"Not by Joram." Biny expelled a short laugh. "Gehazi happened to be at the palace, heard the disturbance, and told Elisha. He told King Joram, 'Send the Aramean to me, and the Arameans will learn there is a God in Israel.'"

This sounded like Elisha, except this was about healing an idol-worshiping enemy, not an Israelite. Yet Jaedon remembered what Elijah did for the widow of Zarephath. He brought her dead son to life, and, though they had been Phoenician idol worshippers, they followed Yahweh afterward.

Biny related details of Elisha meeting with the captain and sending him to wash in the Jordan to be healed.

"I can imagine the man's gratitude," Jaedon said. "How wonderful for Elisha. Such riches will fund his work and that of the prophets for years to come." Jaedon folded his arms, contemplating watching such an amazing miracle. If only he could have been there.

"Except Elisha would not accept a gift." Biny shrugged. "Said he would not accept payment for what God freely gave."

Jaedon cocked his head. "He continues to surprise, and he always has a reason. Yet, perhaps I begin to understand. What happened next?"

Biny paused and looked down. "Then Gehazi received Naaman's *tzara'at*."

This was unexpected, and Jaedon had a stronger urge

to go to Samaria. Ask Elisha why he was willing to heal an Aramean, to start. And why was his servant afflicted?

"Although Elisha refused Naaman's offer," Biny continued, "Gehazi followed the Aramean and asked for silver and clothing."

"Ohhh." Jaedon slowly exhaled. "Both Elisha and Elijah always protected God's word. Did exactly what He commanded, nothing more or less. The Lord told Elisha the healing was a gift, and so he refused Naaman's gifts. Gehazi's action told a different story. That God's mercy was for sale."

"Yes," said Biny, nodding solemnly. "It was not only that Gehazi lied in saying the gifts were for prophets."

"He said that?" Maalik asked.

Savta Yaffa had been listening silently, but now she interjected, "Lying is always wrong. But lying about what God has said is dangerous."

Jaedon scuffed his foot in the dirt. "Who will tell Gehazi's wife and sons what happened?"

"Even though they live near us, I have not spoken to them in a while," Biny said. "Only seen them at a distance. I dread telling them such bad news. Gehazi was sent to stay with the other *metzorim* in the camp outside Samaria."

Jaedon sighed. "Are there many in the *tzara'at* camp? Does the city provide food?"

"The messenger did not say."

"Did he say who will serve Elisha now?"

Biny shook his head.

Jaedon wiped his brow and sighed. "I will tell the family."

When Jaedon approached Gehazi's home, he only saw Lital working in the garden. Walking bent over, a basket slung over one shoulder, she carefully pulled weeds between rows of knee-high barley. She stood a moment, not seeing him, one hand pressed to the small of her back, while the other wiped her forehead. Where were her sons?

He cleared his throat. "Lital."

She jerked upright, her eyes wide and startled.

"I am sorry to have surprised you," he said quietly. "I

have come with news. Where are your sons?" His gaze swept from the house, to the field, and to the hill and woods beyond. He did not want to tell her without her sons. "Have they gone hunting?"

"No," she said hesitantly. "They are in the house."

Why weren't they helping her in the fields? He turned, intending to go speak to them first. Or at least bring them out so they could comfort her. "Do not go inside," she said quickly. "That is, they are not well."

"All three? Shall I send for my mother? She is knowledgeable about draughts and poultices."

She swung her head, as if in pain. "No one should come near. I will care for them. You said you bring news?"

His gaze strayed back to the house. He did not want to tell her that Gehazi was afflicted. Not without her sons by her side.

"I should come back when they are well."

Her eyes grew suspicious. "You have news of Gehazi." Her face took on a strange, knowing expression. Like Savta Yaffa when, as a young boy, he had disappointed her.

"I am sorry." Why was he apologizing? He had done nothing. "But Gehazi"—his throat was closing, he could only blurt it out—"has become ill with *tzara'at*."

She bent, choking. He hurried forward and touched his hand to her shoulder. Poor woman.

But when he turned her around, she was laughing, though tears streamed from her slitted eyes. "Tzara'at! Gehazi, too! Oh, how God must hate us."

Then, as he stood helpless to comfort her, she really did start to cry.

As her sobs subsided, Jaedon promised help. That he would tell others in the settlement, that all would bring food, carry water, and prepare such remedies as would ease pain.

When he told Maalik of their troubles, he said, "If they have *tzara'at*, they cannot stay here. The settlement is too small and their house too close to others. The entire settlement could become infected. They must go to the camp outside Samaria."

Although Jaedon argued that Lital was caring for her sons, that surely they would prefer to stay in their own home, opinions were firmly against him, especially among the elders. "You know nothing of the law concerning this terrible disease. The *metzora* must be kept separate, unless he is healed."

"How will they travel to Samaria when they are ill?" Jaedon asked. It felt vile to even consider sending them away.

Maalik said, "Old Kenan died last winter. We can give them his wagon and mule."

It was not a bad idea. "How can they drive the mule? He was never an easy animal."

Maalik shrugged. "The disease sometimes relents and allows those afflicted to regain some strength. We must pray for that."

Lord, please heal them completely. Or if not, please give them respite. Or if not ... he looked at his own unblemished arms, hands, legs. *Send me?*

So it was decided that Jaedon would drive the wagon to Samaria. Villagers filled the wagon bed with last fall's barley straw and spread blankets on top, making a comfortable bed where the three young men reclined.

At first, Lital had protested. They could not take her boys. Then she declared she would go with them, but her sons would not have it. They swore they were content with the solution. If they should worsen, they did not want her to watch. If they were healed, they would return. "This is best, Imma," said Asriel. We will be at peace, knowing that you will not take the disease from us, and we will be with Abba." The oldest son raised a hand to the cluster of villagers that stood watching them leave. "May the Lord bless you for your goodness to our mother ... and to us."

Miriam stood among the villagers, her arms folded. She had not wanted Jaedon to go. She waved goodbye but stayed back as he had insisted. How could he be sure he did not already carry a seed of the disease, from contact with Gehazi's sons? Maalik had assured him that his youth and strength would protect him if he maintained distance and immersed often in clean water, but he would not be careless of his mother's life.

The thought awoke a feeling of kinship with Lital's sons.

He climbed on the wagon seat and took the reins. "I will care for them, and I will find Gehazi. I will see to them all."

The journey to Samaria took only three days. He tried to think back to the long meandering journey when he'd fled with Imma and Savta Yaffa from Jezebel. After they met Elijah, he often led them deep into the mountains, away from the ridge road.

This time, there had been no reason to take such precautions. Any travelers they came across were anxious to avoid the wagon and let them pass. He had only to call out, "I transport *metzorim*."

As he neared the city, he wondered if he should hide his identity. Call himself Jaedon ben Dov. But he sensed that, as a friend of Elisha, he would not be as vulnerable to Jezebel's schemes as he had been as a young boy. Besides, he didn't intend to make claims on the property she had stolen. Even though King Ahab was long dead, the thought of the old queen made his skin burn, as if he had stumbled into a hive of wasps.

"Jaedon, turn aside here." The eldest of Gehazi's sons, raised his voice to be heard over the rumbling of the wooden wheels.

He almost asked why. But of course, three *metzorim* would not be allowed past the gates. He had not thought to ask where the camp would be.

"I was told the camp is east of the city, past the dunghill."

Jaedon glanced over his shoulder. "Thank you. How do you feel?"

The boy smiled wryly and shrugged. "We're better, now that our fevers are gone. But the rash ..." He shrugged, holding up his arm. His scratching had raised welts. His brothers turned their heads away, misery in their posture.

The youngest, Abner, who had seen about twelve years, asked, "Will Abba still be alive?"

The older brothers stared at the boy, obviously wishing he'd kept his mouth shut.

"One of the prophets sent word that he has settled in and is doing well. He will be glad to see you."

Now all three brothers turned sorrowful gazes on Jaedon. His face heated and he shook his head. "I am sorry. Of course your father would not wish to see you in this camp. Forgive my clumsiness. I will pray for your healing."

They rode in silence a while. Jaedon smelled the refuse before he saw it.

A fire smoked at one edge. Several ragged figures dug through the discards. Their garments hid everything but their eyes, so he couldn't tell if they were men, women, or how far the disease had progressed. At least there were no young children among them. Jaedon glanced at Abner. Except him. *Yahweh, have mercy on these, my neighbors.*

After they passed the highest part of the dump, they came across a flimsy dwelling. Made of branches and rags, it resembled a *Sukkot* booth framed by branches and roofed with palm fronds. A few shrouded figures sat under its patchy shade, eating what might have been porridge.

As the mule plodded along, they came across several dwellings made of scavenged items from the dump—rags, discarded poles, and such branches or roofing materials that were left at the outskirts by charitable individuals.

Jaedon called to everyone they encountered. "Who knows Gehazi of Gilgal?"

Finally, they approached what looked like a fallen log covered with rags. But a log that size would have been scavenged for building or at least firewood. When Jaedon called out once more, the log arched, twisted, and threw off the rags. Gehazi got to his feet, staring at the cart in disbelief.

Jaedon pulled the mule to a stop, staring back. What could he say? Only one thing. "I am sorry to see you here, my friend. Sorrier still to bring your sons to this place."

Gehazi looked away, his face twisted like the trunk of a wind-whipped tree. "Elisha told me they would arrive soon, though I foolishly hoped he was wrong. And you—you are good. But you risk contagion."

He watched as the boys climbed down, but when they ran to their father, he held up his hands to ward them away.

"How can it matter, Abba? Look!" The youngest held up

his hands, and as his loose sleeves fell back, the lesions were apparent. The other two did the same. Then they converged on their father, arms wrapped around each other.

Still seated on the wagon bench, Jaedon heard without understanding their murmured conversation. He stared at his white-knuckled grip on the reins. He never expected to find anyone he knew in a camp for *metzorim*. And Gehazi— after losing his house and vineyard to Arameans—this!

In some ways he and Gehazi were the same. Both had wanted to be mentored by Elisha. Both lost their home and vineyard. Their family legacy.

Gehazi shouldn't have done what he did, but Jaedon almost understood. He, too, ached with unmet desires.

Chapter Thirty-Seven

The Lord is close to the brokenhearted
and saves those who are crushed in spirit.
Psalm 34:18

Samaria to Gilgal, the next day
Elisha

THE THIRD WATCH SOUNDED. ELISHA HAD lain awake through the night, and there were still hours before dawn. It seemed an iron shield pressed upon his chest. Without opening his eyes, he whispered the words of King David when he feared he'd be forced to fight against his own people.

The Lord is close to the brokenhearted ... yes, that was him. Brokenhearted, crushed in spirit, and forced to speak against one he had nurtured in the ways of the Lord like a child. But Gehazi was no child. He had rebelled against Yahweh's known will and the Lord had punished him. Rightly so. Not only for his greed, but the slur against God's character—that Yahweh's mercy could be bought with gold.

The Lord was just. He was good. Elisha's shoulders slumped. He had grown to love his servant. So what was left to him but surrender to the sadness?

Slowly, he got to his feet and felt his way to the ewer on the corner table. After washing, he slid the fringed shawl over his head and went to stand by the eastern window. Only the moon touched the outlines of the city and the torches of the watchmen dotted the walls they stood upon.

"Lord." He could not continue.

I hear you, Elisha.

"He has joined the other *metzorim*, but of course You know. What would you have me do next? Do I stay longer in Samaria?"

You have met with King Joram several times and instructed him to follow My law. It remains for him to obey or not. Return now to Gilgal. Refresh your spirit among the prophets. They need you, and you need them.

Elisha bowed his head. "Yes, Lord." He waited awhile in

silence. Perhaps the Lord had more to say.

Finally, he lit a lamp and moved around the house deciding what he would bring. His cloak, water, and what food was in the house were sufficient. The Lord would supply his other needs. He still had Malka's donkey, so he would ride it to Gilgal. Perhaps the Lord would send him next to Shunem, and he could return the animal.

He was ready to leave before dawn, but as he headed for the shed where he stabled the donkey, the Lord spoke again.

Feed the donkey but wait for Jaedon. You will travel with him.

Why was Jaedon in Samaria? His curiosity pricked, Elisha forked hay into the donkey's manger. She always lay down to sleep, so she was lurching to her feet. Feeling her age, poor girl. As she whiffled her nose into the hay, he grabbed a rag and briskly rubbed her shaggy coat free of straw and manure. Ready.

He returned to the house, rechecked everything, and when he noticed his neighbor step outside to scan the sky, he met him in the space between their two homes. "I'll be traveling for a time."

"Good weather for a journey. I'll keep an eye on your house," the neighbor said. "If a prophet stops by, we'll invite him for supper."

"The Lord will bless you," Elisha said.

The neighbor grinned, ducked back inside, and returned with a cloth-wrapped parcel. "My wife sends this hot flatbread for your travels."

As Elisha packed the bread save one piece, he saw someone approaching on foot. Soon he recognized Jaedon.

"The Lord told me to wait for you," he said, "but not why you have come."

Jaedon glanced down. "I've brought Gehazi's three sons to the camp of the *metzorim*."

Elisha groaned, an ache spreading through his limbs. "Already."

Jaedon raised his eyebrows but asked no questions. "Let me carry that for you," he said, when Elisha returned from his house with his few necessities.

"It's not far to the city's stable and I am not decrepit. I

have taken Elijah's mantle, but I am only old enough to be your father—not your grandfather." He smiled to soften the words.

Gehazi, and now the boys. And Lital. *Lord.*

Be comforted, Elisha. And don't forget Malka's donkey. She will have need of it.

He felt a grin curve his lips. "Jaedon, you can help me with another matter. There is a donkey in the shed. Bring her out."

A few stems of hay protruded from the donkey's mouth as they walked toward Samaria's gate. The stablemaster brought out the mule. Glancing at the prophet, he shook his head at the small piece of silver Jaedon held out. "This fellow cleaned out the manger left by a customer who couldn't wait for his animals to finish their meal. Besides, I did nothing with your wagon. Didn't want to touch it, frankly, after you told me who you carried. You did a good thing, lad. But I don't want to risk ... well, *tzara'at* is a fearsome disease."

He did not refuse, however, when Elisha offered him one of the flatbreads Joshua's wife had given. Jaedon hitched the mule to the wagon and tied the donkey in back. Soon they were on the road to Gilgal. For a while they chatted about Jaedon's journey to Samaria, then how Gehazi's wife had taken the news.

Elisha shared the bare-bones tale of Naaman's healing and Gehazi's actions. "He could not resist Naaman's riches. He did not recognize the wealth he already held in his hands. He could only see what he lost."

Elisha glanced at Jaedon. The boy had not been back to the north since he fled Jezreel with Miriam. Was he thinking of Naboth's vineyard and the fine home built against the city wall that would have been his one day?

"I will be glad to return to Gilgal." Jaedon stared at the reins in his hands. "Samaria is not the same without my grandmother."

"The Lord blessed us all when He sent her to Gilgal."

"For Imma's wedding." Jaedon chuckled.

The cart rattled as they hit a rut in the road. Elisha gripped the wooden bench as it lurched sideways. "I'm glad she stayed."

"Who would not stay with the Sons of the Prophets if invited? Good company, the word of the Lord, the occasional miracle ..." He nudged Elisha with his shoulder as his voice trailed off. A sharp chirp came from a tall tree a ways from the road, and Jaedon's head jerked in that direction. An eagle swept from the branches, angling deeper into a wooded area, then folded its wings and dived. A sharp cry revealed that the raptor had killed its prey.

"I often think of Hevel. Imma and Dov thought they saw her the day Elijah left in the whirlwind. After she left, I never saw her again."

"Perhaps you will."

Jaedon slanted a sly glance. "Only perhaps?"

Elisha flung up his hands. "I do not know. There are many things I do not know. But just as the Lord provides food each day, He gives knowledge when I need it. But I am curious about a matter upon which you can spread light. During times I was away from Gilgal, you have continued to search for your betrothed. What have you learned?"

He listened as Jaedon related the endless roads he had trod, the pagan temples, the sneering or bored priests. "It's not as if no captives had been offered, but they all replied with a similar answer. They had not seen a captive as young and beautiful as Ziva."

Elisha wondered if they had told the truth. If indeed they had purchased her, they would not be willing to part with a lucrative source of income.

As if he'd understood Elisha's thoughts, Jaedon continued, "Dov had given me Imma's dowry, which I freely offered. I saw the greed in their eyes. Later, I made sure to disappear into the hills instead of keeping to the road. If they'd had her, I believe they would have taken the silver."

The boy had matured over the time they'd been apart. Elisha felt a stirring in the wind, as sometimes happened before the Lord spoke. He waited, but the Lord did not speak, Jaedon said no more on the matter, and they drove on as the sun climbed high.

Though no longer fresh from the oven, the flatbread was sun-warmed when they stopped for the midday meal. Elisha directed them off the road and into a hilly area, where they came to a grassy spot, a copse of trees, and a stream. Jaedon hobbled the mule and donkey, and they grazed while Elisha and Jaedon cooled their feet in the stream.

Jaedon grew thoughtful. "When I first met Ziva, we were on our way to return captive children to their village. Biny told us we were approaching Gischala, Eden's hometown. He wanted to stop and share news of her with her parents and younger sister, and the rest ... well, you know. We met and talked as her village welcomed the children and celebrated their freedom. When the day grew warm, we retreated to a date orchard watered by a stream"—he indicated the reflective ribbon of green—"such as this."

Silence stretched between them, broken only by the munching of the donkeys, the burble of the brook, and the chatter of birds hidden by the thick foliage.

Elisha cleared his throat. "You mentioned miracles earlier. Let me tell you how the Lord has worked while you were away, before the healing of Naaman." He told the story that still amazed him—the death and quickening of Malka's son. Various emotions crossed Jaedon's face. Surprise. Confusion. Then something else he could not interpret.

He paused in his description of Malka's reaction. "Yes?"

Jaedon leaned forward and wrapped his arms around his knees, his expression now smoothed like new clay. "This sounds very like what Elijah told. The widow of Zarephath and her son."

"Yes, very like. I first sent Gehazi with my staff. He is younger and would be quicker. As I hurried toward Shunem, I remembered how I asked the Lord, when He gave me the mantle of Elijah, to give me a double-portion of my master's spirit. Elijah was steadfast. Completely devoted to the Lord. But he had the confidence of the Sons of the Prophets who were not all convinced, in the beginning, that I was the Lord's choice."

Once again, conflicting emotions played across Jaedon's face. "Imma and Dov both described how the whirlwind dropped Elijah's mantle at your feet, and how you struck the waters of the Jordan which parted for you as they had for the prophet. That should have been enough to convince anyone."

"Yes. That's what the Lord reminded me. So I prayed,

fervently, as Elijah did. The boy sneezed"—Elisha chuckled—"and came back. The Lord strengthened my resolve that day. Yet … are you convinced?"

"That you are the Lord's choice? Of course I am! Why do you ask?"

"You have asked something of me which I am not able to grant. I am not able to restore Ziva to you, nor even tell you where she is. What good am I as a prophet?"

Jaedon leapt to his feet, strode down to the stream, and picked up a rock. He tossed it back and forth in his hands several times, then reared back and threw it with force toward a distant tree. He missed. He bent to gather several more stones and aimed at the tree again and again, without success. Finally, he stopped and stood staring at the tree, his shoulders trembling. Then he turned, and Elisha saw the boy was laughing.

"Do you feel better?"

"Foolish, but yes, better." He looked at his palm which still held a single stone. "I usually hit what I aim at."

"It can be frustrating to miss your objective and not understand why."

"We are not talking about throwing rocks, are we?"

"No."

Jaedon looked at the ground. "You asked the Lord where to find Ziva. As did I. I suppose I am angry."

"Yes." Elisha hesitated, not wanting to ask who he was angry with. Should he explain Gehazi's mistake? It might help the lad avoid a similar misstep."

Tell him.

"When Gehazi lost his home and vineyard, he felt unworthy. Less of a man. Believed his wife deserved more. She is a good woman. But instead of accepting with gratitude what the Lord gave him, Gehazi decided to take by stealth what the Lord had not given." Elisha waited.

Jaedon seemed to think it over. "The key is accepting with gratitude what the Lord gives. My family. My home. The young vineyard."

"You're on the right path. Don't forget your friends. Including me."

Jaedon walked over and sat down. "Including you."

Chapter Thirty-Eight

The company of the prophets said to Elisha,
"Look, the place where we meet with you is too small for us.
Let us go to the Jordan, where each of us can get a pole;
and let us build a place there for us to meet."
2 Kings 6:1-2

Gilgal, nearly 3 years after ending search for Ziva
Jaedon

TWO SMALL BODIES FLUNG THEMSELVES ACROSS Jaedon, jolting him from a bad dream. Growling, he rolled onto his back and clutched Yuval and Aharon into a bear hug. The two boys had grown as close as brothers since Biny and Eden had adopted Aharon. Nathaniel stood back, eyes wide and a faint smile flitting across his face. Then Jaedon's youngest brother took a breath and jumped atop them all.

"Ooof! Have mercy on your old uncle."

"It's almost daybreak, *Dod* Jaedon," said Aharon. "You promised to take us fishing."

"You're not our uncle," squealed Yuval. "You're our brother." Nathaniel rolled off the pile and grinned.

In truth he was not Aharon's uncle, either. He was the almost-betrothed of the boy's sister. But Biny had adopted the boy, and Jaedon was closer to his friend than a brother, so he chose the title, and the boy happily called him *dod*.

"I am your older brother, *ach katan*. Much, much older." Gently setting the three aside, Jaedon shoved himself up. "You should listen to me because of my great wisdom." He thumped his head with his knuckles and the boys laughed.

What had possessed him to keep the boys overnight? Yes, Dov and Miriam wanted to hunt, and the settlement would welcome meat in this drought. Any of the grandparents or even Biny and Eden would have been glad to keep them.

So was he, though they had kept him awake into the second watch of the night, chortling and asking for just one more story about Elijah and Elisha.

He grinned at their banter, as welcome as the patter of rain would be on his rooftop. They filled his empty house with joy, so that he could almost forget the one for whom he had built it.

He fed them leftover gruel the grandmothers had brought for their supper. As he swallowed the watery stuff, he prayed.

Please, Lord, help us catch fish to thicken tomorrow's soup.

After breaking their fast, they headed toward Biny's house, each boy proudly wearing one of the fishing lines they had braided yesterday from reed fibers. Jaedon had made three more of reddish hairs from the tail of Dov's stallion, Uriel. Five bone hooks were carefully folded into a scrap of leather and a handful of grooved pebbles rattled in a pouch.

He looked down at the dark heads beside him. "Boys, when I was the age of Yuval and Aharon, the prophet Elisha was like an uncle to me. He taught me many things—"

"Like how to make a fishline?" Yuval piped up.

"And train the young eagle?" Aharon added.

Jaedon grinned. Ziva's brother had come a long way overcoming his shyness.

"I want an eagle," said Nathaniel, his youngest brother.

Jaedon cleared his throat. "All those and more. Most important, he taught me to pray—for everything."

"God is up there." Nathaniel pointed at the sky.

Jaedon couldn't help another grin. There was no reason to concern himself about his youngest brother's shyness. With two older companions, he did not lack for examples—or competition.

"If Elisha were with us right now, he would tell us to pray about the fish."

Yuval looked at the braided twine circling his wrist. "Why? We have fishlines and hooks. You said there is a trap at the river."

Jaedon answered patiently. "We will cast our lines in the river and the trap may have fish—or not. But it is God who provides food, for us and the animals. He is in control of everything. That is why we ask His help and thank Him for our blessings."

The boys slid their gazes toward him. He raised his hands toward heaven. "Blessed are you, Lord our God, at whose word all came to be." He paused. This was one of the formal prayers Elijah used when teaching at settlements of the prophets.

Then he added his earlier, silent prayer. More like those Elisha taught him. "Please, Lord, help us catch fish to thicken tomorrow's soup."

"Amen! If we bring home a fish, your imma will be happy." Binyamin was walking toward them.

Aharon ran forward and grabbed him around the middle. "Abba!" He held up his arm, proudly showing the fishing line. "I braided this." He glanced behind. "Jaedon helped."

"Let me see!" Biny knelt beside his adopted son.

Jaedon's throat tightened. Not at the thought of Ziva, though reminders of the abrupt end to his betrothal still felt like he'd swallowed a handful of stones. It was thinking about Biny fathering this orphaned child, as Dov had fathered him. Neither had called it a duty, rather, a joy.

Jaedon rubbed his throat. "Glad you're coming. I'm outnumbered."

"Still are. Should I call Eden?"

"We'll manage. At least we outweigh them."

They found a wide spot in the river under an ancient willow whose roots stretched toward the river's new, lower level. Each boy held a short stick, with the line wound tightly around its middle. Bone hooks were baited with the guts of the solitary fish they found in the trap, and the grooved rocks from Jaedon's pouch dragged the lines down to fish level, out of their sight in the murky water.

It was a pleasant spot nearly hidden around a bend. The current swirled lazily, indicating a deep spot. The willow was not the only tree, a stand of young ash grew thick and straight along its banks.

Having warned the boys not to scare the fish, Jaedon spoke quietly. "If we catch fish this morning, we'll swim before we go home." He quickly shushed as all three boys inhaled and opened their mouths to shout with joy.

Biny grinned and shook his head. He showed them how to check their hooks, and when two of them were found empty, helped them thread fish guts more carefully. Before long, each boy had caught a couple fish and Biny and Jaedon had caught several more between them.

"This is a good spot." Jaedon waded into the river while holding Nathaniel's hand.

Taking another step, Jaedon slipped, went under, and came up sputtering. "Deeper than I thought." He hugged his youngest sibling to his chest. "All right little brother?

Although looking uncertain, Nathaniel swiped wet hair off his face and nodded.

"Let's move to shallower water," Biny said. "I think swimming lessons are in order."

As they moved toward the bank, Jaedon heard men's voices in the distance. He recognized several of the prophets, and as they grew closer, he heard an axe striking wood. Soon the group was upon them.

"Ho, you're swimming? Come out of there and help us, you lazy brutes." Javan, who had built Imma's loom when Elijah had first brought them to Gilgal, brandished an axe above his head.

"Why should we?" Jaedon teased. "We've been fishing with these lads since sunup and we're tired." He yawned, though he had every intention of joining in their project— whatever it was.

"Elisha is with us."

Biny motioned the boys to the bank. "Well then, of course. What are you doing?"

Javan pointed at a cluster of the saplings that lined the creek. "First, cut some of these trees for posts and trusses. We'll build a shelter where Elisha can teach all of us together. The other spot has become too small."

Jaedon heaved the smallest boy up on the bank. With all the noise of voices and activity, there'd be no more fishing today. But a shade structure would make for a pleasant meeting location for the Sons of the Prophets who usually met after morning chores for Torah reading and instruction. Fishermen who arrived with the dawn could find respite in its shade to clean their fish.

He saw Elisha now, at the back of the small crowd, smiling and talking kindly to a new young prophet who walked beside him. His eyes were on Elisha's face as he spoke. Jaedon recognized the expression of rapt understanding, a moment's enlightenment, that had filled him whenever Elisha taught him from the Torah.

A pang hit him, like hunger but not for food. He had missed time alone with Elisha, their times reading the Torah together, and listening to the prophet's deep insights. Circumstance had separated them—Jaedon's search for Ziva, and Elisha's time in Samaria with the king. A prophet was God's voice to the king, and Israel faced war on several fronts.

He reminded himself there would be Torah studies with the school of prophets, though they might not be the intimate discussions of the past.

The prophets took turns using the axe, until each tired and passed it on to another. The rest gathered bundles of the downed saplings and stacked them into a rough rectangle defining the new structure.

Then a sharp cry sounded. It was the young prophet Jaedon had noticed earlier. He held his hand to his head as if he'd been injured. "The axe! As I was cutting, the head flew from the handle into the river. It was a borrowed axe!"

Of course it was. No one in this company could afford an iron tool, and those who owned them were careful in who they allowed to borrow the expensive item. The young man would be hard pressed to replace it.

The other prophets gathered around the young man in commiseration, some turning to gaze in the murky waters of the Jordan. Despite the drought, the waters were deep with inches of silty mud at the bottom. The axe would be impossible to find.

"Show me where it went." Elisha gently touched the young man's shoulder.

He lifted his misery-filled gaze, walked to the bank, and pointed. "Here."

Elisha withdrew a knife from his sash and cut a small stick from one of the saplings. He threw it into the river where the prophet had seen the axe fall. When it hit the surface, a small splash started ripples to spread in ever-widening circles. Something dark and shiny bobbed to the surface, looking at first like the rounded back of a catfish.

"Grab it," Elisha said.

The young prophet reached out and grabbed the borrowed axe head.

Later, Jaedon fixed this as the moment he knew he would follow Elisha. He wanted to, as he had years before when Elisha first received Elijah's mantle. Then, the Lord had not chosen him but Gehazi. Now, Jaedon knew the Lord had approved him. So he approached Elisha with confidence.

"Master, you will need another servant."

Elisha turned to look at him, tucking the knife back into his sash.

"Can you accept what the Lord wills?"

Could he? A rush of the old enthusiasm filled him, but he paused, the weight of experience and loss whispering it was hard, sometimes impossible, to recognize God's will.

"Yes." He leveled his shoulders, hoping his voice sounded firm. "If you will help me understand, should I mistake it."

Chapter Thirty-Nine

*Now the king of Aram was at war with Israel. After
conferring with his officers, he said, "I will set up my camp
in such and such a place." The man of God sent word to
the king of Israel: "Beware of passing that place,
because the Arameans are going down there."*
2 Kings 6:8-9

Samaria
Jaedon

FOR SEVERAL MONTHS AFTER JAEDON BEGAN serving Elisha, they
worked among the schools of the prophets at Gilgal, Bethel,
and Jericho. They went out from each of the towns, traveling
and teaching throughout the hills of Ephraim. At first, Elisha
read from the Torah and Jaedon asked questions then, one
by one, the students in turn read. Always, Elisha interjected
questions of his own or gently revised answers.

Each night as the students performed their tasks,
Jaedon hummed with gratitude as he built the fire and
poured lentils into a stewpot. Though his body ached, his
mind stretched to enfold all he had seen and heard that day.

One night, as the travelers warmed their hands over the
coals, Elisha stood. "The Lord says I must return to Samaria
with a message for King Joram, but I do not leave you
unprepared. You will continue to teach as I have shown you.
If you grow weary or your family needs you, train others."

Amidst murmuring and a few slow nods, one asked,
"When will you return, Master?"

Elisha slowly shook his head. "War is coming. I must
stay close to the king."

Chilled by Elisha's words, Jaedon placed more wood on
the coals. "I will go with you." He took a deep breath. Each
time Elisha had prophesied to the king, he faced danger.
Sometimes from the king.

Elisha turned to face him. "Yes, that is your place."

Jaedon slowly exhaled.

They left that night for Samaria, not even returning to

Gilgal for clothes or supplies. "The Lord will provide for our needs," Elisha said.

When they reached the city, Elisha showed Jaedon his house, pointed out the king's palace, then led him next door where Gehazi had lived. The first thing he saw was a tunic on a peg. His whole body stiffened.

In a few steps Elisha grabbed the tunic and wadded it in his arms. "You will not be wearing this." He paused. "There is no disease in the fabric, but ..." He stopped again. When the silence stretched, Elisha pursed his lips and said, "Well." Then he bustled around the room, peering into shelves, lifting a chest lid, grasping a broom in a corner. He pointed out empty buckets and gave directions to the city well. Except for the tunic, a grinding stone, and a few grains of mouse-nibbled grain, the house was empty and tidy, although a layer of dust covered everything. Jaedon thought about asking Elisha to leave the tunic for him to use as a cleaning rag, then pressed his lips together.

When Elisha prepared to leave, Jaedon almost asked if they could live in the same house. But if Elisha wanted that, he would have said so. He made his own tour of the house, finding folded cloths on a shelf, a cook pot on the hearth, and dishes and utensils in the chest. The pitcher and ewer on a table needed filling.

Jaedon picked up the buckets and headed for the city well.

When he returned, Elisha was bidding two women farewell. One glanced shyly at Jaedon as they left.

"The women brought us a kettle of stew and parcels of food. Barley, I think they said, and vegetables." Elisha led him inside, where the smell of roasted lamb filled his nostrils. "And this tunic and cloak." He held up garments of finely woven, but undyed, wool. "Your size, I believe."

Though he was not dead, the ghost of Gehazi whispered throughout the house. When a cold wind blew through the window, Jaedon wondered if Gehazi's cloak kept him warm in the camp. If sweat beaded his brow, he wondered if the palm fronds that roofed the shelter had withered. When he tended the few rows of herbs behind the house, he wondered about Gehazi's three sons, and if the *tzara'at* had progressed. Did Lital live alone in the house the four had built, still tend the garden they had tilled? Or had she moved in with another family, or they with her?

He often wondered if Gehazi knew Jaedon now held his place as Elisha's servant. Would Gehazi hate his old rival for that?

Each week, Elisha sent Jaedon with food to the camp. Knowing he went, the townsfolk sometimes donated blankets or clothing. Though he searched, Jaedon had not seen the family. It was not surprising. Even though *metzorim* would come forward when they saw the gifts, their faces were covered and they remained far off until he backed away.

When he returned to the city, he recited a Psalm to soothe his troubled spirit.

Elisha was regularly summoned before the king, and Jaedon accompanied him. Each time they conferred, Elisha dispensed strategies worthy of a general.

'Beware. The Aramean army will ambush Israel's soldiers on the pass of Megiddo.' Or, 'The Aramean army is camping tonight at Tamar, in the valley of Arabah, in preparation for battle.'

Then King Joram would send his own army in a stealth attack, befuddling and angering the enemy.

That morning, as Jaedon prepared food for the two of them to break their fast, Elisha had more to tell. "The Lord gave me another vision. Like before, I saw the king of Aram and his advisors planning strategy. They circled around a map of Israel, and it was a simple matter to look over Benhadad's shoulder when he put his finger on the location they would attack. But this time, the king drew back and slammed his fist on the map. 'Will you not tell me, who is the traitor among us! Who is a spy for the King of Israel?'"

"The king will have someone's head," Jaedon said.

Elisha appeared to consider this. "I would not like an innocent person put to death." He stroked his beard, which was becoming heavily threaded with gray. "Naaman is no longer working for Benhadad, but his second in command, Rafiq, is now a lieutenant."

"So there is a spy?" Jaedon served Elisha a bowl of porridge. If there was not, how did Elisha know this? And how did this lieutenant fit into the story?

Elisha tipped his head. "No. As I said, the Lord told me. However, Rafiq was present when his captain was healed. He understands that there is a God in Israel and that I am his prophet."

That was not an admission—or denial—of meeting with a spy, but it was further explanation. Jaedon offered a plate of dried fruit.

Elisha accepted a fig. "The Lord told me none of Benhadad's men will suffer because of his suspicion. When he demands 'Which of you is the traitor,' Rafiq will say 'Elisha, the prophet in Israel, tells the king the words you speak, even in the privacy of your bedroom.'" The prophet threw back his head and laughed, setting off a street dog to barking.

"Once Benhadad realizes I am the informer, we can no longer remain in Samaria with King Joram. We will move on and send our messages."

Jaedon nodded, mindful of his promise to accept the will of the Lord. Elisha had seen a vision, and the Lord had told him what to do. God's will was clear, if not entirely understandable. Jaedon knew *what* was to be done, if not *why*. But he could always ask.

"Where are we going, Master?"

"The Lord has sent us to Dothan."

The road to Dothan was a hard day's journey by foot. The road was rutted and often rocky, but since they had returned the borrowed donkey, and the king's offered chariot would not handle the terrain, they walked.

They did not pass other travelers. Jaedon remembered the ruffians from Bethel who accosted Elisha and him as they traveled from Jericho to Bethel, after Elijah had gone up. He stared into the rocky outcroppings and caves along the road. Hiding places. Jaedon wished for the comfort of other travelers. Someone to help, if they were waylaid.

My help is from the Lord.

Where had that thought come from? Was it a fragment of one of King David's Psalms he had read from Elisha's scrolls? It comforted him, and Jaedon silently thanked the Lord when they reached Dothan without incident. Why had he feared? He was with the Lord's prophet, who had foreseen the enemy's plans and, with Yahweh's help, thwarted them.

Elisha eyed him, smiled, and pointed to a house at the edge of the settlement. A room perched atop the flat roof, overlooking plowed fields and a crescent of hills beyond the plain. Had the Lord directed him there?

The prophet winked. "That is the house of a friend. He will be glad to lodge us in the upper room, which boasts cooling breezes and quite a view."

Elisha had taught in Dothan before, and the couple asked about Gehazi. "Hard news," said the husband when Elisha gave a brief answer, "but you have a new, younger man now. Are you married, lad?" He nudged his wife, as if she would procure a marriageable woman in short order.

"I am betrothed," he said firmly, careful not to look at Elisha. Yes, his betrothed had been taken, and not even the Lord's prophet could help him find her, but that did not negate his promise. Even the fact that he had been unable to deliver the *mohar* made no difference to his commitment.

The supper was delicious. It had been a while since he had eaten a woman's cooking. Jaedon looked around the cozy room, with its woven rugs and colorful cushions. Together with talk of marriage and betrothal, his thoughts drifted again to Ziva. He pictured her sitting under a date palm, upright and smiling demurely. Then chaos and danger forced its way into the scene, for that was where she had been —but not killed. They had not found her body, though they had found many others. And he felt ... yes, he felt that the Lord told him she was alive. Was it possible that the Lord spoke to him, as he did to Elisha?

No, not in the same way. Jaedon was no prophet. But hadn't Elisha mentioned a still, small voice, the whisper of God?

Where is she, Yahweh? He had searched through Aram, checked every temple, every slave auction he could find. Could he have been fooling himself? Was the truth ... that she was dead?

She lives. She is safe.

Jaedon clenched his fists. He longed to believe what his heart was telling him, but not at the cost of knowing the truth.

"Jaedon?"

He twitched and glanced up to find Elisha gazing at him with concern. He realized the wife was offering him a second helping of stew. "I thank you, yes. A small helping please."

After supper, Elisha recited a selection from the Torah. He spoke in phrases, nearly melodic patterns. Jaedon was drawn into the rhythms. The words filled his mind like the current of the river Jordan, dark and peaceful, with sustenance in its depths.

As the mountains surround Jerusalem,
so the Lord surrounds His people
Both now and forevermore.

When they finally climbed the steps to the upper room, Jaedon's soul felt at rest. Ziva was alive and well. If he did not know where she was, the Lord did. Perhaps someday ... he didn't know how to finish that thought, and so he let it be. The Lord knew.

For now, he was with Elisha. The man of God. Respected. The teacher of Israel, the word of God to the king.

Elisha motioned Jaedon to follow him into the tiny room where two pallets were spread. But the night was balmy, so he dragged one of the mats outside under the stars. He lay back, gazing at the scattered brilliance overhead. Was Ziva also staring into this night sky?

He woke smiling. He had dreamed of her. Not in the date orchard, where his dreams usually took him. He was leading her through the vineyard, *their* vineyard, holding her hand. Then they were in the house, she exclaiming in pleasure, running her fingers over the table's smooth surface, running to the window, leaning out and laughing when she saw—

An army surrounded the settlement. He bolted upright

and rubbed his eyes. This was no dream! Countless armed and armored soldiers, horsemen, and chariots flooded over the crescent of hills and onto the plowed fields. He stumbled toward the room to awaken Elisha. "Master!"

Why this army, why here? This small settlement was not worthy of the assemblage. A few raiders on horseback in the dead of night would gain them their captives and such spoil as a rural village would hold. But chariots!

He stood at the threshold looking in. Elisha had risen calmly, rubbed his hands over his face, and smoothed his tunic. He walked onto the roof and leaned over the parapet, motioning to Jaedon to come alongside.

Suddenly he knew. There was a treasure here–and a traitor. "They are here for you, Elisha! What shall we do?"

The prophet nodded, his expression tranquil. "I know, Jaedon. But don't forget who we serve. Don't be afraid, for those who are with us are more than those who are against us."

Jaedon tried to compose himself, to match Elisha's calm. Of course, the Lord was with them, but what was to be done? Elisha stood in plain view, on a rooftop, no less. There was no way they could sneak off and escape by dead of night.

Several soldiers blasted long metal horns, their shrill scream like dying women. Jaedon looked around for something he could use as a weapon. There was not so much as an iron pot or a stone on the rooftop.

He felt for his hunting knife, remembered he'd placed it beside his sleeping mat, and hastily retrieved it. Tucking it into his sash, he asked, "Do you have your knife?"

"We won't need weapons," Elisha replied. Then he looked up. "Open his eyes, Lord, so that he may see."

Suddenly, Jaedon saw what had been there all along.

Brilliance exceeding the sunlight filled the sky. Chariots of fire surrounded Elisha—above, below, and strangely passing through the rooftop he stood upon. Flaming horses pawed the clouds, their sword-wielding riders at the ready. Chariots, horses, riders, and winged soldiers, all aflame, filled the valley and crowded the surrounding hills, as far as he could see.

Then the Aramean army started to move toward the rooftop. They passed through the army of flame, senseless to the danger surrounding them, while the heavenly army waited, looking to Elisha for orders.

Elisha strode to the center of the rooftop and raised his hands toward heaven. "Lord, strike this army with blindness."

The Arameans slowed, then began to swarm into each other like ants confused when a torch lands among them.

Elisha descended the stairs and waded into their midst. Jaedon stayed close.

"This is not the road and this is not the city," he shouted. "Follow me, and I will lead you to the man you are looking for."

The prophet grasped the hand of the Aramean commander, motioning to Jaedon to take the reins of a general's horse. The others followed, trailing along like children making a chain of themselves, hand to shoulder.

The fiery army was slowly fading, but Jaedon still smelled fire. He grasped the front of his tunic and brought it to his nose. Yes. Smoke. They were still surrounded with the army of the Lord.

He felt no fear. How could he ever fear again?

Although Elisha and Jaedon had made the trip to Dothan in one long day, it took them four to lead the blinded army back to Samaria. Along the way, one of the chariots broke an axel. While sightless soldiers stood helpless, Jaedon unhitched the horses and turned them loose. They would follow or make their way to new owners in the hill country.

When the blind army finally entered through Samaria's city gate, citizens stared dumbfounded at the sight of the prophet and his servant in the lead. No wonder. They hadn't seen the enemy surrounded by fiery chariots. Soon they swarmed around, brandishing weapons and cursing the enemy.

Elisha prayed aloud. "Lord, open the eyes of these men so they can see." When the Arameans saw they were tightly pressed within Samaria's city gates, and armed men surrounded them, they threw down their own weapons and surrendered.

"Kill them, kill them," the Israelites chanted.

They only quieted when King Joram pushed his way through to face Elisha. He raised his sword. "Shall I kill them, my father, shall I kill them?"

"No," Elisha said. "Would you kill those you captured with your own sword or bow? Treat these captives kindly. Set food and water before them so that they may eat and drink and then go back to their master."

Jaedon felt his lips turn up in a smile, imagining the guffaws when this amazing story was told around a campfire. Yahweh must like to laugh.

This was not how the Arameans expected to be treated. He had seen their faces pale when they realized where they stood. What stories they would tell.

What did the Lord mean by this? Twice, He had, through His prophet, showed grace to Israel's enemy. Once, when He allowed Elisha to heal Naaman. Again, by pardoning, feeding, and sending this army home. Yet among them, there might be raiders who had attacked Ziva's village.

A section from the Torah floated into memory. *If your enemy is hungry, give him food to eat; if he is thirsty give him water to drink. In doing this, you will heap burning coals on his head, and the Lord will reward you.*

Jaedon had never understood about those burning coals.

Elisha had shrugged. "Who can say? Punishment? Regret for past sins? But the point is that God is the balancer of all accounts."

She is alive. She is safe.

His spirit grasped the promise and held it close. The Lord had comforted before, yet Ziva was still lost. He walked slowly among the Arameans as they ate, studying their faces. He turned his gaze to Elisha, silently asking permission.

Elisha, understanding, nodded.

Speaking Aramean, Jaedon asked, "I seek a young Israelite maiden, who would have seen about thirteen or fourteen years of age when she was taken from the settlement of Gischala. A beautiful girl, but small." He held his hand level with his heart. "Tell me, if you know of such a girl."

They heard his question, and their eyes rounded once more with fear. They were vulnerable. Yet, if they knew something that would help, they would tell him. He saw it written on their faces.

But every answer was no.

Chapter Forty

*Some time later, Ben-Hadad king of Aram mobilized his
entire army and marched up and laid siege to Samaria.*
2 Kings 6:24

Samaria, a year later
Jaedon

IT WAS STRANGE TO WAKE, NOT to a cock's crow, for all had long
since been eaten, not to the greetings of one neighbor to
another, for pleasantries had long been forsaken, but only to
the rumble of his empty stomach.

Aram had stopped sending raiding parties, but when
Israel finally trusted in peace with their neighbor, the king
led his entire army to attack Samaria's walled city.

Jaedon ran his hands over his dry face, sparing the
puddle of water in his ewer, dressed, and walked next door
to pray with Elisha.

The prophet bent over the open scroll, his finger moving
slowly down the lines of text. He lifted his head and smiled.
"The mercies of the Lord are new every morning, Jaedon."

Pleasantries remained with his master.

But this was also a test. "Because of the Lord's great
love we are not consumed," Jaedon responded, "for his
compassions never fail. They are new every morning; great is
His faithfulness."

"Good, good. You will need that today, for sustenance."
Elisha smiled at his little jest, and Jaedon felt his spirit lift,
even as his stomach growled again. Last night, he had found
nothing to purchase in the marketplace, so it was unlikely
there would be food today. If it were his decision, he would
stay with Elisha when he met to pray with those of the city
elders who still worshipped Yahweh. But each day the
prophet sent him out to patrol the city, the marketplace and,
as one would check the weather, to test the temper of the
people inside the city walls.

First, he walked to the marketplace. What was that fly-
infested lump of bone, skin, and fur? A donkey's head? It

didn't matter that no devout Israelite should eat unclean donkey flesh. Desperate citizens were bidding the price up to eighty shekels—several years' wages. A dove keeper appeared to be selling the dung from her birds, who had all been eaten days ago. Or could it be dried pods from the carob plant? He bent to look more closely. Impossible to tell, and in either case the cost was beyond all but the rich.

He ascended the steps to the top of the city wall. Battering rams and siege engines littered the hill upon which the city stood, and racing chariots below filled the air with dust. His gaze swept across a swarm of Arameans, perhaps including some of the very soldiers Elisha had sent home with full stomachs the year before. It was rumored that the Arameans blinded by Yahweh, defected to Egypt in fear, and King Benhadad had to employ mercenary soldiers to replace them.

Either way, a mighty force had imprisoned Israel behind its city walls for months. Unable to replenish supplies or send for reinforcements, Samaria fell prey to famine.

Trudging back down into the marketplace, Jaedon wandered among those seeking something to fill their stomachs. This was where he would glean information.

"My children are growing weak. If I can't find food for them soon, they will die."

"My husband plans to sneak over the wall tonight. See if he can find food among the enemy."

"This is a curse on us from the Lord. He warned us if we worshipped idols, he would stop the rain and send an enemy to punish us."

"That's foolish superstition, Martha. There have always been dry seasons, just as there have always been wars."

Hearing a commotion overhead, Jaedon glanced up. A watchman saluted two well-dressed men. Having accompanied Elisha when he counseled Israel's leader, Jaedon recognized King Joram and his advisor, Hiram. They spoke in quiet voices, peering across the valley, likely taking stock of the enemy forces, then glancing down at the desperate occupants of the marketplace and city streets such as could be seen from the wall.

Then a woman's shrill voice addressed the king. "Help

me, my lord the king!"

At first, the king replied in a cynical tone. "If the Lord does not help you, how can I? My threshing floor is empty, my winepress is dry." Then shaking his head, he softened his voice. "What is the matter?"

"Injustice, my lord the king. A promise not kept. This woman said to me, 'Stop mourning your dead son. Give up his body so we may eat him today, and tomorrow we'll eat my son.' So I did as she said. We cooked my son and ate him. The next day I said to her, 'It's your turn. Where is your son so we may eat him?' But she has hidden her son.'"

Jaedon gagged, and when the king heard her words his face contorted, in what seemed rage and despair. He tore his royal robe, and Jaedon saw that he wore sackcloth against his skin. So he had followed Elisha's counsel that he should repent and seek forgiveness for not removing all idols from Israel.

In the next breath Joram cursed the one whose counsel he obeyed. "May God deal with me, be it ever so severely, if the head of Elisha son of Shaphat remains on his shoulders today!"

Jaedon hurried to the prophet's house, where he was meeting with the elders of the city. Jaedon quickly related what he'd overheard, and as they heard footsteps approach, Elisha said, "You see how this murderer is sending someone to cut off my head? When the messenger knocks, hold the door against him. His master the king will be right behind him."

There was pounding on the door and thuds as someone threw his weight against the door. Even though none of the elders were strong, there were nine of them, and with Jaedon, the door was held secure by ten sets of hands or shoulders.

Finally, the king shouted through the barrier, "I did as you said, Elisha. I am truly sorry, but this disaster is from the Lord. Why should I wait for Him any longer?"

Elisha said to them, "He is calm now. Open the door."

The king stood outside, hollow cheeked and scowling. At a signal, his officer sheathed his sword.

Elisha folded his arms across his chest. "Hear the word of the Lord: About this time tomorrow, twelve pounds of fine flour will sell for a shekel and twice as much barley will also sell for a shekel at the gate of Samaria."

That price was higher than normal, but there would be flour! Yet Hiram, the officer who accompanied the king, scoffed. "Look, even if the Lord should open the floodgates of heaven, this could not happen."

Elisha gazed at him steadily. "It will happen as the Lord said, and you will see it with your own eyes. But you will not eat any of it."

Gehazi stretched, his bones and flesh stiff, having fallen asleep against the cold stone surface of the city wall. Hoping to find something to sustain them in the refuse thrown over the wall, he and his sons had stationed themselves just outside of the city gate. The Arameans would not come near because of their dreaded disease, and so the battering rams had not been wheeled close. Although the enemy could have disposed of them with arrows shot from a distance, Gehazi doubted they felt the need to use siege machines. Three days had gone by since garbage had been thrown over the wall. The situation inside must have grown so dire that the citizens ate their own waste. The city would soon be forced to throw open its gates and surrender.

"Listen," Gehazi said to his sons. "Why should we wait here any longer waiting for food that does not come? Even if we somehow could get into the city—the famine is there, and we will die. If we stay here without food, we will die. Tonight, when they are tired of taunting our countrymen, let's go to the Arameans and surrender. They have plenty of food. If they spare us, we will live. Even if they kill us, we are no worse off."

"You are right, father." Asriel spoke for his younger brothers, who nodded in silent agreement. They had no other options.

So at dusk they walked downhill to the Aramean camp, sniffing for cookfires and listening for voices. But the quiet was broken only by the sound of their own footsteps. When they reached the outskirts of the camp, they saw no one. Soon they realized all the tents were abandoned. A line of horses and donkeys, tied between tents, whinnied and brayed at them as they approached.

Gehazi led them into the first tent. Clothing, food, even bits of silver lay scattered.

"Huh," Asriel grunted. His eldest son picked up a strange purple fruit, bit, and red juice trickled from his mouth. Baruch found a stack of flatbread and tossed rounds to his younger brother and Gehazi.

"What has happened, Abba?" Young Abner spread his arms. "Why would they leave so suddenly? And on foot?"

"Only God knows." Gehazi paused, judged by his own words. He'd answered tritely, meaning 'who can say?' but the truth was that God was the cause of whatever had happened here.

I am sorry, Lord. Why did I not trust you all along?

His heart heavy, Gehazi followed his three sons as they wandered from tent to tent, murmuring "Look at this," and "Taste."

"Put this on, Abba," said Baruch. His middle son held out a finely embroidered linen robe. Despite the fading light, Gehazi realized it was very like one he had hidden in Samaria, never to be worn.

He recoiled. "No, my son. What we're doing is not right. This is a day of good news, and we are keeping it to ourselves. If we wait until daylight, punishment will overtake us. Let's go at once and report what we know."

Baruch nodded as he set aside the garment. "You're right, Father."

Gehazi turned and led his sons out of the tent. It would be a time of rejoicing for the city. For he and his sons—well, they would return to the camp of the *metzorim*. At least there would be food. He looked down and saw a plain homespun tunic spread over a bush, as if it had been washed and left to dry. Quite a contrast to the ragged and soiled tunic he had worn since he entered the camp. He picked it up. This he could wear without fear or guilt.

When they reached the city gate, he called out to the gatekeepers. "Good news! We went into the Aramean camp and no one was there—not a sound of anyone—only tethered horses and donkeys, and the tents left just as they were.

There is food, my brothers!"

Gehazi heard the gatekeepers run along the wall and shout the news. He sighed. At least he had done the right thing this time. He chaffed his arms, wishing for a moment he had kept the fine robe. Its long sleeves would have kept him warm against the night air. Then he stopped. Could it be? He felt smooth skin, not scabs. Turning he saw Asriel, Baruch, and Abner examining their own arms and legs and then staring at him in amazed delight. "Abba! We are healed! We are clean!"

Since the incident with the king's messenger, Jaedon had slept across the threshold of Elisha's house. When he heard excited shouts outside, he sat up. Behind him, he heard the prophet's footsteps. "Go tell the king that the Lord has done what He said."

Outside, the townsfolk were excitedly repeating what they'd heard from *metzorim* outside the city—that the enemy had abandoned their tents. When Jaedon reached the palace, he was made to wait in the antechamber. He could hear the king speaking in the next room. "I will tell you what the Aramean plan. They know we are starving, so they have left the camp to hide in the countryside, thinking, 'They will come out to investigate, and then we will take them and get into the city.'"

Then Jaedon heard a servant announce his arrival. The king summoned him, and after he delivered Elisha's message, said to an officer, "Send out men to find what happened. They can take any horses left in the city. If they are killed, their plight will be no worse than all we Israelites who are doomed."

They were able to send two horse-driven chariots after the Aramean army. Later it was reported that as they traveled the road toward the Jordan river, clothing and equipment were strewn everywhere. When the messengers returned, they were laughing, saying, "The Lord must have chased them with His angels or the fires of the old prophet Elijah, because they fled headlong, lightening their load in fear."

Jaedon and Elisha listened from their house, when the

king shouted the news from the city wall. There was a great sound of rejoicing from the people. Then groups flooded toward the city gate to plunder the food, clothing, and riches from the camp of the Arameans. So it was as the Lord had said. A *seah* of flour sold for a shekel as did two of barley.

Hiram, the king's officer, who had said, "Even if the Lord should open the floodgates of heaven, that will not happen," went to stand in the gateway and direct the crowds, but he was trampled under their feet and died. So it was also as the Lord had said, "You will see it with your own eyes, but you will not eat any of it!"

That night, Jaedon baked flatbread made of fine, pale flour on hot stones while lentils waited over the banked fire. Later, stomachs full, they strolled through the city, listening to sounds carried from all corners of the city on a warm breeze—lutes and laughter, conversation and singing. Stars shone overhead and Jaedon ruminated on all he had seen and heard, from the time he had fled his grandfather's vineyard in Jezreel to now.

He had many questions.

He was no prophet. The ways of the Lord were a mystery to him.

The breeze warmed his skin and peace filled Jaedon's heart, and his thoughts settled there, like an eagle on its nest.

Chapter Forty-One

*Love the Lord, all his faithful people! The Lord preserves
those who are true to him, but the proud he pays back in full.*
Psalm 31:23

Samaria to Gilgal
Jaedon

As far as Jaedon could see, the hills were verdant. It was as
if the heavens declared a curse lifted. Rain had fallen every
day the week after the Lord sent the Arameans away in flight.
It only ceased the evening before the little band set out for
Gilgal.

Elisha led, walking and conversing with Gehazi. Jaedon
and the three brothers followed. Sometime after the Aramean
army had fled, the former *metzorim* and his sons had
presented themselves to Elisha, claiming the Lord had healed
them. The prophet pronounced them clean, for it was true.
But each had retained at least one small lesion on a forearm
or thigh—a reminder of what it meant to rebel against the
will of the Lord.

A reminder it seemed Gehazi understood full well, for
when instructed to burn their contaminated garments and
offered new tunics from those left by the retreating army,
Gehazi had turned pale.

"Master, pride and greed were my sins. I dare not take
Aramean clothing."

"You need not fear to do as I say. I have collected the
simple garments of common soldiers."

"But the design—longer than a working man would wear
and dyed blue, rather than plain homespun or the plant-
based dye with which Lital tints her yarn."

"We will save your wife the trouble of weaving three
tunics on short notice. There is nothing else, after all."

At the mention of Lital, Gehazi's shoulders had sagged,
and an expression that may have been guilt crossed his face.

Jaedon, as well as each of Gehazi's sons, carried a
bundle of garments on his back—more long tunics and thick

cloaks. None in Gilgal would suffer from cold this winter. Elisha had selected the clothing himself, rejecting anything bejeweled, dyed purple, or embroidered with silver or gold threads.

Asriel, Gehazi's oldest, described the moment he realized the Arameans had deserted the camp and how he and his brothers had run from tent to tent collecting riches.

"Abba stopped us. He was overcome with our selfishness. We were eating strange and wonderful fruits, while our countrymen were starving. Our hearts went out to our father and we all agreed. When we decided to turn aside and brought the news to the city, our *tzara'at* faded away."

"As when Moses' sister, Miriam, was healed in the wilderness," his younger brother Baruch declared.

Both brothers nodded their agreement, then they began to discuss how their imma would react when she saw the three of them, healed.

"She will be happy beyond imagining," Jaedon said.

"I suppose so," said Asriel. "But she has suffered." His gaze rested upon his father, who walked ahead talking quietly with Elisha.

Jaedon studied the lad. He had suffered because of his father's sin, as had his brothers. Had they forgiven Gehazi during their time in the camp of the *metzorim?*

Jaedon could not help letting his gaze stray to Gehazi and Elisha. Quickly, he forced his attention to the mountains, where a rivulet glinted among the trees, testament of a hidden spring. Jaedon did not want to overhear what Elisha was saying to his former servant. He no longer needed to be told such things were not for him to know. Instead, he tried to listen for the Lord's whisper.

I am listening, Lord. I will do whatever you ask.

Jaedon looked ahead at Elisha, still deep in conversation. *Whatever you ask.* What might that mean? If the Lord wanted him to continue serving Elisha, he would be content. But if the Lord restored Gehazi to Elisha's service, what then?

They walked until they tired then made camp beside the brook he had glimpsed. Jaedon walked upstream and found a fish trap filled with three fat fish, which he roasted and they shared. In the morning, three more had found their way into the enclosure. They left those for the trap's owner. Instead, they ate flatbread from their packs as they walked.

Late in the third day, footsore and weary, Jaedon spotted the smoke of cook fires rising from the direction of Gilgal. Soon they heard shouts of welcome, even a shofar.

That evening as lentils simmered and bread baked, stories were told. Jaedon sat beside Imma, watching Dov dance among the sons of the prophets.

Ho-ahh, ho-ahh! The shofar's bellow punctuated gentle, resonant lute music, signaling the competitive dancers to ever-higher leaps.

Imma leaned her head against Jaedon's shoulder. "I have missed you, my son."

He slid his arm around her. Had she grown smaller? "I thought of you often, Imma, and of home."

"You had such adventures!" She had heard of the angelic army, the blinded Arameans, and he had related a softened version of the famine in besieged Samaria.

She had seen Gehazi and his sons reunited with Lital. Jaedon repeated Gehazi's story of finding the deserted enemy camp, his resolve to do right, and Yahweh's merciful healing.

"What does this mean for you? Will Elisha take Gehazi back as his servant?"

"Perhaps. They talked for hours as we walked. Though I did not overhear, I think they came to an understanding."

"Did Elisha say nothing to you?"

He shrugged. "That Yahweh has a purpose for me. I am to listen."

Imma wrinkled her nose in concentration. "What has Elisha told you of this Aramean he healed?"

Jaedon paused, wording his answer not to reveal the thought that had troubled him. If the Aramean had not come to Israel, Gehazi would not have been tempted. "Only that his servant said, 'There is a prophet in Israel. If my master could see him, he would be healed."

"That servant must have been Israelite," his mother said. "Else how would he know our prophet had such standing with Yahweh?"

Jaedon smiled at her, enjoying the direction her

thoughts had taken. Upon hearing the news, his had taken a different path—pride in the reputation Elisha had earned in Aram.

"Hmm." Miriam tapped her finger on her chin. "Perhaps I misspoke."

Jaedon tipped his head. "About what?"

"Why must the servant have been a man?"

Elisha was engrossed in conversation with Gilgal's prophets, so Jaedon pulled Gehazi aside and asked the question.

"Yes, the captain was from Damascus. He was called Naaman." A breeze whipped Gehazi's graying hair. His experience had etched deep lines on his forehead, but he faced Jaedon with quiet assurance. "You believe his servant is your Ziva?"

His Ziva.

He had exhausted all leads. Had it been five years? Now he had one more path to follow, and it would take him to the land of the Arameans.

"Elisha once told me, with Yahweh there is no coincidence."

"So you will go? What of serving Elisha?"

He did not want to leave Elisha. He was his friend, as well as his teacher, and he still needed Jaedon's support. Could he trust that to another? To this one, who had failed him before?

Jaedon felt a twinge of guilt. He had cringed at the sight of the Aramean army, massed around Dothan as far as his eyes could see.

Do not forget the fiery angels and chariots. I am the Captain of Heaven's armies.

Jaedon turned his gaze to the leafy bower overhead and the blue expanse beyond. "I will ask Elisha's permission. He has the right to expect my continued service."

Gehazi scuffed his sandal across the ground. "As he did mine." He lifted his gaze.

"Do you wish to be reinstated?" Jaedon asked.

Gehazi nodded.

Jaedon stood. "Shall we both speak to him?"

Routed by the Israelites, Benhadad's army had slunk home confused and ashamed. The appalling news was whispered throughout Damascus. Privately Naaman praised God for protecting His people, the Israelites. Then he asked Rafiq to find his old uniform and sponge it clean.

"Where are we going, my father?" Rafiq asked, holding out the clean garments.

As if for the last time, Naaman allowed his gaze to rest on this young man, well, perhaps no longer young, who had followed him through war, peace, and turning again, like a wheel, to war.

"I am going to speak to the king."

Another change was coming.

Benhadad slumped on his throne, his robes creased and dull as if he'd not changed clothing for days. "If you had been there, my old captain, we would have seen victory."

Naaman cleared his throat. "Oh, king, live forever. I have served you proudly, until I grew too old to fight. I am grateful to you, not only for your generosity but for your support and wise counsel. You sent me to Israel's King Joram when I contracted *tzara'at*, and there I was healed."

Benhadad nodded. "It was an Israelite disease, contracted during your military exploits, and healed by an Israelite king. It was right. Rimmon had no power over an Israelite disease."

Naaman paused, choosing his words carefully. It would not do to say Rimmon had no power over anything. "The king did not heal me. It was the Israelite God Yahweh and His prophet Elisha."

"Elisha!" Benhadad spat. "The one Rafiq said could hear what I spoke in my bedroom?"

"The very one." Then Naaman described his healing in greater detail than he had expressed before.

Afterward, Benhadad stroked his chin thoughtfully. "A muddy river, you say. Yet you were healed on the seventh immersion, just as the prophet said. It seems the prophet wields great power."

Naaman nodded. "He would say His God holds the power, and he, Elisha, is only God's servant. Regardless, great power surrounds Israel. My king, out of my great regard and respect for you and for our country, I plead with you. Contend no more with the God of the Israelites."

When Naaman returned home, he felt something of the exhilaration he had felt bursting through the surface of the muddy Jordan river—clean and drunk on light. But when he entered Amirah's room and saw Ziva combing his wife's hair, he felt a niggle of guilt.

They turned to smile at him. Emet lay at their feet, his chin resting upon a silk cushion he had claimed as his own. The dog did not lift his head, but his eyes swiveled to follow Naaman as he crossed the room to kiss Amirah's cheek. A peaceful scene.

He had not abducted the girl, but she was taken, and he did not restore her to her family. How could he? Her home was gone, her people killed. That much he knew.

He had not cared for the girl as he should have. Slowly he pulled the cloak from his shoulders and hung it carefully where Ziva would have returned it, if he had flung it on a stool as he often did.

He knew Amirah thought of Ziva as a daughter, and the girl—although she was a girl no longer—loved his wife. Even he—though that did not matter, he was not a woman to be driven by his feelings—but Amirah doted on—

"What are you doing with your cloak, Naaman?" Amirah's laughter floated merrily like a string of metal chimes he had given her. He looked down at his hands. He again held the cloak and was folding it into an untidy square.

He shrugged and handed the wadded cloth to Ziva who walked toward him with arms outstretched.

"I've come from speaking with the king," he said.

As Jaedon emerged from the last stand of trees, a breeze whipped over the meadow before him. Biny stood knee-deep in the grassy expanse, bending over something in Aharon's hand. The boy straightened, whipped his arm in a circle, then stretched it out.

"Whoop!" Aharon hopped from foot to foot beside his adoptive father. "Did you see, Abba? I hit the target! Did you see, *Dod* Jaedon?"

Years ago, Elisha had stood just there, yanking a bit of twine-wrapped fur across the meadow as Hevel dived with extended talons. When he ran to take the prize from her, she had danced around it with jealous pride.

"Accurate and deadly swift." Jaedon ruffled the boy's hair. "He is ready to guard your new flock of goats, Biny."

"Soon." Biny lay a hand on the boy's shoulder. "Did you come to practice with us?"

Of course he had not, but he could see that Aharon was not yet tired, and since he would be asking Biny to travel with him, he nodded and bent to gather a few stones. Eden would have her hands full with the children when they departed. Their daughter, Bracha, in her mother's womb the day Elijah went up, was so close to Aharon's age that the two might have been twins, and what trouble one did not discover, the other pointed out.

Later, Jaedon and Biny went together to ask Dov to accompany them. Their strengths—soldier, strongman, and spy—like three strands of a rope. They discussed the benefits and drawbacks of going on foot or riding the only animals available to them—the horse, the donkey, and the mule.

"On foot, we have the advantage of quick concealment," Dov said. "Perhaps that is best since we have only two dependable animals."

Jaedon frowned in thought. It had been so long, and this was such a thin lead. Speed appealed to him more than stealth. "Well, the mule was not as obstinate as I expected on our trip to Samaria."

"Then it was pulling a wagon filled with four men and provisions. Have you tried riding the animal?" Biny asked.

Jaedon shook his head. Since old Kenan's death, the mule had roamed the settlement, resisting capture. Occasionally one of the prophets seduced her with grain, and she submitted to pulling a plow, but none had ridden her.

Rattling grain in a bucket, Jaedon attempted it later that day. The mule had shown her displeasure in a series of stiff-legged hops, mid-air twists, and bone-jarring landings. Blessedly, this happened in the meadow, and long grass softened his inevitable ejection. The mule, honking her victory, had disappeared toward the village, tail carried triumphantly high like a shepherd's crook.

Muttering five different ways of cooking mule, unclean or not, Jaedon had dusted himself off and followed. When he found her munching a tender weed beside Kenan's empty house, he took hold of the bridle and resolutely led her back to the meadow. Seven times.

After that, the mule showed him her smooth gaits. It was like riding a cloud. A good thing, since every muscle in his body screamed in favor of slaying the mule, or at least leaving her behind. But with her rebellion played out, she did seem a more agreeable animal.

The three left the next morning, Jaedon on the mule since neither Dov nor Biny would ride her. As he approached, she flopped one long ear toward him which he took as a good sign, especially for a mule who had worn her first saddle yesterday. He saddled her, adding additional padding over and under the leather.

"Still sore?" Biny asked.

Jaedon shrugged. "At least one of us is."

Dov had procured leather vests from his time as a soldier. "Wear them under your tunics as we travel. If we are attacked, they will stop or at least slow an arrow."

They rode all day, the mule striding along placidly. As they made camp that evening, Dov said, "She did well. Shall we trade tomorrow?"

Jaedon loosened the girth, swung the saddle over a fallen log, and fastened hobbles to the mule's front legs. "No. I believe we have reached an understanding."

He noticed Dov reaching behind to massage his back, and Biny walked a little stiffly.

Jaedon failed to mention the seven hard landings in the meadow and the handful of grain he'd stashed in his pouch where the mule could smell it.

It was working. As he walked deeper into the woods she lifted her nose, left a patch of grass, and followed him.

He returned to the clearing with an armful of kindling

and set to making a fire. Soon a pot of lentils simmered over the flames.

Dov approached and dropped a handful of greens into the pot. "If we keep up the pace tomorrow, we'll reach Hazor and turn off for Damascus. We can camp nearby, but there's an inn where we should eat. Other travelers are often willing to share what they know over a glass of *shekhar*."

Jaedon nodded. Though he disliked the company of strangers, they might learn something to help them gain entrance to the city of Damascus.

They had discussed and discarded various plans. His uncle Kadesh had bargained with traveling merchants around campfires, but with a drought that stretched across long months, there was no grape crop to sell. Though Dov and Jaedon crafted polished bows and fine arrows, it did not seem wise to supply the enemy with weapons. So Dov suggested they pose as Moabite merchants looking to buy a few embroidered robes and mosaic vessels to sell to wealthy customers in Edom and nearby Moab.

"Why Moab?" Jaedon had asked.

"Moab is Israel's enemy," Dov said. "And the enemy of my enemy—"

"Is my friend." Jaedon and Biny said together.

Chapter Forty-Two

Hope deferred makes the heart sick,
but a longing fulfilled is a tree of life.
Proverbs 13:12

Enroute to Damascus
Jaedon

SEVERAL HORSES AND A CAMEL WERE tied outside the inn at Hazor. The horses bunched and eyed the camel uneasily, while it placidly chewed its cud.

Jaedon mirrored the camel's indifference as he, Dov, and Biny entered the crowded room. Hungry, dusty travelers lined wooden benches slurping porridge. Their eyes asked a common question. *Who are you, stranger?*

A handsome young woman strode up to greet them. "Three bowls for a *gerah*. If you are eating."

Jaedon reached into his pouch and dropped a silver nugget on her tray.

The girl eyed a large man who had spread his elbows to claim more space than he needed. "Make room," she said.

He growled and did not move.

"Make room, or you'll receive no extra portions despite my love for your mother."

He slid over and Biny and Dov filled the space. Across the table, two men grinned and made room for Jaedon.

"Where you headed?" The stranger to his left mumbled, appearing uninterested in the answer. Probably expecting lies. On an impulse Jadon decided against their carefully crafted tale.

"I am seeking a wife." He broadened his accent like the Moabites. "A strong woman who can work on my farm. Can't pay a man to help. Hard times, you know."

The girl appeared over his shoulder and plopped steaming bowls in front of them. Dov stared intently into his stew, and Biny's eyebrows scrunched.

"Our Neri here is unattached," said his table mate. "And she's a hard worker. But she comes with a ferocious dog."

Others nearby chuckled. "Neri's always got a dog," said another.

The girl glared at them and whirled off to help other customers.

The innkeeper bustled over, wiping his hands on a rag. "You know the rules. Leave Neri to her work. None of your tomfoolery. You"—he jerked his hand at Jaedon, then at the door—"Out!"

Jaedon stared at him, then started to rise.

"Nay, nay, Samson," said the biggest man at the table. "Leave the lad be. He wants a wife to work his farm, and we teased him about Neri. We're sorry she took affront. It was only good fun. Eh, boys?"

Heads down, shoulders shifting, the others muttered their agreement. The innkeeper flung the rag over his shoulder and turned his gaze to Jaedon. "You the farmer?"

"Yes, sir."

"You are young. Where is your father?"

Dov cleared his throat and lifted a finger.

"I know a widow … but no, she is too old for you. Doubt she'd be any help farmin'." He hesitated and then grinned. "Make a man of you though." He sauntered back to the hearth and attended the stew.

Various men in the room came by to offer their young daughters, sisters, and extra wives before Jaedon, Dov, and Biny departed. As they extracted their animals from the tether, the girl Neri met them outside.

"I packed some provisions for the rest of your trip. You are from Israel, yes? Heading for Damascus?" She extended the parcel.

Jaedon searched her face without answering. Neri had seemed self-controlled, hard even. Now her eyes had softened and something prompted him to speak the truth.

"What is your name?" Her quiet voice reminded him of Imma, praying with him each night.

"I am called Jaedon."

Neri nodded. "I thought I heard in the inn. But … were you also called that by a young woman?"

He froze, somehow knowing what came next.

"Was her name Ziva?" she asked.

Dov and Biny dropped all pretense of being too busy saddling the animals to listen and moved closer.

As the three questioned her, Neri described how she'd met Ziva when Naaman's soldiers stopped for the midday meal. She only knew the captain was taking her to his home in the north.

"I sent my dog with her. It would protect her with its life. Later, one of our customers remarked seeing the dog in Damascus, in the company of a young girl. It has been years, and I don't know if they are still there. But a man as wealthy as he settles into a place. His king's palace is in the city."

Jaedon's breath grew shallow. This made sense. Naaman would have returned to Damascus, and Ziva would belong to his household. The man knew she was Hebrew, and he would have returned from his healing with gratitude toward Elisha and the servant girl who had told him 'If only you would go to the prophet who is in Samaria.'

Jaedon's heart melted as he admired Ziva's compassion on her enemy. Another captive, in her place, would have hoped for the captain's death to pay for those of her family. For a brief moment, another thought planted a seed of fear.

Jaedon sucked in a ragged breath. No. That could not be. Naaman had decided to visit Elisha on Ziva's advice. He would not callously sell her before he set off in pursuit of healing. If the man had faith that Elisha could heal, surely he realized the prophet could see his actions from afar and be angered. Might worsen the *tzara'at*, rather than heal.

Kindhearted girl. Then another thought crept in. His kindhearted, beautiful girl, a captive for nearly five years, might have grown to care for her captor! That was why she'd sent him to Elisha. Perhaps he'd taken her to wife ... or as a concubine.

A pulse pounded in his forehead, pain that grew as he convinced himself. Even if he found her, she was lost to him.

"Jaedon." Dov lay a hand on his arm. "Why the sad face? This is good news, my son. Let's go."

"Watch yourselves," Neri said. "You dress like traders, but the road to Damascus is overrun with thieves, some who would kill you for less than the price of a meal. Not to mention the king's mounted troops, alert for foreign spies."

Dov reached into his pouch and offered Neri a silver piece. She held up her hand. "There is little value in what I've told you. But if you find Ziva, come back this way. I would like to see her restored to her people." She turned her gaze upon Jaedon. "And to you."

Jaedon took note of the way through the upper city, which Dov said would take them to Damascus. Small mudbrick houses crowded together, remarkably similar to those in Samaria. Dov explained that King Ahab had helped restore the city, thus the similarity.

Dov suggested they water their animals at Hazor's elaborate water system. The road led to a huge stone edifice. Peering into its depths, they ogled the wide shaft, broad steps, and gleaming black pool. But even the mule would not put a foot on the winding steps.

Dov turned his horse away. "Ahab also had a hand in expanding this water system."

"He was sensitive to drought." Biny stepped onto the white donkey. "But this land belonged to Israel. Now the Arameans drink from it." His long legs dangled past the animal's foreleg.

"Are you sure you don't want to ride the mule?" Jaedon asked. "Your feet are nearly dragging the ground."

"As long as I don't hit the ground. You were groaning for two days after we left Gilgal."

"Yes, but the mule hasn't misbehaved since."

"I'm glad, for your sake. No, I'll stick with your imma's well-trained donkey." He stroked her brush of mane. "You're a sweet girl, Sheleg."

They stopped at a river outside the city to water the animals. Then they rode at an easy pace, as befit their pretense as traders, but Jaedon longed to urge the mule into her ground-covering lope. "Will we reach Damascus by nightfall?"

Dov shook his head. "Another two days."

Jaedon unclenched his jaw. *Let us find her safe. Make me patient, Lord.*

After a while, they entered a harsh landscape of rock, brush, and pine. Jaedon rolled his shoulders, muscles sore from long days on the trail. The sun glared a hard yellow protest as it crept toward earth.

A black silhouette crossed its face, outstretched wings, protruding talons. An eagle struck an unfortunate coney, gave it an efficient shake, and proceeded to rip flesh and fur. It raised its head and glowered at the approaching riders.

Not just any eagle.

"Hevel." Jaedon shouted.

The eagle clutched its prey and, keeping a suspicious eye on Jaedon, climbed into the sky. Jaedon watched until it disappeared, a tiny speck in the distance.

Dov rode close. "Was it her?"

Jaedon nodded, unable to speak. But had it been? Wouldn't she have come to him? He shook his head, answering his own silent question. When he trained Hevel, she fought against allowing him to take her prey. Finally, realizing he would share it with her, she grudgingly accepted his discipline. But she was a wild thing now and no longer amenable to human rules.

"Perhaps she has a nest nearby." Dov searched treetops in the direction she had disappeared.

Jaedon yearned to follow her path, but the Lord had set his feet on another journey. Giving Dov a brief nod, Jaedon turned the mule back to the road and nudged her into a canter.

They made camp that night in a rocky crevice that hid them from the road. There was little forage for the animals, so Jaedon fed them from the meager store of grain. They made no fire to alert robbers or Arameans to their presence, and they slept, wrapped in their cloaks, on stony ground.

Jaedon woke before dawn, surprised that he had dropped to sleep. After making a quick meal of parched grain and dried figs, they were on their way. The rising sun heated a landscape ever more desolate. The mule grunted and kicked its hind leg at a swarm of flies that darted in and out.

Then Jaedon reined in the mule. "I hear riders." He looked around, more in habit than expectation. The rumble grew louder. "A lot of them."

"There's nowhere to hide," said Dov. "Remember, lads. We are traders, heading for Damascus to purchase their exquisite cloth." Suddenly, his head swiveled skyward.

Jaedon turned his head just as a huge wing knocked his arm, jarring him in the saddle. He stared after the apparition. *Hevel.* The eagle circled around, then dived, casting a shadow. Folding her wings at the last moment, she lit on his shoulder, talons clutching for purchase.

Gasping, he jerked a hand up to cup her warm side, grateful for the leather vest under his tunic.

There was no chance to express that gratitude.

The mule squealed and shot high into the air, as if Hevel bore them aloft. The eagle and the mule parted ways during one of the bone-jarring landings. The eagle beat her wings in a hasty retreat, bearing a strip of Jaedon's tunic. The mule crow-hopped in widening circles, pulling against the reins to bolt in the opposite direction.

Jaedon hung on as best he could, but the mule sent him flying and disappeared over the road ahead. Jaedon landed on his back with a grunt.

He lay not moving, struggling to breathe. A beak tugged a lock of his hair. Rolling his eyes, he saw Hevel standing beside him, head lowered, feathered legs spread, and staring into his face as if confused to find him lying in the road. Jaedon moaned as Dov and Biny jumped from their animals and came to stand over him.

Riders, Jaedon mouthed, not able to find his voice.

Dov nodded, slanting a glance to the road ahead. "They're coming over the hill," he said quietly. "Looks like a prominent family, accompanied by a squad of soldiers. They are guarding a fine wagon. Stick to our plan." He paused. "Except for"—he pointed at the eagle—"Hevel." He glanced again toward the travel party. "They have the mule. I suppose we'd best tell the truth about what happened. It will fit the rest of our story."

"Mmfh," rasped Jaedon, lifting a finger. It was the best he could do.

Biny approached and the eagle flew off, landing atop a nearby pine.

His friend bent over, sliding his arm under Jaedon's shoulders. "Can you sit?" He pulled, without waiting for an answer, and Jaedon groaned again.

"They're coming," Dov whispered. "Move him to the side of the road."

Jaedon struggled to get his feet under him. "No, stand me up." *Help me, Lord.* As the band of horsemen drew close, he whispered, "Those who are with us are greater than those we face."

Biny braced him on his left, Dov on his right, the horse and the donkey formed another wall of protection. Not quite an army of angels.

Jaedon studied the two men at the head of the soldiers. They appeared more interested than threatening. The man on the right was older and larger than the young man to the left. "This your mule? Are you all right?"

"Yes," Jaedon croaked. He cleared his throat. "Yes," he repeated firmly. "Just a spill."

"I see. You are traders?"

"Making our way to Damascus," Dov said.

"What do you have to sell?" asked the older man. "Perhaps I will buy gifts."

"Nothing to sell," Dov answered. "We hoped to buy cloth in Damascus. We have heard it is exquisite."

"Where will you sell it?"

"Moab," said Dov.

"Ah." He turned to the soldiers behind him. "Arrest them. They are lying."

As the soldiers urged their horses forward, Dov and Biny reached for their weapons. Jaedon had lost his knife when he fell. There was a scuffle, but not much of one. Nearly twenty soldiers made short work of disarming the three and tying their hands behind them.

The wagon crested the hill and stopped. The door swung open, and a soldier helped a grand lady to the ground. She appeared somewhat older than Imma but still was very attractive.

"What is it?" she asked the troop's leader. Her voice lilted, but she glared at Jaedon. "Did they plan to attack us?"

"I am not sure. But they purport to come from Moab, and they are not Moabites."

"I did not say we came from Moab. In fact we—"

"They are from Israel!" A young woman peered from behind the wagon's open door. "I recognize their speech." A soldier helped her to the ground. She looked first at Dov, then at Jaedon, and she clapped both hands over her mouth.

"What is it, my dear?" The older woman put her arm around the girl protectively.

She reached for the woman's hand. "It is him." She paused, obviously struggling against strong emotion. "That is Jaedon."

Chapter Forty-Three

*In your unfailing love you will lead the people
You have redeemed. In your strength you will
guide them to your holy dwelling.
Exodus 15:13*

*Home to Gilgal
Ziva*

"Will Eden recognize me, do you think?"

As they drove the final miles to Gilgal, Ziva plied Biny and Jaedon with questions. They had joined her, Amirah, and Naaman in his wagon, while Jaedon's father had ridden ahead to alert the villagers of Gilgal.

"Of course she will. I recognized you at once, little sister." Biny answered.

Jaedon only smiled.

Ziva glanced at him from under her eyelashes. After she recognized him standing in the road and saw Biny nearby, it was easy to run to them, laughing and crying, Emet bounding by her side. "How is it that you are here?" she had asked.

"We were coming for you," Jaedon answered, but it was Biny who enfolded her in his arms.

Which was as it should be. Although there had been an understanding of sorts between her and Jaedon, the actual betrothal had never taken place. Except in her heart.

"Elisha could not tell us where you'd been taken," Jaedon had said. "But he knew you were alive. As did I."

She had raised her eyebrows at that.

"I searched a long time. Far into Aramean territory, when I received leads that took me to ... various locations."

She listened, hungry to know, as the two of them filled in gaps, beginning to understand why they had lost hope of finding her. She ached, hearing her parents had not survived, but felt joy learning Mara and Aharon had.

"We took in Mara and adopted Aharon," Biny said. "Now he has a little sister ... er, niece, and—"

"But tell me—how big is he and is he well? Mara! Alive! I feared her dead or … worse."

"No, in fact she and one of the elder women found Aharon. We gladly took her in and would have adopted her, but she is now being courted by one of the prophets."

Ziva briefly fought an urge to giggle, then let it happen. Mara had informed her that a prophet could not support a family as well as a farmer. Evidently, she had changed her mind. Then gratitude engulfed Ziva. Mara had saved her brother, and she was alive to form new opinions on life. She reached out and grasped Biny's hand as he described Aharon's changes and promised she'd see him soon.

"—and your new niece is named Bracha and a blessing she is! Eden says she looks like you."

Aharon and Mara, safe. A new niece. *Blessing.* So many changes, while she'd been gone. A memory of the early days after her capture threatened to shadow the moment. She patted Biny's hand once more, then sat back, allowing the sway of the coach to soothe her. She'd made a life for herself. Friends who had become almost family. Meaningful work—caring for her despondent mistress, and then for the orphans of Damascus.

Biny answered her questions, but Jaedon grew quiet. She felt shy about asking him the hard questions—the ones to which she most wanted answers. How long had he searched? When did he give up? And … had he taken a wife? She closed her eyes. Impossible. She could not ask.

Naaman cleared his throat. "How long did you search, Jaedon?"

"Until I ran out of places. Nearly a year."

"But you were on the road today. Almost five years later. Said you were bound for Damascus. How did you know she'd be there?"

"We did not know, but the Lord had given us direction … a clue, of sorts. We had heard of your healing from tzara'at. That a servant had told you a prophet in Israel could heal you. At the time, we made no connection with Ziva. Later, as my mother and I talked about another instance of tzara'at, we wondered about the servant who sent you to Elisha. We thought he might have been a prophet or another Israelite who knew of Elisha's powers. Then my mother asked, 'Why must the servant have been a man?'"

Naaman laughed and slapped his knee. He took his wife's hand. "Leave it to a woman to ask the right question. Now, my dear, do you have questions for the young men?"

Her mistress also ignored Biny, leaning toward Jaedon. "Ziva told us your parents stay among the prophets, though they are not prophets. Are they still living?"

Jaedon smiled. "Yes, my parents, my grandparents, and my siblings."

"My, a large family." She closed her eyes and Ziva reached for her hand, knowing the pain her childless mistress felt. Amirah patted her and continued. "Do you all live together?"

"My parents and siblings live in a small house, my three grandparents share another. We manage a vineyard and a stand of young apple trees. I ... I live alone, in the house I built for Ziva."

He had seemed as shy as she, when Naaman had suggested they get out of the wagon and stretch their legs. After several moments of silence, Ziva motioned to the road ahead. "How much farther to Gilgal?"

"We should arrive before nightfall."

They walked again in silence. "You wrote me a letter, but it was lost during the attack. I mourned its loss ... among many others."

He looked at her intently. His lips parted, then closed. He stared at the road a while, then said, "Do you wish to speak of it? I will not urge you, if you find it too painful."

She hesitated, gathering her thoughts, but convinced she wanted to tell him all. "Of the attack itself, I remember only a blow to my head and then blackness. Later, I mostly remember fear. Fear that all I loved were dead. Afterwards came pain, which still comes to me keenly, like waves—sometimes in ripples, other times great billows." She looked sideways at him. "The knowing is better. Knowing Abba and Imma are dead is like an echo of that great billow of fear–but an echo that hurts me less as it returns over time."

He nodded, reaching to briefly touch her elbow. "I am sorry for the pain you endured. I hope ... I want ... I have waited for you. As I said, I knew you were alive. I searched until I had nowhere else to turn. Now that I've found you, I want to bring you to your house and, with Yahweh's help, spend my days making you happy until all your echoes of sadness and fear are gone."

He reached for a string that showed behind the neck of his tunic. He pulled out a small sack made of homespun and handed it to her.

"I could not deliver the *ketubah* I prepared for your father. If you agree, I will present it to Biny when we reach Gilgal. For now, please accept this reminder of my heart's promise."

She pulled open the drawstring and carefully extracted a dirt-stained fragment of papyrus. His letter. She opened it, rereading the honeyed words she had repeated from memory, when she most needed hope. *A house of stone behind the vineyard. Plastered walls, if you desire. Apple trees.*

Ziva swiped at her eyes, trailing grit from the tattered document.

Then she pressed the letter to her chest and looked up. "I agree," she whispered, hoping her smile said more than her words. "Yes. Give Biny the *Ketubah.*"

A small crowd from Gilgal buzzed around the trail from the ridge. They would not be familiar with the huge conveyance nor the strange assortment of Arameans it carried. If Jaedon, Biny, and Dov had not accompanied them or Elisha had not been at Gilgal to welcome them, there might have been resistance.

Ziva wondered at the size of the gathering. Gilgal must be larger than Gischala had been. So many massed together at the road. Biny walked into their midst, arm in arm with Ziva. They stared at her curiously and she saw herself in their eyes—an unfamiliar young woman wearing embroidered Aramean garments.

Then Eden ran out of the crowd. When she wept and called out—*Ziva, my sweet sister, Ziva*—the settlers murmured their sympathy and edged closer, offering muted welcomes.

Jaedon followed with Naaman and Amirah. Ziva understood the villagers' suspicious glances. All they saw was a tall man with a soldier's bearing and a grand lady wearing a long, embroidered tunic. No one who belonged in Gilgal.

Biny shouted. "This is Naaman, the man our Lord healed from tzara'at, and this is his wife Amirah. They have … cared for Ziva for a time and now return her to us."

Ziva loosed herself from Eden's embrace and ran to throw her arms around Amirah. "Amirah has been like a mother to me. She and the captain treated me as gently as a daughter." She kissed both Amirah's hands, wanting it clear that the captain and her mistress, although Aramean, were to be accepted and treated with respect.

They were, especially after both Elisha and Jaedon offered them hospitality. Ziva thought the couple would choose to stay with Jaedon, but Naaman, appearing overwhelmed by Elisha's offer, nevertheless accepted. "I have studied your holy writings and Ziva has instructed Amirah. But we would welcome time with you, learning more about the ways of the Lord."

After making arrangements for the remaining soldiers, wagon, and animals, Elisha led Naaman and Amirah to his house.

Ziva went home with Eden and Biny. Mara, who had remained behind watching the children, greeted her with a hug, then stepped back. Aharon, no longer little, approached. He stood chest high, but he hung back shyly when Eden introduced Ziva as his sister.

"Little brother," She wanted to hug and kiss him, but instead took his hands. "I am so glad you are safe. And so big! You were crawling when I last saw you."

His expression looked troubled. "I … I cannot remember you."

She gave a light squeeze then released his hands. "Of course not, my brother. We will reacquaint ourselves. For now, I am just grateful to be here with you."

A baby started to fuss from a cradle, pulling Ziva's gaze.

"Is that my dear niece, whom I have never met?"

Eden bustled to the corner, picked up the child, and handed her to Ziva. "Let me rectify that. This is our sweet Bracha. I believe her cloths are in need of changing."

Ziva chuckled. "I assure you, dear sister, I am well versed in that skill. In Damascus, my mistress brought many of the city's orphans into her care, including a pair of twins." The babes were now toddling around the estate, cared for, in Amirah's absence, by Gihan and Habib.

A stew was bubbling on the hearth, infusing the room with savory aromas. Ziva's stomach rumbled and she pressed her hand against it with a little gasp. "Sorry! It has been a long journey."

"Of course," said Eden. She hurried to a worktable, washed her hands in the ewer, and removed a clean cloth from a lump of dough. "Everything is nearly ready. Elisha warned me."

Ziva coaxed the baby to smile while Mara helped pat out the dough. Flatbread was ready by the time Bracha was settled and Biny poured water over Aharon's hands.

Ziva saw his hands were no longer pudgy, thinning into the hands of a boy. Nor did he gum his food. "The last time we ate together, little brother, you were the size of your sister. A little bigger, perhaps."

"I will always be bigger. Abba says it is up to me to protect her from older boys." Aharon glanced at Biny, wearing an expression of trust.

"That is true, my son. It is a man's responsibility to care for the women of his household."

Aharon slid his gaze up to Ziva. "You are also my sister. So I will protect you, too."

The room filled with laughter, but Aharon frowned until Biny clapped him on the shoulder. "You are right, my son. Protect her always."

The next morning, after they had broken their fast, someone rapped on the open door. Jaedon waited, a *ketubah* in his hands and the prophet Elisha at his side.

Biny, acting in the absence of Ziva's father, accepted the

thin piece of wood and read the inked terms aloud. Ziva would receive pieces of silver, a pair of gold earrings, and a donkey's colt, which Jaedon would train.

But there was more. Because of their long separation, by circumstance unavoidable by either, Jaedon asked to forego any further waiting period. If Ziva agreed, Jaedon would return sometime the next day and bring her to the house he had built for her. Elisha would conduct the marriage ceremony and the whole village would attend a celebration.

After reading, Biny nodded. "Sounds reasonable. Do you agree to go with this man, little sister?"

Ziva did not recognize the prophets who peeked in the open door and window. Then she caught a glimpse of Elisha, flanked by Naaman and Amirah, squeezed in the back. None remarked on the ketubah's offerings or short term of the betrothal. The room and faces seemed to whirl. She could scarcely remember what Biny had read, beyond that Jaedon's offer seemed wildly generous. She didn't want to wait either.

Shyly, she nodded.

"You must say, *I will go.*" Eden whispered in her ear.

Ziva smiled. "I will *certainly* go."

Then Eden hurried to a shelf, returning with a small ceramic cup. Dov had brought it last night, telling them the cup had been his gift to Miriam at their betrothal. The betrothal cup was plain in shape, but the unusual glaze had gleamed variously green and blue when tilted under the sun.

Jaedon filled the cup with wine from a matching carafe. Ziva sipped and her family cheered.

Epilogue

HOO-AHH! HOO-AHH! THE SHOFAR BLEW, PIERCING the evening's stillness. Ziva jumped up from the wooden chair and hurried toward the window. She had waited all day to hear the announcing trumpets, but Eden intercepted her path and gently pushed her back.

"The bride does not run to her betrothed like a wanton." Hands on hips, Eden tutted. "She waits demurely in the wedding chair."

"You did not," Ziva squirmed in the chair. "I remember."

"But Imma told me to," Eden replied. "At least one of us should obey our mother." She smiled, but the corners of her eyes slid down.

"Should I light my lamp now?" Mara asked.

"Oh yes!" Eden hurried to bring a kindled straw, shielding it with her hand.

It was bittersweet that Ziva, Eden, and Mara were the only ones here who remembered her mother. Who felt her absence deeply. Ziva drew in a breath. For a moment, she imagined the burial caves in Gischala. She had not seen them but would go one day. Jaedon with her. *I wish you were with me, Imma. But are you and Abba watching from Paradise?* She sat again. Biny had carved this chair for the wedding of Miriam and Dov, Jaedon's adoptive parents. Eden and other brides of the settlement had used it. Ziva gripped the smooth sanded edges. Now it was her turn.

Hoo-ahh! Ziva ran back to the window, but this time Eden only laughed.

The flames of at least fifty torches crowded the path to Biny and Eden's door. "He is coming!" Ziva put her hand over her mouth, whirled, and pulled a finely woven veil from a peg. "Help me!"

Eden adjusted it so as to cover her hair and face. She liked how the translucent veil filtered the blue of the pretty wedding tunic. It had belonged to Jaedon's mother, a tall woman. Miriam had altered the garment to fit Ziva, probably working long into the night.

A rap came at the door and Biny went to answer.

Hearing several male voices, Ziva stepped back. Jaedon walked in, followed by Dov and Elisha. "I have come for my bride."

Eden and Mara hastened Ziva back into the chair. Jaedon took one corner, Elisha the opposite, and Biny and Dov grasped the back two chair legs.

"Up, lads," Elisha said. Ziva swayed and grasped for Jaedon's shoulder as they lifted the chair and moved outside.

A cheer rose from the congregants, and they began to sing the king's wedding song, written by the sons of Korah.

My heart is stirred by a noble theme ...
My tongue is the pen of a skillful writer

Ziva looked at the midnight sky, countless stars spilling across its expanse. She imagined King David's scribe across an expanse of years, composing this song for his king. A song now being sung to her.

Your lips have been anointed with grace
Your robes are fragrant with myrrh and aloes and cassia

Jaedon turned and smiled at her. His hair was still damp from a *mikvah* and he smelled of cassia, perhaps because of the garland of the frilled yellow blooms encircling his neck. Ziva smiled behind the veil. A man that upheld tradition.

Then Emet, also wearing a cassia garland, burst from the crowd. A length of twine dragged the ground, and one of the prophets ran up, apologizing and reaching for the twine. But Emet dodged and jumped against the chair, nearly unseating her. The prophet lunged then and took firm hold of the dog. Ziva and Jaedon laughed as the prophet and Emet backed away.

Listen daughter and pay careful attention
Forget your people and your father's house
Let the king be enthralled by your beauty

Hearing feminine voices behind, Ziva turned and saw Eden, Mara, Miriam and several wives of the prophets singing. She had met them briefly, but she could not remember all their names. Yet they were here to celebrate with her. Even Jaedon's grandmother and great-grandmother—the *savtas* he called them—added their high-pitched voices.

All glorious is the princess within her chamber
Her virgin companions follow her—
Led in with joy and gladness

The immas and savtas placed hands over their mouths, hiding smiles.

Ziva grew dizzy on the music, the sweetness of the air, and the swaying of the wedding chair. She wanted down. Perhaps the glasses of watered wine she had shared earlier with Eden and Mara had affected her. She saw the *chuppah*, not far ahead. Her stomach gave a small flip and roll, like a fish under water. Suddenly, she felt she could go no farther, not even the few steps that would put her under the arch.

She gave a quiet moan, and Jaedon, instantly attentive, motioned for the chair to be set down. He took both her hands and leaned close.

Through the gauzy white of her veil, she saw concern in his expression. "Are you all right, my love?"

My love. Her heart warmed. "I am well." She lay a hand on her stomach, making a grimace he would not be able to see through the veil. "The chair, I think. Can we walk the rest of the way?"

"Of course." He took her arm. His hand was warm through the thin sleeve of her wedding tunic.

A trio of prophets continued playing their lyres. The air was sweet. Yellow flowers were everywhere—across the *chuppah*, woven in braids, and though bedraggled, around the neck of Emet, who now lay politely at the feet of the prophet to whom he was tethered.

Naaman, Amirah, and Elisha waited on one side of the *chuppah*, Dov, Miriam, and Jaedon's grandmothers on the other. Dov whispered their names. *Hadassah and Yaffa.* In their crinkled smiles, Ziva found boundless welcome.

Then Elisha began to read from a scroll.

The Lord God said, "It is not good for the man to be alone. I will make a helper suitable for him." But for the man no suitable helper was found.

So the Lord God caused the man to fall into a deep sleep; and while he was sleeping, he took one of the man's ribs and then closed up the place with flesh. Then the Lord God made a woman from the rib he had taken out of the man, and he brought her to the man.

Elisha lowered the scroll. "After Elijah went up to the Lord, and I picked up the mantle he left me, Jaedon asked to serve me. But the Lord told me another would be my servant. Then Jaedon met a young woman, and everything changed. Many of you understand. He was sure she was his *suitable helper.*

"But it seemed the Lord had other plans for Ziva and Jaedon, for I could not help him find the girl. I knew, as did he, that Ziva lived. Though I asked the Lord for sight and Jaedon searched for years, she remained lost to us.

"But not lost to the Lord. He sent Ziva as his emissary to Aram, Israel's enemy. To tell Naaman the God of Israel could heal him. To mend Amirah's hurting heart. To encourage those of Naaman's household to nurture orphaned children.

"All this time, Naaman thought Ziva's family was dead. He and his wife had come to care for her."

Elisha told them what Jaedon had recounted in the wagon and why he had set out for Damascus at the same time Naaman and Amirah were bringing her to Gilgal.

"The Lord planned that their wedding would take place," Elisha said, "perhaps a little delayed—but not late. Not late at all, by the Lord's timing." Elisha picked up the scroll.

The man said, "This is now bone of my bones and flesh of my flesh; she shall be called 'woman,' for she was taken out of man." That is why a man leaves his father and mother and is united to his wife, and they become one flesh.

Then, lifting a cup, Jaedon said to Ziva, "I am my beloved's, and my beloved is mine."

She, after taking a sip, answered, "Let him lead me to the banquet hall, and let his banner over me be love." This was the moment, his promises and hers given. The beginning, which she would remember and hold dear.

Jaedon lifted her veil and ducked beneath. Smiling, he whispered, "Ishah." His eyes were dark and warm, like a summer night. Her gaze traced his face as he moved closer. He had changed since that day in the date orchard. A few lines creased the corners of eyes and lips, hollows defined cheek bones.

Then his lips touched hers, briefly at first, then returning to rest, like a dove who had come home.

After many toasts and congratulations, they moved to a table piled with food. "The specialties of the prophets' wives," Jaedon murmured.

The villagers sat under trees and on logs, eating food carried to them by the older children of the settlement. Torches braced between rocks lit the area, flashing in the deepening night.

Afterward there was more music and dancing. Ziva remembered the night her father had danced with her and Imma. How happy they would have been to see this day.

Eden came near, carrying little Bracha and holding Aharon by the hand, and she thought that Imma and Abba were here, in a sense, in these children, and in Ziva and Eden.

When the drums started to beat, the music picked up the pace. The men made a line, hands on shoulders, knees lifted high. The women, giggling, held hands and danced around them.

Jaedon whispered in Ziva's ear, and she nodded, smiling. Then clasping hands, they walked to the pretty stone house above the vineyard.

"Shall I take you first to see the apple trees?" he asked.

"Yes," she answered, shivering, though the night was warm. Even her teeth clattered.

"You are cold," Jaedon said, removing the embroidered cloak that enhanced his wedding clothes. "Let me cover you with my mantle."

Author's Note

IN THE MIDST OF WRITING *MANTLE*, our family experienced a bear of an ordeal I would have liked to avoid. It began as my husband, who had been cheerfully recovering from knee surgery, began to experience extreme pain. Post-surgical infection and its long aftermath grasped our lives and shook. Another hospitalization and a second surgery. My big strong man grew helpless and I an inept caregiver.

But God is good. When our strength was at its ebb, He showed me verses of encouragement. He sent Christian prayer warriors, yard-care fairies, and meal toters. Though we have prided ourselves on our independence, we learned to say thank you instead of no.

Then came another loss. My mother, who had been bright and spunky, passed on to heaven. She was a committed believer in Jesus and raised me to also trust in God. I was comforted knowing she was with the Lord, grateful that I had visited her in Idaho recently, but grew teary remembering a lifetime of scenes of us together.

My publisher kindly extended my deadline. You, my patient readers, prayed for us. My heartfelt thanks to all.

As I wrote *Mantle* during this time, themes of loss and despair, protection and guidance, and God working blessings behind the scenes—all of which we were experiencing in our lives—emerged from the scriptural source of the book—2 Kings, chapters 1 through the first part of 8.

Readers often ask me, "What is fact or fiction?" Biblical fact: Elijah went up to heaven via whirlwind and chariot, and Elisha received his physical and metaphorical mantle. Also fact: Elisha received a double portion of his mentor's spirit and effected twice as many miracles. The Bible does not name the servant girl who directed her master to Israel's God to be healed of leprosy, but I have portrayed her as she is described. Nor does it name the four lepers who discovered the Arameans had fled, but some Rabbis of the Talmud propose they were Gehazi and his sons. Perhaps this is reasonable supposition, given that in chapter 8:1-6, Gehazi visits the king of Israel on behalf of the Shunamite widow. Surely a leper would not be allowed in the king's court if his disease was not, at least, in remission.

However, other scholars posit that the timeline in 2 Kings is not chronological, instead chapters are arranged topically. If commentators differ in their opinions, perhaps you will not fault me for choosing to include this legend.

I have also named and expanded the character of Ziva. The Bible account of Naaman's servant girl is spare, but it shows she came to care for her master and mistress by the fact that she lovingly sends him to the prophet Elisha to be healed. She knows about the "sons of the prophets," and she has a strong faith! Elisha had healed no one before this time.

As always, I start with biblical truth, layer in customs and history, and imagine a plausible story line where the Bible leaves spaces. Please read 2 Kings for yourself and tell me how I've done.

Thank you for reading and supporting my writing. If you have enjoyed one or more of my books, please consider writing a review and posting on major retailers. Tell your friends. Ask your library to buy. And please keep in touch with me through my newsletter, at this link. I share my news, recommendations, and devotional thoughts. And I enjoy hearing back from you!

Character List

<u>Biblical Characters</u>
Elijah - Prophet in Israel who accurately predicted 3-yr drought
Elisha - Prophet in Israel mentored by Elijah – At Gilgal with sons of the prophets, Samaria with King Joram, Mount Carmel to retreat and pray, many of his miracles mirrored Elijah's
Micaiah - One of the sons of the prophets, in Whirlwind
King Ahab - King of Israel in Rain, Whirlwind, Mentioned in Mantle, though deceased
King Ahaziah - King of Israel in Whirlwind. Jezebel & Ahab's son. Mentioned in Mantle, deceased
King Joram - King of Israel, also in Whirlwind. Jezebel & Ahab's son. Brother of Ahaziah (his story in Whirlwind.)
Obadiah's widow - Add to author's note. Some think this widow was Obadiah's widow.
Naaman - Captain of the Aramean army during the reign of Benhadad
Hiram - Officer in Israel's army, direct report to King Joram

<u>Biblical Characters, but not named in scripture</u>
Amirah - Naaman's wife
Abner - Son of Gehazi and Lital
Asriel - Son of Gehazi and Lital
Baruch - Son of Gehazi and Lital
Kadesh - Jaedon's uncle, deceased, his story in Whirlwind
Ziva - Eden's sister
Samuel - A wealthy older farmer in Shunem, husband of Malka
Malka - Industrious woman of Shunem, married to Samuel
Joel - Son of Malka and Samuel

<u>Fictional Characters</u>
Miriam - Jaedon's adoptive mother
Dov - Jaedon's adoptive father, formerly an officer in Ahab's army
Gershoni - Jaedon's younger sister, about 4 at the beginning of story

Yuval - Jaedon's step-brother (Miriam & Dov), about 9 months at beginning of story
Sheleg - Miriam's white donkey
Uriel - Dov's warhorse - a gift from King Ahab
Savta Yaffa - Jaedon's grandmother by blood, Naboth's widow
Maalik - Jaedon's adoptive grandfather, married to Hadassah
Savta Hadassah - Mother of Naboth and Miriam's grandmother.
Binyamin (Biny) - One of the sons of the prophets, minor character in Rain and Whirlwind
Eden - Married to Binyamin, sister to Ziva.
Bracha - Daughter of Eden & Biny
Hevel - Eagle trained by Jaedon in Whirlwind, now in the wild
Naomi - Elderly woman in Bethel, friend of Miriam and Hadassah
Jezebel - Wife of King Ahab, enemy of prophets of Yahweh
Shimon - Ziva and Eden's father
Chedva - Ziva and Eden's mother
Tobiah - Shepherd from Elisha's home farm
Ocran - Officer in Israel's army. Dov's senior officer in Whirlwind.
Unnamed - Ocran's daughter, about 3-4
Lital - Gehazi's wife
Nathaniel - Miriam/Dov's son, Jaedon's youngest sibling (step-brother) Named after his great-grandfather, his story in The Eyes of the Lord
Mara - Ziva's friend in Gischala
Lotan - Mara's father, an old soldier
Aharon - Ziva's baby brother, about 10 months when introduced
Laban - An older widower in Gischala who wanted to marry Ziva.
Tal - Samuel's servant
Rafiq - Soldier, direct report to Naaman
Emet - Yellow dog given to Ziva by Neri
Neri - Servant at the Inn at Hazor
Habib - Naaman's trusted servant, Rafiq's father
Gihan - Amirah's trusted servant
Rima - Another female servant in Naaman's household
Puah - An old woman of Gishala